Lord of Beasts

Kit Sun Cheah

Days of Fire

Before the events of *Saga of the Swordbreaker*, Li Ming was a soldier in the Special Military Police. Sign up for my newsletter at https://bit.ly/3xdjuIE and receive a *free* ebook showing his origin story!

Notes on Timekeeping and Calendars

To standardize timekeeping across the breadth of its vast empire, and to placate the peoples it had subdued, the Yue Dynasty created a standard clock and calendar across Xiazhou, based on the norms of its subjects. The power, majesty and influence of the Great Yue guaranteed its adoption across the world, with some minor concessions to foreign powers. Even the Celestial Empire dared not tear down this legacy of its former overlords. With the dawn of the Zhongxia Republic, the Yue clock and calendar remained untouched.

1 minute equals 100 seconds.

1 *ke* equals 10 minutes.

1 hour equals 8 *ke*.

1 day equals 12 hours.

Each hour is divided into two halves, upper and lower, of 4 *ke*. In the Continent, each hour is named after an animal of the zodiac.

Only the Continent uses the word *ke* to designate a period of time one-eighth of an hour.

Every week has ten days. In the Continent, the days are named after the ten heavenly stems.

Every month has three weeks. Reckoned by the phases of the moon, each month has either 29 or 30 days, referred to as a minor or major (or small and large) month respectively.

Every year has 12 months. 7 times every 19 years, the calendar adds a leap month of 30 days.

Unlike the rest of the world, which numbers years according to the Common Era, the Republic continues the age-old tradition of regnal years.

Chapter One

Bashe

Legend held that a bashe could grow so huge, it could swallow an elephant. Surely it was an exaggeration.

But not by much.

This close to the giant snake, Li Ming sensed its qi. A river of raw, vital force surging out the mouth of the dark cave that served as its den, emanating from an enormous living loop nestled deep within the bowels of the hill. It was easily the size of a house. And it was all coiled up, looping upon itself in multiple turns. Stretched out to its full length, it could easily cover half the length of a football field. At least.

Slowly, silently, Li Ming ascended the hill. He planted his feet on solid rock and unyielding earth, he leaned forward to counterbalance the bulk of his pack, he held his infinity gun close to his chest. Steering clear of vegetation and loose soil, his senses drinking in nothing and everything around him at once, he cut a serpentine path around countless trees and towards the mouth of the cave.

Below him, to his left, Ghazan followed. The tall, clean-limbed Yue was slightly slower, a little noisier, but he still made good time. Li Ming heard the soft rustle of vegetation, the scrape of steel soles against stone, once a soft curse when he lost his footing. Ghazan was a child of the steppes, not of the hills, but still he adapted quickly.

Bashe were diurnal. So the men made their approach at the third hour, the hour of the tiger, when the land was asleep and the moon hidden behind a sea of clouds. Li Ming navigated with his fusion goggles, seeing the world in infrared and thermal vision. His helmet visor projected a landscape of crisp black and white, low-fidelity daylight robbed of most color. Night-flying birds revealed themselves as swift-moving clouds of orange and yellow, their body heat betraying them.

Li Ming had grown up among hills and forest, farms and plateaus. This hill was steep and slippery, but he trusted in his experience and proprioception, intuitively stepping on solid ground and adjusting his weight for stealth and stability. He made good time, barely pausing, his subconscious mind driving his body to free his conscious mind for the task at hand.

The bashe had to die. There was no question about it. This close to civilization, just ten minutes from the closest town, it was a calamity in waiting. Already it had gobbled up dozens of sheep and goats in the past three days. Left unchecked, humans were next.

But ordinary humans couldn't fight a beast like that, so they turned to biaohang.

And in the armed escort business, Dayong Biaoju was the gold standard.

The slope rounded off and flattened into a flat patch of earth, marking the entrance to the cave. Li Ming halted just below the crest, keeping low to the ground. The snake continued to snooze, ignorant of the biaohang's approach. Li Ming sneaked a peek behind him and saw Ghazan cover the final few paces.

Ghazan pressed himself against the earth, aiming his infinity gun at the cave opening. A bright silvery line betrayed his infrared laser. Li Ming shucked off his backpack, set it next to him, and reached for the smaller bag mounted on its back.

The Shanbang Belt Bag resembled a small clutch-sized bag, the kind of bag a man could wear over his lumbar in the wilds or a woman could sling over her shoulder on the street. On the outside, it appeared large enough to hold only essentials or to supplement a main pack. But on the inside, it was as large as a one-bedroom apartment.

It was no ordinary bag. It was an interspatial storage machine, with the form factor of a bag.

Li Ming worked the controls with both hands, calling up a holographic menu. Set to infrared mode, the floating window glowed in his visor but left the visible world in darkness.

Li Ming touched the first item on his inventory. The menu became a translucent three-dimensional image floating in mid-air. He aimed the backpack just so and pressed the eject button.

The image became a black hole. Within its depths, a tiny mote of white light rocketed to the surface and out into the real world. The mote swelled up, becoming a curved rectangular pouch. The hole closed instantly, and the pouch landed softly on the backpack.

Infinity gun slung over his back, Li Ming grabbed the pouch and crawled up to the cave. The beast's qi grew thicker, stronger, tasting of death and predation and violence. Li Ming's hackles rose. He breathed through the sensation, letting it pass, and opened the pouch to reveal a Type 99 antipersonnel mine.

It was such a small thing, a curved rectangular slab half the length of his forearm, but so much death was packed into it. Seven hundred steel balls packed in front of a layer of high explosive. Clack it off and any living thing within a hundred *chi* in front of it would cease to exist.

Screens large and small sang of the romance of the jianghu, the drama of the monster hunter, the splendid battles with the beasts and bandits of the world. In a role playing game, the intrepid biaohang would quest into the depths of the cave, battling lesser foes, until coming face to face with the serpent king on its throne. In the real world, the best hunts were ones that were boring, because everything went according to plan and the target never knew what hit it.

Li Ming ran his hands down the mine, finding the words 'This Side Towards Enemy' in raised characters on the front face, then deployed its twin bipods and oriented the device towards the cave. The mine had a tiny peep sight for aiming, but he didn't bother with it. It was impossible to align any kind of sight with fusion goggles. He just pointed the mine in the general direction of the opening.

Working by feel, he found the spool of firing wire snug in the pouch's larger outer pocket, took the blasting cap at the end of the wire, and connected it to the mine. He backed up, letting the wire play itself out, careful not to upset the mine, and returned to his pack. He took up his weapon and aimed it—and its laser—at the cave opening.

Now it was Ghazan's turn. He crawled up to the cave and emplaced his own mine, creating overlapping arcs of fire. Li Ming kept his attention trained on the laser dot and Ghazan in his peripheral vision. Ghazan added another step, daisy-chaining the mines together, allowing a single clacker to detonate both.

Ghazan slunk away, took up his weapon, and whispered into the team radio.

"Mines deployed."

The words flowed from his mouth like liquid chocolate, rounding off and muffling the tones that gave meaning and identity to each character.

"Roger. Return to fallback position," Cai Yan replied.

She was the leader of their little expedition, the daughter of the former owner of Dayong. After his murder, her twin brother had taken over the business, holding down the fort in their home city of Bao An. Which freed her—and a few select biaohang—to pursue contracts elsewhere.

The men retreated. The descent was slower, more agonizingly cautious, than the ascent. Li Ming allowed the wire to play out, keeping clear of anything that might snag on it and unbalance the mine. Ghazan cut across the trees, following Li Ming's footsteps.

Down they went, retracing their steps. Li Ming paused at the foot of the hill, long enough to check on Ghazan. He was still plodding along, still behind Li Ming. Li Ming turned back and climbed up another hill.

This hill was bare and gentle, the trees few and far between. He made good time, trekking across grassy earth at an angle away from the cave, allowing the wire to reach—

The spool played out completely.

And he was out in the open.

He cursed, but only in his mind. He'd been so focused on returning that he hadn't tracked how much wire he had left.

"I've run out of wire," Li Ming reported. "Moving to alternate position."

Li Ming reeled in the wire, going back down the hill. Ghazan stood in the dark, glaring silently at him, no doubt passing judgment. He'd picked a poor route. There was no cover, no concealment, not here on this hill. The closest was a tree at the foot of the hill.

The bashe's hill.

The men lay down by the tree, keeping most of its mass behind them and the cave. Li Ming wriggled about until he had a good line of sight to the cave. Ghazan adjusted too, pressing himself up against Li Ming. This close, the Yue's qi was a bonfire, spilling ethereal heat in every direction, threatening to smother Li Ming's. Somehow, over the months, the Yue's qi had grown by leaps and bounds, overtaking Li Ming's.

Li Ming didn't mind. He wasn't competing with Ghazan, not in this. Li Ming set his pouch down and opened the smaller outer pouch.

Here was the firing device. The device that would trigger hell in a small space.

He connected the clacker to the firing wire. And just like that, the mines were live.

Li Ming glanced at his heads up display. It was only slightly halfway past the hour. And there was no telling when the bashe would emerge from its cave.

Now came the hard part. The waiting.

Ghazan had hated this part of the plan. He was a man of action, a hunter and warrior, always eager to run down his prey and put it to the bayonet. It had taken a long time to talk him around and make him see the light.

He'd wanted to charge straight into the lair and kill the monster snake while it was still asleep. But in such close quarters, it was at the height of its strength, and it would be extremely difficult to escape if something went wrong. More to the point, Dayong would only be paid if it brought proof of the kill, and nobody wanted to drag out a humongous elephant-eating snake if they could avoid it. Better to let it come to them and do half their work.

The major downside of this plan was that it would yield a lesser harvest, and with it, lower pay. Li Ming didn't mind. Better to be paid modestly while keeping your life and limbs than to risk everything in chase of a higher payday. There would always be more beasts to hunt.

Fatigue crept into Li Ming's body. Every cell screamed at him to sleep. Li Ming massaged the Zhong Chong point on both hands, a spot just below the middle fingernail, on the side facing the thumb. A subtle bitter taste tingled across his tongue, waste energy flushing through his meridians, temporarily restoring his vitality.

The team was on fifty percent watch, one hour rotation. It was Ghazan's turn to rest. That left Li Ming staring into the darkness, left hand on the handguard of his infinity gun, right hand on the clacker.

The hour of the rabbit arrived with great reluctance. Ghazan signaled his wakefulness with a whisper.

"My turn on watch."

Li Ming handed over the clacker, then closed his eyes and breathed deep.

He drank in the qi of the earth and the air, circulating it throughout his body, replenishing the energy he had lost. He took care not to steal from Ghazan, not consciously at least, but this close to him it would be inevitable. The best Li Ming could do was to limit his body to taking only the excess qi his body expelled, the qi it couldn't use. Even so, it was like drinking from a waterfall.

Energy flowed through him like water, down his nose, lungs, dantian, curving to follow his perineum, up his spine and over his crown and back to his nose, joining the major meridians of his body in an unbroken circuit. Secondary circuits activated, sending waves of hot, heavy energy ebbing and flowing down his arms and legs, fingers and feet. It was healing, soothing, as if he were adrift on an ocean wave under the summer sun.

When he opened his eyes again, dawn broke. The goggles automatically cut off, allowing him to see the world in crystal clear color.

Ghazan stirred. Li Ming reached over to take the clacker.

"My turn," Li Ming whispered.

Ghazan nodded off. Li Ming watched. The snake slept.

Morning crawled past. The men took turns to have breakfast. Strips of mutton rougan for Ghazan, a compressed food bar for Li Ming. The beast continued to slumber. The men continued to watch.

The sun crept across the sky. The world brightened steadily. Sweat gathered in Li Ming's cracks and crevices. Itchiness followed. Li Ming remained still, recognizing the sensation and allowing it to leave, keeping his attention trained on the cave, on the snake. Bashe were cold-blooded, and it would awake only when it was warm enough.

At midday, the snake stirred.

Its energy shifted. It unwound itself, its head rising languidly to taste the air. Li Ming sensed it rather than felt it, a sinuous winding movement in its enormous qi field.

"Stand to. Target is waking up," Li Ming whispered.

"Roger," Wong Wan Lung said.

To the south, the sniper, the final member of the team, lay up among the trees and rolling hills. Wong Biaohang hailed from the Nanguang Federation, from the southern region of the continent. While he'd only recently joined Dayong, he had been in the business for years, longer than Ghazan and Li Ming combined. Li Ming didn't want to think too hard about Wong Biaohang sharing his observation point with Cai Yan. They were all professionals, but...

But that meant he had to focus, here and now.

The snake snapped to full alertness. Its body tensed and coiled. It froze for a moment, then slithered towards the cave mouth.

"The target is alert and exiting the cave," Li Ming reported.

"Think it sensed us?" Ghazan asked.

The bottom fell out of Li Ming's stomach. Of course it had. The enormous beast had a qi field to match its prodigious size, and the men were at the outer edges of the field. It could sense them as easily as Li Ming could sense it.

Li Ming's grip tightened around the clacker.

"Yes."

"Good."

Li Ming heard the smile—and the bloodlust—in the Yue's voice.

"Stand to, stand to," Cai Yan ordered.

Harsh sizzling reverberated within the cave, a primal sound from the dim and distant past, speaking directly to his genetic memory. It was the sound of scales slithering against stone, paired with the hissing of an animal the size of a truck. The sound shook Li Ming to the core, chilling his blood, stealing his breath. The bashe accelerated, its movements growing quicker and surer as its body warmed up. Li Ming glanced at his clacker, checking that, the wire was in, his fingers still safely pressed against its plastic body, and disengaged the safety latch.

The serpent appeared.

A gigantic head emerged from the mouth of the cave, scraping against its sides, revealing shining green scales and flat yellow eyes. Its black forked tongue flickered in and out, tasting the air. It danced back and forth in the air, revealing a pale white underbelly. It rose, higher and higher, rearing up to expose more of its length.

"Sights are hot," Wong Biaohang said.

"Fire," Cai Yan ordered.

A sharp crack rang out, a crack unlike anything Li Ming had ever heard. It was as if the air was tearing itself apart, splitting under a mass of metal screaming forth at ludicrous velocities. Unlike the others, Wong Biaohang had armed himself with a coilgun, and it was the first time Li Ming had heard a kinetic weapon fired in anger.

Blood bloomed from the serpent's eye. Blood erupted from the other side of its skull. Blood showered the world.

And it dropped.

The ground quaked under its mass. Dust billowed. Stones showered down from the heavens. Qi spewed forth from the wound, dissipating in the air.

"Is it dead?" Wong Biaohang asked.

The rest of its qi field was intact.

"No," Ghazan said.

The bashe surged up again, curling up into a gigantic question mark in the blink of an eye. Its jaws opened wide, revealing fangs like sabers, hissing in pain and rage, training its surviving eye on Li Ming.

Li Ming squeezed the clacker.

The mines detonated with a ferocious double bang. Hundreds of high-velocity pellets shattered scales, sheared flesh, broke bones, chopping the beast clean in half. A red cloud burst forth, splattering the mouth of the cave, leaving behind a lingering mist. The beast slammed back down. More qi gushed out into the world. The bashe's upper half twitched and threshed about, snapping and biting at the air, at the dirt, at everything within range of its enormous fangs.

"Is it dead yet?" Wong Biaohang asked.

"Shoot it again," Li Ming urged.

Another thundercrack. Blood burst just behind its head. The monster hissed again, rearing up to its diminished height.

Blood dripped from a hundred tiny wounds. Blood gushed from the enormous stump. White bone, shattered and ragged, peeked out from the wounds. But the elephant-swallowing snake was still in the fight.

Rising to a knee, Li Ming brought up his infinity gun. As if sensing the motion, the snake dropped its head, falling out of his sight picture. Li Ming swung the gun down, and it swerved to the right, surging ever closer towards them.

A third thundercrack. The shot pierced through the beast's body and out the other side, and still the beast charged forward. A trio of plasma bolts followed, chewing away at its huge wound, barely slowing it down. Li Ming clicked to full auto and adjusted his aim and—

Ghazan.

Ghazan charged the beast, sunlight gleaming off his bayonet, bellowing a war cry in his native tongue. His dusky skin flashed white as a star. His platinum hair burned bright as the sun. Qi erupted from his body, spewing out his crown and hands, merging with the beast's own to become a volcano in full fury.

"Ghazan! What the devil are you doing?!"

The snake lunged.

Ghazan thrust.

A ray of blazing fire blasted through his bayonet, spearing the bashe clean through its jaws and out its brain. Everything it touched disintegrated. The killing light faded to reveal a gaping tunnel large enough for a child to crawl through.

The snake hurtled past Ghazan, missing him by a hair's breadth, struck the ground, rolled and flopped, and came to a rest by the tree.

And went completely still.

The bashe's qi was gone. So completely gone it was as if it had been ripped out of its body and scattered to the cosmos. The remaining energy from the bashe's lower half surrounded Ghazan like an aurora for a fleeting moment, and vanished into nothingness.

The Yue stood tall, the conqueror triumphant, spattered in blood, a maniacal grin stretching across his face.

A second chill ran down Li Ming's spine. He knew the Yue was a risk taker and a berserker. Point him at an enemy and he would close in and destroy it with fire and steel. But here, so close to him, it felt like he was standing before a beast that had taken rebirth in the form of a man.

Regardless of how he felt, though, he still had a job to do. Staying clear of its enormous jaws, Li Ming poked the snake's unwounded eye. It remained still.

"Target eliminated," Li Ming said.

"You sure love your bayonet, don't you?" Cai Yan remarked.

"I told you we should have gone into its nest," Ghazan said. "I could have put it down with one blow."

"Ah, but can you process an entire bashe with one blow too?" Wong Biaohang asked.

It wasn't enough to kill the beast. Now they had to clean and gut it, to preserve what was valuable and discard the rest. And to do it before rot set in and spoiled everything.

Li Ming safed his weapon and drew his knife.

"Let's get to work."

Chapter Two

Capital of Abundance

The Capital of Abundance in an abundant land, the Free City of Yudu sat far to the southwest of the Central Plains. A city of stone and a city of water, eons ago its original settlers had built it among many mountains at the confluence of countless rivers. The oldest continuously-inhabited major city on the continent, it predated the Zhongxia Republic, the Celestial Empire, the Yue Dynasty, even the very concept of Xiazhou. Today it was the de facto capital of a nation that was no nation, a city-state that held sway over the other city-states in the Central Plains by virtue of its wealth and size.

Yudu was enormous. Larger than any other city Li Ming had visited, it was home to twenty million souls. Its metropolitan area, easily the size of a country, had a population of double that figure. Standing at the balcony, watching the city as it woke, a secret thrill ran through Li Ming, as though he had a first-hand view of a sight few people would ever know.

Street food carts lined the streets under the shade of ancient trees and the amber illumination of modern streetlamps. Billboards advertised the latest pills and potions, martial movies and high fashion, all fronted by ever-youthful immortals with flawless skin and perfect figures. Rows of semidetached houses formed grids and blocks, anchored by luxury high-rises. Where other cities had skyscrapers, Yudu had vertical forests, its high-rises overflowing with lush greenery and blooming flowers. Buses and trams climbed up and down the steep hills of the city, ready to accept the first passengers of the day. A quiet hush filled the world, a sense of infinite potential waiting to become manifest.

Li Ming found it hard to believe that just a day ago, he had been lying on hard earth waiting to do battle with a monster snake.

Processing and documenting the bashe had taken the better part of the afternoon. As the men dragged the divided halves together, Cai Yan washed down and iced the corpse. Armed with knives and multitools, they stripped the bashe of everything useful, everything the market found valuable.

Snakeskin could be turned to leather, in turn made into clothing, accessories, everything that used the hide of beasts. The fangs were an acceptable alternative to ivory from endangered animals. The venom glands would be synthesized into antivenin and medicines. Bashe gallbladder was valued for its ability to treat a huge range of illnesses, from fever to rheumatism to cancer. Its bones, rendered down to powder and consumed as a decoction, treated cardiovascular diseases. And its flesh, of course, was an exotic delicacy among some circles.

Skinning and gutting the snake, separating the useful from the useless, was hard work. But it offered the promise of an enormous payday, above and beyond what they would already be paid for accepting this contract.

Not that there would be much more money. The mines had blown clean through its intestines, spoiling the meat around them. It had taken delicate and dirty work to recover the gallbladder intact, and even more careful cutting to retrieve the venom glands. Ghazan's beam had vaporized the brain completely, barely missing the glands.

By the time they were done, everyone stank of blood and guts. After wiping themselves down and spraying on deodorant, they hiked back to their vehicle and drove back to Yudu.

It was late by the time they returned to the Eight Points hotel. Late enough that they skipped their usual post-hunt celebration meal in favor of quick and easy rations. They showered, changed, sent their preliminary report, and crashed into bed as soon as their heads were dry and their bellies quiet.

And now, at the hour of the rabbit, everyone else was still asleep. Cai Yan had rented a three-bedroom suite, the better to save money. She had claimed the master bedroom, Ghazan slept alone, while Li Ming shared his room with Wong Biaohang. The southerner was still in bed when Li Ming climbed out, and Li Ming took care not to wake him. He brushed his teeth, stretched, and stepped out into the balcony.

Here and now, he was alone at the heart of the Capital of Abundance. Apart from the people, yet also a part of them. It was the destiny of every biaohang, of every citizen of the world of the rivers and lakes. But days like this, he felt it more keenly than others.

He allowed himself a second more to appreciate the sight. To soak in the feeling. To allow his heart to settle. Then he moved.

Breathing deeply, drinking in the qi of the morning, he brought his hands through a fluid circle, bringing them to his lower dantian, the spot three fingers below and behind the navel, slightly bending his knees and twisting his hips. He shot his right fist straight out, at the same time stepping his right foot forward and planting it at a forty-five degree angle. Torquing counter-clockwise, he crossed his left arm over his right, bringing his left foot to his right, compressing his body and spine just so. In a single swift motion, he uncoiled himself, left hand drilling outwards at heart height, right hand spiraling inwards to his side, left foot dropping ahead of the right.

His fingers spread out and curled into eagle claws and tiger mouths. Seventy percent of his weight shifted to his rear foot. His bent legs resembled the character for the number eight. He tucked in his buttocks, keeping his pelvis and spine neutral, his chest rounded and hollow, his head upright.

This was the Sancai Shi, the Three Powers Stance, the principal battle stance of wuxingquan.

He brought his attention to his soles and worked his way up, making minute adjustments to his posture. He brought his right hand over his Belt Vessel meridian, the better to facilitate qi flow. He pressed and pulled his feet, readying himself to pounce like a tiger. He brought his mind to bear on a single thought, the thought of advancing forward.

He stood and breathed.

This was zhan zhuang. Standing practice, the foundational cultivation practice of the art.

Qi trickled into him, growing into a river, a torrent, a flood. His fingers and feet tingled and warmed, and the sensations rushed down his limbs to cover his body. More qi gushed through the meridians of his inner elbow and the webs of his thumbs, through his skin, through his eyes. It circulated powerfully through him, following his breath like blood pulsing in time with the heart.

He stood and breathed, acknowledging the sensation without dwelling on them, letting the energies flow into and through him, cleansing and charging him from the inside out. On the inhale he visualized streams of golden light entering him, on the exhale he imagined dark clouds blowing out and dissipating into emptiness. His conscious mind counted his breaths, keeping track.

At the fiftieth breath, he changed his posture just so, bringing his awareness to his joints. Now he sank into the posture, into the floor, into the earth itself. All sensation of muscles and ligaments and tendons, of a conscious body, melted away. He felt only the weight of his bones and the force of gravity pulling him down into the earth.

Where the first mindset cultivated martial power, this one tonified and revitalized the bones, blood, organs and qi. Together they promoted health and strength.

Another fifty breaths, and he shifted sides.

Slowly, smoothly, he withdraw his left arm and left foot, then extended his right arm and right foot, a mirror image of his starting position. Then he sank into place and breathed.

The sun peeked above the horizon, splashing the world in golden and orange hues. Cars and bikes took to the roads. Shops opened for business. Lights blazed from windows. A baby wailed. Citizens flocked to a park in between a pair of apartment blocks, ready for morning exercises and gongfu. The warming air grew thick and sticky. Thin fog blurred nearby buildings and distant mountains.

All this he logged, allowing the thoughts to rise in his mind and pass away, like bubbles in a stream, his heart and mind solely focused on zhan zhuang. After a hundred breaths, he lowered his hands to his dantian, brought his feet together, and relaxed.

Brimming with qi, his hands and legs crackling like electricity, Li Ming savored the view for a moment more. Then he returned to the living room.

It was still dark. A soft thumping sound emanated from the direction of Ghazan's bedroom. Ghazan kept to the old traditions of practicing in secret, of never showing the true extent of your skill to outsiders. Li Ming wasn't nearly so paranoid, but in the world of the jianghu it was only common sense. You never allowed a potential rival to know what you could be capable of.

A long strip of empty space ran from the windows to the main door. Li Ming planted himself in the middle of the corridor, away from furniture or anything breakable, and assumed the Sancai Shi. He glanced left and right, making one last check, and began.

He breathed in, taking his lead fist through a circle and over his dantian. With a sharp exhale, he drilled his fist outwards, twisting into a palm-up punch, stepping and angling his foot out. Breathing in, he raised his rear fist to chest height, forming a wedge with both arms, and brought his rear foot up. He stayed there for a moment, frozen in an in-between state, subtly adjusting his posture.

And exploded.

His dantian rotated, mimicking an ocean wave, rising high and rolling forward. His right fist blasted through a parabolic arc, opening into a palm even as it spiraled out to face the door. His left hand drew back to his side. His right foot stomped forward, the energy bouncing off the ground and up his striking arm. His breath expelled from his nose. These motions happened all at once, totally in sync, manifesting as a single energetic eruption. His qi followed the lines of force, surging outwards from his striking hand, and recycling into his dantian and his lungs. A half-beat later, his rear foot shuffled forward, stabilizing his posture.

This was Pi Quan, the Splitting Fist. Representing the element of metal, it was the first of the five fists of the art, containing within it every power of wuxingquan.

He shot out another fist, another, yet another, marching down a straight line, a single uninterrupted chain of splitting fists. He reached the door, smoothly spun around, and continued splitting the air.

It appeared to be a linear motion. Li Ming knew different. Wuxingquan—at least, *his* branch of wuqingquan—was all circles. Circles large and small, circles hidden in straight lines, circles known only to those with eyes to see. They lay in the twist of the hips, the movement of the hands, the rotation of the dantian, the subtle arcs that generated explosive short-range power.

He marched back and forth, splitting and turning, turning and splitting. After twenty strikes, he returned to his starting position. Circled his arms to his dantian, breathed, relaxed. He brought his awareness to his Huiyin, the perineum point, the meridian that united yin and yang, letting it lift and open.

More energy blasted through him, shooting up his spine and through his crown, chasing away the last vestiges of sleep, expanding his capacity to store and generate qi. Deep within him, his lungs vibrated, supercharged with life.

He breathed into the sensation for five breaths, then assumed the Sancai Shi and resumed practice.

Zuan Quan, the Drilling Fist, spiraling like a geyser. Beng Quan, the Crushing Fist, linear punches with the power of an arrow shot from a bow. Pao Quan, the Cannon Fist, rising and expanding like fire. Heng Quan, the Crossing Fist, rotating in harmony with the planet. Together with Pi Quan, these were the five fists of the Five Element Fist.

Within the five fists were the entirety of the art. But it was only the beginning of knowledge. After the Five Elements came the Twelve Animals, showing many of the myriad applications of the fists. Li Ming worked his way through the forms, ending with the Assorted Form, combining the Five Fists and Twelve Animals in a single linked set.

One last movement, and the master bedroom door opened.

Cai Yan.

She stood in the doorway, one hand on her hip, the other propping herself up against the frame, backlit in the warm yellow glow of a table lamp. Her dark pajamas shimmered softly in the light, clinging to her broad shoulders and slender waist. Raven hair, normally tied up, tousled down to her shoulders. Her qi field, silk hiding steel, reached out to caress his own.

She smiled, and the room lit up.

"*Zao an*," she said.

"Good morning," he echoed.

"Training?"

"Of course."

She shook her head.

"You're always training."

"We're martial cultivators. If we're not fighting, we're training."

"*Gongfu zhainan.*"

"We're biaohang. We should be *zhainan* and *zhainü*. Besides, weren't you training earlier?"

"I don't train in the dark like you. Or Ghazan."

Underscoring her point, a string of steady, muffled booms drifted from Ghazan's room.

"I don't have anyone to train with," Li Ming replied.

She smiled.

"*Zhen kelian.*"

How pitiful.

"Would you kindly take pity on your *shidi* and train with him?"

The smile became a giggle.

"You! *Zhen shide!*"

"That's a yes?"

"I'm not going to train in the dark."

She clicked on the lights, revealing the living room in all its splendor. Leather sofas and gleaming wooden tables, delicate ceramic vases holding live plants, shelves laden with miniature sculptures and figurines and books, paintings mounted on cream-painted walls. On the first day of their stay, Li Ming had rearranged the furniture, creating an open space for training.

"What would you like to do?" she asked.

"Let's start with two man sets."

"Yizhang or wuxingquan?"

"Both."

The An Family taught both styles as part of a single integrated art. He grew up with wuxingquan, while she favored yizhang. He wasn't nearly as proficient as her in her style, and she in turn wasn't as much of a striker as he was, but they knew the forms, the principles, the applications, and together they explored the breadth and depth of An Family gongfu.

She stepped up to him. Breathed. And stepped into the Sancai Shi.

"Let's go," she said.

First came the semi-cooperative drills. Baby Catching the Butterfly and Take the Root. These weren't fighting forms, but they developed the attributes necessary for combat. Sensitivity, balance, momentum, impulse, and qigong.

Fresh wave of warmth flowed through him. With every breath, he consciously relaxed his muscles, letting physics and body mechanics to do the work, allowing the qi to flow. Feet hooked against feet, flesh pressed against flesh, bone ground against bone. Through her silken sleeve, he felt her qi, receptive and yielding, and her body heat. Their qi mingled together, becoming a superfield that entwined their energies as one.

A short break. Then came the combative sets.

Li Ming threw a metal fist. Cai Yan slapped it down and drilled in with a water punch. Li Ming fired a wood fist, curving it ever so slightly to deflect the incoming blow. Cai Yan erupted from below, blowing away the jab with a fire punch. Li Ming stepped out, swatting her punch away with one hand, the other crossing over to drive an earth fist into her face. Cai Yan replied with metal, and now Li Ming ran through the same cycle she did.

This was the Productive Cycle. Based on the Five Element theory, it was one of a possible set of responses to an incoming energy. They threw the blows at full speed and maximum intent, aiming for vital targets, simulating sudden violence, training nerves and reflexes.

Next came the Conquering Cycle. Metal and fire, fire and water, water and earth, earth and wood. The cycle Li Ming preferred, the one he used most often, with his fists and his magic.

Another pause. Then they segued into the Bear and the Eagle. Short range power paired with long range strikes, horizontal circles versus vertical, the higher-level principles of the art.

They circled around, crashed together, pulled apart. They swooped from up high and surged from below. Every spiral became a strike, every strike flowed into a spiral. Fingers grasped like the claws of an eagle, fists and palms blasted forth with the raw power of a bear.

They kept tight, stayed close, keeping away from the walls and the furniture, adjusting their positions in real time. She was close, so close he could smell her, clean sweat mixed with subtle a floral fragrance. Her face relaxed, her eyes widened, taking in everything—the room, the walls, the furniture, him.

Now the last set. An Shen Pao. The Serene Body Cannon, the longest form they knew, the most famous form among the many branches of wuxingquan.

He chased her, she fell away, she entered, he yielded, he stepped, she spiraled, she struck, he shielded, he grasped, she released, following the dance laid down by those who had gone before them, a dance that encapsulated the powers of the art and the energies of the cosmos.

One last exchange, and they stepped back and stood down.

"You've improved," he said.

She beamed.

"You're not bad yourself."

"Shall we do yizhang?"

"Sure."

She bloomed.

Head and upper body twisting to face him, legs turning to the side, right arm extending to chest height and opening into a palm, left wrapping around her torso, her entire body moving as a single integrated unit with effortless grace.

He tried to mirror her. But his movements were functional, conscious, lacking that ineffable something that separated mere students from those who owned the art. He needed more practice, but that was why he was here.

They began with circle walking. A deceptively simple exercise, they circled each other around an unseen axis, first clockwise, then counter-clockwise. Beginners simply practiced walking the circle to develop core attributes. But hidden in this practice was the art of footwork, of sneaking up and closing the distance, of ranging out without being seen.

Round and round and round they walked, closer, further, closer still, eyes wide open, taking in each other, sensing energies and movement, maneuvering to avoid the furniture. Without a word, without a signal, they flowed into the sets.

Advance and retreat, palm and grasp, punch and parry, hook and release, they drew circles and cut through them, manifesting curved vectors and straight lines and the infinite gradient between them. They expressed the eight elements of the art, each a reflection of an aspect of the universe, not as the languid arcs of other branches of yizhang, but as the linear blows of the five fists of wuxingquan.

Conscious thought melted away, leaving action and reaction, offense and counteroffense, following the ancient patterns refined over centuries. Their energies swirled and blended. Active and receptive, positive and negative, masculine and feminine. Her movements become jolts of liquid lightning, his own crashed and retreated like black water set on fire. With every touch he felt her, all of her, her structure and momentum and center, her qi and heart and intent, and he sensed her doing the same. An invisible boundary between them fell away, and in that moment, they were two souls unfolding into the great dance of the cosmos.

And just like that, they circled away and stepped out and faced each other.

And it was over.

Someone clapped.

Wong Wan Lung, standing by the television, clapped, his broad face split in genuine delight.

"Kao ban! Nimen de gonfu zen piaolian!"

Li Ming needed a moment to translate his accent into standard speech.

Magnificent! Your gongfu is splendid!

Cai Yan flushed.

"It's nothing. I still have a long way to go."

"Me too," Li Ming said. "Yizhang isn't my principal art."

"That was yizhang? I thought it was more... curved."

"Our lineage combines yizhang and wuxingquan," Li Ming said.

"Ah. Well, I don't know much gonfu myself, but I can appreciate it when I see it."

An odd statement, coming from him. The stocky southerner was an accredited biaohang, a silver-ranked martial cultivator. But his qi score was only 125, only slightly more powerful than an ordinary human. Stranger yet, there were gaps and hollows in his qi field. Li Ming could *see* them, an emptiness that ran the length of his arms and legs, leaving only a thin mist.

"You don't practice gongfu?" Li Ming asked.

Wong Biaohang's face twisted in exaggerated distaste.

"I'm a shooter, not a fighter. I just need enough gonfu to untangle myself from close quarters."

Ghazan emerged from his room, his arms crossed, a skeptical expression on his face.

"You sure don't like getting your hands dirty."

Wong Biaohang pretended to examine his hands and wiped them down on his pants.

"My hands are more valuable to me than gold. I can trust Ga San-*gor* to take care of beasts who get too close, right?"

Ghazan chuffed, then turned to the other biaohang and asked, "Were you two doing two-man sets?"

"Yes," Li Ming said.

"That's not real gongfu. Without sparring, you're not learning how to fight."

Li Ming glanced at Cai Yan. "He's got a point there."

Cai Yan shied back. A little. She wasn't naturally inclined towards sparring. It was the one thing that separated her from the other biaohang.

Normally she let the frontliners do the heavy lifting while she supported them from the rear with magic. But with such a small team, there was no division between the front and back lines. She had to hold her own. More to the point, she had to *show* that she could hold her own in a press-up fight.

"Let's go." She paused. "But nothing hard, okay? We don't have safety gear."

"How long you want to go for?"

"One minute."

Ghazan sneered.

"One minute?"

"We've got a full workday ahead of us, you know."

"Let's do it," Li Ming said.

In the middle of the training space, Li Ming sank into the Sancai Shi. Cai Yan twisted around into her yizhang stance. In that moment, whatever it was that joined them earlier melted away, splitting apart in the face of an invisible and irresistible force.

"Ready?" Wong Biaohang said. "Go!"

Li Ming pounced.

His lead hand found her wrist. Grasping like a vice, he pulled her down and launched his rear hand, arcing into a splitting palm. Her rear hand came up, guarding her head. He hooked her hand down and stepped in again with another splitting strike, and this time his palm found her crown.

She tried to spiral out. He advanced with a flurry of straight punches, driving her against the wall. She slipped away, slapped down a strike, speared in her other hand. He ducked, parrying her away, unleashing a palm of his own, taking her low in the belly. She backed up, trying to shed the energy of the blow, but instead bumped against the wall.

She was at the disadvantage here. The small space restricted her movements, kept her from full turns and flanking circles. Li Ming stepped forward, forward, ever forward, driving her back against the wall. She defended with a lightning-fast flurry of palms and spears, he answered with deflections and parries and counters, the slap of every contact echoing in the room.

She spun out, stepping into empty space. Her left hand went high, her right went low, leaving an opening in the middle. Without a thought, he punched into her gap. She spiraled away from the punch, deflecting with her left hand, loosing a backfist with her right.

Her knuckles caught him below the ribs and scraped across his flesh. Instantly she reversed her motion, right arm rising to wrap around him. Li Ming chopped it down with a splitting fist, spun in a tiny circle, struck her shoulder with his other hand.

She spun into him, shedding the force of the blow, right hand rising to cover her hand, left palm shooting for his exposed rib. He dropped his elbow, lowered his arm and pivoted slightly, sweeping the arm away.

Her right arm shot in and wrapped around his neck. Her other hand reached around his back to grab her wrist. Her weight shifted, setting up the sweep. He shifted all his weight to his lead foot and lifted his other knee, voiding the strike and hitting her in the belly.

But her momentum was too great, his structure too unstable, and he went down.

Instantly he wrapped his lifted leg around her back, then the other, and then they *both* went down. He rounded his back, landing hard on the carpet, slapping the ground with his other hand to break the fall. She tried to rear up, his legs still wrapped around her torso, struggling for dominance. He punched up at her face, a big and obvious movement, and she double-parried it aside. His other hand snaked in, twisting around to bring the palm to face the ceiling, found her muscled throat—

Stopped.

The web of his found her delicate jugular and carotid. A little higher and it might have crushed the windpipe. It was enough to demonstrate that he could have finished her, to touch her just enough that she had felt it.

With a twist of his hips, he unbalanced her. Enough to release her, scoot back, scramble up to his feet. She did the same, assuming her guard and—

"Time!" Wong called.

Li Ming punched his palm over his heart, the traditional martial art salute. She mirrored him.

"Thank you," Li Ming said. "You fought well."

"You too. I could barely stop you."

"You're in close quarters," Ghazan said. "You should have closed in and used your yizhang grappling. Or switched to wuxing striking."

"I tried, but..." she shrugged.

"You need more sparring."

"You want to have a go too?" Li Ming asked.

Ghazan grinned.

"Sure."

Ghazan stepped up, sinking into his guard. Right side bladed towards Li Ming, elbow chambered and aimed at his chest, left fist over his Belt Vessel, legs held wide but high. Li Ming assumed the Sancai Shi.

"Ready? Go!"

Ghazan exploded.

His right hand hammered down, clearing Li Ming's arm. His body twisted around, elbow slashing up.

Li Ming leaned back, shifting his weight, raising his knee. Ghazan's elbow whooshed past his nose. Li Ming's knee found his belly. Li Ming stepped out, left palm coming around to strike Ghazan in the gut.

Ghazan grinned.

And charged.

He threw a nonstop barrage of punches and forearms, a whirlwind of violence in a small space, striking high and low and high again, seeking to clear the way for a killshot. Li Ming turtled up, covering himself up, seeking deflections and counters, striking where he could. But Ghazan had made his bones as a bareknuckle fighter in the Taiping fight circuit, and at infighting range he was in his element.

For every blow Li Ming deflected, another landed. The shots were light, but Ghazan's qi blew into and through him, sending fiery shockwaves radiating through him. Li Ming swirled around, trying to flank him, but Ghazan kept cutting him off, crashing into him, forcing him to answer an incoming fist.

Li Ming peeled away, jumping out into the middle of the training area. Ghazan shifted his stance, spreading his arms and legs wide, then leapt in and whirled around, his rear arm arcing around to split the air.

Li Ming shuffled his rear foot up to his lead foot, angling his arms just so, and blasted in. His right arm rotated in mid-air, catching Ghazan's forearm and camming it away. Li Ming's left palm went low, through the opening he had created, shooting into the ribs.

At the last moment, Li Ming twitched.

He pushed off his rear foot, sending a spiraling force through his body. His left palm angled up, going for the armpit. His joints opened, his spine undulated. Then the rest of Li Ming's body weight accelerated into and through Ghazan.

Ghazan went flying.

He crashed against the wall. Instantly he slapped his hand down, the twin thundering booms reverberating in the room, shaking the windows and paintings and figurines. He launched himself off, advancing once again with windmilling palms, slashing high and low and side to side, covering his inexorable advance. Li Ming stood where he was, reading his body, ready to—

"Time!"

Ghazan stopped.

And relaxed.

Li Ming saluted.

"Good job."

Ghazan mirrored him.

"You too."

Li Ming extended his hand. Ghazan shook. Li Ming reached over and lightly patted Ghazan on the shoulder.

The Yue tensed, as if shielding himself from a crashing palm, ready to whirl around into a hook. And, just as abruptly, relaxed.

Ghazan turned to Cai Yan.

"Want to spar too?"

She hesitated.

"Sure."

It was a bloodbath.

Ghazan went in hard and never let up. She threw palm after palm, trying to range out. He simply blew them aside like an iron bar slapping away a leaf. He was the worst possible opponent for her, taller, stronger, faster, with fight intelligence and experience she couldn't begin to match.

She tried strategy after strategy, but he stuffed them all. When she went long range, he closed the gap and loosed a punishing series of blows. When she tried to circle around, he threw hard elbows and knocked her back. When she tried to grapple, he retreated and answered with long-range chops. For every blow she got in, he landed three more.

She covered up, focusing on defense and counters and escapes. He just kept coming, overwhelming power matched with terrific speed.

Ghazan threw a powerful jab. Cai Yan speared her arm out, deflecting the blow, almost but not quite reaching him. Abruptly she whirled around, elbow slashing. He got his own elbow up, but it was a little too late, and her bone smashed into his bicep.

He punished her with a lightning-fast barrage. She circled round and round, trying to slip away, to slip in, mostly failing. He launched a hook, she torqued in, shielding her face with her forearms, then slashed both palms out as if she were cutting with twin swords. He deflected one strike, but the other reached his jaw. He spun into an elbow to the chest, knocking her back, then launched a pair of straight punches.

"Time!"

Cai Yan was panting, sweating, her qi expended. Ghazan stood tall and strong, his qi field burning like a wildfire, the ghost of a smile twitching across his lips.

"Thank you," Cai Yan said. "I see why you were an undefeated fighter."

Ghazan acknowledged the compliment with a tiny nod, as if it were a fact so unremarkable it was barely worthy of notice.

"You weren't bad yourself."

"You look like you had fun," Wong Biaohang said.

"Fighting is great. You want to try?" Ghazan said.

Wong Biaohang held up both hands.

"I *know* I can't fight at your level. You won't learn anything from sparring with me."

Wong Biaohang made himself look small and self-depreciating. But behind his words and mask, there was a heart of steel. Li Ming realized that Wong Biaohang understood his strengths and knew that he had nothing to prove.

"I hope you've gotten all that pent-up aggression out of your system," Cai Yan said. "We've got a packed morning ahead, and we'll be dealing with civilians."

"Who are these civilians?"

"The Jianghu Association."

Chapter Three

Fixer

If Yudu were the hegemon of the Central Plains, Jinshan District was its crown. The commercial, economic and political center of the city-state, its influence stretched out to touch every corner of the world. The Ten Corporations had found a town of hills and transformed it into a nation of skyscrapers. Financial institutions and megamalls, arcologies and institutes of learning, here was where the elite lived and worked and played, insulated from the general population. Gold flowed like water from these mountains of glass and steel, and where gold went, blood followed.

It had only been two weeks since the Dayong party arrived in Yudu. Li Ming was still orienting himself, still learning the ground. But there was no mistaking Jinshan, no way to get lost. The sheer density of ultra-modern high-rises, some traditional towers, others cutting-edge edifices designed by machine intelligences, set it apart from the rest of the city. He thought he was familiar with urban verticality, but deep inside the district, he once again reminded himself that at heart, he was still a dirt bun from a no-name farming village.

After a quick shower and a leisurely breakfast, the team had set off for Jingshan. There was no rush, but the sooner they finished their work, the sooner they got paid, both in money and, more importantly, prestige.

Half a year ago, Dayong lost almost half of its active biaohang. What began as a beast hunting expedition became a mission to clear and salvage an abandoned military bunker dating to the Yue Dynasty. After fighting through hordes of rapid-spawned genetically-modified monsters, the biaohang had recovered a motherlode of Yue Dynasty tech.

For their reward, they were betrayed by soldiers of the Ten Thousand Swords Society.

Li Ming, Ghazan and Cai Yan were the only survivors. Cai Yan Meng Yang, the boss of Dayong, father of Cai Yan, had been the first to die. The Cais had completed their mourning period months ago, but a veil of sorrow had fallen over Cai Yan's face and never lifted.

They had exacted vengeance on the Ten Thousand Swords. But no amount of bloodshed would bring back the dead and no amount of reparations could undo reputation damage. For a biaoju that had lost so many biaohang in such a short time, the world of the rivers and lakes saw only two possibilities. Either the biaoju's forces were weak, and therefore not worthy of being part of the jianghu, or they had powerful enemies—and no one dared to get caught in the crossfire.

Even now, Dayong still struggled to replace its losses. Three biaohang completed their contracts with the company and moved on elsewhere. Few answered Dayong's recruitment advertisements, even fewer met its standards. Cai Yan stepped up as leader of the company, advised by his grandparents, focusing on the business side of operations. After months of heroic effort, Dayong had finally recruited and retained enough manpower to meet its contractual obligations at home.

But only barely enough.

Fed by the waters of great rivers and blessed with huge swathes of fertile arable land, the Central Plains was the breadbasket of the continent. It also lacked a central government, functioning instead as a loose league of city-states and independent towns only barely united under the auspices of the Central Plains Merchant Association. Rich in natural resources, yet lacking the ability to mount a coordinated defense, beasts and bandits found natural habitats in the Central Plains.

Two weeks ago, the Central Plains reported a sudden spike in beast activity around Yudu. The city government issued an open invitation to biaohang and hunters from around the continent to harvest the beasts. Dayong accepted immediately.

They had to.

The mission to the Central Plains was a signal of strength. It showed that Dayong could send forces outside its home province. It demonstrated their commitment to protecting the innocent and upholding the code of the jianghu. It advertised their skill at arms and cultivation to the inhabitants of the rivers and lakes. Through this expedition, Dayong would prove it was worthy of being named as the finest biaoju of its home province.

Failure was not an option.

Without more clients, more contracts, most of all, more manpower, Dayong was finished. There were always other biaoju around, ready to snatch up lucrative accounts from under Dayong's nose. As an independent company, it could not hope to compete with the large private military and security corporations. If Dayong could not regenerate its strength, it would be relegated to third-tier status forever.

Li Ming would have preferred a larger party. At least ten men, a full squad, with the ability to conduct tactical maneuvers and to absorb casualties. This was a dangerous business, and losses had to be factored into the equation. But most of Dayong's new blood were newcomers to the jianghu. Sending them on a high-risk beast hunting expedition was reckless, even suicidal. Cai Yan insisted that they stay in Bao An to gain experience working regular contracts, with many of the Dayong's senior biaohang showing them the ropes.

Wong Wan Lung, with plenty of successful expeditions under his belt, was the only recruit the Cais felt comfortable deploying to the Central Plains. Sending Li Ming and Ghazan, Dayong's most famous fighters, would increase Dayong's profile, and hopefully attract more attention and recruits. With Cai Yan busy at home, it fell to Cai Yan to lead the expedition.

Four biaohang, for an expedition that would last indefinitely, until Yudu rescinded the beast alert or unless another lucrative contract came up. Li Ming had no idea how the team would make it work, only that they had to.

Where they lacked in quantity, they had quality. Every biaohang was blooded and experienced. Thanks to Cai Yan's brand-new gold rank, they were all permitted to carry top-tier gear, drawn from the company's arsenal. What equipment they lacked, they could purchase from the markets of the Central Plains, world-renowned for stocking anything a martial cultivator ever needed—including many things he didn't know he needed. It was their only advantage. They had to make it count.

But even that wasn't enough, which was why they had hired a fixer.

For such a powerful organization, the local office of the Jianghu Association was a bland affair. Occupying its own city block, it was a three-story cube of brick and mortar, of high narrow windows and broad double doors. But for the three-story pagoda tower it wore as a cap, it was visually indistinguishable from its neighbors. At the main entrance, Zhang Mei Lin waited.

Accredited by the Jianghu Association, she was the team's guide, negotiator, interpreter, facilitator, go-getter. If the team needed to find someone, interface with an official, get something done, she was the woman they turned to.

She was also a civilian. Her long twin braids, running down to her narrow waist, secured with blue ribbons, was proof of that. Today she was outfitted for the city, matching a green dress with white stockings and black flats. A black leather messenger bag lay slung over her shoulder.

"*Zao an!*" she chimed. "How was your hunt?"

"We bagged the bashe," Li Ming replied.

Leaning in, she beamed at them, holding her arms behind her back.

"*Wah! Shuaige men hao lihai wo!*"

You hunks are so awesome!

Wong Biaohang puffed up his chest. Ghazan crossed his arms and smirked. Cai Yan glanced at her, then at Li Ming.

"I didn't do much," Li Ming said. "The others did the heavy lifting."

"You triggered the mines," Wong Biaohang said. "It would have stopped most beasts."

"Not this one. And Ghazan finished it off with his bayonet."

Ms. Zhang's eyes widened.

"You killed a bashe with a *bayonet*?"

Ghazan waved his hand dismissively.

"It was nothing. The bashe was already weakened, and I augmented the strike with magic."

"Ah. But it's still an incredible feat."

"Dayong hires the best in the business," Cai Yan said.

The air inside the Association building crackled with qi. The second he stepped through the doors, Li Ming felt an electric tingling down his spine and palms. It was as if storm clouds were gathering in the air, building up to critical mass.

The workday had just begun, and already the lobby was packed with life. People occupied a half-dozen counters. Knots of young men and women spread out across the many sofas and chairs, staring at screens and talking into devices. Display boards showed queue numbers in bright red numbers. In small cubicles, clients conferred earnestly with Association staff.

They were all cultivators.

It was in the way they talked, walked, dressed. Many of them openly wore weapons, cold steel and reality shapers, the status symbols of the jianghu. They positioned themselves to watch the doors and the room, frequently looking up to sweep the room and peek at mirrors. Those that didn't, or couldn't, had buddies to watch their backs. The professionals wore a variant of the same uniform, long-sleeved shirt with cargo pants and boots, armed with a plethora of pockets and zippers, in muted colors. Others chose flashier and more fashionable outfits, islands of color in a sea of olive drab and urban grays, unafraid to tell the world who and what they were.

The team took the elevators downstairs. Here in the basement, crews of workers stood ready to receive and assess harvested beasts. Ms. Zhang whispered into a few ears and secured priority access to a work bay. Inside the bay, a gang of burly men in stained coveralls waited for them.

Ms. Zhang and the detail leader exchanged profuse greetings in the Yudu dialect. The Central Plains was home to seven dialects, all of them mutually unintelligible with the standard Xiayu spoken in the Zhongxia Republic. Where Xiayu had four tones, the people of Yudu used five. While Yuhua and Xiayu shared many initials, finals and consonants, there were also many sounds exclusive to one or the other. Some words Li Ming thought he recognized, others were so hopelessly alien he couldn't hope to understand them. Without Ms. Zhang, the Dayong team would be fish out of water.

Finally, in halting Xiayu, the detail leader addressed the biaohang.

"Let's see what kind of beast you've brought in today."

The biaohang pulled out their Shanbang Belt Bags. As one, they manifested portable meat coolers. Most hunters were satisfied with chests filled with ice. For this expedition, the Dayong team had procured industrial-grade walk-in coolers, more commonly used for multi-day hunts by a team of hunters.

Each cooler could hold the equivalent of eight elk carcasses from internal hooks. They were all packed to bursting, stuffed with bags of raw meat, organs and bones. The chillers worked overtime, struggling to preserve the harvested tissue.

The detail leader shook his head, muttering something under his breath.

"Mr. Guo says the bashe must have been huge," Ms. Zhang translated.

"It was as large as a long-haul truck," Li Ming said.

Mr. Guo's eyes boggled.

"A truck?! I heard that bashe could grow to great lengths, but…" He shook his head. "I believe it."

The workers moved like a well-oiled machine. They hauled the bags from the coolers, weighed them with precision scales, unpacked and assessed the contents of each bag, transferred them to specialty coolers. Every time they filled one of their own coolers, they carted it off and brought in a replacement. It was like watching an assembly line at a factory, with each man assigned a specific task and doing it supremely well.

The biaohang stood back and watched the process, ensuring every worker did his job right. It was part of the Association's oversight mechanism, optional but highly encouraged. The workers spoke to each other in Yuhua, using jargon and slang only they knew, their conversations brief and utilitarian. Li Ming studied hands and pockets, ensuring no one secreted away something that didn't belong to the team.

In their corner, the assessors tallied up the harvested materials by weight and quality, filling up their ledger. They worked swiftly but methodically, handling every cut of meat, every fragment of bone, every recovered organ with gloved hands and respirators. They looked for signs of decay, disease and damage, and determined what use the harvest could be put to. They compiled their reports using voice dictation, speaking into their headsets. They were like robots, swiftly rotating and studying their items, scanning for imperfections in seconds, before handing them off to the repacking team and receiving the next item.

They had to work fast. Occupational health and safety regulations imposed strict limits on how long raw meat could be allowed to be exposed to the open air. Once a beast died, the decay process began. The coolers suspended the process, but it did not reset the clock. The workers had to complete the unpacking-assessment-repacking cycle before the meat warmed up enough for bacteria to resume activity.

An hour later, the workers carted off the last of the harvest. The assessors discarded their personal protective equipment, discussed their findings and compiled their report for the biaohang to inspect.

Now it was the women's turn to shine. They pored over every line of the report, compared them against the Jianghu Association's beast pay scale, and haggled with the assessors. Li Ming didn't have Cai Yan's business acumen or Ms. Zhang's local knowledge; he simply provided moral support with his presence. Wong Biaohang chimed in here and there, emphasizing the difficulty of the kill and the quality of the beast's hide. Ghazan hung back and said nothing, instead watching the rest of the room.

Finally they agreed on the payout. Eight thousand yuan per biaohang, about a quarter of the average monthly salary of a white collar worker in Bao An. Not too shabby for a single day's work. With a handshake and a digital signature, Cai Yan concluded the contract.

There was still plenty of work left to do. Equipment inspection and maintenance. Scanning news and forums for updates on beast and bandit activity. Searching for new contracts and opportunities on the Association's job boards. Checking in with Dayong back in Bao An. As they headed back upstairs, Li Ming prepared a to-do list, sorting them by order of priority. Cai Yan lowered the visor of her Eight Eyes augmented reality headset and danced her fingers through the air, working the haptic controls.

And startled.

Her body went still. But her qi jolted through her, shooting from her feet up and out her crown, catching Li Ming in the backwash.

"What happened?" Li Ming asked.

"We've been offered an exclusive contract."

Chapter Four

Beast Hunt

I n times of crisis, there was more than enough work to go around for the inhabitants of the rivers and lakes. But it didn't mean everyone had a chance to get paid.

Open contracts were a free-for-all. Available to any accredited biaohang who met the rank and experience requirements, they operated on a first come, first serve basis. Whoever secured—and completed—the contract first got the rewards. There were no second place winners. Most of those contracts were standing bounties on beasts, but some beasts were so rare that there was no way everyone could earn a slice of the pie.

Dayong's strategy was simple. Ignore most of the low-level contracts and pursue only the most dangerous—and most rewarding—prey. Prey like the bashe. Most small biaoju didn't have the experience or the equipment, or both, to take them on. Those who dared usually wouldn't come back. Only a handful of elite teams had the confidence and the capability to handle those contracts, and *those* teams were usually inundated with job offers from governments and businesses. Dayong didn't, *couldn't*, compete with everybody in a red ocean, so they found a niche with little competition.

The only drawback, of course, was that the monsters they hunted were maneaters and living calamities.

But this was the jianghu, where a man staked life and limb for the promise of gold and fame. Everybody in the team knew what they were up against when they signed up for the expedition. No one had backed out. And with three successful hunts in ten days, it seemed to be a winning strategy.

One that had now caught the eye of the right kind of people.

Or so Li Ming hoped.

Most contracts managed by the Jianghu Association were conducted out in the open, in the tables and cubicles scattered among the lobby. But they were only for open contracts, jobs that posed little to no security risk to the participants. Exclusive contracts were always negotiated behind closed doors. For this one, no less a personage than Branch Manager Qiu invited the Dayong team to his office.

As they seated themselves on plush leather sofas around the coffee table, his secretary served them cups of hot bluish-yellow tea. Fresh and grassy, it left a strong aftertaste on the way down. Li Ming wasn't much of a tea connoisseur, but he recognized excellent tea when he drank it.

"Thank you for taking the trouble to listen to our request," manager Manager Qiu said.

Unlike other Yudu citizens Li Ming had encountered so far, he spoke pitch-perfect Xiayu, devoid of regional quirks.

"It was no trouble at all," Cai Yan said. "We were already in the building when I received your email."

"Ah. Lucky. Perhaps it signals an auspicious start."

"What's the contract about?"

"It's a beast hunt. A swarm of hanba have invaded a farming town. We seek your aid in clearing them out."

"I've never heard of hanba before," Ghazan said.

"They're the bane of farmers," Li Ming said. "They cause drought and destroy crops and plantations everywhere they go. Their preferred habitats are rivers and forests. I don't think they're found in the Yue Homelands."

"Quite right," Manager Qiu agreed. "The climate and the geography in the Central Plains is ideal for hanba. Not so much the Yue Homelands. Unfortunately, hanba swarms are a common occurrence here."

"How large is this swarm?" Cai Yan asked.

"Witnesses place the number at between twenty to thirty. But you must understand, hanba breed faster than rabbits."

"Where's the town?"

"An Le. About thirty-five *li* southeast of Yudu."

"An Le isn't part of Yudu, is it?" Ghazan asked.

"It's not, but the town is within our sphere of influence. When beasts and bandits appear, it is our responsibility to defend it."

"Who's the contract originator?" Cai Yan asked.

"The Yudu Military Forces."

"The *military* called this contract?"

"In the Central Plains, the military works hand-in-glove with the jianghu. There isn't as much tension between the private and public sector as you see in Zhongxia," Ms. Zhang explained.

"There isn't as much difference too," Wong Biaohang added.

Manager Qiu and Ms. Zhang frowned, but they didn't argue the point.

"Is the military on site?" Li Ming asked.

"Yes. A platoon from the Eighth Shock Infantry Company, commanded by Captain Bao Chen Ming. He will be your liaison at the village."

"We are new to the Central Plains, and unfamiliar with your ways," Cai Yan said. "If the military is already at the scene, why can't they take care of the beasts?"

"The hanba have infested the rice paddies. Captain Bao is concerned about collateral damage, and so he requested for biaohang with kinetic weapons and precision magic. Dayong fit the bill."

Infinity guns were the most powerful and widely-available man-portable arms on the planet. They also had the distressing tendency of setting vegetation and other flammable materials on fire.

Sighing, Li Ming shook his head.

"This job is going to come down to cold weapons in close quarters," he said.

Wong smiled.

"Don't forget, I have a precision coilgun. I can put down the hanba and leave the rice intact."

"Someone's going to have to poke the bodies when you're done."

Wong Biaohang patted Li Ming's shoulder.

"*Xinku ni le.*"

I've made you work hard.

Coming from anyone else, it might have been patronizing. The veteran biaohang actually sounded sincere.

"How much is the military paying for the job?" Ghazan asked.

"Fifteen thousand yuan, half on acceptance, half on completion. This is above and beyond any rewards you will receive for turning in the hanba to us."

"What can hanba be used for?" Li Ming asked.

"To be blunt, compost. You won't be paid much. However, their internal organs can be used for medicines, research and various industrial processes. They fetch a premium price on the market. But harvesting their organs will be difficult."

"Why? Aren't hanba endemic in your land?" Ghazan asked.

"They have a unique biology. They appear humanoid, but they absorb water, air and qi through their skin. They do not have arteries or veins like we do, rather a dense network of redundant vessels that transport their vital fluids. The fastest way to kill one is to destroy their core. But that is also where their organs lie."

Ghazan frowned.

"I can't stab them in the throat?"

"It will only annoy them, and it will take a long time for them to bleed out. You could try smothering or burying the hanba with magic to preserve the organs, but I've told it's a long and... *disturbing* process."

Li Ming winced.

"I've tried it before. It's time-consuming *and* risky. Better to put them down quickly and cleanly."

"Always a good idea," Wong Biaohang said.

"Would you like to accept the contract?" Manager Qiu asked.

Cai Yan looked at her team.

"What do you guys think?"

"Every day we're not working, we're burning money," Ghazan said.

Lodging, vehicles, supplies, rental of the Belt Bags, Ms. Zhang's rates, the costs added up. The expedition was in the black, but not for long. Li Ming's share of the bashe's bounty would only cover costs for two, maybe three days at most.

"Are you up for another hunt?" Cai Yan asked.

"Always," Ghazan said.

"I've never hunted hanba before," Wong Biaohang said. "Seems fun."

"I have," Li Ming said. "It's not fun. Which means I'll be coming with you."

"We're in," Cai Yan said.

An Le was a town under siege.

Soldiers in green uniforms patrolled the high walls, infinity guns at the ready. The gatekeepers, two Yudu troopers in modern kit partnered with two civilians with ancient gear, scrutinized everyone's biaohang cards before letting them pass.

The streets were empty. Faces peered out of darkened windows. Thick clouds of incense drifted from a small shrine at the center of town. More soldiers stood guard on the roofs and street corners. The monsters had driven everyone indoors, away from the life-giving fields.

The soldiers had turned the mayor's home into a fortress. Inside his humble living room, Captain Bao sprawled out across a couch. Mayor Kong shrank into himself, hands clasped before him, his face shot through with lines. His family served the biaohang tea, brought out chairs and stools for the guests, and promptly banished themselves to their rooms.

Captain Bao didn't look much like a soldier. Short and chubby, his cheeks bulged like a chipmunk and his gut sagged under his plate carrier. His hands were fine and delicate, *too* delicate for a serious soldier. But he wore a pair of sleek reality shapers on his arms, his powered exoskeleton was reinforced with armored plates, and his infinity gun was clean and well-maintained. His aura was powerful, extending to fill the room. Most of all, behind the clear lenses of his Raptor smartglasses, his eyes shone with a keen intelligence.

As the biaohang entered the room, Li Ming had studied Bao's qi. With quick glances and eye blinks, he activated the Raptor's qi assessment app and focused the cameras on Bao, long enough for the instruments to return a result without giving away what he was doing.

16782 qi points. Over two thousand more than his own. Anyone who had the dedication and talent to work himself up to such a score was not a man to be trifled with, no matter how he appeared on the outside.

"Thank you for coming to helping us," Mayor Kong said.

"No problem. It is our job," Cai Yan replied.

"It is rare to see a Yue around these parts," Captain Bao said. "You must have traveled far."

Ghazan grunted and sipped his tea.

"I go where the beasts go."

For the Yue, Li Ming knew it was the height of diplomacy.

"We heard there are many beasts infesting the rice paddies," Cai Yan said smoothly. "Could you tell us more?"

"Not *daotian*," Mayor Kong said. "*Titian*. We grow rice in the terraced fields to the north."

"Ah. Apologies. Are the farmers safe? How many beasts are there?"

"When we arrived, we evacuated the farms, locked down the town, and sealed off the terrace," Captain Bao said. "Everyone is safe and accounted for. Our drone spotted twenty-five hanba."

Wong Biaohang grinned.

"A target rich environment. Nice."

"The terraces are our lifeblood, and it is harvest season," Mayor Kong said. "The hanba are destroying our rice and fish. Please act swiftly, but preserve the terraces."

"Wait a second," Li Ming said. "Did you say 'fish'?"

"Yes. No one told you?"

Cai Yan shook her head. "We were only told you grew rice."

"We cultivate carp along with rice. It is a mutually beneficial relationship. The rice shelters the carp. The carp in turn feed on pests and weeds, and their constant movements loosens the soil, which improves fertility and reduces diseases. We've practiced dual rice and carp cultivation for over a thousand years. I'm surprised no one told you about it."

Even in the jianghu, intelligence failures and miscommunication still occurred.

"How are the hanba destroying your crops and carp?" Ghazan asked.

"I heard farms are rare in your country."

"Yes. Only about one percent of arable land in the homelands is suitable for crop production. Hanba do not exist over there. I wish to know more about them."

Mayor Kong's hands tightened into fists.

"Hanba are the scourge of our land. They drink copious amounts of water. One hanba can drain a terrace in a day. While drinking, they gorge themselves on everything they can find around them. Rice shoots, fish, everything they can stuff into their bellies. They reproduce quickly, too. Their young mature in a week, and their females spawn at least a dozen of them in every breeding cycle."

"Ordinarily we would handle hanba ourselves, but their presence in the rice terraces creates many complications," Captain Bao said. "We felt it was best to hire specialists."

"You don't have kinetics?" Wong Biaohang asked.

"Not at the platoon level. Only specialist sniper units have kinetic weapons, and it will take hours to mobilize them."

Wong Biaohang shook his head. "In Nanguang, kinetic weapons are commonplace."

"They also have higher lifetime costs."

"That is true."

"What about magic?" Li Ming asked.

"Our textbook tactic is to electrocute hanba with lightning bolts. But with the fish… we felt it would cause more harm than good."

"I heard you could smother or bury hanba," Ghazan said.

"If they were in an open field, with rice sprouts or seeds, we would gladly try that. But now, with the rice ready for harvest, and with fish in the fields, we don't want to disturb the soil dynamics and risk burying the crops and the fish too."

"That leaves us with long-range kinetic fire," Wong said.

"Essentially, yes. But if you have magic that can pick off the hanba without disturbing the rice and the carp, go ahead."

Li Ming did. But Wong's coilgun had far greater range.

"I don't mean to cause offense, but the more time we spend talking about the beasts, the more time they have to destroy the livelihood of my town," Mayor Kong said. "Please hurry."

"Do you have any more questions?" Captain Bao added.

Cai Yan glanced about the room. One by one, the men shook their heads.

"Let's get started," she said.

Everyone rose to their feet.

"Good hunting," Captain Bao said. "We look forward to seeing what Dayong can do."

"We won't let you down."

Chapter Five

Down the Way of Devils

The rice terraces began where the northern walls of An Le ended. Flights of steep steps cut into rolling hills ranged to the horizon, covered in a sea of swaying golden-green stalks. The terraces emphasized the natural contours of the slopes, yet simultaneously served the needs of Man. Gazing upon the panorama of rounded curves and sharp lines, shaped by the hands of men yet respectful of the seasons and cycles of the natural world, a place that gave forth life in the service of the living, Li Ming stood in quiet wonder.

He would have liked to visit here as a tourist, but fate had placed him here as a hunter.

Wong Biaohang paced the wall walk, hunting for the perfect spot. From here he could dominate the terraces, deliver death from above at ranges beyond the comprehension of mere beasts. But the walls were narrow, built at a time when the height of military technology was the repeating crossbow. There was no space for him to properly deploy his coilgun.

The coilgun was enormous. With the butt resting against the ground, its muzzle ended just past Wong Biaohang's jaw. Sleek and angular, there was no mistaking its lethal purpose. Every component was custom-built for the singular purpose of delivering a long, thin dart at hypersonic velocities exactly where the shooter wished it to go.

The pistol grip was molded exactly to Wong Biaohang's hand, the cheekpiece crafted for his face, the trigger a flat-faced bar that offered a longer reach and greater contact area than a traditional curved design. A cosmic tap ran flush against the hand-facing side of the buttstock, drawing qi from the universe and converting it to electricity. Forward of the trigger group, a huge box magazine as wide as Li Ming's palm was locked in place. Its skeletonized handguard sported a single accessory, a fantastically complex bipod. Mounted atop the upper receiver was a digital day/night scope with integrated ballistic calculator, a scope as expensive as a new motorbike.

This was Wong's weapon, and his only. He allowed no one else to shoot it, handle it, not even touch it. Li Ming could respect that. After all, he wouldn't let anyone touch his swordbreaker.

As the shooter set up, Li Ming ran through his own preparations. He snapped on his battle belt and helmet, leaving the rest of his armor in his Belt Bag. He drew out his infinity gun, slung it over his neck, and ran through a quick function check. He patted down his mismatched reality shapers, one on either arm, inspecting the crystal housings. Finally, he drew his swordbreaker.

The cold weapon he had taken with him since leaving Fuyang, it was patterned after the swordbreakers used by the Imperial Bodyguards of the Celestial Empire. It was a strange weapon, a sword that could not cut, a cross-shaped mace with an armor-piercing tip, a hefty chunk of meteorite steel designed for thrusting and crushing.

It was also a magic weapon.

Hidden in the pommel was a five element primordial crystal. The grip panels contained the dense circuitry needed to channel and transform raw qi into cosmic power. It was a weapon worthy of the ancient protectors, a cold weapon and a reality shaper in one, a weapon that, but for legal loopholes, he would not be allowed to carry. He was, after all, only a bronze-ranked martial cultivator, unworthy of such a powerful implement of battle.

Which made it his trump card, one he would play only when he needed it.

Wong produced a sandbag from his Belt Bag and planted it against a battlement. He smoothened it, patted it, kneaded it, compacted it into just the right shape. He rested the huge coilgun on the sandbag, leaving the bipod folded, and folded his arm across his chest.

"Shooter ready," Wong Biaohang said.

Li Ming scanned the terraces, seeking flashes of color, of movement, of anything that betrayed the presence of a beast. By the northern gate, Ghazan and Cai Yan stood ready to repulse a counterattack.

Against such a vast vista, a hanba was a tiny target. They could crouch low in the water, hide among rice stalks, and wait for an unwary human to pass by. In Fuyang, hunting teams resorted to systematically stabbing paddies and ditches with spears when hanba were about.

Here, they had fusion goggles.

In thermal vision, heat showed up as flashes of yellow, orange and red. Qi vision visualized a qi field as translucent clouds of ethereal colors. A hanba would show up clearly in a fusion imager.

If calibrated properly.

Li Ming worked the controls of his fusion goggles, adjusting the gain and sensitivity. Originally set for night use, he saw nothing but reds and oranges everywhere he looked. In the sweltering summer sunlight, the sensitivity would be sharply reduced. He would have preferred to hunt at night, but Mayor Kong insisted—*demanded*—that the team leave now, and Cai Yan had acquiesced.

Finally he found the right setting. The visor shaded the world in cool greens and blacks, leaving flashes of red where the sun reflected off the water. He investigated each patch of red, first in thermal, then with qi view, hunting for hanba.

And found a bloom of orange and amber.

Li Ming clicked off the thermal view. A dark shape crouched behind drooping stalks of rice, encircled in bubbles. Most of the terrace had been ravaged and drained, leaving only a handful of intact stalks poking through shallow, brackish water. Smaller shapes darted across the water, keeping clear of the intruder.

"Go to glass," Li Ming said.

"Ready," Wong Biaohang said.

"Second hour, one hundred twenty, twenty-five degrees depression. Go to the berm."

"Contact."

"Go the rice stalk halfway between the berm and the slope."

"Contact. I have eyes on humanoid figure. Possible target. Shows up hot in my scope."

"Engage."

A slight pause.

A soft, polite cough.

The coilgun recoiled gently into Wong's shoulder. There was no muzzle flash, no streak of blinding light, just a whisper-quiet sound like the swatting of a metal brush against wood. Wong had set the weapon to subsonic mode, the better to avoid spooking the prey.

Downrange, the round tore into the target. Water splashed around the point of impact. A clump of strange matter ripped away. Clear amber fluid gushed from the wound.

And the hanba rose.

The beast was neither animal nor plant, but something in between. Its mottled gray-green skin faded into the background. Bright yellow eyes, huge and unblinking, gazed at the world from what passed for a head. It had no neck, only a small dome atop a rotund belly. Tendrils extruded from its sides, bunching into four crude limbs, separating into dozens of delicate grabbers. Yellow liquid dribbled from a hole in between and below its eyes.

"Target still up," Li Ming warned.

The shooter fired again.

The round drilled through the middle of the hanba. More amber blood burst out. The creature toppled on its back, twitching and thrashing.

"Want me to shoot it again?" Wong Biaohang asked.

"Sure."

A third thump. The hanba shuddered. And went still.

"One down, twenty-four to go," Wong Biaohang said.

The hunt stretched through the morning and past midday. Drawing upon his childhood experiences in Fuyang, Li Ming learned to read the rice terraces and adapt what he knew.

The hanba hid among weeds and rice, but they always left signs of their presence. Drained paddies. Chewed-off stalks. Bubbles. Whenever Li Ming saw all three signs, he went to thermal and inevitably spotted the beast.

For his part, Wong Biaohang's already formidable skills sharpened. He learned to place his shots carefully, in the exact center of mass, through the hanba's heart, brains and lungs. Anywhere else would merely annoy and alarm the beast.

The hanba came in all sizes. Most were the size of large dogs, engorged on water and rice and fish. A few specimens had grown to the height of men. But some were tiny, no larger than a watermelon. Hanba young.

His heart quailed at the thought of slaughtering the young. His rational mind reminded himself that they were beasts that brought drought and devastation everywhere they went, and that if they were allowed to mature, they would once again revisit calamity on the people. They *all* had to die.

Yet every time he called a shot, he felt a tiny part of him die too.

The monsters were helpless. They intuited that they were being picked off one by one, but they neither saw nor heard the shooter. Only the death throes of their companions. Most of them chose to remain still, to hide in the water and imitate the rice. Wong took his time with those, lining up his sights for a perfect kill shot. The rest tried to run. Li Ming prioritized the runners, guiding Wong to them. The few he missed, Ghazan and Cai Yan eliminated.

When Ghazan spotted a runner, he called it in to Cai Yan. She tracked the target, watching it flee across the paddies. The moment it stepped on dry land, she called down a lightning bolt from the heavens, striking it through the head, shocking and shutting down its organs while leaving the fish intact.

The thunder spooked the hanba, sending more of them fleeing. Wong gunned them down as quickly as he could, leaving the rest to Cai Yan.

Her range was incredible. Two, three, four, even five hundred *chi*, and she was still capable of accurately striking a target with a lethal lightning bolt. If she could see it, she could kill it. The best Li Ming managed with his own magic was a hundred *chi*, and that was with his swordbreaker.

He had a long way to go. But then, she was a gold ranker, and he a mere bronze.

Halfway past the hour of the goat, they finally called for a stop. Li Ming swept the terraces three times, finding no more threats. Cai Yan and Wong tallied their kills, finding a total of twenty-eight.

They broke for lunch, taking turns to stand watch. Li Ming went first and stared out the battlements the second he was done. Once he'd seen a majestic view of man and nature existing in harmony. Now he saw only hiding spots, corpses, spatters of amber blood.

The military drone whooshed over the terraces, sweeping the farms. It was a black whirring spot against a clear blue sky, zigging and zagging in a precisely-programmed search pattern. Li Ming looked where it wasn't looking, letting his awareness expand to embrace everything before him, allowing his subconscious to identify and flag incongruities in the landscape.

There were none. Not anymore.

Immediately after lunch, the team moved out. Fanning out across the terraces, they retrieved the bodies, stuffing them inside the Belt Bags. Processing them could wait until they were back in the village, where they would have room to deploy the coolers and work in relative peace.

And when they were sure the hanba were dead.

Ghazan believed in the finality of the blade. With fixed bayonet, he roughly prodded the corpses, ready to deliver the finishing blow as needed. Li Ming wasn't as keen on bayonets, not when he had his swordbreaker.

Infinity gun slung over his neck, he held his swordbreaker in one hand, his Hellcat subcompact pistol in the other. He covered a body with his sidearm as he approached, and once in range he poked it in the eyes with his blade. The first time he'd did that, he felt sick, but that was years ago, when he still wore the greens of a Special Military Policemen. Now he just felt nothing but strange flesh yielding to hardened steel.

It was slow work. The waterlogged soil sucked in his boots and held him back. Curious fishes swam up to him, their tails tickling his calves. The afternoon sun baked him, plastering his clothes to his body with sweat and water.

For all that, he made good time. Glancing over his shoulder, he realized he'd left Cai Yan and Wong Biaohang far behind. Ghazan was somewhere off to his left, stabbing through rice stalks with gusto.

The plan was for the frontliners to collect the bodies, while the back liners provided support near the city walls. Were they hunting mere animals, it wasn't right for the killers to leave the prey for others to clean up. But they were hunting beasts, and beasts could come from anywhere. The wise biaohang knew that you never went anywhere alone, without overwatch and backup close by.

Li Ming forged ahead, sloshing through the paddies, carefully descending the terraces. The bodies would rot quickly under the sun. He was almost certain that the assessors would pronounce the hanba fit only for compost, but he still had to try. Still, he couldn't afford to get careless. Every paddy had a sump at the base of the berm, a water-filled ditch where the fish could hide during the dry seasons and in case of emergencies. The murky water hid the sump from casual view. He'd almost tripped a few times before he realized why. It wouldn't do to fall flat on his face. Not in front of the others.

He planted a soggy boot on a berm and gathered his bearings. He'd collected six carcasses already, and he was halfway down the hill. There were three more hills to go, with ten more bodies scattered between them. The work was deceptively fatiguing, and he was only going downhill. He had to pace himself. But if he went too slow, they would only be paid compost.

He wiped his brow with the back of his right hand, his swordbreaker hand. He could rest when they were done. He just had to push on and finish this. He pushed himself off and—

Qi rushed through him. Hot and fiery, it burned bright as a flame, igniting his heart and mind.

He was a hunter, a beast slayer. Work like this was beneath him. What the devil was he doing, slopping through the mud like this? He should—

He shook his head. That wasn't right. He had work to do. He should—

A dark shape hurtled off to his right.

He spun around, bringing his pistol to bear.

Nothing.

He lowered the weapon a fraction and scanned. Nothing but golden rice and green hills and terraces. But...

"Li Ming! Did you see something?" Wong Biaohang called.

"I thought I saw movement to my right!" Li Ming replied. "Anyone see anything?"

"I don't—"

A screech split the air, echoing among the hills. Bestial and bellowing, it sounded like a word.

"*XIAO!*"

"Beast! Contact right!" Li Ming called.

He scrambled up on the berm and—

The soil crumbled under his boot.

Instantly he stamped down, regaining his balance. He picked another spot and stepped up, planting his feet solidly on the earth.

He'd made a mistake. He had to keep at least one hand free, to keep his balance, to pull himself up, to catch himself when he fell. Perhaps he really should invest in a bayonet like Ghazan.

As the thoughts raced through his mind, he pivoted like a tank turret, eyes soft and wide open, breathing softly and deeply, sweeping the world before him. His ears, already augmented by his headset, pricked up, listening for the tiny sounds that betrayed a moving target.

Water splashed. Stalks rustled. Heavy foot thumped rhythmically. It approached him, just below the crest of the terrace, curving around to the right.

"Wong Biaohang! It's going your way!" Li Ming yelled.

"Roger! Any sign of it?"

"I hear it! I don't—"

"*XIAO!*"

A huge black blur burst into the air. Its titanic arms stretched like wings, guiding its flight. Li Ming fired at it, but it was fast, too fast, his bolts spearing harmlessly into the sky.

"*YAOGUAI!*" Li Ming yelled.

A whisper-quiet shot punched through its arm. The beast screeched.

And dove.

On Wong Wan Lung.

It smashed into him with tremendous force, knocking him down into the paddy in a burst of dirty water, sprawling over him. Wong Biaohang thrashed about, arms flailing, but it crushed him under its tremendous weight. It reached down with both hands and ripped his arm off.

Wong Wan Lung screamed.

It tossed the limb aside and reached down again, pressing itself against him, huge arms scrambling for purchase.

It's trying to drown him!

Li Ming snapped up his pistol and blasted off a triple tap. The three full-power bolts streaked through the air just under the speed of light, searing bright lines across his field of view, and—

Decohered.

The star-bright bolts disintegrated halfway to the target, becoming no more dangerous than a cloud of hot steam.

Li Ming screamed in rage. Wong Biaohang hollered in pain, his voice suddenly cutting off. The monster shrieked.

And tore off Wong's other arm.

Cai Yan shouted, her voice echoing like thunder. A white bolt slashed forth from her outstretched arms, striking the monster in the chest. The beast rocked back. Shouted again. And extended its right arm.

The beast's palm flashed. The world rippled. An invisible pulse tore through the world, distorting and contracting the air before and around it. At the last moment, a steel-gray barrier appeared in front of Cai Yan. Shield and shot annihilated each other in a burst of light and fury, throwing her back into the water.

This wasn't an ordinary beast. It was an Evolved beast. A cultivator among beasts, one capable of using magic.

"GHAZAN!" Li Ming yelled.

A plasma bolt struck the creature in the upper body. Now it felt it, bellowing in rage. It jumped.

At Li Ming.

It hurtled through the air, arms spread out. Now he saw it clearly, great mass of dirty fur hiding tremendous muscles, the body of a snake with the arms of a monkey and the face of a man. Its muscular serpentine body ended in a single, massive hoof. Blood gushed from a hole in its left arm. Claws extended from massive paws. An unnatural wind blew, accelerating it. In the middle of its forehead, a green crystal gleamed.

A shanxiao.

An apex predator of the mountains.

Time slowed. Thought ceased. With crystal clarity, Li Ming saw the monster swoop down on him, teeth bared and fangs dripping. His heart stilled, his mind blanked, the entirety of his spirit poised in perfect readiness, ready for the right moment.

Now.

His gun swung up. The red dot framed its chest. He fired.

The bolt smashed into an invisible veil. The energies exploded on impact, but the nova-hot plasma leaked through, scorching its chest. With a howl, the shanxiao dropped from the sky, crashing hard into the paddy.

Right in front of Li Ming.

Li Ming swung his swordbreaker. The shanxiao threw up its good arm. Steel crashed against hardened bone, blowing it down. Hissing, the monster recoiled. Li Ming thrust for its throat—

It leaned back, just barely dodging the blow.

Li Ming chambered for another strike. The beast leapt back, crashing through rice stalks, keeping out of range. Li Ming swung his handgun back up—

"LI MING! ON YOUR RIGHT!"

A gust of wind. A sharp tearing crackle. Reality crumpled and reformed.

And suddenly Ghazan was *there*, right next to Li Ming, infinity gun held out like a spear, his skin the color of deepest night, his eyes burning red, his fair hair a pure burning white.

"With you!"

Ghazan's voice was now a harsh, gravelly boom, the sound of burning brimstone-covered rocks crashing against each other.

A strange sensation rippled through the air, a blast of weird qi spiraling past Li Ming, cutting him in its wake. Li Ming recoiled from it.

And the shanxiao picked itself up, gnashing its teeth. Red blood spewed from the massive hole in its left arm. Its other arm hung at an odd angle, broken by the swordbreaker. The wounds should have put down a lesser being, but this shanxiao was a cultivator among beasts. It coiled up, balancing itself on its sole hoof, and lowered its head to aim its forehead crystal at the biaohang.

Li Ming fired.

The Hellcat's bolts splashed against an invisible barrier, boiling off the water around it, leaving the monster untouched. White-hot balls spiraled around it, vaporizing everything it touched. With a sinking feeling, Li Ming realized it had captured his shots, and was preparing to use them against him.

"Ghazan—"

The Yue lunged.

The shanxiao turned, too little and too late. With a thunderous bellow, Ghazan thrust, plunging his bayonet deep through its armpit. Twisted. And retracted.

Its qi collapsed.

The energies peeled off from the shanxiao as if it were shedding its skin. The plasma bolts disintegrated in bright flashes. Ghazan drank down the raw qi, claiming it for his own. His qi field grew larger, brighter, hotter, a black hole gobbling down a sun.

The shanxiao fell.

And went completely still.

"Ghazan," Li Ming said quietly, "what the devil did you just do?"

Ghazan lowered his weapon and turned to Li Ming. It was like looking into the heart of a dark star.

"Saved your life. And you're welcome."

"Thanks. But what kind of magic is that?"

"High-level Night magic. One I am experimenting with."

The Yue had their own magic system, based on the cosmic principles of Sky and Night. Li Ming didn't begin to understand it, only that Ghazan had consistently executed magic no one else in Dayong had seen before.

"You consumed the beast's qi, didn't you?"

"What about it?"

"That's illegal!"

"Only if you do it on humans. There is no law forbidding the use of such powers on beasts."

"But—"

"It is in the bylaws of your Jianghu Association. And in my country, people care little about how you kill a beast."

Li Ming felt the earth crumbling beneath him. Ghazan had saved his life, yes. But that kind of qi-eating magic had been taboo since the days of the Celestial Empire. He'd read about it in the Li Family magic weapon manual. It was one of the few branches of magic his ancestors had explicitly forbidden their descendants from exploring.

But why?

Was it simply the norms of those days? Or were there longer-term consequences? Was there an ethical way to use such magic? Or did it lure men down the way of devils?

He didn't know.

Over the radio, Cai Yan's voice cut through his thoughts.

"Status report. Is everyone okay?"

Ghazan shuddered. His skin brightened to a light olive. His hair reverted to a soft shade of shade of platinum. His eyes faded to amber. But his qi field remained larger, stronger, more powerful than before.

Li Ming patted himself down, found no wounds, and hit his push-to-talk switch.

"Ghazan and I are okay," Li Ming replied. "And you?"

"I'm fine. What about the beast?"

Ghazan touched his bayonet to its eye. It remained still.

"It's dead."

"Good work! Where's Wong Biaohang?"

A cold shiver ran down Li Ming's spine.

"Wong Biaohang, check in. Are you alright?" Cai Yan asked.

No response.

"Wong Biaohang! Are you there?"

Wong Biaohang yelled at the top of his lungs.

"I'M HERE! I CAN'T REACH MY RADIO!"

"Are you injured?"

"I'M DOWN!"

Li Ming's heart stopped.

"Stay where you are! We're coming!"

Weapons sheathed, Li Ming charged up the slope. Ghazan trailed behind, checking his back. Cai Yan hustled across the terraces, apparently none the worse for wear.

"I'm over here!" Wong Biaohang shouted.

He had propped himself up in a seated position against a slope, hip-deep in water.

"Can you move?" Li Ming asked.

Wong Biaohang waved, but there was something wrong. His sleeves were loose, floppy, as if...

Stumps.

He was waving stumps.

"MEDIC!" Li Ming roared. "MEDIC UP!"

Cai Yan flashed white. Fire qi blasted through her muscles. Muck sprayed out behind her, as if she were running on the surface of the water.

"I'm fine! Really!" the downed man protested.

Li Ming hopped over one terrace, two, a third, and now he was in right in front of Wong Biaohang.

"How bad is it?" Li Ming asked.

Wong Biaohang flapped his stumps pathetically.

"I'm fine, really. I just need my arms back. Could you help me pick them up?"

No good. He wasn't making sense. His fair face was pale, his chest heaving. His clothes were so soaked through, Li Ming couldn't tell where he was bleeding, or how much.

Cai Yan was a certified medic, but so was he. He set his backpack down and grabbed his first aid kit. Cai Yan stopped in front of Wong, splashing water everywhere. She peeled off her tactical gloves. Li Ming grabbed a pair of nitrile gloves and handed them to her.

"I'm fine! I don't need first aid!" Wong Biaohang protested.

"We all know you're hard, but you don't have to put up a front," she said. "Does anywhere hurt?"

"*Everything* hurts. But look, I'm—"

She knelt over him, feeling his vital signs.

"Talk to me. What did the beast do? Other than your arms, what did it do to you?"

"Bruises, that's all. I—"

"Okay. I'm going to do what I can. Once you're stable, we'll get you to a hospital—"

"I *am* stable! I just need my arms back!"

"You mean this one?" Ghazan asked.

The Yue bent over, fishing an arm from the water. Despite the trauma, it looked remarkably intact. No breaks, no bleeding, no wounds, there was only...

Metal?

Li Ming blinked.

The arm was completely lifelike. Its musculature was convincing, its skin covered with hair, but the end of the arm terminated in a matte metal ball joint.

"You're a cyborg," Li Ming said flatly.

"I was trying to tell you guys that!" Wong Biaohang protested. "You wouldn't let me speak!"

Li Ming shook his head, wondering if he should laugh or sigh. He compromised with a smile.

Cai Yan held out her arms. Her crystals glowed white. The light leapt from her shapers and engulfed Wong, sinking into him. Wong exhaled in relief.

"Thanks," Wong Biaohang said. "I'm fine now."

Ghazan retrieved Wong's other arm from the mud.

"How do we put your arms back together?" Ghazan asked.

"We can pop them back into the sockets. But it's not critical. I'd rather do it at the cybernetics clinic in Yudu. After violent trauma like that, they need to be examined. Maybe even replaced. You should go and recover and process the bodies first. That's more important."

"Roger. I'll get to it," Li Ming said.

He pivoted around and—

"Wait!"

"Yes?"

Wong Biaohang's sleeves flailed miserably.

"I need a hand."

Li Ming blinked.

And laughed.

"What's so funny?"

Li Ming doubled over, his laughter violent and gusty. He couldn't help it. There was just something about the way he said it, juxtaposed with his armless sleeves.

"What?"

"You need... A hand..."

Li Ming abandoned his senses to a gale-force guffaws. A second later, Cai Yan erupted into giggles. Even Ghazan smiled.

"*Wei! Mm ho siew lor!*" Wong Wan Lung exclaimed.

They laughed. And laughed. And laughed.

Chapter Six

The Natural Order

By necessity, the team took the following day off. Wong checked himself into a hospital to fix up his cybernetic limbs. The rest of the biaohang handled the routine but necessary tasks that would make or break a hunt.

Equipment cleaning and maintenance. Laundry. Administration. Paperwork. Scanning newspapers and job boards.

And training.

Martial cultivation in the morning. Intense bodyweight exercises in the evening, paired with a long distance run in the hotel gym. They trained their martial skills in private, in the balcony or in their rooms, away from prying eyes. The last time Li Ming practiced in public, he'd attracted the attention of a cultivator who had tried to lure him into a pointless duel. In Yudu, with so many martial cultivators seeking opportunities for gold and glory, among them there were bound to be fools who thought themselves heroes.

In the evening, after dinner, after everyone began to wind down, Li Ming headed up to the rooftop garden. In a quiet pavilion, away from prying eyes, he fired up his smartglasses and called his family.

He tried to call them as often as he could. Once a day if possible. But they understood that the demands of his work overrode his call schedule. He tried not to call *too* late if he could. Fuyang was an hour ahead of the Central Plains.

For the first fifteen minutes, the Lis exchanged pleasantries and updates. Mother complained about inflation and the rising costs of groceries. Younger Sister chatted amicably about homework, events in the province, her efforts to prepare for her final term in school, and the Higher Education Examination that would determine the course of her academic career.

Father said nothing of importance.

At last, the women were all talked out. Li Ming seized the opportunity to speak.

"I need to discuss some work stuff with Father."

"Again?" Sister whined.

"Work never ends. You know how it is."

She huffed.

"Have fun with your work."

Rustling and crackling passed through the line. Then a strong male voice spoke.

"We are secure."

Li Guo An presented the image of a gentleman farmer to the world. But before his retirement, he was a gold-ranked armed escort, one of the elite of the jianghu, tirelessly traveling the continent to hunt beasts and bandits. Before *that*, he was Colonel Li of the Special Forces. Some habits never died.

And Father being Father, he would already have known that his son needed to speak to him in private.

"Yesterday I saw some... weird magic. I wanted your thoughts on them," Li Ming said.

"What kind of magic?"

"I was told it was high-level Night magic, the magic of the Yue people. But it looked a lot like qi eating magic."

Father's voice went cold.

"Tell me about it."

Li Ming described the showdown at the terraces, leaving out Ghazan's name.

"This Yue colleague of yours... he is dangerous. Do not get close to him," Father said.

"Why?"

"His magic. Sky and Night exist outside the cosmos. They are not yin and yang, they are not like any of the elements we are familiar with, but they have the power to subvert them all. Yue magic is chaotic magic, designed to overthrow the natural order of things and bend the cosmos to the user's will. It is extremely powerful, but also extremely dangerous. To the enemy *and* the user."

"How is it dangerous to the user?"

"When we cast magic, we draw qi into our bodies, fuse them with the qi of a primordial crystal, and use our intention to manifest it. The elemental energies touch us *and* the cosmos. Yinyang, wuxing, bagua, they are part of the natural universe, and to express them in the outer world is to draw them into our inner world. It reinforces the elements and powers that exist within us.

"Sky and Night are *not* natural. If you draw Sky and Night into you, it alters you in deep and subtle levels. The Yue you spoke of transforms his body with Sky and Night, magnifying this effect. This transformation enhances the user's power, but it also magnifies the changes within. Using this magic turns you into... something else. Something that isn't human anymore."

"He is still human."

"For now. But for how long? And now that he uses qi eating magic, it's not going to end well."

"Our ancestors warned us against it. But I don't understand what they meant by 'break the golden stove, burn the crimson palace and drown the mud pill'."

The manual of the Li Family Magic Weapon Style was written in classical script, composed entirely in poetic verse. Many key concepts and terms were referred to in oblique terms, using colorful language and vivid imagery that revealed absolutely nothing about them. The only way to understand the style was oral transmission from teacher to student, father to son.

"Those terms refer to the three dantian: lower, middle and upper. Overuse of qi eating magic will overload the three dantian. In the late Yue Dynasty period, it was a common occurrence among their elite warriors, common enough that many historians argue that it contributed to its collapse."

"How can the dantian be overloaded?"

"Imagine your dantian as a boiler. You pour in water, start a fire, and you get steam. The water is the jing you absorb from the air, from the food you eat, from everything around you. The fire is your innate capability to refine jing. The steam is the refined qi that your body uses to sustain life.

"When everything is in balance, qi is clean and abundant, and the mind, body and spirit are healthy. The use of qi eating magic floods the boiler with water, more water than it was designed to contain. This drowns the mud pill, the upper dantian, because now the fire is struggling to boil the water. There's a lot of jing, but so much that it cannot be easily transformed into qi. If the body cannot produce sufficient qi, poor health follows. The qi eater may have to resort to stealing the qi of others just to survive."

"What if he grows the fire?" Li Ming asked.

"Then he burns the crimson palace, which is the middle dantian. A boiler is designed to specific tolerances. If you try to shove in more fuel and increase the temperature of the fire beyond safe limits, you could damage the boiler. In the same way, if a qi eater supercharges his fire, he could overload his metabolism and hurt his body."

"Where does breaking the golden stove come in?"

"The golden stove is your lower dantian. A boiler is designed to hold hot steam under high pressure, but it has limited volume. If you increase the water *and* the fire, you will produce a huge amount of steam, more steam than the boiler can hold. What do you think happens after that?"

"An explosion."

"Exactly. Martial cultivation methods prevent this through holistic development. It increases your ability to absorb, transform, store and use qi simultaneously. This is like upgrading your boiler. It is slow work, but it also prevents disasters like this. Qi eating magic absorbs a huge amount of raw energy, but it does not develop the dantian."

"I see. The ancestors weren't just being poetic. They were describing specific effects. And... I think I know what they are."

"Really? What are they?"

"The mud pill refines the spirit into emptiness. By drowning the mud pill, the spirit sinks and becomes heavy, and becomes unable to grasp higher truths and abstract concepts.

"The crimson palace refines qi into spirit, and governs respiration and the health of the internal organs. When the crimson palace burns, the organs burn also. This internal fire hurts the lungs, which affects breathing. When breathing becomes dysfunctional, the rest of the body, mind and spirit follows.

"The golden stove refines and purifies jing into qi. But if there is too much jing, the stove overloads and breaks. When it breaks, the jing and qi are dispersed. Without jing and qi, death follows.

"Did I get it right?"

Li Guo An laughed.

"Wonderful! You're beginning to understand the teachings of our ancestors."

"You taught me how."

"And now you're learning for yourself."

They spent another *ke* discussing more concepts and principles from the manual. The slim volume contained a lifetime of teachings. With every read-through, every discussion, Li Ming gleaned new information. But there was always more to learn, greater depths to plumb. In that regard, it was little different from gongfu.

Finally, Li Ming asked the question weighing on his mind.

"What should I do about someone who uses qi eating magic?"

"He is walking the path of the devil cultivator. If you can, if you dare, bring him back to the orthodox path. If not, you must cut all ties with him, lest he sees you as meat."

"What if I can't?"

"Then you must put him down."

Chapter Seven

Land of Immortals

Wong Wan Lung returned the following morning. To celebrate, they enjoyed a buffet breakfast in the hotel lounge.

Li Ming had never seen so many kinds of food in such a small place. There were traditional dishes, international cuisines, fusion foods. There were salads, breads, eggs, meats, fruits, buns, soups, noodles, congee, all of them prepared with a myriad of methods. There were so many kinds of foods, Li Ming didn't know where to begin.

Ghazan stuck to what he knew. He stacked his plate high with boiled meats, filled a tall glass with milk, and called it good. Cai Yan went vegetarian, choosing a bowl of cold noodles with assorted vegetables and eggs. Wong Biaohang assembled a small collection of buns.

Li Ming wandered the tables and selections, reading signs and ingredients, marveling at the many ways of preparing seemingly everyday meals. This was his third visit to the lounge, and every time there were new items on display. Finally, in the local cuisine section, he selected an enormous pork guokui. And tea.

Back at the table, the biaohang lifted their glasses.

"*Ganbei!*" Cai Yan called.

"*Ganbei!*" the men echoed.

They clinked their cups and drank.

None of them had alcohol. No one minded. The toast was their post-hunt ritual, and if they couldn't drink in the morning, they'd drink something else.

Li Ming tore off a bite of his guokui. The flatbread was thick and crispy, stuffed with thick chunks of roast pork and thin slices of assorted vegetables drowned in chili sauce.

Everything was hot and spicy in the Central Plains. The hotter the better. His tongue, accustomed to the mild sweetness and natural tastes of his home province, was still unused to the copious spices the locals used. The Yudu region was famed for its chili, but consuming spices in summer felt like a violation of common sense.

But, as he kept reminding himself, he was a long way from home.

"Wong Biaohang, how are your arms now?" Li Ming asked.

"*Aiya*, I keep telling you, you don't have to be so formal. Lung-gor or Wong-gor will do."

It didn't feel right, calling someone over ten years his senior 'elder brother', much less use a nickname like that. Li Ming was still the junior man around the table.

"I'll try," Li Ming said.

"You know that's not going to happen," Cai Yan said.

The men chuckled.

"I had to inspect, test and recalibrate my arms," Wong-gor said. "The technicians were afraid of water and impact damage, especially to the cosmic taps. They went and replaced the damaged artificial skin too. I told them they didn't have to, but they insisted. It took them all day to complete the repairs."

"From where I was, the damage looked dramatic," Li Ming said.

"Nah, artificial limbs can be easily removed. Watch."

Wong-gor rolled up the sleeve of his right arm, all the way to his shoulder joint. He pressed the fingers of his left hand against unseen catches hidden beneath his clothes. With a soft *click*, the entire arm detached.

"See?" he said, waving the arm about. "Pops right off."

"Makes maintenance and replacement easier," Ghazan remarked.

Wong-gor casually reinserted his arm and rotated it through a circle.

"Absolutely. It also detaches if it is placed under bone-breaking stress. This preserves the joints and makes field repairs easy."

"Was there any damage?" Cai Yan asked.

"Only skin deep. My insurance plan covers it."

"I heard there are different kinds of cybernetic limbs," Li Ming said.

"There's a limb for every job out there. Mine are designed for precision motor skills. I can play the piano, flip a coin, pull a trigger with total accuracy. It's the same kind of limbs dancers use."

Ghazan snorted.

"You? Dancer?"

"Hey, don't knock it. My hands, legs, fingers, even my toes do exactly what I want them to do, go precisely where I want them to go. Best of all, my heartbeat and breath won't throw off my aim."

"It can be useful for long-range shots," Li Ming said.

"*Incredibly* useful."

"How did you become a silver-ranked cultivator? I thought you had to meet a qi threshold before you could be promoted."

"The Jianghu Association makes an exception for cyborgs. Especially those with prosthetic limbs. Between the surgery and the... trauma, the qi body is permanently diminished. We can't possibly cultivate at your level."

It also meant he couldn't use magic. Which explained why he never wore reality shapers.

"How do you live without magic?" Ghazan asked.

Wong-gor grinned.

"Easy. I keep my distance and shoot the enemy in the face. A civilized method of warfare, yes?"

"'Civilized'? Really?"

"You like to work up close and get your hands dirty. *Ho wat dat eh.*"

Li Ming had no idea what the last sentence meant, but the look of mock-disgust on Wong-gor's face was enough.

"I heard you southerners are soft and elegant," Ghazan said.

"Yes, yes, absolutely. We are the center of arts and culture in Xiazhou. We leave the fighting to strong men like you."

Ghazan leaned back with a smile. Li Ming sipped his tea, hiding his amazement. Wong-gor had disarmed Ghazan just like that. Incredible. He never knew such a feat were possible.

"Why do you use kinetics instead of infinity guns?" Li Ming asked. "Aren't they harder to use?"

"They're also cleaner. A plasma bolt blows off a huge chunk of flesh. A coilgun flechette fragments on impact and carves out smaller but deeper wound channels."

"It has less stopping power," Ghazan said.

"True, but with proper shot placement, you'll have a beast carcass in an almost pristine condition. That means more money. It's why you love your bayonets, yes?"

Ghazan shrugged.

"True. But your coilgun is too long for close quarters."

"I'm a sniper, not a fighter. If I have to work in close quarters, something's gone terribly wrong. But if it does, I've got an infinity sidearm with me."

"What would you do against a threat armed with magic?"

"Shoot first, shoot lots, shoot from long range."

"Always a good idea," Li Ming said.

Wong-gor was a cyborg among cultivators, an outsider in a land of immortals and those who aspired to become immortal, a brick in a world of magicians, and yet he seemed... comfortable. He had carved out a place for himself among the rivers and lakes, one that made him an equal of, even superior to, those who walked the way of the martial cultivator. How had he done it?

And would Li Ming find a place of his own too?

"How did you become a cyborg?" Li Ming asked.

A twinge ran through Wong-gor's shrunken aura.

"Surgery. I was told it was long and intense, not to mention bloody and messy, but at least I slept through it."

"Sounds like you didn't enjoy it."

Wong-gor held up his arm and rotated his forearm through a full three hundred and sixty degrees. Then his hand. He spread his fingers and bent them back, far further than any man could without touching them.

Li Ming gaped.

"I never asked for this. But I made the most of it," Wong-gor said.

"You didn't choose the surgery?"

Wong-gor shrugged. Sipped his tea. And spoke.

"When I was younger, I lived in an apartment complex near a park. It was a quiet place. A nice place. The kind of place far from anywhere dangerous, a place where you could go to school, go to work and go to bed without worrying about beasts and bandits.

"My younger sister and I played in the park often. Father was working at the office, Mother was working at home, so they left us to do our own thing.

"One summer day, when I was six years old, I was playing with Younger Sister at the swings when I heard a growling sound. I looked up and saw a beast. A yugou.

"I had no idea what it was doing there. I didn't even know what it was. But I saw its eyes locked on us, the set of its jaws, the saliva dripping from its muzzle, and I knew it was dangerous.

"I told her to run back home. I dashed away from her, yelling at the yugou at the top of my lungs. She was just four years old. I had to draw it away from her.

"The plan worked.

"It jumped on me, and…"

He shrugged. Looked away. Said nothing.

"It must be difficult," Cai Yan said.

"I don't remember much of it. Just a lot of blood and a lot of pain. Uncle Bo, the security guard, ran over, kicked it off me, and shot it in the head. Then he called an ambulance. I blacked out soon after that.

"When I woke up, I was in the hospital. And I had brand-new arms and legs."

"I'm sorry," Li Ming said.

"Nothing for you to be sorry about. Everyone lived. Except the yugou, but who cares about it?"

"You did the right thing."

Another shrug.

"Yeah, well, after that I developed an allergy to close work."

"Did it take long to get used to your new limbs?" Ghazan asked.

"Three weeks, thereabouts. As I grew up, I swapped out limbs, and I needed to re-train them. My parents were relieved when I finally stopped growing."

"Was there any way to heal your qi field from the trauma?"

"We tried everything. Herbs, pills, supplements, experimental therapies. You're looking at the result. Slightly better than the average person, but not enough to be a cultivator."

"I see. You've survived a lot."

"All of us have."

A hush fell around the table.

Ghazan gnawed on a strip of barbequed mutton. Cai Yan folded her hands in her lap and looked down. Li Ming breathed.

Wong-gor lifted his cup.

"Here's to us. Survivors, hunters, biaohang. *Ganbei!*"

They raised their glasses.

"*Ganbei!*"

Chapter Eight

Bridge of the Martial Immortal

Yudu, with its eight shopping districts, was a paradise for tourists, fashionistas, youths, and every species of consumer. But among them all, only one catered to the specific tastes of the martial cultivator. Wuxianqiao, the Bridge of the Martial Immortal.

The bridge itself spanned the mighty Yu River, the river that gave the city its name and fed the countless farms of the Central Plains. Collapsed and rebuilt a dozen times in the span of its existence, today it took the shape of what the architects believed to be its original appearance during the Warring States Era, embellished by artists for contemporary tastes, reinforced by engineers for the city's civil engineering codes.

Great arches of time-worn stone admitted water taxies, cargo carriers, cruise ships. Wide piers of waterproofed concrete sank beneath the green-tinged waters. Scarlet pillars rose at regular intervals between sections of ornately-carved handrails, holding up roofs of teal tiles. In the center of the bridge, a pavilion with an upswept roof loomed over the river.

The narrow bridge was for pedestrians only. Cyclists were supposed to dismount and push. Few did. Li Ming kept to the sides, close to the guardrails, ceding the center of the bridge to the unlawful riders. Wong-gor followed. Ghazan strode straight down the middle, as if he owned everything in sight. Cai Yan zigzagged down the length of the bridge, swooping into empty spots by the rails whenever they appeared, taking photos of the river.

The pavilion was a popular tourist attraction. Overhangs on either side looked out onto the river. Vending machines chimed advertising jingles in the corners, offering canned drinks, fresh-made fruit juice, ready-to-eat snacks. People crowded the rails and benches, capturing the sights and sounds on smartglasses and headsets, leaving a wide aisle in down the middle of the road for foot traffic. Slipping through the crowd, Li Ming scanned faces and hands and hips, looking for signs of trouble.

At the other side of the pavilion, a trio of young men loitered about a vending machine. They scanned the crowd too, peering out at the world behind mid-range smartglasses. The man in the middle did a double take. He nudged his buddies and whispered something. All three turned to Li Ming, locking eyes and lenses on him. They were reading his qi field.

He read their bodies.

Empty hands. Reality shapers, plain and functional, consumer-grade designed for work instead of show. Loose short-sleeved shirts tucked out over faded jeans. Comfortable shoes. They weren't biaohang, not high-ranking ones anyway.

The leader swaggered over. His body bore the marks of a mildly experienced street fighter: many-broken nose and bulging biceps, scrawny neck and stick legs. His friends fanned out, sealing off the aisle. The one on the left had a big mole on his left cheek, the other sported a pair of crooked lips.

Here we go, Li Ming thought, and bladed his body towards him.

"Excuse me. Are you Li Ming?"

Li Ming kept his hands low. The rest of the team spread out around him.

"Who sent you?" Li Ming asked.

Broken Nose blinked.

"Excuse me?"

"You know who I am. Did someone send you?"

"No, no. I just recognized you from the *Jianghu Times.* You're the one who saved Bao An, right?"

"That was half a year ago."

Broken Nose smiled and cupped his fist over his heart.

"Your skills must have grown since then. I wish to exchange pointers with you."

His voice carried across the pavilion. Conversation stopped. Nearby civilians turned to look. The air crackled with qi.

Broken Nose was a name maker. In the world of the jianghu, the easiest way to climb the leaderboards was to duel someone placed higher than you. Victory in a challenge match would pull down the loser's score and elevate the winner's. With the prestige that followed victory came the contracts, sponsorships, and bragging rights.

In the Zhongxia Republic, all duels had to be formally sanctioned and regulated. Here in the Central Plains, anything goes, so long as both sides could produce proof of consent.

Li Ming wasn't here to play this game. But Broken Nose was more polite than the name makers he'd met in Bao An. That alone gave Li Ming pause.

Slightly.

Li Ming approached the challenger, his hands low and visible, his shapers charged and ready to go. Ghazan sidled up next to Li Ming. Li Ming saw no sign of Cai Yan or Wong-gor, but they'd doubtless be behind him, ready to step in.

Out the corners of his eyes, Li Ming saw bystanders backing away. Others hung back, waking their devices. Madness. Any sane person would stay far away from a battle between cultivators. Did these people think they were invincible?

He couldn't control what the other men would do, but he could hold himself back.

"Sorry, we're busy now," Li Ming said.

"Surely you can spare a few minutes—"

"We are not interested in matches."

Broken Nose spread his arms wide.

"We're at the Bridge of the Martial Immortal. By tradition, any martial cultivator who wishes to cross must be prepared to fight."

Ghazan cracked his knuckles. The civilians retreated to the rails, still watching the scene. Still advancing, Li Ming raised his hand.

"We are new to your city and ignorant of your ways. We are not here to challenge anyone. We merely wish to cross," Li Ming said.

Broken Nose smirked.

"Are you afraid of losing?"

Ghazan pounded his fist into his palm. The sound echoed in the suddenly-quiet pavilion.

"I am more afraid of what would happen to you," Li Ming said.

"So confident you'd win?"

Li Ming fixed Broken Nose with a steely glare. His qi flared, blowing over the challenger's own. Broken Nose blinked. His buddies closed in protectively around him.

"You're new to the jianghu, aren't you?" Li Ming asked.

Broken Nose blinked.

"No. We've been here for two years."

"Ah. You are my seniors. My respects to you. Allow your junior to point out that the jianghu is deep and wide. Surely there are safer ways to build your names."

"But there is no faster or better way than to cross hands," Broken Nose said.

Li Ming sneaked forward again, now bringing both palms up, facing out.

"We came here to protect Yudu from beasts. If you could just let us pass—"

"You may pass, after we cross hands."

One last step, and Li Ming rooted his weight on his lead leg.

"We're not fighters. We're just hunters. We're not—"

"Enough talk. Show me your gongfu."

Broken Nose sank into his stance. Legs spread wide, left arm extended, right fist close to his face. Highly stable, but thus also immobile.

"I have no gongfu worth mentioning."

"Your friend, then. I recognize Ga San from the—"

Li Ming blasted off from his weighted foot. His arms shot out, forming a spear of bone. Forearm clashed against forearm. Rotating into Broken Nose, Li Ming hooked his left wrist with his left hand, pressed his lead leg against the opponent's own, and pulled him down. Broken Nose fell into Li Ming, suddenly off-balance. Li Ming blasted into him, palms driving into his chest, his entire body weight blowing through him.

Broken Nose went flying.

Flailing, spinning, he yelped in surprise, and crashed into Big Mole. Both men went down in a crumpled heap.

Li Ming turned to the last man. Crooked Lips charged in, throwing a long-range punch. Shooting off-line, Li Ming slapped it aside, first with his left hand, then his right. His right arm hooked back around, wrapping around his neck. Li Ming grabbed his wrist with his other hand and torqued his hips sharply, lifting him off the floor and sending him crashing back down. Li Ming guided his fall, dumping him on his back instead of the back of his head.

Li Ming released him and leapt away. He took three long steps, then spun around to face the men, resting his left hand on the pommel of his swordbreaker.

"I trust that was enough of a lesson?" Li Ming asked.

The Broken Nose rolled off Big Mole, rubbing his chest.

"You cheated!" he growled.

"I didn't want this match. You insisted."

Broken Nose grunted, planting his palms on the ground.

"You cheated!" Broken Nose repeated.

"Stop!"

Li Ming's voice thundered across the pavilion, freezing him in place.

"If you move, my friend will beat you up some more. I'm sure he'll enjoy it. I don't think you will," Li Ming said.

Ghazan grinned.

Broken Nose spat a curse and stayed where he is.

"My team and I have other business to tend to," Li Ming said. "I trust there'll be no more trouble from now on?"

He mumbled something.

Ghazan stomped over and placed the sole of his boot on the man's knuckles. And leaned forward.

"Did you say something?" Ghazan asked.

"No trouble!" he squeaked. "Please, stop!"

"Good."

Ghazan stepped off.

"Let's go," Li Ming said.

They hustled down the bridge. The men took turns looking over their shoulder, watching their backs. Cai Yan led the way, cutting through the crowd. The civilians, their bloodlust sated, gave them room.

"Was that yizhang?" Ghazan asked.

"Yizhang, wuxing, they are all part of the same gongfu," Li Ming said.

"I recognize what you did," Cai Yan said. "We drilled them together."

"It paid off."

She smiled.

"You went easy on them," Ghazan accused.

"Ah?"

"You didn't do any real damage. Only bruised muscles and egos."

There was so much he could have done. He could have punched the name maker in the face, jabbed his eyes, struck his throat. He could have spiked the second guy head-first into the ground. He could have stomped the fallen men when they were down. If he were on the battlefield, fighting for his life or those around him, he'd have done it without a second thought.

But it wasn't.

"It wasn't worth doing more harm than this," Li Ming said.

"Never do an enemy a small injury. Crush him so thoroughly that you need not fear his revenge," Ghazan said.

"There were witnesses, cameras, no other avenue of escape. Mercy makes us heroes. Brutality turns us into villains."

Ghazan grumbled something in Yue, then switched to Xiayu.

"There will be consequences. They may come looking for revenge."

"Then we shall have to be ready for them."

Past the bridge was the Wuxianqiao district proper. Rows of houses built in the traditional style, from brick and mortar, wood and silk, snaked along the riverbank. The narrow roads were paved with regular rectangular slabs of flagstone, roads for pedestrians first and bikes second and four-wheelers not at all.

Strolling down the sidewalk, Li Ming drank in the overhanging balconies propped up with columns of timber and stone, hand-painted signboards, the ornate *dougong* joining pillars to roofs. The aesthetics hailed from previous centuries, but everything else was planted solidly in the era of the Five States and Ten Corporations.

Modern pop music blared from loudspeakers, a riot of modern medleys, classical tunes, foreign songs and Zhongxia hits. Screens and holograms advertised products and services, everything from clothing to computers to acupuncture to supplements. Street vendors hawked their wares, yelling prices and products and promotions, competing with their neighbors. Perfumes, deep-fried meats, fragrant tea, a hundred scents combined and clashed and vied for supremacy. Crowds of cultivators thronged the streets, hunting for the best bargains and the latest gear. Everyone was looking for an edge here, buyer and seller alike, an edge over their competitors, their targets, themselves.

The windows hinted at a stupendous array of goods. Hot and cold weapons, chained to racks, from subcompact pistols to infinity cannons and everything in between. Elixirs and pills promising to bolster qi cultivation, ward off diseases, enhance a man's stamina. Mannequins modeling the latest in tactical and civilian attires. Widescreens played action videos of gorgeous young women and athletic men showing off products.

Anything a martial cultivator wanted, he could get here in Wuxianqiao. But for the professional armed escort, there was no better place to shop than the Three Worlds Emporium.

It stood tall over the street, a three-story pagoda towering over all other buildings in the district, so large it occupied its own city block. It might have been mistaken for a temple, and indeed a temple it was, one dedicated to the worship of war.

Weapons. Armor. Reality shapers. Primordial crystals. Everything a man needed to challenge the evils of the world, he could find in some corner of the emporium. If a rookie needed a cheap starter gun to mark his debut in the jianghu, he could find it here. If a gold ranker needed to outfit her hunting party, the Three Worlds had everything she needed. If there was something a discerning customer needed that the Emporium didn't stock, a squad of engineers and specialists stood ready to assemble it by hand.

More than arms and accoutrements, the Emporium stocked everything needed for sustainment and development. Backpacks, tools, clothing, journals, ammunition, more, it was a one-stop shop for beast hunters and manslayers.

Li Ming grabbed a basket and went shopping.

On the ground floor, he stocked up on bottles of beast essence, enough to last him a month. Rendered down from double-boiled beast flesh, the black liquid was superconcentrated with vitamins and nutrients. The cheapest brands offered essence and nothing more. Higher-end recipes included herbal mixtures to boost the immune system, improve concentration, and achieve peak performance. Li Ming picked the most expensive option, formulated for the needs of the martial cultivator seeking maximum qi growth.

Li Ming drank two bottles a day, once after breakfast and once before bed. Coupled with his daily cultivation practice, he increased his qi score by a hundred and twenty points a month—an extra twenty points than if he cultivated without supplementation.

Twenty points might not seem like much, not for the money he had to spend for it, but it compounded over time. It was what separated the gold rankers of the jianghu from everybody else.

Cai Yan filled her basket with a staggering array of products. Pills, elixirs, more pills, broth, even more pills, all of them designed for women. As a magic user—as an immortal—she had to keep her body, spirit and qi in top form. He didn't dare to glance at the price tags; his own beast essence was expensive enough. He wondered if she were caught in an infinite loop, hunting beasts and bandits so she could afford the supplements so that she could continue to hunt.

It was the loop that defined life in the jianghu—the loop that trapped so many martial cultivators.

In the cold weapons section on the second floor, Li Ming purchased a bayonet. The same government-issue bayonet he had used in his military days, complete with mounting bracket for an accessory rail. Ghazan favored folding bayonets for rapid access, but Li Ming saw no reason to use his unless he absolutely had to. He preferred the reliability of a fixed blade. Ghazan had accepted the possibility of breaking his bayonet in combat—and had worked around it—but Li Ming didn't wish to replace his weapons every few months.

Among the guns, Li Ming spotted Wong-gor stocking up on ammunition. He chose flechettes designed for deep penetration and rapid fragmentation, the most expensive type of flechette on the shelves. Li Ming didn't know if he could stand the thought of spending thousands of yuan on ammo—infinity guns were expensive enough—but it worked for him.

Perusing the weapons accessories, Li Ming examined upgrades for his Hellion pistol. Every infinity gun needed to find a delicate balance between power, range, heat capacity and rate of fire. If Li Ming could have engaged the shanxiao from a distance, if he could have dropped it with one shot, the hunt at the rice paddies would have turned out very differently.

His primary weapon, an Avenger from the Sima Clan Arsenal, could have easily done that. But what if he didn't have his Avenger on hand? His Hellion had to step up to finish the job. But was it adequate for the job?

Only up close. But if he weren't fighting up close…

Li Ming waited for Wong-gor to finish his purchase. The second Wong-gor stepped away from the counter, Li Ming accosted him.

"What sidearm do you use?" Li Ming asked.

"Looking to upgrade your own?"

"When I shot at the shanxiao at the rice terrace, the bolt disintegrated in mid-air."

Wong Biaohang's eyebrows arched sharply.

"What do you use?"

"A Hellion."

"Ah. No wonder. It's a subcompact. Great for deep concealment and up close work. But it has a limited range. Past twenty *chi*, the bolt will fall apart. You wouldn't have that problem with a kinetic weapon. The bullet will keep on going until it hits something."

"I was wondering if I could extend the range."

"On a subcompact frame? Not likely. The bolt integrity is based on three factors: bolt intensity, velocity, and the strength of the magnetic field. The more powerful the bolt, the faster it will rupture. To prevent that, you need higher speed and greater magnetic field intensity. A tiny pistol like that won't fit the parts you need to push the range past twenty, twenty-five *chi* at most."

"What do you recommend?"

"I use the Viper hand cannon. An amazing piece of kit. It'll reach out to a hundred *chi*, it's got select fire capability, it'll blow clean through a shanxiao. Better yet, if you fit it with a brace, you can transform it into a compact carbine, with greater accuracy and stability out to its maximum effective range. Look, you can see it over there."

Wong gestured at a display case near the counter. Dozens of handguns lined up in neat rows, spread across three shelves. The Viper nested apart from them, perched atop a black plastic case.

Large but sleek, its matte frame drank in the light. It seemed top-heavy, a large upper frame married to a stubby handle, but the elongated trigger guard seemed to balance it out perfectly. The reflex sight was big and beefy, reassuringly overengineered for hard use.

Right next to it was a Force Multiplier brace. It looked like the shell of a gun, a long upper receiver, a folding telescoped stock, accessory rails, but no grip or sights or anything that would rain thunderbolts on a target.

"It seems... big," Li Ming said.

"It's a big gun, for big work," Wong agreed. "It's not for concealed carry, especially when fitted with the brace. It's for field work, for times when you need range and firepower. You can keep your Hellion for urban use and everyday carry, but if you're going on a high profile operation, you need something more substantial than a tiny little piece like yours."

Li Ming worked his smartglasses, calling up the Viper's spec sheet from the manufacturer's site.

Range: 100 chi

Sustained rate of fire: 8 shots / second

Maximum rate of fire: 15 shots / second

Overheat capacity: 30 shots

Overheat cooldown time: 30 seconds

It was incredible performance. Almost the equal of a full-sized infinity gun, but in a smaller package. The brace turned it into tiny carbine, closing the gap even further. Li Ming understood why Wong-gor had picked this weapon.

Then Li Ming looked at the price.

"Ten *thousand* yuan?"

"Yeah, it's priced as much as a mid-range infinity gun," Wong-gor said. "The brace costs another five thousand. But they are well worth the money, *if* you see yourself going into situations where you need this kind of capability."

Li Ming frowned. And when he looked at the fire control unit, his frown deepened.

"This model only has safe and single fire."

"Ah, right. This is the civilian model. Only silver rankers and higher can purchase select-fire weapons. But it's not necessary if you ask me. Besides, if you buy the civilian model, you can upgrade the fire control unit once you rank up."

"What other upgrades have you made to your Viper?"

He laughed.

"Lots. Deeper heat sink, more powerful magnetic field, vertical grip, magnifier, offset sights... I don't expect to need it often, but if I do, I need the firepower of an infinity gun in a small and light package. I think the total cost of the accessories match that of the weapon."

"I see..."

"It's an expensive gun, especially for someone new to the jianghu. You don't need a gun exactly like mine. You need a gun that fits *your* needs. As a frontliner, you'll have a different use case for sidearms than me."

"The Viper is out of budget now."

"There you go. You don't need it now. Take your time to think about it some more, figure out your use case, and when you have the money you can revisit the gun again."

"Alright. Thanks."

Wong-gor's words made sense. Still, it took sheer effort of will to tear himself away from the Viper.

Not now. Not today. Maybe in the future.

Li Ming shoved his purchases into the Belt Bag. It was a useful piece of tech, though it required a cosmic tap. If the power ever cut out, its pocket dimension would collapse and everything stored within would be destroyed. There was no substitute for the old-fashioned backpack, at least in critical situations. Would be nice if he could buy one for himself, though.

Someday. When he could afford it. Whenever that was.

Chapter Nine

The Same Sky

Down the street from the Three Worlds Emporium, at the end of the district, stood a temple. An actual place of worship, but one that catered to the demographics of the district. Side halls honored various tutelary spirits, including the city gods of Yudu, but the main hall was dedicated to General Guan and Marshal Yue. Once mortal men, in life they were legendary heroes, in death they were venerated as gods of war.

Here they sat side-by-side upon golden thrones, illuminated by a hundred burning oil lamps, constantly engulfed in thick clouds of sweet incense. Tapestries showed cherubic Fo and lesser immortals meditating and frolicking around them, a nod to the rich pantheon of divinities that populated the myths of the continent, but Li Ming knew it was a subtle message that all beings enjoyed peace and prosperity only because warriors stood ready to defend them.

Li Ming, Cai Yan and Wong-gor paid their respects. Ghazan stood outside and waited. Li Ming didn't know if the Yue were religious, only that the Celestial Empire had obliterated nearly every shrine and temple of the Yue people across the Continent, and that outside the Yue Homelands no one was in a hurry to rebuild them.

A small army of hawkers and fortune tellers set up shop along the street. Some flogged incense, lamps, flowers, and other traditional offerings for the gods. Others sold religious paraphernalia: statuettes, prayer beads, singing bowls. But the most popular ones offered more esoteric services.

Palm readers, face readers, yi jing coin readers, even an old woman who claimed her pet parrot had the power to divine the future from a weathered pack of playing cards. It was a natural fit. After entreating the gods, believers could come here to calculate their fates and expunge their doubts. With red and yellow signs, the fortune tellers advertised their services. Li Ming recognized a few of them. But for every method he knew, there were three he had never seen before.

A sign leapt out at him.

Master Chen's quick bazi consultation. 100 yuan for 5 minutes.

Li Ming gestured at the sign.

"Does anybody want to try that?"

"I already know my bazi, thanks," Cai Yan said.

"I don't believe in *suan ming*," Wong-gor said. "Do you?"

"We're here. Might as well," Li Ming said. "Ghazan, what about you?"

He frowned. Shrugged.

"Why not?"

Master Chen was a rotund old man, a bright smile plastered on his face, seated at a table covered in a wrinkled yellow tablecloth. His bald pate shone in the sun. He was a small man, but he had an unusually huge qi field. As Li Ming approached, he swore he saw a *third* eye, a bright blue orb above and in between his eyes. But when Li Ming looked directly at his face, he saw nothing but age-spotted skin. Probably.

"Hello!" Master Chen beamed. "Who would like to go first?"

Li Ming raised his hand. "I will."

As he sat down, Li Ming suddenly realized that no one in the group had told Master Chen they'd wanted a reading.

"What's your date, time and location of birth?" Master Chen asked.

Li Ming told him. Master Chen punched in the information into an old, stained slate. The screen refreshed, showing an irregular grid filled with characters and numbers. Written in the classical script, Li Ming needed a few seconds to translate them into the simplified script he had learned.

Master Chen squinted, mumbling to himself, tapping at the screen. He scrolled up and down, left and right, eyes flicking over the sea of information. Frowned.

Then looked up and grinned brilliantly.

"Young man, you are a hero."

Li Ming blinked. Blinked again.

"Eh?"

"You have a Jia day master. You have an honest, direct, and noble character. Like a great tree, you protect and shelter everyone below from you the sun and rain. You support your friends, family and loved ones without a second thought.

"You have the ability to see everything around you, both the big picture and the tiny details. If you plan your actions properly, nothing is beyond you. Be organized, craft a solid plan, work hard and you will achieve your goals.

"You are hardworking, reliable and self-sufficient. Everyone can count on you to get the job done. You love helping others, and you have a reputation for being virtuous and upright. However, you are prone to aggression and recklessness, and you can blunt at times."

"Interesting..." Li Ming said.

"Am I right?"

"Yes. Especially the reckless part," Cai Yan said.

"*Wei.*"

Master Chen laughed.

"It is in your nature. You have the Goat Blade star. You are brave and daring, aggressive and assertive, with an indomitable will. You are driven to protect the innocent from the powerful. It gives you the strength and energy to carry out your life's mission. However, you are also at risk of violence, both giving and receiving violence. As your day master is the element of Yang Wood, this effect is especially pronounced."

"Explains a lot," Li Ming said.

"You are extremely intelligent. You were born with the Intelligence star. Learning comes easily to you. With your expertise and intelligence, people will turn to you for advice.

You also attract many helpful people into your life. You have *two* Noblemen stars. Lots of people will want to help you. You just need to ask for help, and they will appear."

"That is *definitely* true."

"You're a very lucky man," Cai Yan said.

"You're going to need all the luck you can get," Master Chen said.

"Why's that?" Li Ming asked.

"You have the Year Breaker in your chart. Money comes easily, but it also flies away just as easily. You just can't seem to hold on to it, no matter what you do."

"My job needs me to buy a lot of expensive gear."

"See what I mean? You must force yourself to save money. Better yet, invest your money. Training, insurance, stocks, shares. Grow your skills and your capacity to grow wealth. The money is considered spent, but it will come back to you in even greater amounts."

"That makes sense."

"Do you like traveling?"

"I have to travel a lot."

"You have the Sky Horse star. The star for travelers. You will make a lot of money if you travel. Your wealth is not at home."

Li Ming chuckled. "There's not much wealth where I came from."

"Exactly. You have a balanced day master. You have a smooth life ahead. In fact... now is the most important period of your life."

"What do you mean?"

"Your current luck pillar."

"Wait. What's that?"

"A luck pillar is a period representing different phases of your life. Your first luck pillar starts from birth and ends at the age of six, and the following pillars run for ten years each.

"You have Direct Wealth in your current luck pillar. Not only that, you are also in a wood frame. You have the Pig, Rabbit and Goat in your chart. Everything you do will be richly rewarded. If you work hard, you will make a huge amount of money."

"That sounds amazing."

"But it's not all good. You have the Seven Killings in your hidden stem in the luck pillar. It will bring danger, stress, disease, even serious injury. Since it is hidden, you may not even see it coming. You must be careful."

"Comes with the territory," Li Ming said.

"You are twenty-one now, yes? Your luck pillar will run for the next five years. The rest of your luck pillars are also smooth, but you are now in the prime of your life. What you do for the next five years will decide the rest of your life. You must make the most of what you have now."

"What can I do?"

"Be a hero."

Li Ming chuckled. "Really?"

"Really. It's in your chart."

"Where?"

"Your weakest career element is water. You will find it easy to make money in water-related industries. These are jobs that require lots of traveling, consultation and strategy, or anything to do with water. But you won't make a lot of money from it.

"Your next-best career element is fire. Fire is about energy, heat, light. Cooking, technology, the energy sector, these are all fire careers. Religion and spirituality too.

"Your absolute best industry is metal. Everything to do with metal. Jewelry, finance, manufacturing. Metal is also about weapons and rule of law. Military, police, and the legal profession are metal careers."

"I'm a biaohang."

"See what I mean? Hero."

Li Ming shook his head. "I just want to be the best I can be."

"That's a good attitude. But listen carefully. Metal offers the highest potential for wealth, but also demands the greatest amount of work. Wealth—true wealth, wealth that lasts—won't come easily. You must put in a lot of effort. Given your profession, and the presence of Goat Blade and Seven Killings, you will face a lot of danger."

"Can I not be a hero?"

"You could. But could you live with yourself if you don't?"

A fair point.

"Do you have any questions so far?" Master Chen asked.

"What are my relationships like?"

Master Chen glanced at the chart.

"You enjoy strong relationships with your family. You may not be physically present with them, but they hold a strong place in your heart. Your father is especially supportive of you."

Li Ming goggled. How could he see that?"

"With your Noblemen stars, you also attract high-quality friends and mentors. However, you also have the Robbery Devil star. You are smart, intense, impatient and demanding. You also attract people with a similar nature to you. Be careful about the friends you keep. You may be betrayed by false friends. You must see people as they are, not who they want you to see."

"Understood. What is my health like?"

Master Chen referred to the chart once again. This time, he tapped his fingers against his table, a tiny frown creeping across his face.

"You have strong wood, but your earth is weak. Your wood attacks your earth, causing various health issues. You were sickly when you were younger, right?"

"Yes. Then my parents adjusted my fengshui and I took up martial arts."

"Good. It helps. You are at risk of chronic illnesses affecting your blood and digestion. You tend to think too much. Not only that when you get angry, you will upset your stomach. You must relax and be happy."

"Easier said than done."

"No, really, if you want to be healthy, you must be happy. Fire produces earth, and fire is the element of happiness. Allow joy into your life. It will reinforce your stomach and immune system."

Li Ming sighed.

"All right."

"*Aiyo*, don't sigh like that! Makes things worse, you know!"

This time, everyone laughed. Master Chen laughed too.

"You said I'm at high risk of violence and danger," Li Ming said. "What can I do to reduce the risk? Quit?"

"No. It will follow you all your life. The only way not to get hurt is to hide away at home forever. But you can't do that, can you?"

"I can't."

"Then you have to do the next best thing. Train hard. Be extra careful when you're working a job. Get proper health insurance. And a will."

The specter of death, disfigurement and disease haunted everyone who inhabited the rivers and lakes. It was just the price of gold and glory.

"What else can you tell me about my character?" Li Ming asked.

"You have a complex personality. Bazi has ten gods that influence your personality, and you have nine of them. But your main influences are Direct Officer, Indirect Resource, and Friend. You have a strong sense of honor and morality, but that you may also be inflexible and indecisive at times. You are rather unconventional, innovative and spiritual, and also overly-idealistic, introverted and secretive. You are independent, disciplined, and self-assured, but you may lack social skills, secretly feel insecure, and lack self-worth."

"Didn't you just contradict yourself?" Li Ming asked. "I thought I had two Noblemen stars. How do I lack social skills? And how can I both be innovative and inflexible?"

"Like I said, you are a complex person, and complexity creates contradictions. The Noblemen stars bring noblemen to you, but whether you keep them is something else. Likewise, you may be so inflexible, you only want to do things your way, if only because it is innovative or unconventional."

"I see... Is there anything else I need to take note of?" Li Ming asked.

Master Chen pointed at a character on his screen.

"You have Death and Emptiness in your chart. Worse, it falls in Chen, which is Yin Earth. Your earth is already weak, and Death and Emptiness makes it even weaker."

"What does this mean?"

"Death and Emptiness is like dispersal. There is no support, and the element is floating in a void. When earth floats in space, it falls apart. Earth is related to material goods and wealth. You don't have much in the way of material desires, do you?"

Li Ming shrugged.

"I have everything I need."

"See? There you go. It's not necessarily bad, but it means you don't value money as much as others. It can be very troublesome in your current luck cycle. You can squander all your earnings if you're not careful."

"Is that why you said money comes easily, but also leaves easily?"

"Yes. You should get a financial adviser when your money comes in. A good one will help you invest and grow your money, or at least keep you from wasting too much of it. Or you could just be a monk."

"A monk?"

"Why not? A monk releases his material desires to gain enlightenment. Or, if you prefer, an immortal. To become a Fo or an immortal, you must leave behind the red dust of the mortal world, go up the mountain, and cultivate your mind, body and spirit."

"I don't want to be a monk."

But what about being an immortal?

"Your life, your choice. While Death and Emptiness brings illness, oftentimes it also brings the gift of spiritual insight. You are free to live your life as you wish, but if you make the most of your innate strengths and weaknesses, you will live the best life possible."

"I see."

Master Chen set his slate aside and looked squarely into Li Ming's eyes. His gaze was deep and piercing, yet soft and warm. His aura flared, and a field of bright blue flashed across Li Ming's sight. Once again, Li Ming had the uncanny sensation of a third eye staring into him, through him, seeing everything he was, is, and would be.

"When we are born, Heaven lays down a road for us. Using bazi, we reveal the shape of the road and calculate our lives. While we are free to live as we please, if we deviate from this road, there will only be pain, suffering and regret. By aligning our lives with the Will of Heaven, we gain absolute freedom in the Way."

"If Heaven lays down a way for you, how can you be free?" Ghazan asked.

Master Chen grinned and shrugged.

"I don't know. I don't have the words to explain it. Just meditate on it and see for yourself if there is any value in the ramblings of an old man."

"Thank you," Li Ming said. "I will."

Li Ming paid with Aitan Pay, transferring funds from his digital wallet to Master Chen's. It amused him to see an old man taking so readily to a next-generation all-in-one app, even more to read his Aitan profile. Master Chen had a modest social media presence on Aitan Circles, one he used extensively for marketing. Somehow he had found a way to blend the old and the new.

"Who's next?" Master Chen asked.

Another strange sensation fell over Li Ming. No one had even hinted at their interest, yet Master Chen spoke as if he knew there was someone else who wanted a reading.

"Me," Ghazan said, sinking into the chair before Master Chen.

"Ah. Are you a Yue?"

"What about it?"

"Few of my customers are Yue. Do you mind if I share this moment on Aitan?"

"Only if you're accurate."

"It's a deal!"

Ghazan recited the details of his nativity. As Master Chen ran through his arcane calculations, a grin crept across Master Chen's face.

"Saw something interesting?" Ghazan asked.

"You two should be brothers."

"Us?" Li Ming asked.

"Yes. Your charts are incredible. They complement each other very well."

"Really," Ghazan said. "What do you see?"

"You have a strong Geng day master. You are like a sword, sharp and powerful. You are a born survivor and thrive under pressure. You enjoy challenges. They forge you, shape you, transforming you from raw steel into an invincible blade.

"You are extremely confident, action-oriented and competitive. You love to be the best in everything you do. When your mind is clear and focused, you can achieve anything you set out to be. Strategy and planning is vital. If you don't plan, you're just swinging a sword all over the place. You could cut yourself. Once you have a plan, nothing will stop you."

"That sounds right," Ghazan admitted.

"Pride is your greatest flaw. Face is especially important to you. You cannot bear to be seen as imperfect, and so you hate making mistakes. When you are winning, you feel confident in yourself. But when things don't go according to plan, you may lose your temper very quickly."

Cai Yan laughed.

"That's *definitely* him!"

Ghazan scowled.

"Pride is poison to the soul," Master Chen said. "Learn to be humble, set your ego aside, and remain cool under pressure."

Ghazan grunted and nodded.

"You are twenty-nine. Three years into your current luck cycle. It's been a challenging time, but also rewarding. Am I right?"

"Yes," he said guardedly.

"You are in the Seven Killings luck cycle. Normally this brings chaos. However, you have an auspicious formation in your chart. You have a Seven Killings star in your natal chart, as well as an Indirect Resource star. This is known as *shayin xiangshen*. Instead of chaos, your Seven Killings produces resources. Whenever you enter a Seven Killings year or luck cycle, you will enjoy great wealth, fame and promotion."

Ghazan blinked.

"It's certainly happened."

"See? Not only that, but your personality profile is also primarily Seven Killings. This is the star of warriors. You are fierce and aggressive. You prefer to shoot first and aim later. Power is everything to you. You want to take the top spot.

"Your Seven Killings element is fire. Fire with metal produces total destruction. You will encounter many situations that will completely transform you. These experiences are necessary. The fire forges you. Without these experiences, you will just be a useless hunk of metal.

"With your personality and your talents, you have the power to overturn heaven and earth."

A ghost of a smile played across Ghazan's face.

"You could just be telling me what I want to hear."

"Go to another bazi master and he'll tell you the same thing. It's right there in your chart."

"What other stars are in my chart?"

"You have the Goat Knife, Robbery and Sky Horse stars too. Which is why I said, you two could be brothers. Like attracts like, and you are both similar and complementary."

"What stars do I have that he doesn't?"

"The Lonely Star."

Ghazan gestured behind him.

"I'm not lonely."

"Loneliness is a state of mind. It is a sense of emptiness in your heart. You feel isolated from others and come across as cold and eccentric. Your Lonely Star is also your Sky Horse. You will drift from place to place without a permanent residence. This star could bring harm to those around you. However, you can make use of this star to gain deep spiritual insights. The best leaders are also loners."

"Everything sounds spot on, doesn't it?" Li Ming said.

Ghazan grunted.

"Yes," he admitted. "But I don't mind being a loner."

"Make the most of it," Master Chen said. "You can't eliminate that part of your personality, but you can use that trait to achieve great things."

"What else can you see?" Ghazan asked. "Health? Wealth?"

"There is a risk of chest, heart, joint and muscle diseases and injuries."

"From my work?"

"It's possible. You only have one major wealth element: metal. You are all in the same profession?"

"Yes," everyone said as one.

"Ah. Being a biaohang suits you perfectly. Your chart is very imbalanced. You are extremely slanted towards Seven Killings and Metal. An imbalanced chart isn't always bad, as it concentrates your strengths in one direction, but it also exposes you to a lot of potential difficulties.

"Grief is the emotion of metal. With so much metal in you, you must strive to release it. Cultivate joy as well. Joy is the emotion of fire, and fire melts metal. With emotional balance, you can mitigate health risks."

A complex expression crossed Ghazan's face.

"I am not sad."

"For now, maybe, but grief will surely be a major theme in your life."

"I'll be the judge of that."

"Of course, of course. Do you have any other questions?"

"Why do you say Li Ming and I should be brothers?"

"You are both intelligent, ambitious and forceful. You have complementary strengths. You can focus on execution, while he networks with people. You are better at managing money, while he can use that money to manifest new ideas. You are both in the middle of superb luck pillars. Since you are both biaohang, if you partner up, you can easily dominate the jianghu."

Pleasure surged through Li Ming. His mind expanded and exploded, allowing the universe to pour into his soul. All at once he saw the mechanisms of Heaven, the twisting strands of fate that joined him and Ghazan and propelled them towards a future where they stood side-by-side as equals. A future where he could steer Ghazan away from the path of devils.

"What if we can't, or don't work together?" Ghazan asked.

Master Chen pursed his lips. Called up Li Ming's chart. Switched between both nativities at rapid speed.

"You are both highly ambitious and highly competitive. If you do not see each other as equals, then you will be in constant competition, forever struggling for dominance. This competition could sharpen the two of you. But if you allow pride and ego to arise between the two of you, if you cannot reign in your natural aggression and impulses, if you allow suspicion and spite to cloud your judgment...

"You will never share the same sky."

Chapter Ten

Shuanglong

I n the morning, they awoke to disaster.

After cultivation, after training, after breakfast, the team gathered in the living room. The second Li Ming opened his news app on his Raptor smartglasses, headlines blasted across the screen.

Beast Surge Declared in Shuanglong

6 Biaohang Dead, 18 Missing in 2 Weeks

Shuanglong Mayor Declares State of Emergency

"Guys, read the news," Li Ming said.

His tone was calm and even, but something in his voice caused everyone to drop everything and turn on their devices.

"*Tian ah...*" Cai Yan whispered.

"Where is Shuanglong?" Wong asked.

Ghazan unfolded his scroll to its full length. Half of the screen displayed his news app. With the other half, he called up a map of the region.

"A hundred and fifty *li* east of Yudu. Right on the border of Yudu's sphere of influence."

"Did the beasts migrate to the east?" Li Ming asked.

"The beast surge warning hasn't been lifted in Yudu," Cai Yan said.

"There hasn't been any major beast activity recently," Wong-gor said. "If anything, the open contracts have been falling off."

"Are we moving to Shuanglong?" Ghazan asked.

Cai Yan frowned.

"The plan was to hunt in the Yudu region. There's still plenty of work around here."

Li Ming called up the Jianghu Association's job boards. There were dozens of available beast hunting contracts in and around Yudu. But most of them were small vegetables, easily taken by teams less experienced and equipped than them.

"There's work in Shuanglong too," Ghazan said.

"But not as much," Cai Yan said. "Thirty-eight over there, fifty-nine over here."

"There are more high-value contracts in Shuanglong than in Yudu," Wong-gor said. "Eight here, twelve over there."

"But how many of those contracts can a four-man team take on?"

Too few.

Those contracts spanned a gamut of missions. Convoy escort, sweeping roads and forests, searching for the missing biaohang, security audits, and of course, beast hunts. Most of those contracts required parties with at least a half-dozen shooters, more often ten to twenty.

Still...

"There's no state of emergency in Yudu," Li Ming said. "Not anymore."

"It doesn't mean that we should chase every emergency that crops up," Cai Yan replied.

"We go where the beasts go. That's what we're here to do."

"The contracts show that the beasts are in Yudu."

"Only for now. There's going to be lag time between the declaration and the contracts."

"Why are you so keen on going to Shuanglong?"

Li Ming pursed his lips, trying to find the right words.

"We are biaohang. We are all part of the jianghu. When our fellow biaohang are in danger, we cannot abandon them. Furthermore, any beast surge capable of taking out so many biaohang in such a short time will pose a grave threat to the people."

"A real hero, aren't you?" Ghazan remarked.

"Just saying it as it is."

"There's only four of us. Just *one* shanxiao almost wiped us out. If there were more of them... I can't lead this expedition into the jaws of death," Cai Yan said.

"Are there any shanxiao in Shuanglong?" Li Ming asked.

Ghazan pecked at his screen.

"The contracts don't mention any shanxiao."

"What about bashe? Or other dangerous beasts?" Cai Yan asked.

"Lots. Bashe, jiaolong, nuhou…"

"It's dangerous. *More* dangerous than what we've done so far."

"Lady Boss, we are biaohang. We run *to* danger, not away from it," Wong-gor said. "That's why we're here."

"We had a week to prepare for the Yudu expedition. If we relocate to Shuanglong, we'll have to kick off from a cold start."

"We have our gear, we have local contacts, we have the Jianghu Association behind us, we have everything we need to do business. We can adapt to the situation as needed," Ghazan said.

"There's plenty of work around here. We don't have to go to Shuanglong."

"If we go, we'll be ahead of the curve. We can snatch the most lucrative contracts before the major players do."

"Why are you so reluctant to go?" Li Ming asked.

Cai Yan looked down. Frowned. And spoke to the floor.

"I… I don't want to lose any more men."

"Without danger, there is no glory," Ghazan said.

"*Yaoqian buyao ming,*" she muttered.

You want money, but not your life.

"I'm not in this for the money," Ghazan replied.

"What *do* you want?"

A shark-like smile split his face.

"I came here to hunt beasts."

"*Zhen shi de…*"

"Me too," Wong-gor said. "It doesn't matter to me whether we're hunting in Yudu or Shuanglong, so long as we can bag monsters and get paid."

"Li Ming, what about you?"

"I joined the expedition to protect the innocent. And that means hunting the most dangerous beasts of the Central Plains."

Cai Yan shook her head.

"*Ni men zhexie ren ru yaoshou yiyang shixue wuqing.*"

You're all as coldblooded and unfeeling as beasts.

Ghazan touched his palm to his chest and bowed.

"Thank you very much."

"*Li Ming mm hai ye sau. Taa hai yinghung,*" Wong-gor said.

"Eh?" Cai Yan and Li Ming said as one.

"Li Ming isn't a beast. He's a hero."

"Heroes are dead. I'm still alive," Li Ming said.

"You're all dead set on going to Shuanglong?" Cai Yan asked.

"You're the boss, but I think you can read the room."

She massaged her temples.

"Let's get going before I regain my sanity."

Shuanglong. The City of Twin Dragons, though the only dragons Li Ming saw were carved of stone, adorning the high walls surrounding the city. Centuries ago, Shuanglong was a fortress city, the jewel of the ancient state of Ge, occupying a strategic position along the Yu River. Ge had vanished into the dim and distant past, but the great ramparts and watchtowers remained. Once they had stood against bandits and invaders, now they defended the people against beasts.

Old Shuanglong packed sixty thousand inhabitants into a dense square enclosed by six and a quarter *li* of walls and fortifications. Eight gates, two for each cardinal direction, controlled access into the ancient bastion. New Shuanglong, population one hundred and fifty thousand, sprawled along the riverbank and across a plain. Each district of the new city sported walls of their own, none so high or thick or grand as the old city, but adequate for keeping out monsters.

Driving through Shuanglong was like navigating a labyrinth. Walls within walls, quarters within districts, every block a city in miniature. Life happened behind the walls; the roads were empty, solely for getting from one block to another. Without the North Star satellite navigation system, Li Ming would have been hopelessly lost. Before the advent of modern barriers and standing armies, this was how the ancients defended their homes from beasts and bandits. The Zhongxia Republic had torn down most of its walls, replacing them with barriers and drones and conscripts. Lacking a large standing military, the people of Shuanglong had chosen to preserve their heritage.

It had taken just over a half hour to pack up, book a hotel in Shuanglong, settle outstanding charges, and depart. Zhang Mei Lin agreed to follow them to Shuanglong, but she had other affairs to tend to, and would arrive in the evening. The drive had taken another two hours. The biaohang rolled into Shuanglong just ahead of the rush from Yudu and surrounding cities.

But not ahead of the military.

Shuanglong had a small standing militia, but it was well-funded. Troops formed checkpoints, guarding the roads in and out of the city and key districts. More soldiers manned the watchtowers. Robot tanks reinforced the men. Drones orbited the skies, swarms of black dots ready to swoop down from the heavens.

Civilians and cars still roamed the streets, but they moved with purpose. People going to work, heading to shelter, stocking up on emergency supplies. No dawdling, no lingering, no sightseeing. The soldiers thoroughly inspected every car with out-of-town plates, scrutinized the identities of drivers and passengers, issued warnings concerning the state of emergency.

But the emergency was why the biaohang were here.

The second the news hit the wires, biaohang quickly snatched up lodging all over Shuanglong. The closest—and best—accommodations Cai Yan could find was at the Shuanglong International Hotel. Sited at the northernmost end of the old city, it was one of the few high-rises within the ancient walls, one of the few concessions to the demands of the modern world.

No suite this time. Just four separate rooms. Li Ming didn't mind. He'd rather trade comfort for privacy. From his window on the tenth floor, he could look down on the city walls.

Tripod-mounted infinity cannons and robots fitted with heavy weapons dotted the battlements, positioned to create overlapping arcs of fire. Soldiers paced the length of the walls, staring out into the darkness, checking in on the gun emplacements. Lights and shadows played across the windows of the watchtowers.

But despite the display of firepower, the militia was undermanned.

Many battlements stood empty. Even fewer towers were occupied. Only a handful of troops walked the walls. Although this part of the city looked out onto the river, aquatic and amphibious beasts were endemic in this part of the Central Plains.

The city was like an egg. A thin, hard shell surrounding a soft gooey center. A sharp tap and the defenses would collapse. There were *just* enough militia to control the approaches to the city and drive off stray beasts, but if Shuanglong were attacked in force, the defenses would rapidly crumble.

The walls were key, Li Ming decided. If an invading horde broke through, the defenders would have to close the gates, retreat to the walls and watchtowers, force the attackers to run a gauntlet of fire. It was the only way such a small force could hold such a huge city. If the police, biaohang and armed civilians chipped in, all the better. But without the walls, or if the walls were breached, Shuanglong would fall.

Could the Shuanglong militia carry out this strategy?

Li Ming had no idea. He was a stranger to this city, and there was precious little about the militia on the Net. He made a note to ask Ms. Zhang when she arrived.

The second they set their stuff down in the hotel, the biaohang set off again. There was still a lot left to do before they could pick up their first contract.

They registered themselves with the Shuanglong branch of the Jianghu Association, the local police department, and the city militia. They purchased guidebooks and maps of the city and its environs. They studied local laws and regulations pertaining to biaohang, magic, weapons, and beasts. Li Ming sent a text message updating his family on his location.

In the early evening, they regrouped in the hotel for group physical training, and found the gym packed with a small army of strongmen. They hogged the weights, the exercise machines, the punching bags, everything that let them work their bulging muscles. The few women around them were banished to the treadmills, or else took turns with the men.

One of them was a Yue.

In a dark sports bra and sweatpants, she cut a lean, almost androgynous figure. Her skin, darker than Ghazan's, attested to countless hours under the summer sun. She had a broad face carved from brass, thick and solid, yet smooth and unlined, framed in a messy cascade of black hair that fell to her shoulders. She moved with unaffected grace, completely aware of the attention she received and completely indifferent to it.

But she glanced at Ghazan.

Held his gaze for a second.

And went back to pumping kettlebells.

Dayong left her alone. They left *everyone* alone. Everybody here was a cultivator. Their qi blended into a superfield, a hot, wet, heavy fog weighing down on Li Ming. They were here to train, to show off their training, to spy on everyone else training. All of them had eyes like tigers, ultra-focused on their workouts and their potential rivals.

The Dayong team headed to an empty section of floor and burned through high intensity bodyweight workouts. A nonstop two-*ke* regimen of push-ups, squats, bridges, leg raises, and more. As they burned through the program, a small group of martial cultivators set up a circle in a corner, taking on all comers in full-contact empty-hand sparring. The sound of meaty smacks and heavy thuds resounded in the room, overpowering the canned pop music drifting from the speakers.

Li Ming would have preferred to finish with empty hand techniques. But that might be seen as a challenge. They were here to hunt beasts, not pick fights with other biaohang.

Back in his room, he did just that. Just a quick run-through of his favorite techniques. Then a quicker shower, and it was off to the restaurant, where he met the rest of the team. And Ms. Zhang.

Ms. Zhang was a rose among thorns. Everyone in Dayong wore the non-uniform uniform of a long-sleeved shirt and cargo pants and assault boots, the signature style of the violence professional on the prowl. Ms. Zhang had matched a dark blue knee-length dress with black strappy high heels, emphasizing her femininity. Makeup lifted years from her face, adding color to her cheeks and red to her lips. Next to her, Cai Yan faded into the background, her posture and attire trumping her looks.

Somehow, by accident or design, Cai Yan wedged herself between Ms. Zhang and Li Ming at the table.

Ms. Zhang insisted on ordering, showing everyone the delights of local cuisine. For starters they had mapo doufu, bean curd cooked in a thick mixture of oil and flaky spices that burned the lips and numbed the tongue. Then came gung pao chicken, laden in chili but balanced with sweet marinade. Stir-fried green beans in soy sauce cooled the mouth between bites of spices. The final main course was shredded pork cooked with fish sauce and garnished with even more chili. For dessert they had bingfen. The cool, refreshing jelly, mixed with dried fruits and soybean milk, cut through the tingling in the tongue and settled the palate.

Throughout dinner, the biaohang pumped Ms. Zhang for information. Prime hunting grounds around Shuanglong. The relationship between the jianghu and the authorities. No-go and high-risk zones. Names and addresses of trustworthy merchants and scammers. The competency of the security forces.

"The Shuanglong militia isn't a proper military," Ms. Zhang said. "More like a... a self-defense group. This is their first major operation in decades. In fact, they've never seen real combat before, not since the Revolution over a hundred years ago."

"Are they any good?" Ghazan asked.

"They've kept out beasts and bandits. But that's all they're good for. There's only about... two hundred and fifty soldiers in all. Maybe a bit more if you count the robot pilots. I can't see them holding off a beast surge, not without the cooperation of the police or the jianghu."

"What's the local police like?" Li Ming asked.

"They're all right, by the standards of the Central Plains. Nothing much to complain about. But a beast emergency like this is not something they're trained or equipped to handle. There's three hundred police officers here, but many also serve as reservists in the militia. Altogether, the city can muster maybe six hundred soldiers and cops."

"So few? Only way to hold the city is to turtle up inside the miniature fortresses," Wong-gor said.

"I heard from the local Association office that that's the defense plan," Ms. Zhang said. "If the city were invaded, everyone must retreat into the nearest walled district and wait for the all clear."

"What if the beasts come by air?" Ghazan asked.

"Flying beasts are not endemic to the region. Besides, we have the towers."

After the meal, everyone returned to their rooms. They stayed on the same floor, side by side with each other. The moment he stepped inside his own, a profound weight fell on him.

The room was small and cramped. It felt like it was boxing him in, squashing him down, trapping him inside a tiny box. Outside the window, the bright lights of the city beckoned. Past those were the walls, and beyond them were the dark waters of the Yu River. The wilds called out to him, promising a refuge from the noise and colors of civilization.

Dayong had an early start tomorrow. But they had no contracts on the horizon. The night was young. He had time. And he had to know what the city was like after dark.

He drew his swordbreaker from his Belt Bag and wore it on his left hip. He checked his Hellion, nestled snugly in its holster on his other hip. Over his forearms he donned his reality shapers. Company property, a gold-ranked shaper, on his left, his iron-ranked shaper on his right. He patted down his pockets, finding his knives and tools. Over everything he wore his dark jacket. He locked up his luggage and stepped out.

Just in time to see Cai Yan leave her room.

"What a coincidence!" she exclaimed. "Going out too?"

"Yes," Li Ming said.

They stood in the hallway for a moment, gazing at each other. Her eyes were large and warm and soft, inviting him in, waiting for him to act.

"Want to come with me?" he asked.

"Sure!"

Down in the lobby, he realized that this was the first time since they'd arrived in the Central Plains that they'd finally had some alone time. Wong-gor or Ghazan or both were usually in the same room, same building, same area of operations. But now, *now*, it was just him and her and the night streets.

He allowed himself a moment of exhilaration. Then reminded himself that, however beautiful and charming she may be, she was still his boss and they were still here for work, and that her position in the Dayong hierarchy would always stand between them.

They stepped out into the humid summer night. Streetlamps cast the world in hard shades of amber, complemented and contrasted by lights and signboards of a hundred dazzling colors. Cars trundled down the streets, guests entered the hotel, pedestrians hustled to their destinations. In this world of color and motion, they were dark and still.

"Where are we going?" she asked.

"Let's explore," he said.

Spiraling outwards from the hotel, they walked in ever-wider circles, exploring the neighborhood.

They found a street lined with temples, temples to the gods of the city, to the sages who had won immortality and now lived among the gods, to the Fo and Pusa who had attained enlightenment and remained in this world to bring happiness to all beings.

They walked an avenue dating to the Warring States era, preserved for millennia, built and designed according to timeless fengshui principles and the teachings of the ancient sages. Instead of streetlights, lanterns hung suspended from long lines bridging opposite roofs. There were no cars, only a footpath of flagstones. Despite the external aesthetics, the shops here offered modern-day food and beverages, electronics and souvenirs, consumer goods and clothing.

They found a deserted alley, dark and empty. Right next to it was a megamall blazing with light and life, an invader from the future in a land sanctified to the past. Li Ming and Cai Yan glanced at the directory and saw no brands of interest.

They arrived at the northern gates.

The gatehouse loomed tall over the three- and four-story buildings before it. Its wide mouth fed into a courtyard enclosed on all by sides by thick walls. Ramps flanked the city-facing entrance, leading up to the wall walks. At the other side of the courtyard stood the archery tower, controlling the outer gate.

This was the *wengcheng*, the barbican, a killing ground that trapped an invading force if they breached the outer gate and exposed them to fire from above. In ages past it was an indispensable part of a city's defenses. Today it was a parking lot.

Large trucks and cars painted in olive green were parked against the walls. Light poles filled the barbican in warm amber light. A quartet of militia stood around the outer gates, infinity guns slung, bored the way young men on guard duty everywhere and everywhen were bored out of their minds. Behind them, the massive gates remained open.

As Li Ming and Cai Yan approached, the detail leader held up his hand and mumbled something. It took Li Ming a moment to penetrate his accent.

"No exit after dark."

"Why's that?" Cai Yan asked.

"Beast alert. Without permission or a permit, we can't let you through."

"Why are the gates open, then?"

"Humans can enter. They just can't leave."

"We're biaohang," Li Ming said. "Martial cultivators."

The leader raised an eyebrow, the rest of his face expressing utter boredom.

"Congratulations. What's that got to do with us?"

"We came here to help you defend your city. We can't do that if we don't know the layout and defenses."

"You can wait until morning."

"The Jianghu Association assured us that the militia will provide full cooperation."

"*My* orders say no one leaves the city after dark."

"We will consider it a personal favor if you let us pass to inspect the walls," Cai Yan said.

And she held out her biaohang card.

The guard looked at her face. And the card. And the field that indicated she was a gold ranker.

Behind his visor, his eyes goggled. He snapped up straight. He blinked several times, hard, training his helmet-mounted goggles on her aura. And blinked again.

"Cai Yan *furen*, you are a long way from Bao An."

"We go where the guaishou go."

"And this... gentleman works for you?"

"Yes," they said as one.

A complex expression crossed the young man's face. Biaohang enjoyed great status and power here in the Central Plains, greater than in the Zhongxia Republic, greater than the official city militia. Ms. Zhang had told them once that few cultivators willingly served in the militia, not if they could join the private sector. The ones who did were always officers like Captain Bao or senior specialists, revered as demigods.

"Let them pass," the leader said.

The soldiers stepped aside.

"Thank you very much. We shall remember this," Cai Yan said.

Past the gate, a walkway led to a set of working piers. Long fingers of waterproofed wood, supported by complex structures of pillars and struts, extended into the waters of the Yu River. Harsh white lights banished the darkness around the piers, leaving clear fields of fire.

The river here was wide and deep and dark and deceptively placid. Fleets of riverboats were tied up to the piers, rocking gently in the currents, their engines cold and their cabins quiet. Li Ming imagined that in the day, fleets of riverboats trawled up and down the length of the river, carrying goods and people from town to town, city to city, following ancient routes and routines that stretched back to the birth of civilization in the Central Plains. Here and now, in the dark waters he saw only a rippling, distorted reflection of the walls and the gates.

To the east and the west, rough gravel walkways circled the walls. White lights illuminated the perimeter, leaving solid darkness beyond. Nothing stirred. No one appeared.

They were alone.

"What's there to see here?" she asked.

"The piers," he said.

"You sure it's safe?"

"Is anyone going to stop us?"

Powerful odors drifted into his noise. Fish and rot, wood and decay, water laced with chemicals and organics. On the far side of the river, irrigation channels siphoned away precious water. Distant lights glowed in the dark, suggesting huts, sheds, farmhouses.

He set it all aside and looked with the eyes of a soldier. The piers were long and the water deep, but the river was slow and the riverbanks shallow. Aquatic and amphibious beasts could easily make landfall here and rush the city. While guards and drones manned the walls and gates and towers, there was a massive dead zone in the shadow of the walls, where the shooters could not easily fire upon.

The drones' turrets didn't have the depression needed to engage threats in the dead zone. The few soldiers up top would have to rush to the arrow holes and fire straight down. The lights illuminated the piers and the perimeter, but they barely reached the rivers. The dark waters offered excellent concealment.

"If there's an attack, it's going to come through here," Li Ming said.

"Oh?" Cai Yan said.

"The plains around the city are vast and flat. The guards will see a monster swarm coming a long way off. But here, the river—"

A strange sensation pulsed through him. His qi field fluttered, his organs trembled, his muscles twitched. The feeling came from everywhere around him, from the sky, the water, the city. It penetrated him, reaching deep, waking the blood and firing nerves and sinew, readying the body for the hunt, for the kill, for war.

It was the same feeling he had right before the shanxiao attack.

"What's going on?" Cai Yan asked.

"Get your gun!" Li Ming yelled.

He swept his jacket aside. The textured grip of the Hellion filled his hand perfectly. He drew the subcompact handgun, grabbing its reassuring weight in both hands, holding it close to his chest. In the darkness, the reflex sight burned a brilliant red.

A loud bellowing filled the air. Deep and husky, guttural and primal, it vibrated unpleasantly in Li Ming's chest. It was the purring of a truck engine, the rumbling of a train, the growling of an apex predator on the hunt.

And another.

And another.

And another, joining in a chorus, rapidly reaching a crescendo.

"The water!" Cai Yan yelled, drawing her Golden Legion handgun. "They're in the water!"

Dark shapes broke the surface of the river. Li Ming aimed at the closest and activated his pistol-mounted light.

Cold yellow eyes narrowed against the spotlight. Slick scales, hard as rocks, large as pebbles, reflected the light as matte olive. A long row of curved spines whipped back and forth, ending in a muscled tail. With a splash, a fat, blunt snout broke the surface of the water. Heavy jaws opened to reveal sharp yellowed teeth. Elongated limbs ended in huge paws and curved claws.

"Yaotuo!" Li Ming called. "Yaotuo in the water!"

Chapter Eleven

The Shadow of the Walls

The ancients had called them muddy dragons. They weren't so far from the truth. The reptilian creatures, distant and gigantic cousins of the common alligator, preyed upon anything they could crush or rend with their enormous teeth. In the water a yaotuo glided like a snake, on land it could stand and walk like an ape, and in both domains it was an apex predator.

There were at least two dozen of them.

The yaotuo surged, rushing the piers. The boats rocked violently. Claws scrambled for purchase on the wood. The bellowing grew louder, angrier, a chorus of hate and malice aimed at the humans. At the end of the pier, a yaotuo hauled itself up and out, roaring at the top of its lungs.

Li Ming shot it in the head.

Its skull vanished in thunder and pink mist. The creature crashed back into the water. Undeterred, the other yaotuo continued their rush.

"Run! We have to run!" Cai Yan shouted.

She sprinted. He followed, three steps behind, looking behind his shoulder.

"There's more of them! They're coming up the riverbanks!"

A dozen, two dozen, more, an entire army of yaotuo swelled up from the dark waters, scrambling up on the riverbanks. Behind the walls, sirens wailed.

"BEASTS! BEASTS IN THE RIVER!" Cai Yan screamed.

Li Ming fired, fast as he could press the trigger, spraying a stream of white-hot plasma downrange. Earth exploded. Monsters screamed. Wood ignited. A boat caught fire. No time to aim, just point and shoot, shooting at a yaotuo caught in the light.

The muddy dragons pressed on.

All along the battlements, a barrage of blue-white bolts ripped forth. Infinity guns firing in single shot, repeaters thundering out short bursts, cannons spraying cones of small bolts. The blasts ripped into the monsters, into the earth, into the piers. Everything they touched detonated, deflagrated, disintegrated. Sand fused to glass, grass burned to ashes, flesh exploded in clouds.

Past the gates, the four gate militiamen fanned out in a circle, weapons at low ready.

"Come on!" the leader shouted.

Until Li Ming and Cai Yan were clear of their lines of fire, the guards couldn't shoot. Li Ming sent fire to his legs, supercharging his muscles. Wind brew up around Cai Yan. They accelerated, rushing past the outer gates, down the dark and narrow tunnel, out the other side.

Past the militiamen, the biaohang skidded to a sudden stop.

And a sudden silence.

All along the walls, the guns had stopped shooting.

What's going on?

"OPEN FIRE!" the militiaman ordered.

The sentries opened fire, filling the fatal funnel with light and fire.

The walls remained dark.

"Close the gates!" Li Ming yelled.

The leader threw his head back and screamed at the archery tower.

"CLOSE THE DAMNED GATES! WHAT THE DEVIL ARE YOU WAITING FOR?!"

Dark figures shot out the left side of the tower.

"*WEI!* WHAT ARE YOU DOING?!" Li Ming yelled.

An explosion ripped through the lower floor of the archery tower. Tongues of fire burst out the windows. Shards of glass rained down on the world. Li Ming ducked, covering his head, fragments whistling past his head. Standing in the shadow of the city wall, the shrapnel just barely missed him.

"ENEMIES ON THE WALLS!" Li Ming yelled. "ENGAGE!"

Frozen to the spot, torn between the charging yaotuo, the burning tower, the new threat from above, the leader gaped, his eyes popping, his jaw dropping, torn between a thousand choices and locked in indecision.

The saboteurs fired.

Twin streams of fire tore through the guards. The leader exploded into hot steam and bone shrapnel. Bolts cut down another guard, a third, walking towards—

Li Ming screamed.

Right hand blasting at the shooters, left hand extended, he reached for the primordial crystal loaded in his reality shaper. The crystal blazed with light, ready to be unleashed. He touched the element of fire and launched a ball of flame into the sky.

Cai Yan fired her own shapers. A translucent dome materialized, moments after the fireball screamed out. Plasma bolts smashed uselessly against the shield, shattering in storms of blinding light.

The fireball arched over the ramparts and detonated. The blast flung a man through the air and over the battlements, screaming as he fell head-first into the *wengcheng*. The other shooter lurched away in the opposite direction, out of Li Ming's sight.

The first shooter landed by the gates with a terrible wet crunch. The yaotuo, scenting fresh meat, howled and charged.

"Fall back to the inner gate!" the surviving militiaman yelled.

Li Ming supercharged his legs, sprinting ahead. Cai Yan flew on a gust of wind. The militiaman—

"DON'T LEAVE ME BEHIND!" he screamed.

He's not a cultivator!

Li Ming stomped the ground, forcing himself to a stop. Cai Yan killed her airspeed and turned around. The straggler, still on the other side of the barbican, sprinted towards them, one arm shooting blindly behind him.

"COME ON!" Li Ming urged, raising his left arm, ready to—

Plasma streaked from the walls, cutting the militiaman down.

And the yaotuo fell on him.

Blasting away at the beasts with one hand, the other raising her shield dome, Cai Yan yelled, "The other shooter is still up there!"

Li Ming stared for a moment, entranced by the sight, by the way the many lights caught her face and accented her fine features in white and blue and gold.

Then his brain remembered where he was.

"Up the walls! We have to get to the gatehouse!"

They sprinted to the inner gate. The shooter harassed them, bolts splashing harmlessly off Cai Yan's shield. Li Ming fired blindly behind him, loosing a fireball, then a string of unaimed shots, unloading into the slavering swarm.

"CLOSE THE GATES!" Li Ming screamed at the gatehouse.

Nothing happened.

"We have to get up there!" Cai Yan yelled.

"Let's go!"

The shield dispersed.

The monsters charged.

Cai Yan stopped at the mouth of the inner gate and aimed her palms at the ground. A cold breeze blew around her, condensing into twin pillars of howling wind. She flew up into the air, safely out of the yaotuo's reach.

Li Ming breathed.

Sent fire qi to his legs.

Jumped.

He shot straight up into the sky. A yaotuo lunged at him, claws barely missing his boot. Upwards he climbed, as high as a two story house—

And fell.

He detonated the air at his feet.

The fire qi rocketed him into air, higher and faster. The ancient stone walls hurled past. The muddy dragons howled and jumped and slashed and snapped, but he was far above them. They continued to surge from the water in droves, and they continued to die in droves.

Li Ming began to descend. He touched his reality shapers again, exploded again, rose again. Now he saw Cai Yan just above and ahead of him, reaching out for the walls. He reached out too and—

His fingers scraped stone.

He fell.

And his crystals were empty.

His left hand flew to the handle of his swordbreaker. He touched his mind to the two-thousand-point qi crystal stored within. He drew it out into the essence of fire.

He erupted once again.

And now he burst up and into the air, arms outstretched. He gripped the battlement and hauled himself up and over, landing next to Cai Yan.

They were now on the right side of the gatehouse. The main door was firmly shut. Light spilled out the tinted windows. Li Ming grabbed Cai Yan's wrist and pulled her down.

"You—"

Plasma chewed the ancient brick battlements. Cai Yan flinched down, rolling into a ball. Crouching low, Li Ming scooted around her, angling off around the corner of the wall—

A dark figure appeared against the bright night.

Li Ming lit him up. The wide cone of his weapon-mounted light revealed a man in a militia uniform, carrying a steaming infinity gun, carrying a helmet and body armor. Li Ming lit him up again, this time with his Hellion, stitching bolts up his chest, neck, face, and the target went down.

"We've got terrorists disguised as guards!" Li Ming snarled.

Cai Yan peeked over the walls.

"The yaotuo are overrunning the barbican, the gates are still up, the drones are still silent!" she reported.

The drones. What the devil happened to them? And what about the other guards on the walls?

"Come on!" Li Ming urged. "To the gatehouse!"

The door was locked tight. It didn't budge under Li Ming's fist and boots. Cai Yan waved him aside and aimed her dual shapers at the lock. She closed her eyes, focused her qi, and shouted.

The door exploded inwards, tearing off its hinges, flying deep into the room beyond. Li Ming charged in, Hellion held in both hands.

Blood.

Pools of blood covered the floor. Men lay slumped over smoking consoles, yawning holes blown into the back of their heads. Kneeling behind an overturned table, a pair of men reeled, shaken by the sudden blast.

Both had infinity guns.

Instinct took over. Advancing on the men, Li Ming fired them up, dumping bolts into them as fast as he could work the trigger, left and right and back again. The low-powered bolts disintegrated against shimmering shields. He continued the onslaught, circling around the table. The closer man's shield failed abruptly, and Li Ming's follow-up shot blew through his neck.

The other lunged.

His entire body mass crashed into Li Ming, destroying his balance, knocking his arms aside, driving him against a filing cabinet. The shooter pinned him to the cabinet, left hand reaching for his belt, right hand seizing Li Ming's throat.

Pain burst through Li Ming. His lungs seized. Li Ming exhaled, yielding into the force. He drew his arms through tight outward circles, the opening movement of entering Sancai Shi, reached over the threat's own arm, and seized the hand gripping his throat. Pinning the threat's hand in place, he torqued clockwise and peeled off the enemy's thumb.

The grip broke. The threat's elbow hyperextended. The threat lost his balance. Flowing with the momentum, Li Ming continued to turn, driving the threat's face into the cabinet. Li Ming released him, leapt back, raised his gun—

Cai Yan fired.

Her shots raked up the shooter's side, going for his arms, neck, ears, everywhere that wasn't covered in armor. The shield failed under the rapid-fire assault. Cai Yan kept up the fire, blasting away. His head exploded. His helmet went flying. What was left fell to the floor.

"Clear!" Cai Yan shouted.

Li Ming looked about. No more threats. A flight of stairs led up to the second floor.

"Clear!"

A quick peek upstairs revealed empty bunk rooms. They rushed back to the consoles and pulled off the dead men. One computer was destroyed. The other was still intact. Words blazed bright across the screen.

GATE CONTROLS

"They haven't destroyed it yet?" Li Ming wondered.

"Maybe they were going to destroy it after they leave," Cai Yan suggested.

"Or maybe..."

Li Ming knelt and checked under the table.

Four rectangular blocks, taped together, lay atop the processor. Lengths of cord ran out from the closer end of each block, neatly bundled and daisy chained together, joined to a long cord that coiled round and round to feed into a narrow metal cylinder resting quietly atop the package.

A bomb.

Li Ming's blood ran cold.

His demolitions expertise was minimal. The military had taught him just enough to blow up dangerous ordnance and obstacles. His biaohang training focused on identifying bombs, not defusing them.

"Li Ming?" Cai Yan asked.

"Close the gate," Li Ming said.

"What did you—"

"Close the gate," Li Ming repeated.

Crouching low, he inspected the bundle with his flashlight. It was just sitting there, inert and innocent. He played the light around, looking for sensors, tripwires, anything that suggested a trap. Meanwhile, Cai Yan leaned over him, clicking away, hammering at keys.

Li Ming turned his attention to the narrow cylinder. It was a fuse igniter. Pull the pull ring, release, let the striker ignite the fuse, and run like all the devils in the underworld were chasing you. Mechanical, foolproof, easy to use.

And the safety pin was in.

With quick, deft movements, Li Ming detached the igniter from the fuse. Just like that, the bomb was rendered safe.

He heaved a sigh of relief.

Heavy metallic clanking reverberated in the gatehouse.

"The gate is closing," Cai Yan said.

"Can we call for help?"

"They blasted the radio."

"*Gaisi...*"

"The gates won't close in time. The yaotuo are going to leak through."

"We've got to stop them. Head out the closer door. I'll take the further one. We'll station ourselves at the ramps and shoot down the yaotuo."

Li Ming swept up a fallen man's infinity gun. A Type 82, the most common infinity gun in the continent. Cai Yan grabbed another. Together, they charged out the gatehouse.

A roiling, seething swarm of beasts massed in the wengcheng, growing and hissing and roaring and snapping. Li Ming felt the urge to rain death and fire on them all. He tore himself away and rushed to the ramp.

And came face-to-face with a yaotuo.

His thumb swept down the fire selector. His hands raised the weapon to his shoulder. The yaotuo bellowed, its breath hot and stinking, and charged.

Li Ming fired.

A white-hot bolt blasted into the yaotuo and tore out the other side. The beast kept coming. He speared out the weapon, striking it in the muzzle, and launched himself clear. The yaotuo stumbled, but remained upright. Li Ming fired again and again, working up the side, until a final shot blew off its head and the creature collapsed in a twitching heap.

More gunshots. Li Ming rushed to the ramp. A group of yaotuo broke through from the gate, spilling out onto the street. Cai Yan fired them up with quick, precise, single shots. Li Ming clicked down to continuous fire and hosed them down.

Starfire scorched the street, incinerating hide, vaporizing flesh, obliterating bone. The ground erupted, detonated, cratered. The yaotuo screeched and twitched and jerked and fell apart in great bloody chunks. Hot steam roiled from the kill zone. The remaining yaotuo howled in fury, in bloodlust, in savage hunger.

With a resounding *BOOM*, the gates slammed shut.

Li Ming heaved a sigh of relief.

"All clear?" Cai Yan called.

"Looks like it!" Li Ming yelled. "Back to the *wengcheng!*"

The yaotuo were retreating.

The great swarm of muddy dragons lumbered through the open outer gate, suddenly calm and docile. Some jostled against their neighbors, others cut ahead of their kin, but they moved with an eerie civility, almost as if they were humans joined in a common goal to go somewhere, but in no rush to get there.

Odd.

One moment they were blood-maddened beasts, tearing up everything in sight. Now they were as meek as mice. Whatever had driven them to rise from the waters had worn off, and now their collective temperament had swung the other way.

It was so strange, Li Ming hadn't even thought of firing upon them.

"MILITIA! MILITIA! DROP YOUR WEAPONS!"

To his right, a team of militia raced down the wall walk, weapons trained on him. Li Ming unslung his gun, tossed it aside and stepped away, hands held high.

"BIAOHANG! WE HELD OFF THE YAOTUO!" Li Ming yelled.

"We are biaohang from Zhongxia! We're here to help!" Cai Yan added.

"Hands up! On the ground!" another militiaman yelled from Cai Yan's direction.

Li Ming went to his knees.

The soldiers rushed up to him, weapons pointed at his head. Blinding flashlights pierced his eyes, forcing him to look away.

"What the devil happened here?" the leader shouted.

"A swarm of yaotuo attempted to invade the city. My colleague and I were at the piers when it happened. We rushed into the *wengcheng* and called for help. Terrorists destroyed the archery tower and allowed the yaotuo into the city. A second team massacred everyone inside the gate house and held the gates open. We killed the terrorists and held off the beasts."

The leader gaped.

"Yaotuo? Terrorists? What the devil?"

"What were you told?" Li Ming asked.

"Shooting at the outer gate. Beasts. The drones mysteriously shutting down. That's all. Who are these terrorists? What do they want?"

The terrorists were all dead. They couldn't answer any questions ever again. Li Ming thought of the last man he had struck. If he had tried to grapple with him instead, tried to take him alive...

"I don't know," Li Ming admitted.

"Show me your identification?"

"It's in my breast pocket."

"Take it out. Slowly."

Li Ming complied, going slowly and deliberate, mindful of the five muzzles trained on him and the barely-visible shadows behind the guns.

"He checks out," the leader announced. "You can stand up now."

The soldiers relaxed. Li Ming picked himself up.

And a strange sensation fell over him.

His qi quivered. His body shivered. Waves of pure heat lapped against him. Fire touched his heart, blossoming into... anger.

More than anger, it was killing rage, a wildfire yearning to bring death and destruction into the world, to consume everything and leave behind nothing but ashes. His heart pounded, his fingers clenched, his teeth gnashed—

But why rage? There was nothing going on right now.

"Did you feel that?" Li Ming asked.

"Feel what?"

"Anybody sensed that?" Cai Yan called, her voice carrying across the air. "It's the same feeling right before the yaotuo struck."

"What did you feel?" the leader demanded.

"I felt... something. Like a wave," another militiaman said. "Don't you feel it?"

"No. I don't feel anything at all."

"I do," Li Ming said, gritting his teeth. "It's stronger."

"What's going on?" Cai Yan asked.

The sirens continued to wail. Infinity guns howled across the city, from walls and rooftops. Bolts seared up into the heavens. Full-throated shrieks and screeches tore split the night.

And from every direction, swarms of dark shapes fell upon the city.

Chapter Twelve

Target Rich Environment

Shrieking, screeching, black shapes swooped from above, diving upon the city. In their wake, small dark objects sliced through the air, showering down like lethal darts on streets and walls, roofs and windows.

Men shouted. Windows shattered. Alarms rang.

And the sounds grew closer.

"TAKE COVER!" Li Ming yelled.

He spun on his heel and ran for the gatehouse. Behind him, hard hail rattled against stone. A man cried out. He burst through the door and held it open.

Too late.

Wet thuds rang out. The militiamen went down, screaming and shrieking, then curled up and moaned in agony.

"Coming in!" Cai Yan called.

A half-dozen militiamen trooped into the gatehouse. Then came Cai Yan, her qi field bright.

"What the devil was that?" a soldier demanded.

Glass windows cracked and spiderwebbed over. Everyone ducked. Cai Yan raised her hands, reinforcing the windows with translucent brown plates.

"Air attack?" someone else called.

The thuds faded into the background. The beasts had moved on, carpet-bombing another section of the city. Infinity guns continued to scream into the heavens. Li Ming shuffled to the open door, clicked on his flashlight, and peered out.

Three fallen troopers lay curled up on the ancient stone, twitching and groaning, frothing from the mouth. Two more lay completely still. Arrows, long and sharp and feathered, lay embedded in their flesh and sides, turning them to pincushions. More arrows lay scattered across the road.

Not arrows.

Feathers.

"What the devil happened?" Cai Yan demanded, peering over his shoulder.

"Poison feathers," Li Ming said. "The beasts are zhenniao."

The most dangerous species of bird in the world, zhenniao brimmed with poison. Poison pumped through its veins, saturated its flesh, filled its vital fluids, concentrated in its razor-sharp feathers. Assassins bred zhenniao to harvest their poison. Superpowers deployed zhenniao as dive bombers and terror weapons in wars past.

But zhenniao were *not* nocturnal.

"Zhenniao aren't active at night!" Cai Yan exclaimed. "What the devil are they doing here?"

"Something's messed up with this place."

"We have to help the wounded!"

"A single drop of zhenniao poison is fatal. If you don't have the antivenin on hand, they are already dead."

Cai Yan cursed up a storm. The team had prepared an abundance of supplies to meet and counter the beasts known to inhabit the Yudu region. Zhenniao was not among them.

"Do we have zhenniao antivenin here?" Li Ming asked.

"No," a militiaman replied. "Zhenniao attacks are unheard of over here!"

"We have to go out. We can still perform first aid," Cai Yan said.

Feather storms swept through the city. Windows shattered, people screamed, tires burst, infinity guns screamed.

"Are you courting death? A single feather could kill you if it touches bare skin!" the militiamen replied.

She clenched her fists. Qi rushed into her arms, into her reality shapers, into the primordial crystals within.

"Xun," she said.

The essence of wind. The feathers, while fast, were tiny and light. A wind barrier would easily sweep them away.

"Go for it," Li Ming said.

She stepped up to the door. Sucked down a deep breath. And swept her arms up and out.

A cool breeze brew around her, spiraling into a gentle whirlwind. The concentrated winds filled the guardhouse, sending a mug clattering to the floor, stirring ripples through the lake of blood, caressing Li Ming.

Cai Yan stepped out.

And poison feathers moved.

The mild winds gently swept the feathers aside, clearing a path. She moved slowly, deliberately, with total concentration, keeping the winds from blowing the feathers up into the air. The briefest lapse of concentration, the slightest miscalculation, the smallest irregularity in the flow of qi would kill the spell and send the poison feathers billowing about in a deadly storm.

It was a masterful display of magic, of controlled power and superb focus. Li Ming didn't know if he could ever do anything like that, only that with his five element crystals, he could never do it. While the three major magic systems of the Continent had much in common, there were some things one system could do that the others could not.

Cai Yan moved from soldier to soldier, creating a clear space around them, maintaining complete awareness of the feathers fluttering around her. She moved in curves and straight lines, brushing the feathers away with her wind barrier, keeping them from contacting the downed men, sweeping them up against the battlements. Now and then, she flicked her fingers, sending a tiny impulse of wind to move stray feathers aside.

It was like watching her perform a solo yizhang set, walking in circles large and small, her arms and hands flowing in constant motion, her body twisting this way and that. Li Ming stared, mesmerized, then reminded himself that there was still an ongoing air raid.

He tore his eyes away and scanned the sky. The zhenniao screeched in the distance. White-hot bolts seared the city skies in every direction, but none came close. The sirens continued to wail, though many speakers were now broken and distorted.

Li Ming turned to the guards.

"Stay here and watch the *wengcheng*. More beasts and terrorists might come this way. Keep them from breaching the gates."

"We won't let them through," a soldier vowed.

Cai Yan came to a sudden halt, swirled her arms about, rested her hands in front of her dantian, and exhaled.

"I'm done," she said. "The floor is clear."

"Put up a wind shield to cover us," Li Ming said. "Zhenniao are still in the area."

Her left palm corkscrewed upwards, reaching for the heavens. The wind shifted, becoming a dome encapsulating the wounded men. She aimed her right palm at a soldier, and focused. Gently, gingerly, the feathers extracted themselves from his body.

He'd heard of subtle, sustained magic like this, but until now he'd never seen it before. She carefully regulated the qi flow from her primordial crystals, keeping it just below the shapers' recharge rate, ensuring she had a steady stream of energy. It was delicate work, and she would need total concentration.

Li Ming stepped into the wind dome. A gentle breeze caressed his skin as he passed. He illuminated the nearest downed soldier and knelt over him. He was already gone, his life energies bleeding into the earth to leave an empty husk behind.

Lying next to him, his buddy was slightly more fortunate. He wriggled and writhed, foam spewing from his mouth, his eyes rolling. Feathers broke off from his body. Needle-point wounds ran up and down his arms and legs.

His seizure had removed the feathers, but he was still rolling about a few of them. With his boots, Li Ming swept the feathers away. Then he rolled the trooper onto his side, careful to avoid touching the wounds, bending the soldier's knee and bracing his head on the back of a hand to keep him from rolling and choking. Li Ming tilted the trooper's head back and opened his jaw, allowing the foam to spill out freely. He was still breathing, but barely.

Li Ming placed his hands over the trooper's body and felt the man's qi.

Fires roared through his body, burning him from the inside out, producing black tar in its wake. The corrosive substance dissolved everything it touched, attacking his organs and scattering his qi. A damp, evil wind fed the flames, emanating from every wound.

Li Ming was no medical specialist. Treating something like this was far beyond him. He barely knew what he was looking at. He had no idea how the energies interacted with each other, and he knew he had to be missing something.

But he had to do something.

Li Ming pumped water qi into the casualty. Cold, pure liquid gushed into him and onto the fires raging through his body. The fires flickered, resisted, clinging on to existence. The winds continued to feed it, its dampness soaking into the black tar. The tar drank in the dampness and the water, growing deeper, stronger.

He had to stop the wind. Cut off the fire from sustenance. Wind was wood, and metal conquered wood, so with his left-hand reality shaper, his good one, he injected metal qi into the wounds.

Metal was hard and cutting and unyielding. It refused to be used like this. Li Ming pressed his will into it, shaping it, letting it take the form of a sturdy hatch bolted shut against a whirlwind, a septic tank containing toxic sludge.

The wind resisted, attempting to flow around it, to batter it down. The metal stood fast, expanding swiftly, cutting it off, containing the wind to the entrance wounds.

Metal produced water, strengthening the water Li Ming poured into the wounds with his other shaper. The fires died down to sulking embers buried in muck.

Li Ming's head pounded. His shapers cut off. He was exhausted. He stepped away, massaging his temples, drinking down qi. He'd slowed down the poison, buying the man more time. That was all he could do. The muck was *probably* earth, and wood conquered earth, but wood also produced fire. He sensed that, with what little he knew of medical magic, if he tried to dissolve the black substance now, he might reignite the fires.

Li Ming wasn't good enough to heal him. He didn't even know if he had saved him. He'd done his best, but... was it enough?

Of course not.

If he lived through this, he had to get better. He had to expand his skills. Being the most powerful martial cultivator in the world was nothing if you didn't know how to use that power wisely.

His Raptor buzzed.

A translucent window popped up in his field of view. Wong-gor was calling him. Li Ming blinked hard, his head still swimming, and the smartglasses interpreted the movement as one of acceptance.

"Li Ming! Where are you?" Wong-gor asked.

"At the northern gates. Cai Yan is with me. We just held off a beast invasion."

She perked up as he spoke her name. He tapped his glasses. She tended to another patient.

On the other side of the line, Wong-gor heaved a sigh of relief.

"*Tai ho le*. Ga San and I are on the roof of the hotel, engaging a swarm of zhenniao. Are you two okay?"

"Yes. We're tending to zhenniao casualties."

"If you don't have the antidote, you can't do much."

"We have to do something."

"Then help us stop the zhenniao. Take Lady Boss and get over here. We're setting up a base of fire."

"Roger."

Li Ming hung up and turned to Cai Yan.

"Was that the guys?" she asked.

"Yes. They're on the roof of the hotel, preparing to fight off the beasts. They want us to go to them."

"Give me a moment."

A wave of white light emanated outwards from her arms. Washing over him, it re-energized his body, chased away minor aches he'd barely noticed, soothed his headache. The surviving soldiers stayed down and continued breathing.

"I've alerted emergency services. We've done all we could. Let's go," Cai Yan said.

"It's still raining poison feathers. Keep up the wind barrier. I'll cover us."

"Roger."

Li Ming drew his Hellion. He didn't dare to touch one of the infinity guns lying around, not with bare hands. They could be contaminated with zhenniao poison. Cai Yan lowered her arms, compressing the dome to cover the two of them. High above, the zhenniao continued to shriek, competing with the sirens. Li Ming scanned the skies, pistol ready. Shooting at such a far target with a tiny gun was insane. He'd have to conserve his heat reserve for dive bombers.

The duo descended the ramp and dashed down the road. Cai Yan breathed audibly through her mouth, arms outstretched, keeping the dome up. Feathers whirled about her, blowing up into the air. Pedestrians lay groaning and twitching and dying on the streets.

Civilians hid inside their homes, their qi like dying oil lamps. A few heroes took to the rooftops, blasting away at zhenniao.

Poison feathers lanced down from the sky, striking metal, stone, flesh. Men fell, screaming and gargling. A gun discharged into a roof, producing an eruption of smoke and shrapnel. Feathers struck the wind shield and flew off to parts unknown. Cai Yan sucked in a breath, recharging her qi.

"Slow down," Li Ming said. "The wind is too strong."

She slowed to a walk. The whirlwind stabilized and slowed.

And a beast screeched.

Li Ming shot his pistol up to chest height. Scanning in all directions, he realized he and Cai Yan were completely alone. The shooters around and above him were all down.

And, dead ahead, a tall black shape rushed out an alley.

Li Ming lit it up.

A zhenniao strode forth on long rooster-like legs, ending in sharp claws. It spread its massive wings, spanning the road, revealing feathers a vivid shade of iridescent green, dissolving into a royal purple over its abdomen. A small head, perched above a long neck, rose high above the humans, darting back and forth, its slender scarlet beak seeking an opening.

Li Ming fired.

The bolt blasted through the base of its neck, igniting feathers, vaporizing meat, obliterating bone, leaving behind two thin strips of flesh. Blood gushed out the wound like a geyser, splashing across the road. Droplets touched the shield and sprayed outwards. The zhenniao stumbled, its head flopping forward, and collapsed at Li Ming's feet.

A wet, gurgling noise issued from its blasted throat. Its scratched and pecked at the air in its death throes, still trying to reach Li Ming. Its feathers shed in great piles, covering the street.

"We're not going down this way," Li Ming said.

They backtracked. Made another turn. Headed down another feather-covered street. Zhenniao circled the skies above, screaming in blood-maddened hate. Bolts—plasma, fire, lightning—scourged the sky. Wind hammers howled in the night, chasing down the beasts.

The hotel loomed ahead of them. Lances of blue-white light flashed from rooftops and windows. A string of high-pitched cracks rang out at irregular intervals. The bodies of zhenniao littered the street. Cai Yan maneuvered around them, Li Ming next to her, keeping to empty space.

Behind them, zhenniao screeched.

Li Ming spun around, pistol raised in both hands. His white light revealed three zhenniao diving from the sky, screeching at the top of their lungs, swooping down at him.

He stood tall, all thought fleeing his mind, his conscious mind going quiet, his heart pumping at a steady beat. From deep within, a place still and unshakable, an urge arose, spreading throughout his body, firing nerves and muscles, guiding his body of flesh and blood.

He fired three times, fast as lightning, blasting them all in the center of mass. Full-power bolts blasted from up high, spearing through the zhenniao, digging great holes into the road, so close he felt the blasts of searing heat. What remained of the beasts crashed down in crumpled heaps of broken bone and charred meat, skidding to a stop at his feet.

Li Ming stood in quiet wonder. What was that? Had he really just done that?

"Come on!" Cai Yan called.

They charged the entrance. The doorman quickly unlocked the door and held them open. The second they burst through, the doorman shut and bolted the door again. Li Ming patched through to Wong-gor.

"Cai Yan and I are in the lobby. We'll get our guns and head up to you."

"Roger that," Wong-gor said, his voice cool and smooth and low. "We've got a target rich environment. Better hurry if you want to get some."

They didn't bother with the elevator. Instead, they burst into the stairwell. Cai Yan manifested her wind, flying up to the tenth floor. Li Ming rose on bursts of detonations, the sound of his passage reverberating in the tiny space. The walls trembled, dust fell, but Li Ming pressed on. Every three floors, he grabbed the guardrails and waited for a few seconds, long enough for his crystals to recharge, and carried on.

Cai Yan reached the landing before him. She held the door open, waiting for him. Li Ming reached the landing, vaulted over the handrail, and squeezed past her. Together, they returned to their rooms.

Li Ming summoned his armor and infinity gun from his Belt Bag. He clipped on his plate carrier, strapped on his auxiliary armor plates, fastened his helmet, slung his weapon around his neck. Within a minute, he was ready for war.

Not fast enough, he knew. The next time he went operational, he had to carry his Belt Bag with him everywhere he went.

He met Cai Yan in the corridor. She, too, was kitted up for combat, helmet and armor and weapon ready. Back in the stairwell, they flew up to the top floor, and stepped out into a hallway of blood.

Casualties lay on blankets down the length of the corridor, bleeding and moaning and trembling. More patients occupied the lift lobby. Cultivators walked among them, soothing energies spewing from reality shapers. Medics armed with first aid kits conducted field surgeries and deployed syringes. In the center of it all, Zhang Mei Lin strode up and down the corridor, offering water and medical supplies, speaking into her headset, coordinating actions.

She beamed at Li Ming, and Cai Yan.

"You're here!" she exclaimed.

"How bad is it?" Li Ming asked.

Her face quickly sobered.

"The zhenniao struck the rooftop bar. Many of the patrons were caught in the open. We've evacuated the casualties here. Ambulances are on the way, but emergency services are stretched thin. There's a group of fighters on the roof holding off the beasts."

"We're going up," Cai Yan said. "We've got beasts to hunt."

"Stay safe out there!"

Cai Yan and Li Ming wound their way around the bodies and headed up the roof access stairs. Stepping out on the rooftop, the sound of gunfire greeted them. The snarling of infinity guns—pistols, long guns, repeaters—mingling with the roaring of Wong's coilgun.

A dozen cultivators lined the roof, their qi fields hot and bright. Illuminated in bright yellow lights, they fired at the fast-moving zhenniao, flung balls and bolts of concentrated magic, called out targets and sectors of fire. At the other end of the roof, Wong discharged his weapon, the only coilgun in the crowd.

Cai Yan brew up a wind shield. Poison feathers drifted across the stained wooden floorboards, gathering safely under tables and chairs, and leaping off the edge of the roof. She walked to Wong-gor, and Li Ming followed.

There were three people on this side of the roof. Wong-gor, perched in place, swiveling like a turret. Ghazan, weapon lowered, scanning the battlefield. And the Yue woman Li Ming had spotted in the gym.

"Coming to you," Li Ming called.

"About time," Ghazan said. "Where were you?"

"Area recon," Cai Yan said smoothly. "What's the situation?"

"We've taken out twenty-three zhenniao," Wong-gor said, still behind his scope. "Radio says there's at least two hundred in the swarm."

The woman fired.

"Twenty-four," she said.

Li Ming stepped up to the rail, in between the woman and Wong-gor.

"Need a spotter?" Li Ming asked.

"I've got this covered," Wong-gor said. "We need every gun in the fight."

"I'll hang back and generate a wind shield," Cai Yan said.

"Don't," Wong-gor said. "The wind will throw off my shots."

Cai Yan pursed her lips.

"How about I create something like a cave? It'll shield us from the top and flanks. You can shoot through the opening."

"That works."

A wind wall swirled around Cai Yan, bending in strange ways, contouring to cover the biaohang. It was profoundly unnatural, guided not by the urban cityscape but by simple force of will, hardening into a hollow half-dome. It swept poison feathers away from it, blowing them clear to empty space.

Li Ming allowed himself a second to marvel at her magic gongfu. Then he turned on his fusion goggles, recalibrated them from the night, and scanned the skies.

The zhenniao showed up as bright patches of red and orange. It was almost unfair, hunting them like this. But war wasn't about fairness. It was about destroying the enemy as quickly and efficiently as possible and coming home in one piece.

Li Ming clicked on his infrared laser. A solid straight beam of bright white light burned into the darkness, blooming against a distant wall, joining the other aiming lasers searching the dark. He rotated the fire mode dial, setting the gun to half-power, then snapped up the gun.

The laser found a distant zhenniao, framed against the night. Li Ming tracked its flight, bringing the laser to bear. It lanced out into the infinite darkness, a tiny pinprick against the infinite heavens. Suddenly a bright dot bloomed against the zhenniao's breast. Without conscious thought, he clicked off the safety and fired.

The zhenniao fell from the sky.

"Target down," Li Ming announced.

Li Ming snapped to the next one. The zhenniao swooped down from the air, taking cover amongst the buildings. Li Ming's dot bloomed against its back, but right behind it was an apartment tower. Li Ming held his fire, swiveling with it, trying to keep his dot on target.

To his left, a laser fell on the zhenniao. A bolt ripped through its wing and exploded against concrete. The wounded beast squawked, flapping its intact wing, trying to guide its fall, but crashed into a lamp post and vanished from sight.

Li Ming glanced to his left. The Yue woman was already looking away, servicing other targets.

"Did you shoot the zhenniao in the wing?" Li Ming asked.

"Was that your prey?"

A touch of cold arrogance colored her voice.

"Set your weapon to half power."

"Half the power means half the range."

"A full power bolt will punch through the beast. We're not here to burn down the city."

She humphed. A dial clicked.

"Done."

Something whistled to his right. Turning, Li Ming saw a black cloud fall the skies. It separated, becoming a cluster of poison feathers. Li Ming flinched—

And the wind barrier flung the feathers aside.

Li Ming rotated in place, hunting for the beast. There, high above him, a shrinking orange splotch, so far away his laser dot vanished against the blot of false color.

"Target, directly above us, five hundred *chi!*" Li Ming called.

He fired, missed, fired, missed again—

CRACK

And the zhenniao dropped.

"Good shot," Li Ming said.

"No problem," Wong-gor replied.

Li Ming swept the city before him, eyes soft and wide open. When he spotted a moving blob of heat, he snapped the laser to the target and tunneled in on the target. He engaged zhenniao in the open, zhenniao on the streets, zhenniao in an alley. But with every shot, he checked what was in front of the threat, what was behind it, what else might be struck by a stray bolt. Whenever he doubted a shot, he held his fire and looked for the next one.

High above, thunder cracked.

Fire and lightning, hail and bolts, a barrage of concentrated magic roared through the city. Night flashed to false day. Detonations echoed and blended into a long and booming roar. Flat rectangular shapes raced in from the northwest, skimming over walls and rooftops.

"Airships!" Cai Yan called. "Airships incoming!"

"Any more targets?" Li Ming called.

"All clear here!" Ghazan shouted.

"East side clear!" a biaohang shouted.

"West is clear!"

"South! All clear!"

"Is that the military?" Wong asked.

"Likely, but whose?" Li Ming asked.

"Not the local militia," the Yue woman said. "They don't use Tai airships."

For airships, the Tai were tiny, barely the size of a passenger car. They peeled off, spreading to all directions of the compass. One of them approached the hotel, navigation lights winking red and green.

"Attention, attention! Friendlies incoming! We are landing on the roof!" a loudspeaker called. "Please make room!"

Wind screamed from its thrusters, blowing poison feathers about. The biaohang threw up wind shields, deflecting them before they got too close. Cai Yan cursed under her breath, sending the feathers over the edge of the roof.

The Tai landed on a flat patch of roof and dropped the side doors. Six heavily armed and armored men jumped out. The leader swaggered over, infinity repeater in hand, a bright smile on his face.

"Greetings! We are here—"

"What the devil did you think you were doing?!" Cai Yan thundered.

The commander recoiled.

"What do you—"

"There were poison feathers scattered over the roof! You could have *killed* someone with that stunt!"

He held up his hands.

"Sorry. Is anyone hurt?"

"No, but you just spread hazardous materials all over the place!"

"We're here to help. My men and I are ready to provide aid and to clean up the feathers. Do you need assistance?"

"Who are you?" Li Ming asked.

"We are from the Ten Thousand Swords Society."

Li Ming's heart hammered in his head. Heat roared into his arms and legs. Fire raged from deep within. The leader continued speaking, but Li Ming didn't hear it. He was back in predator mode, his world shrinking down to the newcomers, his brain crunching numbers and calculating solutions.

"We are here to help," the leader said.

"No," Li Ming replied.

And snapped up his infinity gun.

Chapter Thirteen

The Good of Mankind

The world froze.

Time stretched out into infinity. Electricity flashed through the crowd, jumping from man to man, heart to heart. The aiming laser bloomed bright within the man's open mouth, the one point of vulnerability between his body armor and his helmet. Li Ming's thumb clicked off the safety. His finger yearned to leap to the trigger.

But stopped.

"HANDS UP!" he ordered.

In that moment, time exploded forward. Men yelled, women shouted, hands flew, qi flared, weapons rose, but Li Ming's perceptions shrank down to the six men before him, all of them gone completely still, holding their hands out.

"What the devil is going on?"

"*You* drop your weapon!"

"What are you doing?"

"SHUT UP!" Li Ming roared. "You! Wanjianhui! Put your weapons on the ground now!"

The leader wavered.

"I think there's a misunderstanding—"

A second laser, visible red, flashed from Li Ming's right.

"Weapons down! Now!" Cai Yan shouted.

"This is a mistake!" the leader replied.

The red dot traced a small circle over his groin.

"We won't ask again! Put your weapons down!"

Behind Li Ming, Wong-gor whispered, his voice so soft, Li Ming's Raptor barely picked it up.

"Things are getting tense. We need you up here."

"What are you doing?" a biaohang demanded. "They helped us!"

"The Wanjianhui slaughtered half of Dayong!" Li Ming said, his laser still aimed on the squad. "We want answers!"

"My condolences, but—"

"Weapons down! NOW!"

The newcomers reluctantly disarmed themselves. They moved slowly, with great precision, doing nothing that could be interpreted as a hostile act.

"You want to tell us what's going on?" Wong-gor asked.

"Dayong discovered a Yue Dynasty ruin during an expedition half a year ago," Cai Yan said. "We requested for backup from White Tiger. Wanjianhui operatives disguised themselves as White Tiger troops and landed at the ruin. After we cleared the ruin, they turned on us."

"Where was this?" the leader asked.

"Southernmost edge of Dongshan Province, close to the border of the Central Plains."

"We had nothing to do with that. We're here to protect the people."

"*Bizui!* *Shut up!* "We're handing you over to the Jianghu Association."

The door burst open. Zhang Mei Lin sprinted out.

"What's going on?" she asked.

"These men are bandits," Li Ming said.

"We're from the Wanjianhui!" the leader said. "We're not bandits!"

"Their comrades killed our brothers! We will have justice!"

"We are a self-defense organization! A biaoju, just like you!"

"*Feihua!* What kind of biaoju betrays, robs and murders fellow biaohang?"

"He's right," Ms. Zhang said.

"What do you mean?" Li Ming thundered.

"In Yudu, the Wanjianhui is a registered biaoju. They are not bandits."

A volcano erupted in Li Ming's heart. Li Ming had read about that, but witnessing it in person set his blood boiling. His finger strayed closer to the trigger.

"Their comrades attacked us in our country! How the devil are they not bandits?!"

"None of my men have anything to do with what happened to you! I swear it!" the leader yelled.

"Let me scan their biaohang cards," Ms. Zhang said. "I can run a background check on them."

"Go ahead," Cai Yan said.

The Wanjianhui soldiers slowly produced their cards from chest-mounted pouches. Ms. Zhang lowered the visor of her headset, inspected them one by one, and compared the photos against the faces.

"They are lawfully-registered biaohang," Ms. Zhang said. "No criminal record, no active warrants. They are not bandits, not by the laws of the Central Plains."

"What about the laws of the Jianghu Association?"

Ms. Zhang smiled sadly.

"Here in the Central Plains, they must bow to the Central Plains Merchant Association."

And the Association would do nothing that would hinder the free market.

"Are you saying we have to let them go?" Cai Yan demanded.

"They are not bandits. They have committed no crimes. You have no legal basis to detain them."

"*Ni kai shenme wan xiao?*" Li Ming exclaimed.

Are you kidding me?

"Can you present any charges against us?" the leader asked. "Have we committed any crimes? We came here to save this city from beasts, and you repay us with suspicion and hostility."

Murmurs passed through the crowd.

"You are part of a secret society," Li Ming said.

"Look around you. You're in the Central Plains. Not the Zhongxia Republic. We have different laws here."

Li Ming's grip tightened. The beast within him bayed for blood. It was easy, so easy, to gun them down on the spot. But the human yanked its leash and stayed his finger.

Was this the right thing to do?

"He's right," Cai Yan whispered.

"You are clearly suffering a great deal. My condolences for your loss. If indeed a Wanjianhui soldier caused you such grief, I apologize on our behalf. We came here simply to help defend this city. That is all."

"That's it?" Li Ming said. "This is a trick. The Wanjianhui plots in darkness and strikes from the shadows."

"What's the trick? We open the city to monsters, then come swooping down to save the day? This isn't a wuxia story!"

"The northern gate guards were murdered," Cai Yan said. "The killers shot them at point blank in the head, opened the gates, and allowed a swarm of yaotuo to invade Shuanglong. We found the bodies. And killed the killers."

The leader's qi field wavered. But only slightly.

"If that's true, then there are terrorists prowling the city. Not us. We just arrived."

"You could have planted agents in Shuanglong. Right before the beast attacks, a huge wave of qi surged through the city. I felt it, Cai Yan felt it, you cultivators must have felt it too."

Murmurs of agreement rippled through the crowd. The Wanjianhui leader bared his teeth.

"Listen to yourself! You're accusing us of terrorism and spinning wild stories! Terrorists might have organized this invasion, but do you have any proof that *we* did it? Any evidence that my men and I are implicated in some grand scheme to destroy the city?"

Li Ming sucked in a breath and said nothing. Cai Yan went quiet.

He was right.

"It's been a terrible night, and after what happened to you, I'd be paranoid too," the leader said. "It's perfectly understandable. But we had nothing to do with what happened to Dayong. We're only here to help. If you let us go now, we'll chalk it up as a misunderstanding and we'll leave it at that. All right?"

His finger yearned to press the trigger, to unleash hell and exact bloody vengeance. But if he did, there was no turning back. There would be nowhere in the jianghu he could hide.

Li Ming lowered his weapon.

"Take your things and get out of here."

"We've got a cargo of zhenniao antivenin and first aid supplies. We'll leave them and evacuate the most critically wounded. Fair enough?"

Li Ming snarled.

"Fine."

"Can we retrieve our weapons?"

Li Ming jerked his muzzle at them.

"I'll be watching you."

He watched as they re-armed themselves. He watched as they unloaded crates and bags from the airship, clearly marked with white crosses against green squares. He watched as they carried the cargo downstairs and came back up with patients draped over their shoulders.

The biaohang dispersed, returning to their posts. Gunfire rang anew, the interval between shots growing longer and longer. Cai Yan and two other biaohang swept up the poison feathers and gathered them in a hazardous waste bag thoughtfully provided by the Ten Thousand Swords.

Li Ming stood his ground and watched.

The men of the Wanjianhui loaded the final casualties aboard the dropship. Their leader turned to him.

"There's no more room inside our airship. We'll move out on foot."

"Go. I'll be behind you."

The Wanjianhui shooters took the elevator. From there they had a straight shot to the ground floor. Li Ming didn't care to cram himself into the narrow car, not with so many potential hostiles in sight.

As he approached the stairs, Ghazan sidled up to him.

"Do you need backup?"

"Yes," Li Ming said.

Ghazan nodded.

"See you downstairs."

He ran.

Glowed white.

And leapt off the edge of the roof.

Li Ming shook his head. The Yue had a penchant for drama. He could do something similar, but gongfu was not something you show off to others. Instead, he ran downstairs, burst into the internal stairwell, and leapt down.

He discharged copious streams of earth and water qi from his arms, manifesting it as tall block of translucent gel. The gel caught him, absorbed the force of his fall, slowed him down, gently lowered him to the ground, dissolved the second his boots touched earth.

When he stepped out into the lobby, Ghazan was already waiting for him. A moment later, the Wanjianhui shooters stepped out the elevator.

The leader seemed impressed.

"I'd ask how you got here ahead of us, but…"

Ghazan said nothing. Li Ming let the sentence hang and gestured at the exit.

The shooters filed out one by one. As they stepped out, they took up a cigar-shaped formation, covering every angle, scanning streets and skies. The leader was the last to go.

"I hope we've eased your suspicions," he said.

"The Wanjianhui and I cannot live under the same sky," Li Ming said.

"Once again, I apologize for the harms you have suffered. But as you have seen, we are not like the men who betrayed you. Here in the Central Plains, the Ten Thousand Swords Society works for the good of all mankind."

"If you do, why is your organization listed as a secret society in Zhongxia? In three of the Five States?"

"Politics. Who knows what transpires in the minds of rulers and politicians? We of the Wanjianhui are above that."

"What do you really want?"

"To protect people. That's all."

Ghazan barked a laugh.

"That's not what we heard," Ghazan said.

"What have you heard?"

"You wish to end the era of the Five States and the Ten Corporations by reforming the jianghu, breaking the power of the corporations, and uniting the continent under a single ruler," Li Ming said.

The leader's brow furrowed.

"What's wrong with that?"

"What do you mean, 'what's wrong with that'? You use subversion, treachery and underhanded means to achieve your goals. The only thing that matters to you is power. The weak are meat to the strong, and only the strongest rule."

The leader smiled. "Ah. What about it?"

"You don't deny this?" Li Ming asked, incredulous.

"How long have you been in the jianghu?"

Li Ming hesitated. But only for a moment.

"Eight months."

"Eight months!" The leader laughed. "No wonder, then."

"What do you mean, 'no wonder'?"

"What is the purpose of the jianghu?"

"To protect the people."

"No, no, that's the mission of the Jianghu Association. What is the meaning of the words 'jianghu'?"

The jianghu was just the name given to the world of the rivers and lakes, to the world of outcasts and vagrants, bodyguards and bandits, martial cultivators and armed escorts, to the realm where men and women lived and died by the sword.

"The word 'jianghu' used to have a noble meaning," the leader continued. "It was a world apart from the world of men, yet also a part of it. It is the world that honors the strongest, most skillful, most dedicated men. Men like that are like tigers and dragons. They cannot be confined by lesser mortals. How can the laws of mortal kings govern immortals who can outlive them?

"The laws of men are fit only for men. Warriors, martial cultivators, and immortals need a different set of laws. Laws that impose order on their world, yet also empower them to realize their full potential. Laws in harmony with the cosmos and the Dao.

"The Jianghu Association was born from this need. But over the centuries, they have lost sight of their purpose. Today it exists to regulate the flow of money, not the hearts of people. Gongfu is now about entertainment, wealth, status. Immortality, that most prized of goals, is now just a commodity.

"Tell me: does it sicken you?"

It did. During his probation period in Bao An, he had seen this around every corner. Even in the Central Plains, in Yudu, nothing had changed. But to open his mouth would be to invite the devil into his mind.

"It sickens me," the leader continued. "It should sicken everyone who studies history. The Yue Dynasty could not control their martial cultivators and fractured into civil strife. The history and legacy of the greatest civilization in the world vanished in the fires of the Warlord Era. The Celestial Empire scarcely lasted for a hundred years before it committed the same mistakes as the Yue. The Summer Revolution brought peace and prosperity only to a corner of Xiazhou. The revolutionaries claimed they were respecting the terms of the Beiyang Treaty, but in doing so they allowed the rise of beasts and bandits.

"We live now in the Era of the Five States and Ten Corporations. The Five States are powerless before the Ten Corporations, and the Ten Corporations care only about profit. The Central Plains reflects the ideal customer of the Ten Corporations. Atomized, soft, worshiping only money and the means to make money.

"It is disgusting.

"Honor. Strength. Gongfu. This is what the Ten Thousand Swords Society stands for."

Ghazan stood where he was, absorbing every word. Li Ming clenched his fists.

"You use treachery and call it honor. You rob from fellow dwellers of the jianghu and call it strength. You take what you want by force and call it gongfu," Li Ming said.

"Once again, we apologize for any harm we've caused."

"You can apologize by dissolving your society and confessing to your crimes."

"We have committed no crimes. But I think I see why you see things that way."

"What do you mean?"

"Huashuo tianxia dashi, fenjiu bihe, hejiu bifen."

It is said that all under Heaven follows this trend: what is long divided must unite, what is long united must divide.

"The Ten Thousand Swords are the agents of history," the leader continued. "We shall bring together what is long divided, but it also demands dividing what is long united. Such a goal demands power. Wealth, resources, might, the ability to achieve a desired outcome. When people see our actions, they believe we only lust for power. We seek power that we may achieve our goal."

"What is your goal?" Ghazan asked.

The leader smiled.

"To restore the jianghu, to resurrect true gongfu, to create a united civilization where only the worthy rule. In so doing, we will bring all under Heaven in accordance with the Dao."

Ghazan maintained a poker face. Li Ming just shook his head.

"Huangquan lushangtu you haoyi duo."

The road to the underworld has plenty of good intentions.

"The city is still in danger. I'm afraid I can't discuss this further with you. Just think about my words. If you want to learn more about us, our office in Yudu is always open."

"You have an office?"

"We are a registered biaoju in the Central Plains, no less in standing than Dayong in Zhongxia."

With those words, the leader spun around and marched out. His men regrouped around him and headed off.

"Unbelievable. Do those people even listen to themselves?" Li Ming grumbled.

Ghazan checked his gun.

"He has a point."

"Seriously? What point?"

Ghazan went completely still. Then looked up, his eyes burning.

"There are still many beasts and terrorists running around this city. We have plenty of work to do."

"Ah. Yes, well, let's get back to it."

Weapons slung, they headed back upstairs.

Chapter Fourteen

Sarantuya

Dayong stood watch for most of the night. The militia, reinforced by the Ten Thousand Swords, swept through the city, destroying every beast they encountered, driving the survivors towards strongpoints held by the hunters, biaohang, and private citizens.

The sirens finally cut out at midnight. It took another two hours before the authorities sounded the all-clear. Li Ming dragged himself into his room, scrubbed down with baby wipes, changed into fresh clothing, and fell on the bed.

He awoke at daybreak, groggy and disoriented. His weapons lay on a nearby chair, ready for immediate action. His swordbreaker stood propped against the table. His old clothes lay in a ragged pile at the foot of his bed.

It had been a while since he'd slept in for so long. On the other hand, he'd had only two hours of sleep. His body yearned to fall back into bed. His brain reminded him that he had commitments and timelines to keep.

He splashed water on his face, brushed his teeth, and began morning cultivation. Zhan zhuang and a hundred fists. That was all he had time for. His qi was weak and sluggish, and he felt only tiny waves of liquid lightning slowly sloshing through him.

He took a long shower, alternating between hot and cold water. He stepped out feeling half-alive. A slight improvement.

Sitting by the window, he drank in the sunlight. Pure yang qi soaked through his skin, penetrating tissue and bone. His body barely registered it. Breathing in qi, he touched his third eye, the spot above and between his own, and applied firm pressure.

Qi trickled through him. A cloud of fatigue lifted off.

He worked his way down the body. The Gates of Consciousness at the base of the cranium. The Wind Mansion, slightly above it, where the head met the neck. Zhong Chong on the middle fingers. The Outer Gates, three fingers below the outer wrist crease, in between the radius and ulna. Zu San Li Ming, the three *li* point, the point of longevity and the point of a hundred diseases, under the kneecap and between the long bones of the legs.

He massaged each spot for a minute, going clockwise and counter-clockwise, working with the qi. By the time he finished, he was reasonably awake. Not energized. But alive. And that was good enough.

Dayong regrouped in the restaurant. Everyone seemed ragged and drained. Even Ms. Zhang, normally bright and chipper, sported dark circles around her eyes.

Except Ghazan.

His aura was full and luminous, his movements crisp and clean, his bearing sharp and alert. It was if he had enjoyed a full night's sleep and then some. Li Ming wondered if he had used his qi eating skill again. But Li Ming had stayed next to Ghazan last night. If he'd used his power, it had to have been before Li Ming returned to the hotel, or after they had retired for the night.

Or maybe Ghazan was just naturally overflowing with qi.

Cultivators, many of them openly armed, occupied most of the tables. Loud conversations filled the dining hall, melting into background babble, obscuring whispered conversations and quiet toasts. There were a handful of civilians in the crowd, all of them dressed in the hand-fitted no-label clothing of the super-rich, but the peasants stayed far away from the ones who had saved the city.

The customers scarfed down huge amounts of food and drink. The kitchen staff struggled to keep up. When Li Ming finally had a chance to visit the buffet tables, there were few choices remaining. He dumped a mass of steaming fried noodles on his plate, topped it with pork dumplings, and grabbed a cup of black coffee.

The food, of course, was ferociously spicy.

At least the restaurant provided complimentary glasses of cold water.

When everyone had a chance to sample their meals, a smile brightened Ms. Zhang's face.

"Did everyone sleep well?"

Wong-gor laughed.

"After the night we had? Of course! Not."

The team chuckled tiredly.

"Everyone worked hard."

"You too," Li Ming said.

Ms. Zhang waved her hand.

"*Aiya*, small matter. You took care of the beasts."

"You took care of the casualties," Cai Yan said. "That's counts."

"I just walked around and made a few calls. You went out and risked your lives. Next to that, what I did was just a drop in the ocean."

"You put in the work," Ghazan counts. "It counts."

Her dimples deepened.

"Thanks!"

"Did you call in the Ten Thousand Swords Society?" Li Ming asked.

"No. Just the emergency services and the Jianghu Association. I didn't even know they were coming until you called me."

"You sure hate the Ten Thousand Swords Society," Wong-gor remarked.

"They killed my father and half my company," Cai Yan spat. "I was *this* close to killing them all."

"My condolences."

"What they did was unforgivable. I can't believe they have an office here."

"I don't know how it is in Zhongxia, but they are a legal entity in Yudu," Ms. Zhang said. "For the past ten years, they've operated as a biaoju. An extraordinarily successful one too. They've single-handedly wiped out the major bandit groups operating in the region."

"Leaving themselves as the biggest bandits," Li Ming said.

"They haven't committed any crimes."

"That we know of."

Cai Yan leaned in. "Are you sure they are aboveboard?"

"*En...* There are rumors of shady business, but nothing verified," Ms. Zhang replied.

"What kind of rumors?"

"Ties to smuggling rings and secret societies. Mercenary work outside the Central Plains. Trafficking in primordial crystals and high technology."

"Have they been investigated?" Li Ming asked.

"The laws of the Central Plains are vastly different from Zhongxia. Where you come from, you're used to the idea of city laws, provincial laws, national laws. Here, there are few laws that span the breadth of the Central Plains, and most of them govern commercial activity. Each city, town and village is free to set their own laws.

"It can be... troublesome to investigate allegations of criminal activity, especially if they extend beyond the borders of a single city. There is a thicket of laws and regulations to cut through, some of them contradictory.

"What is called smuggling in Zhongxia is simply an informal agreement in the Central Plains. Some cities like Yudu allow biaoju to operate openly with minimal regulation, others require extensive licenses and permits. A secret society in one jurisdiction is a fraternal organization in another. We don't have a central government that imposes its will upon the people and decides what is a crime and what isn't. The closest we have to one is the Merchant Association, and they are focused on ensuring free trade and commerce. They prefer to have as few laws and regulations as possible."

"How can the Central Plains *not* have a central government?" Li Ming wondered.

"It's been that way since the Summer Revolution. We made it work for us."

Li Ming couldn't begin to imagine how that worked. How did they not have warlords, bandits, widespread chaos? They had great difficulty controlling their beast population, with hordes swarming neighboring states at regular intervals. How was the Central Plains not a hotbed of crime, terror and instability?

"Who was the leader of the Wanjianhui squad?" Cai Yan asked.

"Chen Bingrong. Operations Director of the Ten Thousand Swords Society, gold-ranked martial cultivator. He is currently ranked 8732 in the Jianghu Association leaderboards and has a qi score of sixteen thousand eight hundred and ninety-four."

Li Ming bit down a curse. He'd been so overwhelmed with rage, he'd forgotten to assess the Wanjianhui leader. A tactical oversight.

"You've made a powerful enemy," Ghazan observed.

"He seemed diplomatic enough," Ms. Zhang said.

"What do you know about him?" Li Ming asked.

"The Jianghu Association doesn't know much about how the Wanjianhui operates. We know they are profitable, even thriving. They turn in beasts, bandits and bounties regularly enough. Of their personnel, we know even less."

"Not even social media? Everyone is on Aitan these days."

"They are very old school. No Net presence worth mentioning."

"In this day and age, it's highly suspicious," Wong said.

"Maybe, but Chen and his men haven't been linked to any crimes, not in the Central Plains. There's nothing we can do about them."

"All we can do is stay clear of them," Cai Yan said.

"And keep an eye on them," Li Ming added.

A woman drew up to the table, carrying a tray of food.

"Excuse me. May I sit here?"

It was the Yue female from the roof and the gym. This close, in the light, Li Ming saw her for the first time. The lines of her face were smooth and delicate, but the set of her jaw and the narrowness of her lips lent her the severity of the distant, barren steppes. Her black hair, shimmering in the light, ran down to her shoulders in straight locks. Her long red dress, flowing down to her knees, accentuated her lean figure, all bones and muscles and nothing more. Over her right shoulder she wore a modest handbag. Li Ming might have thought her pretty, bordering on beautiful, but she had the eyes of a tiger, a deep pitiless black, scanning everyone at the table.

"Sure," Cai Yan said.

"Thank you."

The men shifted aside, making room for her. She set down her tray and pulled up a chair next to Ghazan. Her plates were piled with white food: milk, bean curd, yoghurt.

"You fought well last night," she said. "I heard you prevented a swarm of yaotuo from invading the city."

She spoke slowly, carefully, enunciating every word, as if compensating for lack of facility with the language. Her accent, too, was stronger than Ghazan's, the fricatives and vowels blending into each other.

"We were just doing our job," Li Ming said.

"The militia and the biaohang were hard-pressed dealing with the zhenniao. If you hadn't sealed the gates, the result would have been disastrous."

"We all did our part," Li Ming said.

"The terrorists responsible are still out there," Cai Yan said. "Coordinating an invasion like this requires resources, skills, manpower. The two men we defeated were only the foot soldiers."

"I hope the police will find them soon," Ms. Zhang said.

"Don't count on it," Li Ming replied.

The city's lax attitude towards law and order disquieted Li Ming. In Bao An, there would have been a police investigation, an interview, a media circus. Here, he and Cai Yan had killed four men and the police had done nothing more than to take his statement. After the all clear signal, he and Cai Yan had walked the local cops to the scene of the shooting and explained the situation. The police reviewed footage of nearby cameras and let them go. Li Ming didn't know if mortal police revered or feared martial cultivators. Or both.

Only that this was the Central Plains.

"You're Dayong Biaoju, based out of Bao An, correct?" the Yue woman asked.

"Yes," Cai Yan said.

"Are you hiring?"

The table went quiet. All eyes looked at the Yue. At Cai Yan. Back again.

"Can I see your biaohang card?" Cai Yan asked.

The woman produced it from her handbag and handed it over. Cai Yan lowered her Eight Eyes headset and studied the card.

"Please tell us more about yourself," Cai Yan said.

"I am Sarantuya, a freelancer. I was contracted with the Black Eagle private military company, based in the Yue Homelands. Last month, Black Eagle sent two teams to the Central Plains, one to Yudu and the other to Shuanglong, to service beast hunting contracts. I was part of the Yudu team.

"Two days ago, we lost contact with the Shuanglong team. After hearing of the state of emergency in Shuanglong, we shifted our operations here.

"When the beast alarm sounded, we raced up to the rooftop bar. I was among the last to arrive. Shortly after I stepped out, the zhenniao struck.

"They strafed the roof with poison feathers. In the first minute, they wiped out almost everyone on the roof. I was lucky. I managed to dive under the bar. The others... Twelve men. Gone. Dead or incapacitated."

"I'm sorry," Cai Yan said.

Sarantuya shook her head.

"When the zhenniao left, I dragged the casualties to safety. I climbed back up on the roof just as your men arrived, along with the second wave of biaohang. You know what happened next."

"Why do you want to sign up with us?" Cai Yan asked.

"Black Eagle is finished. With one team missing and the other destroyed, they have to fold up overseas operations and focus on operations in the Homelands. As a freelancer, the head office gave me the option of returning or signing up with another company."

"And you chose to come to us," Ghazan said. "Why?"

She looked at him, an intense expression in her face. He met her gaze with matching intensity. Their qi crackled and collided, blending and becoming something new, something greater. The backwash surged over Li Ming like superheated static, setting his hair standing on end.

"You fought well. I wanted to fight alongside the best," she said.

"Why not return home?" Cai Yan asked.

Her qi field shifted. She drew herself straight, resting her hands on her lap. Her eyes widened and blanked, staring at a point beyond infinity. Gone was the woman, in her place a warrior princess of the steppes, come from her native land to follow the footsteps of her nomadic ancestors, seeking fame and fortune—or die trying.

"The best way to honor the memories of the fallen is to continue the work and see the expedition through to the end. It is too dangerous to hunt alone, so I seek to sign up with the mightiest warriors I could find. And I found you."

"I like your spirit," Wong-gor said.

She remained completely still, a statue impervious to praise or condemnation, daring the world to judge her for who and what she was.

"Where are you from?" Cai Yan asked.

"Kharodon."

The capital of the Yue Homelands. Ghazan said something in rapid-fire Yue. The woman replied in the same language. The exchange continued for half a minute. Li Ming listened in total ignorance, paying attention to body language and tone of voice. At last, Ghazan's eyes flickered, as if he'd remembered that there were others at the table.

"You said you were a freelancer," Ghazan said, now in Xiayu. "Why did you choose this path?"

"I enjoy traveling. As a freelancer, I've worked all over the Yue Homelands. This job was my first overseas contract."

A touch of anger and regret crept into her voice.

"How much work experience do you have?" Cai Yan asked.

"Eight years as a hunter. Two years ago, I broke through the ten thousand qi point barrier, and since then I made my way as a martial cultivator—though I continue to specialize in hunting beasts."

"Your card says you're a bronze rank," Cai Yan said. "Impressive, for just two years of work as a martial cultivator."

"How much experience do you have?" Sarantuya asked.

"Twelve years," Wong-gor said. "But this is my first contract with Dayong."

"Four years," Cai Yan said.

"Year and a half," Ghazan said.

"Eight months," Li Ming said.

Sarantuya's jaw dropped.

"What's wrong?" Li Ming asked.

"After what I've heard of Dayong, I thought you were all veterans of the jianghu."

"Most of our experienced staff are in Bao An," Cai Yan said. "For this expedition, we sent everyone we could spare. But these men are all superb biaohang."

Sarantuya turned to Li Ming.

"Even you?"

"We all have to start from somewhere," Li Ming said wryly.

"Li Ming earned the Medal of Valor in the military," Cai Yan said. "He's defeated more high-ranking martial immortals than all of us combined."

Sarantuya's gaze shifted from skepticism to respect.

"You served in the military before becoming a biaohang?"

"Only two years," Li Ming said.

"Special Forces?"

"Special Military Police."

"Only two steps down from the Special Forces, if I recall."

Li Ming shrugged. "The nation called, I answered. They saw fit to post me to the Special Military Police, I saw no reason to object. They give me my orders, I carried them out. That's all."

"You're a modest one, aren't you?"

"Everyone here is my senior. How can I boast of what I have done?"

"An excellent attitude. How about the rest of you? Do you have any prior service?"

"Eight years in the Yue military," Ghazan said. "Contract soldier."

"Ah. You have the bearing of a soldier. You and Li Biaohang."

"Service leaves its mark."

She cocked her head.

"You have… close to ten years of experience, yes? How long have you been cultivating?"

"Twenty years."

"Twenty? But your qi field… It's as powerful as someone who's cultivated for four or five decades. As powerful as a martial immortal."

Ghazan smirked.

"I work hard."

"Ghazan's the most dedicated cultivator amongst all of us," Li Ming said.

Sarantuya turned to Cai Yan.

"Are you the boss? I thought the most experienced among you would lead the team," Sarantuya asked.

"I inherited the company from my father, along with my brother," Cai Yan replied.

"Dayong is a business, and she's the best among us at business decisions," Li Ming said.

"But you are also the field leader?" Sarantuya asked.

"I've hunted many beasts alongside my father and brother," Cai Yan said, "but the men have more training and experience than me. When they speak, I listen."

"A wise policy."

"You said you were a hunter. What skills and experience do you have?"

"I have hunted the most dangerous beasts in the homelands and have participated in over thirty multi-day hunts along some of the most prestigious biaoju of the nation. Black Tiger, Silver Arrow, the Golden Horde. I am no stranger to long-term expeditions like this.

"My specialty lies in marksmanship, along with combat and support magic. As you've heard, I am also fluent in Xiayu and Yueyu. In addition, during expeditions, I have also handled administrative and logistics matters. This includes liaising with clients, the Jianghu Association, and local governments; and managing contracts and negotiations."

"We are a small team," Cai Yan said. "All of us here have to be generalists. When we go out into the field, the back line and front line merge together. You must be prepared to fight alongside us like you did last night."

"I am accustomed to operating in small teams. I ran most of my jobs in parties of five or less, and many of them were solo."

"Solo?" Ghazan said. "You hunted solo? How?"

She smiled.

"I see my prey before they see me. I shoot them before they reach me. It works out well."

"What about martial arts?" Cai Yan asked.

"I studied some martial arts on and off, but my preference is the gun."

"Me too!" Wong-gor exclaimed.

"If it comes down to a close-up fight, we may not be able to help you," Cai Yan said. "You'll have to fend for yourself, at least long enough for us to get to you."

"If a threat gets close, I'm not going to wrestle with it. I'll stab or shoot it."

"I like the way you think," Wong-gor said.

"What kind of magic system do you use?" Li Ming asked.

"Night and Sky."

Ghazan smiled. "Me too."

"Is it common among the Yue people?" Li Ming asked.

"Of course. The system came from us," Ghazan replied. "It is part of our heritage, as much as yinyang, the five elements and eight trigrams is part of yours."

"Do you have your own gear?" Cai Yan asked.

"Yes. Weapon, armor, supplies, crystals, everything I need for a hunt. I don't need to rely on Black Eagle property," Sarantuya replied.

Or yours, Li Ming heard.

"What rates do you charge?" Cai Yan asked.

"For this expedition, Black Eagle paid us in shares of the bounty we brought in. Because of my experience, I rated three shares."

Li Ming was entitled to just one share. But he was still the junior man in the company, and he was also paid a day rate.

"Sounds reasonable," Cai Yan said.

"We're bringing her in?" Ghazan asked.

"We could also use another gun," Wong-gor said.

"The more the merrier," Ms. Zhang said.

Cai Yan looked at Li Ming.

"What do you think?"

He thought of the zhenniao she had shot down. Of the plasma bolt that had burned through it and into the building beyond.

"We take collateral damage very seriously here," Li Ming said. "Our priority is to protect people. We need to take care not to cause more harm than necessary, especially to innocent bystanders."

"I understand," Sarantuya said.

He turned back to Cai Yan.

"We're undermanned as is. With another shooter, we'll have more tactical options."

"We need to run a background check, study your resume, check your references," Cai Yan said. "But if it works out, I see no reason to object."

Sarantuya smiled.

"Thank you. I look forward to working with you."

Chapter Fifteen

The Real Prize

The first order of business was to clean up the city. Hundreds of beast corpses lay scattered within and without its walls. Uncounted thousands of poison feathers lay scattered across roads and roofs. Until they were disposed of, the city ordered a mandatory lockdown save for emergency services, the militia, and everyone who volunteered to join the cleanup effort.

And there was no greater way to motivate volunteers than to offer monetary incentives.

There was no way to confirm direct personal kills of beasts. The sheer chaos of the invasion prevented the Jianghu Association from accurately crediting kills. Instead, any biaohang who could prove they had participated in the battle of Shuanglong would be awarded a share of the total value of the recovered corpses. Anyone who turned in poison feathers would also be compensated by weight of feathers recovered.

The battle outside the walls was supposed to have been the exception. Only Li Ming and Cai Yan had left the city from the north prior to the yaotuo uprising. Security videos confirmed their side of the story. Under ordinary circumstances, there would have been enough proof to justify a rich reward.

Except for one tiny problem.

"There are no yaotuo bodies," Ms. Zhang said.

"How?" Li Ming demanded. "Did they take their dead with them?"

"Yaotuo in the Central Plains practice cannibalism. After the assault, they would have needed food to recover their energy. And there were plenty of corpses right there."

"The soldiers didn't stop them?"

"They report seeing the yaotuo drag their dead into the water, but didn't do anything to stop them. They saw no threat and therefore no need to engage."

"They can confirm we engaged the yaotuo," Cai Yan said.

"The issue isn't whether you fought the beasts. It's that there are no recovered bodies. The Jianghu Association raises funds by selling beast cadavers and parts on the open market. If they have nothing to sell, they have no money to pay you."

"We killed a few beasts inside the city walls," Li Ming said. "What happened to them?"

"The militia did not report finding any bodies."

Li Ming burst into a bout of swearing.

"The bodies were right there, just past the gates!"

"I'm sorry. Scavengers must have stolen them."

The bane of the jianghu, scavengers swooped down on kills abandoned by their killers, harvested the bodies, and sold them on the black market. They thrived in chaos, appearing whenever biaohang and beast hunters could not guard the bodies of their prey.

"The militia didn't stop them," Li Ming said. "Why?"

"They were busy defending the city. The terrorists had destroyed the consoles controlling the drones, shutting them down, so they had to spread themselves thin along the walls to watch for beasts. They didn't notice if there were scavengers about."

"A convenient excuse, isn't it?"

"That's what they told me. Doesn't mean I believe them."

"How much will we be paid?" Cai Yan asked.

"One share of the city defense bonus, like everyone else," Ms. Zhang said.

"Just how much is the bonus?" Li Ming asked.

"We'll only know after we recover and assess the bodies."

"Assuming scavengers haven't stolen them all."

"Or the militia," Li Ming said coldly.

Many scavengers were policemen and soldiers. Ostensibly deployed to guard the bodies, they were also the ones who came closest to them. And the ones who controlled investigations into scavengers. Li Ming had no doubt that he would never be paid for holding off the yaotuo.

"I know you're angry, but this is how things work in the Central Plains," Ms. Zhang said. "If you want to make more money, you could participate in the clean-up effort."

"How much will they pay for that?" Li Ming asked.

"I'm not going to lie to you. You'll be paid little more than dirt for the bodies. After so long in the open, the only use we have for their flesh and bone is compost. More intact bodies can be rendered down to extract the poison from their tissues. However, zhenniao are dangerous creatures, so you'll still be paid decently.

"The real prize is the feathers. We can extract the poison from them and use them in various industrial and medical practices, including the manufacture of antivenin. Each feather will be graded as if it were a chunk of recovered flesh. Gathered in bulk, they will add up to a decent amount. And they don't degrade as fast as meat."

The trick, of course, was to gather the feathers without killing yourself.

The slightest brush against a feather would numb naked skin. Pricking a finger against its razor points and edges would introduce a dangerous dose of toxin into the bloodstream. Regulations demanded full-body protective suits and gloves and boots, rated for resistance to cuts and punctures and biochemical agents. There were only enough such suits in the city to outfit a squad of militia.

Undeterred, the biaohang and civilian volunteers outfitted themselves the best they could.

Li Ming donned his field clothing, long-sleeved shirt and thick pants. Over his shirt he wore his trusty jacket, turning up the collar to protect his throat. He wore a double layer of socks under his combat boots. He donned his tactical gloves, impervious to cuts and chemicals and easy to sanitize, and shielded his forearms with his reality shapers. Finally he put on his helmet and plate carrier.

It was hot. It was heavy. In the humid late summer heat, it was a beast of an outfit. But it covered most of his skin, leaving only his jaw exposed. An acceptable risk.

Wong and Cai Yan had kitted themselves up in similar fashion. Ms. Zhang covered herself head to toe in clothing and departed for the Jianghu Association office, claiming she had other duties, but promising she would secure favorable rates for the team. Sarantuya wasn't officially part of Dayong, not yet anyway, but for a cleanup job like this, there was no harm letting her tag along. She wore a two-part camouflage hunting suit, long pants and hooded jacket, leaving only her eyes exposed, and donned a pair of safety goggles.

Ghazan slipped on a pair of gloves and called it good.

"You're going out like that?" Cai Yan marveled.

"It is adequate protection. With heavy clothing like yours, you are more at risk of heatstroke than poison."

"Urban environments generate their own weather," Wong-gor said. "A strong wind could blow a feather into your face."

"Skin contact with a poison feather only produces some numbing. It is not dangerous."

"And if you get cut?"

"I secured antivenin."

Zhenniao antivenin, a rarity in the open market in the best of days, had vanished from every shelf on every supply store in the city. How Ghazan had accomplished a feat, Li Ming couldn't begin to guess.

"The poison causes paralysis. You won't be able to perform self-aid. At least wear something to cover your face," Li Ming said.

Ghazan, with great reluctance, donned a hood. And a helmet.

Armed with large garbage bags and large tongs, they dispersed from the hotel.

It was easy but tedious work. Poison feathers were *everywhere*. Hiding under cars, hanging from branches, snagged on fences, lying on rooftops and balconies. Dayong worked in a spiral, clearing the city street by street, block by block. What feathers they couldn't reach, they used magic to draw towards them. Whenever they found a zhenniao body, they shoved it into a Belt Bag or a freezer. And reported human corpses to the police.

Other cleaners had other strategies. Some sprinted down the streets or hopped from roof to roof, snatching up as many feathers in the open as they could, leaving behind the snagged and hidden feathers for others to deal with. Some secured brooms and dustpans, ladders and vacuum cleaners, doing their best to maximize physical distance from the feathers. A few dedicated teams focused on collecting and securing the bodies of beasts and men alike, wrapping them in sheets and rags and tying them up in neat bundles. Many citizens were content to clean up their immediate neighborhoods, many biaohang ranged across the city.

All of them improvised what protection they could, or wanted to. Gloves for everyone, masks and hoods for almost everyone. Jackets, rags wrapped around limbs, thick towels, or just bare limbs and deep confidence in their skills and luck. Many cultivators forewent any kind of physical protective equipment, trusting instead in magic.

Neither the police nor the militia stopped them or censured them for having inadequate protections. If anything, they joined in too, picking up feathers and bodies along with the volunteers. Ms. Zhang claimed that they would also receive a bonus for turning in harvested beast materials.

It was a discombobulating sight. In the Zhongxia Republic, the military and police were expressly forbidden from receiving rewards for putting down and harvesting beasts. It was merely part of their duty to the people. More prosaically, they drew their salaries from taxes. The government wanted to keep taxpayer burden to reasonable levels and prevent civil servants from being swayed by private sector monies. Li Ming had spent much of his short-lived military career destroying beasts with no more reward than a generic letter of thanks and congratulations.

But this was the Central Plains, and they had their own laws and culture. He couldn't change them. Only operate within their bounds.

At midday, Dayong broke for lunch. They gathered at the office of the Jianghu Association and dropped off their bounty with Ms. Zhang. As the fixer negotiated on their behalf, the biaohang lingered in the lobby, sprawling across the sofas and coaches, cooling off, wiping themselves down, sheltering from the heat. And the stench.

The air in the city was fetid with the odor of rotting meat. As unrecovered bodies and limbs succumbed to decay, they spewed a noxious fog of foul gases, a fog that *might* be mixed with zhenniao poison. Everybody in the Society knew that poison-soaked particles could cause respiratory irritation and discomfort if inhaled, nobody knew if there was enough in the air for a lethal inhalation dose.

The Society offered respirators. They vanished in moments. Fortunately, Dayong had their own. As they rested, prepared their kit, planned their next move, Li Ming looked up to see a familiar face enter the lobby.

"Captain Bao!" Li Ming called.

Unlike so many others on the street, Captain Bao wore his standard military uniform and nothing more. No helmet, no mask, no armor. He carried himself with a sense of personal invulnerability, utterly unperturbed by the events and people around him. Waving, he walked over.

"It's been a while," Li Ming said. "What are you doing here?"

"Shuanglong has requested Yudu for reinforcements. My superiors sent my company."

"Isn't Shuanglong an independent city?"

"Yes, but Yudu and Shuanglong enjoy a strong and harmonious relationship."

"The cities and towns of the Central Plains are bound by shared history, culture and language," Ms. Zhang added. "If one is in danger, everyone sends help. It's like being part of the same neighborhood."

"Like being part of a nation," Wong-gor said.

She shrugged. "Well, yes, but they are also independent and sovereign entities. They are not obliged to follow laws set down by any other entity, except perhaps the Merchant Association."

Li Ming had no conception of how such a realm could exist. The only frame of reference he had was fiction, from the canon of work that collectively described a mythological jianghu from some long-distant golden age, an age where civilization was little more than a loosely-organized collection of widely-separated villages and cities ruled by a faraway emperor.

"What's your mission in Shuanglong?" Ghazan asked.

"We are to reinforce the local militia, support them with heavy weapons and drones, and assist the jianghu in its efforts to control the beast population. In fact, I'm here to post a contract."

"Beast hunting?" Sarantuya asked.

"Yes." Captain Bao paused. "I believe we haven't met."

"Sarantuya, of the Yue Homelands, formerly of Black Eagle, now a freelancer."

"Interesting. Are you working with Dayong?"

She turned to Cai Yan. Cai Yan raised an eyebrow.

"We fought side-by-side during the attack on the city. We're now working together to clean up the city. She hasn't formally signed up with us yet, but we don't have any jobs lined up. Yet," Cai Yan said.

"Well... I believe we can help each other, if you're up to it."

"Tell us more."

"My drone operators have spotted a zhenniao nest up in the Ba Mountains. We believe it is the surviving remnants of the swarm that attacked the city last night. We count twenty of them. We wish to hire a biaoju to destroy the swarm."

"You have a company of troopers," Li Ming said. "More than enough to take them."

"Ordinarily, yes, but I have my orders, and my orders are to stay in this city."

"Orders can be so inconvenient," Wong-gor said.

Captain Bao barked a laugh.

"Hah! Sad but true. On the other hand, this is an opportunity for you."

"You're extending the contract to us?" Cai Yan asked.

"If you're willing to take it."

Zhenniao were among the most dangerous beasts on the planet. If the Dayong team accepted the contract, they'd be facing odds of five to one against. Li Ming, intimately familiar with the mass of contradictions that called itself military intelligence, knew that that they had to prepare for at least double the number of expected beasts.

They'd have to bring in Sarantuya.

"How much is the contract worth?" Cai Yan asked.

"Fifty thousand yuan, half up front, half on completion. Plus the bounty from any beasts you manage to bring back here."

"Will you support us?" Li Ming asked.

"I only have four drones. They are all needed to monitor the area. But once you're on site, my man can talk you into the nest."

"There won't be a single nest," Sarantuya said. "Zhenniao are parasocial animals. Adults will care for their own young, and only occasionally mingle with each other to forage and hunt. Members of the same clan may share a home range, but each family and individual has its own territory. Females freely travel through inter-clan boundaries, but the males often keep their distance. Mate pairs cluster their nests together to protect their eggs and young, but unattached adults live separately."

"You're a real encyclopedia, aren't you?" Bao remarked.

"I have hunted zhenniao before. It pays to study your prey. Which makes their behavior so troubling."

"How so?"

"Zhenniao do not normally gather in large numbers like this, not unless they are defending their range against intruders or hunting large prey. They are active in the day and rest at night. Is this some new breed of zhenniao?"

"Or did someone find a way to control a flock of zhenniao?" Li Ming asked.

It wasn't unheard of. Beast masters of previous dynasties used magic and training to dominate the minds of beasts and send them to war. Zhongxia officially condemned those methods as inhumane, but the techniques remained.

But he'd never heard of a domination method that used wide-area qi before.

"We don't have any intelligence on that," Captain Bao said.

"Seems to me there's more going on than just a simple beast hunt," Wong-gor said.

"I'll direct the relevant authorities to launch an investigation. Meanwhile, we have many bloodthirsty beasts roaming the forests and the mountains."

"Every one of them is a pot of gold."

"Exactly."

"We came here to hunt beasts, not sweep the streets," Ghazan said. "I'm in."

"Me too," Li Ming said.

Cai Yan turned to Sarantuya.

"What about you? We could use someone with your experience."

The Yue smiled faintly.

"Are you signing me on with Dayong?"

"For this contract. And for future jobs, if this works out. But only if you're comfortable working with us."

"The zhenniao killed and wounded my comrades. Blood must be answered with blood."

"We'll take the contract," Cai Yan said.

Captain Bao grinned.

"Good hunting. And good luck."

Chapter Sixteen

The Living Cosmos

Spanning thousands of *li* and dozens of peaks, the Ba Mountains was a country unto itself, a nation claimed by the beasts of the land and sky. It began at the farthermost ends of the Yu River, where the wide waters narrowed into a fast-flowing river, swept through a dramatic curve to become a half-formed hook, and branched off into lesser mountains to define the eastern and southeastern borders of the Central Plains.

The tiny slice Li Ming saw stole his breath away. Before him stretched a vast evergreen forest, an ancient growth that had seen the rise and fall of nations and dynasties. Thick, clean, cool mist shrouded the treetops, softening colors and contours, blurring the boundaries between earth and wood and mountain and heaven. A bubbling stream wound between the woods, following the shape of the ground, in so doing inexorably shaping it. Beyond the mist, the silhouettes of high peaks beckoned him, daring him to discover them.

Beautiful though it may be, navigating it was a beast. The ground was rocky and uneven, pitilessly rising with every step. Fallen branches and loose stones threatened to betray a careless foot. Plunging into the forest, the woods loomed high and tall and solemn over Li Ming, robbing him of visual references. Unseen birds chirped, insects buzzed back, leaves rustled. Rubbings and droppings betrayed the presence of animals—many kinds of animals.

During the long drive over, Sarantuya had briefed the team on zhenniao habits. They marked their territory with droppings, pecks, and poison feathers. They had a keen sense of hearing and investigated suspicious sounds. Naturally aggressive, they would defend their terrain against all intruders, and with complex calls they could organize their clan for a coordinated attack.

The single greatest sign of their presence was prey.

Zhenniao were voraciously omnivorous. They could, and would, consume anything—but they loved animals and plants only slightly less toxic than themselves. Anywhere there was a concentration of poisonous flora, fauna, fruits, fungi, there they would be.

Sarantuya saw signs of zhenniao everywhere. She pointed to patches of dug-up earth where there were once mushrooms. She highlighted deep chips in tree trunks where an iron-hard beak had plucked beetles and other insects. She uncovered piles of tiny bones and skeletons, mounds of droppings, scratch marks carved deliberately into the ground.

"The zhenniao won't stay here forever," she said. "They must consume huge amounts of food. The adults hunt for themselves and their young. Eventually they will start competing with each other. Their nature will drive them to spread out, especially the single adults. When they grow desperate, they will attack farms, livestock, and people. Or each other."

It was late afternoon by the time Dayong reached the forest. The drone operator reported that the zhenniao had spread out, the mate pairs clustering together and the individuals dispersing across the forest. The drone orbited the main nest, but the remaining zhenniao were out of its sight.

The hunters moved with an abundance of caution. Stealth and senses were their first line of defense, guns and magic and reflexes their second, armor last of all. At Cai Yan's insistence, everyone was in full body armor, plus gloves and helmet and cut-resistant clothing. Everyone carried at least two doses of zhenniao antivenin in their first aid kits. And everyone had powered exoskeletons.

Time passed in slow, grueling, motion. They moved in a modified arrowhead formation, Sarantuya on point, Li Ming and Ghazan on flank security, Wong-gor and Cai Yan hanging back. Li Ming moved from cover to cover, minimizing his time exposed in the open. He placed his feet on hard earth, cold stone, soft grasses, everywhere that would silence his steps and minimize his footprints. He kept his eyes peeled, scanning left and right and high and low, watching for a flash of vivid green or royal purple.

The drone operator tried talking the team into the main nest. A straight line advance, insertion point to objective area in shortest possible time. Sarantuya would have none of that. She simply marked the nest's location on the team's map and led the group in a serpentine search pattern, spread out as far as they dared.

"Zhenniao may not like each other as individuals, but they will defend the clan to the death. If anything threatens the young, anything that alerts the parents, the clan will come rushing down to protect the nest. If we attack the nest head-on, the remaining adults will swarm us from all sides. We do not have the numbers to defend against a massed attack.

"Instead, we must nibble our way around the edges of the clan. Take the unpaired males first, for they are the most aggressive. Then the unpaired females. Only after removing the fiercest fighters will we strike at the nest."

The drone stayed where it was, its unblinking eye trained on the nest and the birds snoozing within. The humans searched for the solitary birds.

They found plenty of sign. But of the zhenniao, they found none.

Sarantuya called a halt at sunset. They made camp in a patch of open ground close to the river, close enough its soothing burbling carried clear through the trees and the leaves. They pitched one-man tents in a tight circle and dug a fire pit in the center of the circle.

The pit had two chambers, a main hole to contain the flames, a smaller tunnel for airflow. Wong filled the main chamber with kindling, Li Ming ignited it with his reality shaper. The fire burned hot and bright, gulping down fresh air from the ventilation shaft, forcing out hot air from the central opening. The concealed flame grew hotter, brighter, cleaner, generating heat without smoke, light without exposure. Contained within the chamber, the fire was invisible from ground level.

Controlled fires drew the attention of beasts and wild animals. They signaled the presence of humans, and humans carried food. Or were food.

Conventional zhenniao hunting doctrine was to rest in the day and hunt them at night. When beasts were asleep, they made easy prey. But the team unanimously decidedly against it. If these zhenniao came from the same flock that attacked Shuanglong, they were likely nocturnal too. It did not do to hunt an apex predator while it was awake. Instead, Dayong would hunt in the day and rest at night. Or until and unless they found proof that these zhenniao displayed more typical activity patterns.

Camping guidebooks emphasized singing, loud chatting, making loud noises. Dayong did none of that. They ate and drank quietly, speaking softly and only when necessary, mainly to plan the next day's movements. They concealed themselves inside their tents, watching over each other's shoulders, weapons close to hand. They ate from military ration packs, either consuming them cold or taking advantage of their flameless ration heaters, carefully sealing and stowing the retort pouches and food packages when they were done.

At the close of dinner, the drone operator called Cai Yan on her scroll. She extended the device to its full length, set it on speaker, and answered.

"The drone's running low on power. We need to land and recharge it," the soldier said.

Most military aircraft ran on cosmic taps. They could stay in air practically forever, landing only for repairs or reloads. The drone had to be ancient. Or cheap.

"Any sign of zhenniao activity?" Cai Yan asked.

"Negative. They seem to be settling down too."

"Roger. Are you able to get another drone in the air?"

"Negative. All our other drones are tasked out or recharging. We'll prioritize your mission, but it'll take at least six hours before we can send the bird airborne again."

Six hours. All night and into the morning. But there was no rush. You never wanted to rush against a superior force if they didn't know you were in the area.

As full darkness fell, they took turns to clean up, take care of toileting, and change into fresh clothing. They moved in pairs, leaving their scents fifty *chi* downwind of the tents. When they were ready for sleep, everyone nestled themselves inside their tents and sleeping bags, reality shapers fastened to their arms, guns slung and held close to their bodies, ready for instant action.

Everyone but Li Ming.

He had volunteered for first watch. The others would rotate through one-hour shifts, starting with the hour of the pig, ending with the hour of the rabbit. He tried not to think of himself as a helpless herbivore hiding in the dark, hoping to live through another monster-haunted night.

He paced the perimeter of the camp, attention trained outwards at the world beyond the tiny circle of tents. Through his fusion goggles, he saw a world of black and white and little else. The only flash of color came when the optics chanced upon the deeps of the fire pit and revealed it as bright splashes of red and orange.

Sound carried further than the unaided eye could see at night, so he pricked his ears and tuned up the sensitivity of his headset. A universe of sounds filled his head. Frogs croaking, long and low and deep. Cicadas singing to the woods. Nocturnal birds chirping to each other. The hooting of owls, answered by a chorus of wolves.

There was another sense, older and deeper and truer, against which the five common senses were but secondary. A hidden sense, one the ancient sages had uncovered and studied in their deep meditations, at once the legacy of all mankind and yet also a gift so strange it had to be trained, perfected, cultivated.

The qi sense.

Qi was all around him. It imbued all living things, all things that were a part of the natural universe. It was in the ground beneath his feet, the great trees surrounding him, the biaohang he guarded, the very air he breathed. It was the foundation of the living cosmos, the quintessence that composed all things and all things would return to. Everyone had the ability to sense qi, if they but learned how.

Here in the mountains, away from the clamor and bustle of civilization, in a forest dense with life, his qi sense expanded to engulf everything around him. His own qi field, unconstrained by the edifices of men, released from the worries and cares that ground down the heart, distanced from the distractions that eroded the will, swelled and surged, becoming a bonfire in the night.

He tuned into this sense, listening intently, allowing raw data to flow unimpeded and unfiltered into his conscious mind. All at once, like a veil falling away, he *knew*.

Cai Yan slumbered like a princess, lying still on the flat earth, hands folded elegantly over her dantian, her Avenger infinity gun lying next to her, grip facing the right for easy access. The crystals within her reality shapers burned with qi, waiting to be given form. Her own qi, like a glove of silk hiding a mailed fist, overflowed her tent and leaked out. Dark wounds over her chest revealed her hidden grief, long-suppressed, not fully released, holding her back.

Wong Wan Lung was still awake. Sitting cross-legged on the floor, back straight, he stared intently at something only he could see. Now and then his fingers drew lines across empty space. His headset, black and chunky, molded itself to the shape of his skull. His qi was strange. His torso radiated powerful qi, his head spiked with mental activity, but around his arms and legs there was only the ghost of a qi field, weak and pale, barely anchored to his body.

Sarantuya tossed and turned about. Spikes and needles extruded from her head, her heart, her dantian, reflecting her inner state. Her qi was not much stronger than his own, but it was unfocused and unsettled. The more powerful a cultivator grew, the more he had to practice remaining calm. Without stillness, without inner control, the power at his command would easily lash out at the world around him—or the world inside him. Li Ming sensed she was still too agitated to rest, and until she rested her mind she would find no comfort no matter how many times she rolled about.

Ghazan was a sun.

His qi field was an all-consuming fire, burning white-hot. Passing through the thin fabric of Ghazan's tent, it engulfed the tents, the clearing, the woods beyond. Li Ming felt the white heat of his qi field, licking at the edges of his own, threatening to set him ablaze. At the heart of the human star, Li Ming sensed a man seated in the lotus position, hands folded over his dantian. Pure white light streamed down from a secondary star floating above his crown, a star that seemed to be an extension of something beyond the observable universe, a tendril of some fabulous realm interposed with this one, yet invisible to mortal sight. Below his feet, tendrils reached deep into the earth, into and through a black hole, a black so perfect no light shone through, leading to another neighboring domain just past the threshold of perception.

Was this Yue cultivation? Li Ming had never seen anything quite like that before. He recognized the seated position, but the energy sources were alien to him. Were these the mythical realms of Sky and Night?

Ghazan shifted. Energy rippled through his field. It tasted of suspicion, of irritation, of hostility. Somehow he had sensed Li Ming's presence and attention. Immediately the white and black stars closed, leaving only the fires of his native qi.

Li Ming suspected it was a secret cultivation method. Over the past half year, he'd seen Ghazan's qi had grown by leaps and bounds. Sarantuya's surprise confirmed his observations. His explosive growth had begun shortly after the expedition to the Yue bunker, in his downtime and Li Ming had caught him reading an ancient Yue scroll. Li Ming had no idea how to read the Yue language, but Ghazan jealously guarded the scroll and his practices all the same.

Had Ghazan discovered a qi eating method? It explained what he had seen in the rice paddies. But this cultivation method didn't consume qi, at least not deliberately. Were these different arts? Or merely different aspects of a more comprehensive style?

Li Ming reminded himself to talk to Ghazan privately about this someday. But not in front of the others. Not when anybody else was around. Ghazan was obsessed with preserving his privacy, and he wouldn't react well if anybody but Li Ming spoke to him.

It had to wait until after the hunt. After the expedition. After he had learned more about Ghazan's secret arts.

Li Ming continued his patrol. Ghazan continued his cultivation. But it was ordinary meditation, breathing while sitting still and no more. Still beneficial, though likely much less powerful than his previous method. To hold himself back like this, Li Ming suspected Ghazan felt like a tiger forced to dine on putrid carrion.

A cool wind whistled through the woods. Wong-gor set his headset away and went to sleep. Sarantuya finally found a measure of peace. Ghazan maintained his meditations. The symphony of the night went on, transforming into a dynamic improv, each player responding to the actions of every other being around it. Li Ming walked the circle around the camp, taking in everything around him.

The sounds stopped.

Li Ming's hair stood on edge. He planted himself beside a tree and listened.

Nothing.

The frogs, the night birds, the prey animals that inhabited the area around him, all had gone quiet. There was only a profound silence, ripe with potential. In the night, small ripples of qi lapped up against his field, tiny but numerous, coming from every direction.

He spun in a circle, eyes and ears wide open. No sound. Black and white. No blobs of color. But the faraway qi signatures continued to converge on the camp. He exhaled, emptying his lungs, his heart, his mind, allowing the universe to speak to him.

Qi blasted into him. It was a hammer from heaven, a spear falling from the sky, a column of concentrated light smashing into and through him, pounding him flat, smearing him across the soil. Shockwaves roiled forth from the point of impact, shaking and shattering everything in their path. He quaked where he stood, unable to stand against the sheer mass of energy trained on him, a tuning fork trembling in resonance with another, more powerful, signal. Lava roared through his body, melting and burning him, setting him alight.

Emotions rushed through his heart. Rage. Alarm. Threat. Fear. Fury roused from deep within him, supercharging his sinews, hardening his bones, strengthening muscles. He gripped his infinity gun, gnashed his teeth, widened his eyes, his heart pounding in his chest. Thoughts thundered through his mind, inarticulable words coagulating into barely-intuited concepts. Intruders, aggressors, threats, they were here, they must be destroyed, the nest had to be—

He exhaled.

Those thoughts weren't his. Those emotions didn't come from him. They came from the qi blast, not his heart. Already the qi bomb diffused, diffusing into the universe, leaving a subtle crackling as it bled from his fingers and feet.

He knew this. He'd sensed it at the rice paddies, just before the shanxiao struck. He'd felt it again at Shuanglong, heralding the beast attacks. Here it was again, this time aimed squarely at *him*, at a time when he had tuned up his qi sensitivity.

He inhaled.

Gulped down a deep breath, drawing qi into his muscles, his lungs, his dantian.

And yelled.

"STAND TO! STAND TO! STAND TO!"

And in the night, an army of beasts screamed back.

Chapter Seventeen

Night Rains on the Ba Mountains

T he qi wave had caught Ghazan by surprise.

One moment he was sitting in total stillness, the next overwhelming hatred and aggression swelled through him. The energies fired his blood, kindled his muscles, ignited his brain, compelling him to rise and kill and feast.

A small part of him observed this phenomenon with complete detachment. He was no stranger to sudden emotional outbursts during deep meditation. The body stored old emotions deep within, and meditation brought them back to the surface, like long-buried bombs rising from the earth to detonate at the slightest touch. In his life he had surely amassed enough unexploded emotional ordnance to shatter the stoutest heart. But this, *this* was different, alien, emanating from a source high above and outside of his body.

The emotions were not his.

Even so, his qi surged like the tides responding to the gravity of the moon. A sharp, sudden wind blew through the tent, whipping the fabric, tugging at the stakes. The air heated, dispelling the nighttime chill. His heart pounded, his fists clenched, his eyes shot wide open. His guns beckoned, his shapers sang, yearning to fulfill their purpose.

At the edges of his awareness, qi spots bloomed. Keeping low to the ground, stalking through the trees, closing in on the campsite. Ten, fifteen, twenty, thirty of them, assembling in a horde, approaching from all sides.

Images flashed through his mind's eye. Yellow eyes burning with hate. Hooked beaks red as blood. Muscled legs and gripping talons. Vivid green and royal purple feathers.

Zhenniao.

"STAND TO! STAND TO! STAND TO!" Li Ming shouted.

The zhenniao shrieked back, first the senior mating pair, then the other parents, the singles last of all, simultaneously signaling and coordinating the charge. In their voices he heard the same primal fury that had so thoroughly gripped his heart mere seconds before.

He shot to his feet. Stiff muscles strained and protested. He ignored them, snatching up his infinity gun and running his fingers down the side. His left hand found the hard plastic handle of his spring-loaded bayonet, a humongous model akin to a short sword. He found the firing stud, rotated his fingers clear, and pressed.

The blade snapped out the front of the handle. It was still dark, but he sensed its presence, killing steel ready to be unleashed upon the world. He sensed *everything* around him, the weight of his gear, the qi flaring from Li Ming, the others scrambling to their feet.

And the zhenniao.

While charging in from all sides, their main force was concentrated to the south. Twenty-three zhenniao, rushing in an uncoordinated mob, animal rage paired with lethal poison, but no tactical sense beyond a straightforward rush.

Ghazan burst out his tent. His helmet was still on the ground, he had no night vision devices, but it didn't matter. He read the qi of the world, writing a mental map of void and density, sentience and stillness. He *felt*, rather than saw, the approach of the zhenniao and the motions of the biaohang.

At the other side of the camp, Li Ming snapped off a shot. He sensed the bolt as it truly was, a train of a hundred pulses of nova-hot plasma, searing through the night at just under the speed of light. The bolt smashed into a bird, destroying itself and the beast in mutual annihilation. More qi, the qi of life and vitality, erupted from the great wound, dissipating in the universe.

A waste.

Cai Yan yelled orders. Wong Wan Lung's coilgun cracked. Sarantuya emerged from her tent, calling out to the men. Li Ming shouted something. Their words faded into meaningless babble. He heard nothing but noise, saw nothing but energy, felt nothing but the flows and bursts of qi in violent motion.

He spun on his heel.

Charged.

His boots landed with unconscious ease, every step propelling him forward, forward, ever forward. He leapt over the stakes and ropes of his tent, sensing instead of seeing their presence. The darkness before him separated into shades of shadow, hinting at trees, branches, stones, bushes. He rushed into emptiness and around solidities, his brain completely on autopilot, his heart-mind anchored in a profound nothingness.

The zhenniao came.

Five of them, rushing towards him, forming a crescent. A white-hot bolt caught the furthest in its breast, producing a blast of hot steam, sending it tumbling and crashing into the earth. The others, filled with rage, ignored their dying brethren, continuing their rush. Spotting him, they spread their wings like archers nocking bows.

Ghazan lunged.

He flew across the earth, burning his qi to augment and accelerate his motions, his muscles firing in a precise sequence trained countless millions of times before, covering the length of a room in a single leap, swallowing up the distance between himself and the nearest zhenniao, bayoneted gun chambered low.

The zhenniao responded in a flash, killing its forward velocity in an instant, spreading its wings out for balance, its head swooping down to bring its beak crashing down on Ghazan's skull.

Ghazan lunged again.

And thrust.

As he stepped off to the left, the beast's head swooshed past, missing him by a hair's breadth. His bayonet rose from below, sinking deep into its neck. His shapers grabbed the qi of his crystals, transformed them into Night and Sky, and blasted them down his weapon, down the length of his bayonet, transmuting into a spear of burning white. The energy bolt parted everything before it, feathers, flesh, bone. Its neck separated in an instant. The spear kept on going, decapitating the monster bird.

Blood gushed from the tremendous wound. The body went slack, falling straight down. The neck and head flopped somewhere behind Ghazan forgotten. Feathers caressed naked skin, fields of numbness and tingling bloomed where they touched, but Ghazan barely noticed. He retracted his weapon, drawing his qi back into himself. The Sky energy peeled off first, revealing a shaft and head of pure Night. The spearhead became a forest of hooks and barbs, tearing out the zhenniao's qi. He reeled the spear into him, dissolving it, reintegrating it.

And consumed the beast's qi.

Life rushed through him. Hot and electric, lightning expressed as liquid, the bones of the earth and the drew from the heavens and the elements of everything in between condensed into a golden elixir. He drank it down, filling his lower dantian, letting the energy spill out and into his middle and higher dantian, burning the beast's qi to make it part of his own.

There was too much qi. There was always too much. The human body could only hold so much qi at a time. Cultivation practice sought to expand that capacity, increase the amount of energy the dantian could absorb and process at once. Even so, there was only so much excess qi a person could take in. Past that limit, the body would reject it. Any cultivator foolish or brave enough to blow past that limit would blow himself up from the inside. This was a hard limit, imposed by biological design, impossible for a mere mortal to break.

So he sidestepped it.

Deep below his feet, he opened a portal to the Night. Existing beyond what humans thought was space-time, it was a timeless, formless, eternal void, capable of holding an infinity of anything, yet at the same time filled with energy that modern science barely understood.

The sorcerer-scientists of the Yue Dynasty explored the Night, plumbing its secrets, producing unimaginable technological wonders. The Xia civilization stole their legacy, what they hadn't destroyed, and attempted to reproduce their findings. Modern scientists were pleased to call interspatial storage the highest expression of their sciences. But it was simply a parlor trick, nothing more complicated than creating a temporary partition of a tiny slice of the surface layer of the Night for one to put away and retrieve items.

The portal he had created touched the depths of the Night itself. Here was the source of the power that fueled interspatial storage, and with this source came great wonders.

He seized the qi he had plundered and sent it deep into the Night, joining a vast reservoir of life qi, the qi of the targets he had slain at close quarters. In the strangeness of the Night, instead of dispersing into the cosmos like it normally did, the qi coalesced together into a huge, perfect sphere. When the last of the qi trickled through, he closed the portal—but left open a tiny crack. Just enough for him to draw upon his reserves at will.

This was the Foundation Method of the Way of Conquering the Heavens. Killing, pillaging, storing, a three-part cycle smoothly executed in the space of heartbeats.

The other three zhenniao, still caught in the grip of bloodthirst, too simple to understand what Ghazan had done to their kin, beat their wings. Less a flap, more like a vibration, they flung a storm of razor-tipped poison feathers from three different angles.

Already Ghazan was in motion, preparing his own defenses. He drew the essence of the Night into himself, transforming every cell in his body, *becoming* the Night itself. His skin, his eyes, his hair, all of him turned blacker than black. His blood chilled, his breath froze, all heat vanishing into the absolute zero of the abyssal void.

The feathers struck.

Disintegrated.

Vanished.

The Night consumed them all, reducing them nothingness. The moment the last feather dissolved, he cycled out his energies, taking on the aspect of pure Sky. Now he burned like a newborn star, white upon white, a white so pure it burned and blurred most of his features. He opened the tap into his hidden reserves, fueling his dantian, and leapt.

The air parted before him. Gravity surrendered to his will. By thought alone, he sped across the ground, his toes barely brushing the earth. Everything he touched, everything he did not wish to preserve, burned in the cosmic furnace that was the Sky. Leaves, branches, a flying bug, they vaporized in an instant. The zhenniao stared at him, transfixed at the sight.

And he thrust.

The steel plunged deep into a living breast. His sense of touch was so finely-tuned, he felt a beating heart split itself against his bayonet, tearing itself apart. The zhenniao howled, discharging its feathers at close range. The Sky burned them all up, fueling the fire within. Ghazan yanked out his bayonet, and the beast's qi, drinking it all down. He offered the qi to the Sky, transforming it into a shield, a great globe of white flame that incinerated all it touched.

The Second Method of Conquering Heaven and Earth: the transmutation of captured qi.

He turned to the remaining two zhenniao. A plasma bolt screamed out the darkness, striking the closest monster. Bloody mist and life qi geysered from the point of impact, spilling profligately on the soil. Naked rage screamed through Ghazan's heart. That qi was his! His by right of war and conquest! How dare they steal his kill?

Distracted, he allowed the surviving zhenniao to reach him. With a lightning quick-motion, it struck at his neck.

Its beak struck the shield.

And burned.

Momentum carried the rest of the beast into the shield. Ghazan embraced it, spreading his arms wide, crushing the zhenniao into him with a massive bear hug. The Sky shield consumed the holocaust whole, growing thicker, hotter, brighter. Ghazan gulped down the excess qi that remained, siphoning them into his dantian, recharging what energy he had spent—and gathering even more.

He extended his palms, feeling for the qi bleeding out the other zhenniao. There was still some left, not a lot, but every drop was precious. He grabbed it all and sent into the Night, into his reserves.

The Third Method of Conquering Heaven and Earth: the scavenging of raw qi.

Life, red and raw, coursed through his veins. Every muscle, every sinew, every nerve thrummed with power. He was *full*, full of vitality, every subsystem running at a hundred and twenty percent, synergizing into a living weapon greater than the sum of its parts, the offspring of a union of steel and skill and will, dominating everything it touched.

The world fell into sharp relief. Behind him were his allies, weathering the assault, the crackling and snarling of their guns carrying through. Around him the zhenniao called out to each other, preparing to surround and slay him. He was alone and unafraid.

He threw his head back. A roar erupted from the depths of his lungs, hearkening to the days of his long-gone but ever-revered ancestors, the battle cry of the warriors and conquerors of the Yue Dynasty.

"UUKHAI!"

He shouted defiance and challenge to the world, daring one and all to come to him, to become a part of him.

The zhenniao accepted.

They crashed through the undergrowth, shrieking and cawing, madly dashing towards the madman. They surrounded him, boxing him into a circle, cutting off every possible avenue of escape. Bolts cut through the forest, cutting a few down. The others closed the gaps, continuing the charge, single-mindedly focused on the man burning as bright as the sun. In the heart of the scrum, Ghazan did the one thing he could do, the one thing he was best at.

He charged.

"UUKHAI!"

With a powerful thrust, he tore the heart out of the nearest beast. As he drank down its qi, he stepped off on a diagonal, thrusting at a bared neck. Quick as an eel, the zhenniao swerved its too-flexible neck, and the blood-soaked bayonet grazed past its armor of poison feathers. Ghazan retracted the weapon through an arc, weight and muscles shifting and playing in a well-oiled rhythm, cutting down and through its feathers. The blade bit into feathers and flesh, but it was too shallow to be decisive. As the zhenniao launched a riposte, he went low, striking its ankle.

Bone snapped, blood sprayed, and the creature went down. He stomped it in the face, feeling its bones break and burn under his shielded boots, its essence sucking into the whirlpool of the Night. Alarm bells sounded around him, and as he turned to the source a zhenniao bulled into him.

Or, rather, his shield.

It incinerated in a flash, half its mass disintegrated in an instant. Sensing only heat and pressure, Ghazan turned around, just in time to see the rest of it tumble into darkness. Before Ghazan could recycle its qi, his shield fell apart too, and two zhenniao lashed at him.

He went low, sliding in between them, bayonet cutting through an arc. Bone cracked on bone, and with a grin he knew they had crashed their heads in the dark. The closest zhenniao was too close for the bayonet, so he simply released his infinity gun and transmuted his hands to Night and punched.

His fist melted through feathers, skin, bone, flesh, plunging deep into its chest cavity. Wet heat surrounded him, dissolving into the night. He pulled his arm out, taking its essence with him. The other zhenniao cocked a wing, ready to strike. He turned himself completely into Night and exploded in with an elbow.

Feathers vanished against his skin. His elbow carved neatly into and through the beast, melting everything it touched. His qi exploded outwards like a bomb, liquefying organs and bone. He stepped clear, dragging their life force into the Night, and screamed again.

"UUKHAI!"

And the zhenniao fell upon him.

The nearest beast lunged for his head. Ghazan shot in low, cycling Night to Sky, and seized a leg in a crushing grip. Skin, muscle and sinews dissolved under his touch. He yanked just as the leg gave out. As the zhenniao toppled, he surged up in an uppercut, the line of force flowing from feet to dantian to Sky crystal to fist, exploding a tunnel clean through the zhenniao.

He changed to Night, recycling the qi. A zhenniao raked his back as he changed, and for its trouble its talons fell apart. Ghazan launched himself into the direction of the force, striking with the whole of his broad back. Softness melted before him, hardness broke, and the zhenniao went down hard. Spinning around, he kicked the closest part of it, disintegrating an arc of flesh and bone in the ever-hungry Night, and stomped through its chest.

A zhenniao lashed at him. He covered his head with his elbows and swung his whole body into the strike, cycling through his energies. His left forearm, shielded in Night, crashed into its long neck, shearing off a swathe of feathers. His elbow, burning in Sky, became a fiery blade, cutting through flesh and veins and spine. He launched himself off the ground, spearing his Sky-elbow into his chest, erasing its insides. He sucked it all into himself, into the Night.

This was Shifangquan, the Fist of the Ten Directions, a fist built around a beast-slaying spear, adapted to the Way of Conquering the Heavens.

Ghazan's head pounded. His blood burned. Lightning tore through flesh and bone. He'd absorbed too much qi, far too much. It was tearing him apart. He had to dump it all. Now.

And he had plenty of targets.

The remaining zhenniao hesitated, now finally recognizing the nature of what they were facing. Backing up, they extended their wings, ready to drown him in poison feathers. He sensed them all in space-time, surrounding him in a rough fan-like formation. He felt them, their legs coiling and tensing, their eyes locking on target, their throats vibrating as they coordinated their assault, tiny muscles vibrating and loosening their weaponized feathers, their wings spreading to create wind funnels. He mapped them all in space-time, a super-conscious *knowing* that came from outside the limited perception of mere mortal senses, identifying and targeting them all in an instant.

He flung his arms towards the sky.

"*UUKHAI!*"

Spears of Sky and Night burst from the ground underneath the monsters' feet, impaling them from cloaca to crown. The Sky burned all resistance, disintegrating their defenses, vaporizing blood and bone and meat, turning them all to energy, to qi. The Night seized their qi, gobbling it all down, replenishing his qi and expanding his reserves. All at once, the zhenniao became burnt husks, falling apart into charred heaps.

Ghazan exalted in the moment. His enemies were all fallen at his feet. He had taken everything from them, increasing all of himself. Their qi coursed through him, becoming one with him, adding to his strength. He was the victor, and to the victor went the spoils. *This* must be how his ancestors had felt, standing astride a continent, the lords of a vast realm stretching from sea to sea, holding within their hands the fates of millions.

"*UUKHAI! UUKHAI! UUKHAI!*"

His battle cry echoed into the night. The world around him went still, the stillness that came from an absence of life, of resistance, of war. He savored the moment, the taste of iron-rich blood hanging in the air, the scent of death and decay mingling with mist and ash, the adrenaline fading into a pleasant afterburn.

Presently he grew aware of the other humans. His conscious mind reminded him of the existence of his companions. He knew that the Xia—Li Ming, Cai Yan, Wong Wan Lung—were facing the wrong way during the fight. Sarantuya had seen glimpses of him, but everything he did could be easily explained away as Sky and Night magic. The Xia knew too little of the arcana of his people, and the Way of Conquering the Heavens was built on the foundations of Sky and Night. Anyone who hadn't fought alongside him, who hadn't seen the plundering of living qi up close, couldn't possibly identify it.

His secret was safe.

And he had grown powerful. Tremendously so.

"Ghazan! Are you alright?" Li Ming called.

"Yes!" Ghazan replied.

"Regroup! It's dangerous out there!"

"Coming in!"

Ghazan trudged towards the camp. With every step, he siphoned the raw qi around him into the Night, into his ever-growing reservoir. Tempting though it was to open the floodgates and boost his qi now, he didn't care to explain an expanded qi field to anyone. Li Ming least of all.

Li Ming was a good man. He could be a great man. And that was why he would never understand Ghazan. This world was wealth and power and nothing besides. He with power wrote the rules, he without obeyed or be destroyed. You could never reach the highest heavens if you did not break through the rules the ones on top set to keep you down.

In the end, Li Ming was a Xia and thought like a Xia. Ghazan was a scion of the Yue Dynasty, a product of his heritage and culture and lineage, and would always be so. No matter how deep their bonds might grow—and, he admitted to himself, he was closer to Li Ming than any other Xia—this would always stand between him.

This was the way of the world, and how it had to be.

A cold wind blew. The skies thickened and darkened. Cold qi concentrated in faraway clouds. Lightning crackled.

A night rain fell upon the Ba Mountains.

Chapter Eighteen

What We Can Live With

Safely ensconced in the campsite, a circle of guns aimed at the world, the biaohang stood watch until daybreak. No more zhenniao came swarming out the darkness. Still, they didn't drop their guard. In the early hours, they rested in shifts. Li Ming stole maybe an hour or two of sleep before the team stood up for their morning routine.

After breakfast and coffee, they discussed the attack, reviewed their tactics, evaluated their performance. All through the night, everyone had remained in the clearing, firing at targets of opportunity as they arose.

Everyone but Ghazan.

"Why did you charge the zhenniao?" Cai Yan demanded.

"The proper response to a close-range assault is to counter-assault through," Ghazan replied. "The zhenniao were so close, my instincts and training kicked in."

"It was dangerous! They had surrounded you. We were too busy fighting off the other zhenniao to help you."

"I had my *qiang*, my bayonet, my magic. With a shield up, the zhenniao couldn't touch me. It was perfectly safe."

"You had the perfect opportunity to use your *qiang* too," Li Ming said.

The word for 'gun' and 'spear' was pronounced the same: *qiang*. Li Ming deliberately kept his words ambiguous, watching Ghazan's reaction.

His eyes hooded over, his lips parted to reveal even rows of white teeth, his hands clenched and unclenched.

"Indeed. They were in perfect range of my *qiang*. The thrust was faster than a shot."

"Nets you more cash too, if you place it just right," Wong-gor said.

"Yes, but money wasn't anywhere near my considerations. I was focused on ending the threat as quickly as possible."

"What about the other zhenniao? After you finished the beasts close to you, you stormed deeper into the forest."

"They were extremely close. If I ran, they would have a free shot at my back. I had to maintain the momentum and destroy them."

"It wouldn't have happened if you'd stayed put," Li Ming said. "By rushing into the woods, you opened a hole in our defenses. It might not have been dangerous to you, but it exposed our flanks. Mine and Sarantuya's."

Ghazan tilted his head, as if considering his words deeply.

"Apologies," Ghazan said at last. "I was too rash. In the Yue military, I was trained to charge the enemy and run him down at close quarters. We did not have a policy of digging in while under fire. It didn't occur to me that you weren't following me until it was over."

"You were in the middle of a beast scrum," Wong-gor said. "No wonder you didn't notice."

"Correct. Nonetheless, I pulled most of the beasts away from you. That decreased the danger to the camp, didn't it?"

"Yes," Cai Yan admitted. "But it was a very risky move. They could have killed you."

"But they didn't."

Arrogance radiated from every pore of the Yue's being. But it was well-earned, Li Ming admitted. He'd engaged over two-thirds of the enemy force at close quarters and walked away unscathed. That move he pulled at the end, spears of searing light shooting up from the earth, was an incredible feat. Only once in his life had he seen someone do something similar, and that soldier was a member of the Immortal Commando Unit. Was Ghazan the equal of a warrior who had spent decades honing mind and body for combat?

Or his superior?

"We're a team," Li Ming said. "We fight as a team. By charging ahead you put us at risk. You must think of the team, not just of yourself. The next time you feel tempted to counter-assault the enemy, call out to us. If only so we can follow your lead."

"I'll keep that in mind," Ghazan said.

"Sarantuya, do you have anything to add?" Cai Yan prompted.

She blinked, as if startled from a reverie.

"I... I think you fought well," she said.

"Really," Ghazan said.

His voice was steady and neutral, revealing nothing. Which was odd. The Yue enjoyed praise like this, even if he wouldn't admit it.

"I covered you as you charged the zhenniao. The way you fought, the magic you cast, it was... amazing."

"Looks like you won a fan," Wong-gor said.

She sighed exasperatedly and said something in Yue, a river of words growing in velocity and density. Li Ming caught only two words: *tenger* and *shönö*. Sky and Night.

Ghazan said something curt, also in the same language, then smoothly transitioned to Xiayu.

"There are great depths to the system of Sky and Night. Great flexibility and complexity too. There are no set techniques, only principles and the best way to use them. This is why the Yue Dynasty chose this system above all other systems."

Re-energized, they moved on the tedious work. Recovering, cleaning and processing the bodies.

There were so many of them, spread out over such a wide area. The dawn's early light revealed the devastation man and beast had visited on the world. Shattered tree trunks smoldered on the forest floor. Poison feathers buried in trees, stumps and soil gleamed evilly. The wind carried ashes and rot in the breeze. The biaohang donned protective gear and set off.

Decay had set in. Torn innards had spilled waste and acids over punctured flesh, permanently ruining it. Flies buzzed around the corpses, competing with swarming ants and crawling worms. Sacs of trapped gases bulged from bellies and breasts and throats. In such an advanced state of decomposition, few people would pay for them. They could harbor dangerous pathogens.

Li Ming had anticipated it. It was late summer, and rain accelerated decay. The hunter within lamented at the loss of so much valuable meat. The soldier understood that the risk of a counterattack while they were busy harvesting flesh was too great, and the risk of brushing bare skin against poison feathers even higher.

Li Ming simply photographed the bodies as proof of kill and harvested the feathers. The Jianghu Association would pay a basic rate, even less than paying dirt, but better that than not being paid at all.

But there were some bodies that seemed mostly intact. Beasts struck in the head or neck, clean shots through the heart, bodies with minimal damage. These could be safely composted at least. Li Ming processed those, preserving the flesh but dumping the viscera.

Ghazan's work was obvious. The bodies had been ruined. The wounds were unlike anything he had seen before, tunnels and arcs and swathes of destruction passing clean through flesh and bone. Ghazan preferred his kills neat and tidy, the better to harvest maximum profit. For him to do this was unheard of. Or maybe he was so desperate he had pulled out all the stops.

Nonetheless, Ghazan worked on his kills without complaint. If anything, he seemed… content. As if he had gained what he had wanted from them.

Li Ming suspected he knew what it was. But he had seen nothing and had no evidence of qi consumption. He couldn't confront Ghazan, not here and now.

With the bodies processed, the biaohang set off for the nests. The drone was finally back up in the air, so high overhead that seen from ground level, it was little more than a fast-moving dot. As the drone swept the forest, the hunters wended through the forest, taking the fastest way to the target.

Barely half a day ago, Li Ming had seen this forest with eyes of wonder, drinking in everything in sight. Now he saw it with the eyes of a soldier, seeing not trees and rocks and the river, but cover and concealment and angles of fire. How odd, he thought, yet after last night, it was not so odd at all.

Li Ming heard the nests long before he saw them. Strings of high-pitched chirps, feeding off each other, becoming louder and more insistent by the second. Li Ming's grip tightened around his Avenger. His senses kicked up a notch. He scanned, searching for signs of the parents, of guards, of opportunistic beasts.

Then he saw the chicks.

Twelve of them, sitting in a depression in the forest floor. Their tawny feathers shone white in the sun. They chirped, chittered, fluttered their little wings, crying out to long-dead parents, pecking at the air, at the earth, at each other. Some were tiny, no larger than his palms cupped together, huddled together for warmth. Their older kin, only as tall as Li Ming's knees, sat in a protective ring around them, hissing at the intruders, yet unwilling to attack.

"They're babies," Cai Yan said, an unreadable expression her face.

"Spread out and search the area," Wong said. "Look for eggs and signs of adults. Beasts don't leave their young unguarded like this."

"I'll stay here and keep an eye on them," Cai Yan said.

"Me too," Li Ming said.

Side by side with Cai Yan, he watched the young zhenniao, weapon at compressed ready, ready to snap up and kill. The beasts, unable to understand the language and posture and tools of man, continued to cry out, to hiss, to stay put.

Li Ming stayed put too.

One by one, the other biaohang reported back in. No signs. No adults. Wong had found a dozen eggs in another nest.

"Keep the eggs," Sarantuya advised. "We can turn them in for a reward."

"What do we do with the chicks?" Ghazan asked.

Sarantuya didn't reply.

The biaohang regrouped around the surviving zhenniao, their weapons close to hand, but not quite aiming them at the young beasts. Except for Ghazan, covering the beasts.

"What do we do with the chicks," Ghazan repeated, his voice dropping so low it became a statement.

"Are they dangerous?" Li Ming asked.

"No," Sarantuya said. "Their feathers are still white. Their poison glands only fully develop when their feathers turn green, half a year after they hatch. The youngest of the chicks are two or three weeks old, the oldest less than six months."

"Is there a reward for harvesting them?" Ghazan asked.

Sarantuya hesitated.

"A small one."

"But they are babies," Cai Yan insisted.

"They'll grow up to become omnivorous adults. Man-killing adults."

"They're not dangerous now," Li Ming said.

"They're beasts," Wong-gor said. "We all saw what happened at Shuanglong. If we don't deal with them now, they'll attack the city again."

"They attacked the city only because of the qi wave," Cai Yan said.

"You sure about that? Correlation isn't causation," Wong said.

"Zhenniao don't normally attack cities, not without provocation," Sarantuya said.

"Then what do you want to do? Abandon them?" Ghazan said.

"They are not going to survive in the wild. Not without parents," Sarantuya said.

"Killing them now would be a mercy."

"Look at them!" Cai Yan insisted. "They're too scared to hurt anyone! How can you even *think* about—"

"If you can't do the job, I will."

The chicks chirped louder, more insistently, more desperately. Their older kin coiled their necks, ready to strike.

Li Ming held up his hands.

"Is there a reward for taking them alive?"

Everyone looked at each other.

"Give me a moment," Cai Yan said.

She pulled out her scroll, called Ms. Zhang, and set her on speaker.

"We found twelve baby zhenniao. Is there a reward if we bring them in to the Jianghu Association?" Cai Yan asked.

"*En*... I haven't seen anyone do it before, but I heard the Association sells live beasts to collectors and farmers. They'll probably share the profits with you."

"Is the reward greater than bringing them in dead?"

"Give me a second. I need to check."

The line went quiet. The biaohang watched the chicks. The chicks chirped and stared back. Li Ming turned away, remembering to cover everyone's back.

When Ms. Zhang called back, her tone was unusually apologetic.

"The Shuanglong office says they're not equipped to handle live beasts. You're the first group in years to talk about bringing in young beasts. If you hand over the zhenniao to them, they can't do anything."

"What about veterinarians? Or wildlife rehabilitation services?"

"There are no animal doctors in Shuanglong capable of handling beasts. While the Central Plains Wildlife Care Center has an office in Shuanglong, they don't deal with beasts either. Nobody cares about live beasts."

"What can we do about the chicks?" Li Ming asked.

Ms. Zhang hesitated.

"Butcher them and sell them to the Association. They can be rendered down into beast essence."

Cai Yan clicked off. Ghazan smiled triumphantly.

"There you have it."

"No," Li Ming said.

"No? We came to the Central Plains to hunt beasts, didn't we?"

"We came here to protect people by putting down dangerous beasts. These chicks are not dangerous."

"They're only beasts."

"We are men."

"Noble words. But sadly misplaced. If we leave, they will starve to death. It is quicker, cleaner, more ethical, to put them down now."

Li Ming wavered where he stood. Ghazan made sense. Misplaced compassion was just as corrosive as lack of it. Worse, it could delude him into thinking he was doing good when he was merely visiting more suffering upon the world.

And yet...

"The older chicks are protecting the younger ones," Li Ming said.

"And?"

"They already have some vestige of nesting and protective instinct. They could learn to feed their siblings."

"If they do not?"

"Their blood is not on our hands."

Ghazan laughed. The chicks squawked in protest, turning to him.

"Is that what you care about? We killed all the adults in the clan. All the zhenniao who could tend to the chicks. Even if we find a way to sell them to the Association, the Association will likely sell them to farmers, who will kill them later. By killing the adults, we killed the young also. The only difference is the manner of their death. End their suffering now."

"There's another difference. What we can live with."

"You can't?"

Li Ming locked gazes with Ghazan. Twin spears flashed from the Yue's eyes, aimed at Li Ming's soul. Li Ming met them, launching spears of his own, crashing spearhead against spearhead, tip against tip, force against force, a connection so power and so tremulous it could snap in a moment.

"We came here to protect people. Killing defenseless beasts is not part of the mission."

Ghazan sneered.

"You're soft."

"I'm not going to do it. Cai Yan is not going to do it either. As the leader of this expedition, what she says goes."

"And I say we've wasted enough time arguing with each other," Cai Yan said.

"We are leaving?" Ghazan said.

"Yes. The job is done."

Ghazan shrugged. As his shoulders lowered, he deflated, shrinking into himself.

"Let's go."

Wong patted his shoulder.

"There'll always be more beasts to hunt."

Chapter Nineteen

Hunted

It was a long hike back to the vehicles. During the trek, Li Ming reviewed the hunt in his mind, reconstructing the timeline, examining it from multiple angles. Then we went back into the past, thinking about the previous hunts. The team hadn't mentioned it yet, they were too focused on the tactical and the immediate, but now that they had time and distance, and safety, it was now time to address the strategic.

They had parked their rented trucks by the side of the main road, covered under camouflage netting. The team pulled off the nets and inspected the vehicles. Li Ming took extra care, examining the tires, the engine, the windows, anything that betrayed signs of damage. Or sabotage.

When he was satisfied that everything was in order, he stood up and addressed the group.

"I think we are being targeted."

The warm air chilled. The team turned to Li Ming. Sarantuya looked puzzled. Wong-gor checked his weapon. Ghazan glanced around. Cai Yan inched closer to her car.

"You too?" Cai Yan said.

"What's going on?" Sarantuya asked.

"Anybody felt that rush of qi right before the zhenniao attacked us?" Li Ming asked.

"Yes," Ghazan said.

"It woke me up," Sarantuya said.

"Me too," Cai Yan said.

"I felt this... crawling sensation over my skin," Wong-gor said. "The same feeling at Shuanglong, just before the attack."

"Exactly. It's the same qi wave I felt at An Le," Li Ming said. "Sarantuya, that was before you joined us."

"Someone is using magic to send beasts against us," Ghazan said.

"And cities and villages," Cai Yan added.

"I didn't sense anything at An Le, but I *did* feel something at Shuanglong," Wong said.

"It's a qi wave that only cultivators can sense at long range," Cai Yan mused. "If he's not directly targeted by it, a non-cultivator can't."

Wong-gor's lips twitched.

"Fortunately, Li Ming sensed the wave. Saved our hides, that's for sure."

"What was this wave? A mind control spell?" Sarantuya asked. "One that overrides the beasts' natural instincts and compels them to attack us?"

"Is such a thing possible?" Li Ming asked.

"It's not impossible," Ghazan said. "After all, it was used against us."

"Who's responsible? And why?" Sarantuya asked.

"The Yudu military," Ghazan said.

"The Ten Thousand Swords Society," Cai Yan said.

"Both," Li Ming said.

"We can make a case for Captain Bao being our prime suspect," Wong-gor said. "He sent us on two jobs that ended in beast ambushes. But the rest of the Yudu military? The Ten Thousand Swords Society? How are they connected?"

"Captain Bao was in An Le during the attack," Li Ming said. "That meant he needed someone to call the beasts on us. We have to assume his men are in on the plot too."

"Drones," Cai Yan said. "There was a drone providing overwatch at An Le. There was another orbiting us in the forest. Maybe whatever they are using to control the beasts is mounted on the drone."

"The drone crew is suspect too," Wong-gor agreed. "But what about the Wanjianhui?"

Half-formed concepts, weighed down by fatigue and run ragged by constant alertness and action, abruptly crystallized into a single focused thought.

"Captain Bao incites a beast invasion in Shuanglong. The Ten Thousand Swords Society swoops down to save the day. They become heroes."

"Yes, but why?" Wong-gor asked. "What do they get out of it?"

"The Central Plains is one of the few places the Wanjianhui can operate openly," Cai Yan said. "They are cementing their position."

"They are already established," Sarantuya said. "What more profit will they get by collaborating with these... these beast lords?"

"Maybe they are field-testing new or recovered technology," Li Ming said.

"And maybe they are also using the opportunity to build up their image even further," Ghazan added.

"But why? What's the endgame?" Wong-gor said. "It can't just be that, can it?"

Li Ming had no answers. But Wong-gor was right. A secret society as powerful and ruthless as the Wanjianhui would not be content with simply portraying themselves as heroes. Not in a land where they were already allowed to operate openly. There was something else here, something they weren't seeing.

"We need to find out more," Li Ming said.

"We can't go back to Shuanglong," Ghazan said. "When Captain Bao learns we've survived the ambush, he may escalate."

"Yudu," Cai Yan said. "We can turn in our bounties there."

"We should just eliminate the threat."

"Not without proof," Wong-gor said. "Most certainly not without knowing who all the players are."

"We can't leave Ms. Zhang alone in Shuanglong. We need to pick her up and brief her on the way to Yudu," Li Ming said.

"And when we return to Yudu, we bring this to the attention of the authorities," Cai Yan said.

"Are there any authorities who will even listen to us?" Li Ming asked. "*Zhongyuan de baoanju doushi lanni fuhu shangqiang.*"

The security agencies of the Central Plains are as useless as sodden mud, unsuitable for building walls.

"There is," Cai Yan said. "The Jianghu Association."

Chapter Twenty

Proof of Guilt

The last rays of the setting sun scorched the world as Dayong rolled into Yudu. Every fiber of Li Ming's being screamed at him to sleep, to rest, to shut down and recover from the exertions of the hunt. But as the office of the Jianghu Association rolled into view, a fresh electric charge surged down his spine.

During the long drive from the Ba Mountains, the biaohang took turns to drive, to rest, to watch out for retaliatory strikes. They had picked up Ms. Zhang at the outermost walls of Shuanglong and briefed her on the road to Yudu. Ms. Zhang listened in wide-eyed amazement, then disbelief, and finally horror.

She didn't argue with Dayong. She'd quickly reached the same conclusions they had. The moment the biaohang fell silent, she clicked on her headset and made a series of calls.

The moment the team entered the Jianghu Association building, a pair of grim-faced security guards greeted them. The guards escorted them through the building, saying not one word more than necessary, and deposited them inside the office of Branch Manager Qiu.

Li Ming had remembered Manager Qiu as a smooth, elegant executive. Now he seemed ruffled, his hand-fitted suit crumpled, his head of black slicked-back hair slowly falling apart. Behind his smartglasses, his eyes were wide with concern.

"Ms. Zhang told me you've been targeted by dark forces," Manager Qiu said. "Are you all right? Did anything happen on the way here?"

"We are fine, thank you," Cai Yan said. "Have you experienced any... undue influence from the Yudu military?"

"No. No one from the military has reached out to us yet. Captain Bao and his men are still stationed in Shuanglong on security duties."

"What about the Ten Thousand Sword Society?"

"Radio silence. But they filed a report claiming will return to Yudu within the next two or three days."

Li Ming heaved a sigh of relief.

"Good. We're ahead of the curve. For now."

"Could you please tell me in detail what happened to you?" Manager Qiu asked.

He sounded polite, but there was steel in his voice. It was a command framed as a request.

Over cups of hot, soothing tea, the biaohang related their missions and suspicions. Manager Qiu took it all in, an intense expression on his face, growing more serious as Li Ming and Cai Yan outlined their suspicions.

"Do you have any clues as to the identity of these beast lords?" Manager Qiu asked.

"Captain Bao and his men," Li Ming said automatically.

"No, you have suspicions. Do you have *evidence*?"

"The fact that every time we've been attacked by beasts *and* experienced the qi wave, we were on a job for Captain Bao."

"That is circumstantial. We need hard evidence."

"The men who killed the gate guards at Shuanglong," Cai Yan said. "The terrorists. Do we have any idea who they are?"

"The autopsies are still ongoing. But I have heard through my contacts in the police that the remains have not been identified."

Li Ming wondered if he could have taken any of the terrorists alive. Probably not, he supposed. Even with magic, a swordbreaker, gongfu, if the enemy offered a fight in close quarters he had to be destroyed, lest he destroy you first.

"They could be foreigners," Ghazan mused.

"Patsies," Wong-gor spat.

"Let's not jump to conclusions here," Manager Qiu said. "Before we can act, we must have proof."

"Is there any proof of collaboration between the Yudu militia and the Wanjianhui?" Li Ming asked.

"The military works hand-in-glove with accredited biaoju, including the Ten Thousand Swords Society. There *are* connections between them. The only question is how deep these ties go."

"Captain Bao must be plotting something with the Wanjianhui."

"Do you have evidence? Do you even know what that something is?"

Li Ming sucked down a breath. And said nothing.

"I understand you've clashed with the Wanjianhui back in the Zhongxia Republic. But it doesn't necessarily follow that they must be working with the beast lords, or that Captain Bao and his men are the beast lords," Manager Qiu said.

"They are the prime suspects."

"Without evidence, the judge will laugh the case out of court."

Li Ming *knew* Captain Bao and his beast lords were conspiring with the Ten Thousand Swords Society. He could feel the contours of the plot in his mind, taste it on the tip of his tongue. But it was intuition and suspicion and nothing more. Enough to investigate, nowhere near enough to declare war.

"Why is the Ten Thousand Swords Society a legal biaoju in the Central Plains?" Cai Yan asked. "They've been blacklisted as a secret society in Zhongxia."

Manager Qiu sighed. Ms. Zhang sighed too. They shared a glance. Ms. Zhang shrugged a little. Manager Qiu sighed once more and spoke.

"The Central Plains Merchant Association will do business with *anyone*. They do not care about criminal allegations or records, backgrounds or labels. They only care about profit. The Ten Thousand Swords Society has not broken any laws in the Central Plains, and they have brought plenty of profits into the region. So long as this remains so, the government will not act against them."

What kind of country was this? A land that embraces devil cultivators but will not support biaohang in their hour of need? A nation that worshiped the free market and did nothing that would choke the flow of gold into their coffers? How could such an society survive?

"The Central Plains is not the Zhongxia Republic," Ms. Zhang said, for what must have been the umpteenth time.

"Why do you allow the Wanjianhui to work here? Don't you regulate the jianghu?" Li Ming asked.

Manager Qiu crushed down into himself. With every word he spoke, he aged a year.

"The world of the rivers and lakes exists in a state of symbiosis with the world of nations and laws. We may operate freely only if we maintain the trust of the people and the rulers. We may have our customs, but we must also obey the laws of the states where we operate."

"You choose to frolic under another man's rule than to suffer under your own," Ghazan said.

"We are a society, a society within a society. There are laws. Customs. *Guanxi*. We cannot throw them all away. Not without consequences, and most definitely not without proof."

Ghazan shook his head. "I do not understand your people."

"We are all joined in the great web of life. Everything we do affects everyone else and comes back to us. We must act appropriately," Wong-gor said.

"We have to do *something*," Li Ming said. "We need to know what the Wanjianhui and the beast lords are planning."

"Then you must find out what it is," Manager Qiu said.

"Are you able to help us?" Wong-gor asked.

Manager Qiu massaged his temples with his knuckles.

"I have friends in the Yudu police. Friends I can trust. I can ask them to launch a quiet investigation, to determine if there are improper relationships between the military and the Wanjianhui. I can also ask them to identify any unusual purchases by Captain Bao or the Wanjianhui."

"Can you sanction Bao and the Wanjianhui?" Cai Yan asked.

"Not without evidence. In the Central Plains, the Wanjianhui is still an accredited biaoju in good standing with the lawful authorities. But…"

"But?"

"On my own authority, I can cancel and blacklist all contracts originating from or awarded to the Yudu militia and the Wanjianhui. I can also hold any bounties and compensation the Wanjianhui may receive for their contracts."

"But if you do that, people will ask questions," Cai Yan said.

"Worse, you will tip them off," Wong-gor added.

"That is all I can do, in my official capacity."

"But unofficially, you *could* encourage all biaoju within the Central Plains to avoid taking contracts from the Yudu militia," Ms. Zhang suggested.

Manager Qiu stroked his chin. "Yes, I could do that. I could rearrange the workflow so that biaohang who wish to take a contract from the Yudu military must go through my office. I could brief them here, in private."

"There is one possibility we haven't considered," Ghazan said lightly.

"Which is?" Manager Qiu asked.

"You, or your staff, are collaborating with the beast lords and the Wanjianhui."

All the qi sucked out the room. Ms. Zhang went white as a ghost. Manager Qiu's eyes popped, his jaw dropped. Li Ming rested one hand on his pistol, the other on his swordbreaker.

Ghazan had lied. They had discussed this possibility in the drive to Shuanglong but breathed not a word of it to Ms. Zhang. It was the possibility they had to eliminate first—and here, deep within the Jianghu Association, they were up close and personal with a key suspect.

Manager Qiu.

"I can prove we're not," Manager Qiu said, keeping his hands conspicuously visible.

"How?" Cai Yan demanded.

"We did not know where you were. We know you went to An Le, but not the specific rice paddy where the shanxiao attacked you. We know you went to Shuanglong, but not which hotel or street. We know you accepted a job from Captain Bao to hunt zhenniao, but the contract did not state your precise location. We did not send anyone to An Le or Shuanglong."

"That's thin," Li Ming said.

"Our contracts and records are stored on a blockchain-based document management system. The documents are permanent, traceable and impossible to be forged. Every alteration is recorded and timestamped. You can read them yourself."

"Show us."

Manager Qiu led the team to his workdesk. He called up multiple windows on his screen: Contracts, Personnel Records, Inventory.

"Here you go," Manager Qiu said.

As Cai Yan and Wong scrolled through the documents, the others watched Manager Qiu and Ms. Zhang.

"There is no reason for us to betray you," Manager Qiu said.

"Then you have nothing to hide," Wong-gor said.

A cynical part of Li Ming wanted to scoff at Manager Qiu's words. On the other hand, what did the beast lords or the Wanjianhui had to offer the Jianghu Association? The same Association that had supported them against the Ten Thousand Swords?

Then again, this was the Central Plains. Not the Zhongxia Republic.

"It doesn't benefit us one bit to turn against our own members," Manager Qiu said.

"Maybe not the Jianghu Association, but what about individual employees?" Li Ming asked.

"We can't betray your position if we had no knowledge of where you went."

"The paperwork doesn't cover phone calls, emails, face-to-face meetings…"

"I understand how you feel, but this is paranoia!"

"It's not paranoia if someone is out to kill you."

"Manager Qiu is right," Cai Yan said. "There's nothing in the records to suggest that the Association knew our location."

"On the other hand, a kill team could easily set up nearby and call in the beasts," Li Ming said.

"What do I have to say so you will believe me?" Manager Qiu asked.

"Now you know how we feel," Wong-gor said.

He spoke not with bitterness or recrimination, but with simple lightheartedness and a wide smile. Just like that, the energies of the room shifted and lightened.

"Take a look at the contracts awarded by the Yudu Military Forces," Sarantuya said. "Do you see anything unusual?"

"Beast hunts… beast hunts… and more beast hunts," Cai Yan said.

"What about contracts taken by the Wanjianhui?" Li Ming asked.

"Mostly beast hunts, with a few escort contracts."

"I could give you a copy of the records," Manager Qiu said.

"Please," Cai Yan said.

"We want everything," Li Ming said. "Contracts, personnel records, inventory—"

"I can't give you *all* our documents! There's confidential data in there."

"Give us what you have on the Wanjianhui and the militia," Cai Yan said.

Manager Qiu pursed his lips.

"Fine."

Cai Yan wired her headset to the computer. Manager Qiu's hands blurred across the keyboard, occasionally working the mouse.

"Done," Manager Qiu said. "This will leave a record on our blockchain, but under the circumstances I'd say it's perfectly acceptable."

"Thank you," Cai Yan said.

"No problem."

"I still don't believe you're innocent," Ghazan said.

"But you have no proof of guilt," Manager Qiu said.

"We will run our own investigation," Cai Yan said. "I trust that you will understand if we don't update you on our actions and locations."

"Of course," Manager Qiu said.

"Ms. Zhang, we are sorry to have dragged you into this. However, we may need your help in the future. If you're up for it, we would like to maintain our contract with you."

"You don't suspect me?" she asked.

"We didn't tell you about the Ba Mountains, only that we were going on a job. And you weren't at An Le. You're not on our suspect list."

For now.

Ms. Zhang nodded.

"I'll help however I can. Just call me and I'll be there."

"Thank you," Cai Yan said.

Chapter Twenty-One

The Depths of A Man's Heart

Once Li Ming had seen the crown jewel of the Central Plains, the city where anyone who worked hard enough to win a fortune. Now, standing at the window, locked in the Sancai Shi, Li Ming saw only a city built upon greed and schemes.

The logos of the Ten Corporations blazed bright in the dawn light. The emblem of the Merchant Association adorned advertisements by every major company in sight. The opulence of the skyscrapers before him whispered of backroom deals and black funds, of unbridled avarice and secret lusts. Here in the heart of the Capital of Fortune, the cries of the street hawkers were nowhere to be heard, the streets were kept scrupulously clean, the cars and people bedecked in the latest finery. But across a river, run-down tenements and worn-out shops stared at Li Ming, testifying to the absence of fortune everywhere else in Yudu.

Last night, Cai Yan booked the first hotel she could find that offered a two-bedroom suite. Cai Yan and Sarantuya occupied one room, the men had the other. Li Ming just about passed out the second he collapsed on the bed. Sheer force of habit pulled him back into consciousness a half hour before daybreak.

The classics advised standing still and breathing deep, doing nothing more than counting breaths. Try as he might, he couldn't focus. Li Ming's thoughts churned in his mind, coagulating into plans and possibilities, concepts and connections.

Even with the Five Fists, the Twelve Animals and the various forms, his mind wouldn't settle. He caught himself dreaming about imaginary actions and potential consequences instead of focusing on the here and now, on the union of the six internal and external harmonies. Often he had to pause and bring his mind back on track, or risk throwing his body out of balance and his qi with it. There was only one thing he could think of to bring himself back on track.

Li Ming drew his swordbreaker.

Everyone was asleep, or at least still in their rooms. Even Ghazan, for whom cultivation was a religion. Li Ming had heard none of the stomping that was the signature of shifangquan. Now was a fine time—maybe the *only* time—to practice the magic weapon style.

He enkindled the blade with qi, sending energy flowing down its length. As he flowed through the elements and forms, he shifted the qi from one element to the next, studying how each shift changed the properties of the weapon in ever so subtle ways. Metal augmented chops and swings, water lightened the blade and encouraged it to twist, wood favored the thrust, fire sent it rising, earth sank it back down with a heavy rotation.

One more swing, and the bedroom door opened.

Ghazan stepped out, his eyes bleary, his aura blazing hot.

"Training?" Ghazan asked.

"Yeah," Li Ming said.

He casually lowered the swordbreaker, dropping the point to the floor, and in that moment recalled the qi flowing within.

"It's been a while since you trained with a weapon."

"Didn't have time or space for it until now."

"You don't have short weapons?"

"Not for training."

"Me too."

"You up for empty hand work?"

Ghazan grinned.

"Always."

For the next five minutes, they exchanged blows across the length of the living and the dining room. Ghazan was a human battering ram, relentless driving forward, seeking to smash through Li Ming's defenses and strike his openings. Li Ming honed his evasions and counters and deceptions, trying to work around the Yue's attacks instead of opposing him directly.

It didn't always work.

The ruckus awoke the other cultivators. One by one they spilled out into the living room, watching the men trade blows. They offered neither encouragement nor criticism, just watching the exchange in silence. But when it was over, Wong-gor clapped. The women followed.

Li Ming wasn't sure why Wong-gor clapped. He knew he'd struck Ghazan at least six times. But for every strike he got in, Ghazan landed two or three more. It wasn't as terrible as his early days sparring with Ghazan, but there was still much room for improvement.

On the bright side, Ghazan had learned to pull his blows. Mostly.

Battered bones and muscles and nerves aching, Li Ming took a long shower. He stepped out to find the team ordering breakfast from room service. As they waited, Ghazan showered, Wong-gor and Sarantuya read the news, and Cai Yan set up her device at the dining room table.

Breakfast came in the form of a huge spread. Fruits, breads, eggs and ham, buns and dumplings, coffee and tea. Li Ming steered clear of everything that contained even a hint of spice. Cai Yan ate a bit of everything. Ghazan went full carnivore as always, while Sarantuya nibbled on buns along with Wong-gor. As they ate, they discussed their next step.

"The Wanjianhui and the Yudu military will learn we are here sooner or later," Li Ming said. "We must harden our defenses."

"I don't think they'll act against us in broad daylight," Wong-gor said. "They have to live by the local laws too."

"They could bring in cutouts. Or beasts," Cai Yan said.

"True. But the room and hallway are hardened, right?"

Last night, Li Ming had installed a heavy-duty wedge and alarm on the door, while Cai Yan reinforced the windows and doors with earth and mountain magic. Nothing short of a full-blown assault would breach the room.

"Yes," Li Ming and Cai Yan said as one.

"They might act against us on the streets," Ghazan said.

"Then we must be extra careful, and travel in groups wherever we go," Li Ming said.

"We need to recon the Wanjianhui headquarters. If we see a significant guard presence, street patrols, any indicators of an elevated alert status, it's a sign they know what we're up to," Cai Yan said.

"We've never been there before. It could easily be business as usual."

"Have you *ever* seen a legitimate biaoju being guarded in times of peace?" Wong-gor asked.

"A biaoju is a business entity," Cai Yan said. "In times of peace, it cannot afford to have men standing around, not working contracts or making money."

"At the very least, if you're planning on visiting them, it would be wise to know the baseline activity," Ghazan said.

"Exactly. Ms. Sarantuya, could you perform the recon?"

Sarantuya blinked.

"Me?"

"Yes. You're still a freelancer. You're not officially part of Dayong. Among everyone in this room, you're the least likely to be recognized by the Wanjianhui."

"Captain Bao saw me. Mr. Manager Qiu and Ms. Zhang met me too."

"We haven't introduced you to anyone at the Jianghu Association building. As Captain Bao is still in Shuanglong, the risk of recognition is reduced. It's not that there's no risk, but if the Wanjianhui pulls up our personnel files now, you won't be among them."

Sarantuya pursed her lips. "What do you need me to do?"

"Recon the area around the headquarters. With your smartglasses, take a video of the office and the surrounding area. Pay attention to entrances, exits, windows, security, and activity levels. We need to know what the area looks like at ground level."

"What if I'm spotted?"

"Break contact, get away, and contact us as soon as you can. But try not to start a fight if you don't have to."

"I'm not comfortable sending her to the enemy's doorstep alone," Wong-gor said. "If something goes wrong, it will go very quickly and very badly."

"Could you back her up?" Cai Yan asked.

"Pretend to be her boyfriend and walk the road with her?"

Sarantuya's voice frosted over.

"Most Yue women do not date foreign men."

"Wong Biaohang could hang back and follow Ms. Sarantuya from a distance, and keep an eye out for security or countersurveillance," Li Ming said.

Sarantuya nodded.

"Yes. I will pretend to be a tourist in the area, taking in the sights and sounds. It will give me an excuse to linger in the vicinity, look at shops and signboards, and see everything you need to see."

"That'll only work in a shopping or tourist area," Wong-gor said. "We need to do our research and adapt accordingly."

"Of course. Are you up to the task?"

Wong-gor smiled.

"I've spent my career blending into the background. They won't see me coming."

"Why not you recon and I guard you?"

"No offense, but you will stand out everywhere you go. Everyone needs a reason to be somewhere, and it will be harder for you to disappear than me. If you play the tourist, people will be less suspicious than if you aimlessly wander around. They might even be more forthcoming with information."

"That makes sense. I trust you'll be my shadow."

Wong-gor puffed up.

"You can count on me."

"What about the rest of you? What will you be doing?" Sarantuya asked.

"We'll go through the documentation Manager Qiu gave us," Cai Yan said. "There could be a clue in there."

"That sounds tedious," Wong-gor observed.

"Someone's got to do it," Li Ming said.

A strange smile played across Ghazan's face.

"When I came to the Central Plains, I didn't expect I would be inspecting paperwork."

"*Zhongren shicai huo yangao.*"

Ghazan frowned.

"I am not familiar with that *chengyu.*"

"It takes many people to gather firewood to build a huge fire. Likewise, a large project needs many hands to succeed."

"There's only five of us."

Wong-gor patted Ghazan's shoulder.

"Ni xinku lo."

As Dayong planned the recon job, the team polished off breakfast. The second Ghazan and Sarantuya left, Cai Yan turned to Li Ming and Wong-gor.

"Last night, Cai Yong sent me an email. I'll forward it to you."

Li Ming turned on his Raptor smartglasses. Moments later, his inbox chimed. As he read the subject header, his heart skipped a beat.

Artifact auction sales results

"Artifact auction?" Ghazan said. "Was this for the artifacts we recovered from the bunker?"

"Yes," Cai Yan said, trying and failing to hide her excitement.

The email was the last link in a long chain connecting the Jianghu Association, Cai Yong, Dayong's finance and accounting team, and Cai Yan. Li Ming realized he'd never seen the finance and accounting team before; they had to be remote workers. Cai Yong's own message was brief and to the point.

Please see attached report.

The report stretched over a hundred pages, breaking down every single item recovered from the site in exhaustive detail, as well as assessments and opinions from Society experts. There was so much detail, *too* much for any sane man to read in a short time. Instead he skipped to the final section, describing the auction proceeds.

A large number shouted at him.

He stared at it.

It stared back.

81783192 yuan.

He blinked again. Re-read the number.

The figure remained unchanging. 81783192 yuan.

He counted the digits in disbelief. One by one, the eight digits arranged themselves in his mind's eye.

"Eighty-one million, seven hundred and eighty-three thousand, one hundred and ninety-two yuan," Li Ming said out loud.

An unbelievable number. A number that existed in newspapers, in movies, in fiction, anywhere but in the real world. A number that was rightfully the province of governments and corporations. Surely this couldn't be his.

"We earned this much from the auction?" Li Ming asked.

"Actually... that's your share," Cai Yan said.

Li Ming blinked. Blinked again. And re-read the line by line breakdown.

She was right.

This was his share. Not Dayong's. Not the total earnings. *His.*

The world trembled. The foundations of Heaven and Earth crumbled, collapsed, compressed, becoming a super-dense singularity smashing together all things known and unknown. It dragged him into its center, breaking him down, crushing his entire being into a tiny cube smaller than an atom and heavier than a galaxy. At the point of maximum compression, the universe exploded outwards, reconstructing itself, the stars, the planets, the moon, every drop of water and every grain of dust, putting everything back in its place, yet somehow subtly rearranged into different configurations, reverting to their outward appearance yet changing their very substance to become something newer and stranger. Within that crucible he emerged, whole and intact, but his insides, his *soul*, permanently transmuted into something else, something he scarcely recognized.

He read the report once more. 81783192 yuan remained, fixed and unchanging, the North Star in a sky swirling with strange stars, both the engine of unfathomable change and the anchor that held him in place.

With money like that he... He didn't even have a frame of reference for it. Within those eight digits danced the promise of infinity and eternity. He could quit Dayong immediately, retire on the spot, go anywhere he wanted and do anything he pleased. He could buy out Fuyang and be the lord of his village, and still have enough money for his grandchildren.

He could become immortal.

"How are you feeling?" Cai Yan asked.

"I... I don't know how I should feel."

Ghazan grunted. "You're still in shock. It'll wear off after a while."

"Ghazan, you don't seem happy," she said.

His face soured.

"This is a lot of money, more money than I'd ever dreamed of. To earn it, all I had to do was to sell the history and heritage of my people."

"You could have objected to the auction."

A bevy of micro-expressions crossed his face. Disgust, regret, sadness. It was the first time Li Ming had seen Ghazan so conflicted before.

"The Yue Dynasty was the greatest empire of all time. Even today, modern science barely understands and imperfectly reproduces many of its wonders. The remnants of the Great Yue, confined to the Yue Homelands, are unable to recreate the glory of their ancestors. It falls to those who can do it. And they were willing to pay us a premium for the right to study the artifacts."

"But you feel like you dishonored your inheritance by selling them," Li Ming said.

Ghazan's lips compressed into a tight line.

"These artifacts are the treasures of my people. But we lack the capability to study them in the same detail as the scientists of the Zhongxia Republic. To rebuild... to one day understand the legacy and the glory of our forefathers, we must give them to... to those with the technical and scientific ability to understand them."

What about the scroll you took?

Li Ming almost gave voice to that thought. But Cai Yan was still in the room, and Li Ming suspected Ghazan would not react well if he said it out loud. He had to speak to Ghazan about it when they were alone.

"It must be a hard decision, but I think it was the right one," Cai Yan said. "The Jianghu Association sold the artifacts to research foundations and organizations specializing in Yue Dynasty relics. If anyone has the capability to study them, they do. In fact, they've already learned much from the bunker and the artifacts they've been allowed to examine."

"What did they discover?" Li Ming asked.

"Everything is infused with magic. The walls, floor, furniture, the gravity lifts, the power plant, everything was coated with a layer of qi. They think it's some kind of preservation magic. They've seen some relics coated with this same magic before, but never so many of them in the same place."

"That explains how everything still works after hundreds of years," Li Ming said.

Including the bioprinters. The source of the horrors deep within the bunker.

"These are among the most well-preserved Yue artifacts ever recovered. The magic itself is rare, and it's a wonder how it managed to remain stable after centuries. Brother complained to me about how the bids were too low," Cai Yan said.

"Too low?" Li Ming repeated. "But the money..."

"This isn't the most valuable find of Yue artifacts by far. Just among the most recent. The largest motherlodes were valued at billions of yuan."

"Billions," Li Ming stated stupidly.

The sounds came out of his mouth. His brain failed to grant them meaning.

"The bioprinters alone are priceless," Ghazan said. "The organization that studies them will re-sell them to the government at a hundred times the price of what they paid for it."

"Ah... *nai ge...* The government seized the most dangerous technologies. That includes the bioprinters. They paid us for them, but it's a pittance compared to the other artifacts we sold to the private sector. Brother says he wants to press the government for more money."

"I thought your government is very generous with taxpayers' money."

"Only when they pay the Ten Corporations and their lobbyists," Li Ming said.

Everyone laughed. Cai Yan was the first to sober up.

"It's a huge amount of money," she said.

"We earned every fen," Ghazan said.

"Yes. But..."

"But?" Li Ming prodded.

She clenched her fists. Bit her lip. And looked at the men.

"We don't have to worry about money. The expedition is in the black. We can leave the Central Plains any time we want."

You can leave Dayong anytime you *want,* Li Ming heard.

"Is this why you sent Sarantuya and Wong-gor out on recon?" Li Ming asked.

"Yes."

Money united people, money divided people. Such unthinkable sums of money would bring out a person's true nature. When around people you don't know, it might be wise not to summon what lay in the depths of a man's heart.

"I think the Wanjianhui and the beast lords—Captain Bao and his men—are up to something," Cai Yan said. "I don't know what it is, but I don't think we can leave them alone. I intend to focus our efforts on uncovering their plot. My share of the auction proceeds will go towards funding the investigation."

The men went quiet.

"If you wish to leave, I understand completely," Cai Yan continued. "I'll make arrangements for you to collect your pay back in Bao An."

The men glanced at each other.

Yue and Xia, dark and fair, men from opposite ends of the continent, but brothers of the spear and fist, brothers in blood and arms. They had bled and killed for each other, and though they might not always see eye to eye, Li Ming sensed the bond between them, a line of bright fire that transcended time and space. Wherever one went, the other would follow.

They sat there for a second longer, Ghazan looking at Li Ming with unaided eyes, Li Ming studying Ghazan's own through the dark lenses of his Raptor. The men went completely still, their qi condensing and concentrating and merging into a superfield that touched both souls.

At last, Ghazan spoke.

"I came here to hunt beasts. There are still many beasts to hunt, including beasts in human skin, so I will stay."

"Thank you," Cai Yan said. "Li Ming, what about you?"

Li Ming sensed himself standing at the precipice of the unknown. He had everything he needed to become immortal, a martial immortal. He could strike out on his own and become the youxia he said he would be. Before him lay a boundless expanse of immeasurable potential. He was free to shape his life however he wanted, and no one could stop him.

And yet...

The old fortuneteller was right. With hard work, Li Ming had earned a vast sum of money. Ghazan, too, had secured a fortune. But if he were right about that, would he not also be right about the suffering in store for them? About the suffering Li Ming wouldn't see coming?

If Ghazan had the power to overturn heaven and earth, and if he paired it with his qi eating magic, then hell awaited at the end of that road. Li Ming couldn't close his eyes to that.

Not only that, the Wanjianhui and its allies were still at large, scheming in the secret corners of the world. Li Ming couldn't walk away from it either.

The fortuneteller had said absolute freedom in the Way came from alignment with the Will of Heaven. What was the Will of Heaven? How should Li Ming act? What was the way to freedom for all?

In framing these questions, Li Ming constructed his answer.

"I'm staying," Li Ming said. "All the way to the end."

Color crept into Cai Yan's cheeks. Or was it just a trick of the light?

"Thanks."

"We're all in this together," Li Ming said.

Her lips arced into a small smile.

"That's right."

Ghazan loudly cleared his throat.

"The money is fine and all, but shall we return to our mission?"

Cai Yan held up a finger.

"Before we do, I have to ask: is this the first time you are handling such huge sums of money?"

"Yes," the men said at once.

"Then there's someone you need to speak to right now."

"Who?" Li Ming asked.

"Our financial adviser."

Chapter Twenty-Two

The Romance of the Jianghu

Li Ming was a dirt bun from a poor farming village. He knew little about high level finance, and had no experience handling such vast amounts of money. Father had drilled him incessantly on the need to save money and invest for the future. Savings he understood well, investments not at all.

Feng Haibin, Dayong's chief financial adviser, sought to correct that.

"Eighty-one million seven hundred and eighty thousand yuan sounds like a lot of money, but it can disappear very quickly if you're not careful. My job is to make sure that money grows instead of disappearing," he said.

On Cai Yan's scroll, Mr. Feng cut an earnest but intense image. His unblinking eyes burned behind a pair of frameless glasses, boring into Li Ming's own. A posed smile failed to soften the set of his cheeks and jaw. But his face was broad and open, and Cai Yan had vouched for him.

"After such a huge windfall, it is tempting to blow that money on luxury expenses," Mr. Feng continued. "Don't. You need this money to last a long time—for the rest of your life, even. You need to play it smart.

"I heard many biaohang follow the code of the Xia, and the code says you should disregard wealth. That kind of thinking is for a previous era. In this era, if you disregard wealth today, you will have to chase it tomorrow. You wouldn't want that kind of lifestyle. We need to preserve your wealth, then grow your wealth.

"My first piece of advice is simple: lock the money away in the bank. Do not touch it for at least three months. You may use it to clear your debts, *all* your debts, and purchase necessities, but that's all you should use it for."

"My sister's still in school and—"

"Worry about *your* debts first," Mr. Feng interrupted. "Do you have any?"

"No."

But he wondered if he should repay his parents for everything they'd done. They'd spent so much time, energy and money on him. It was only right, wasn't it?

"Excellent. You already have more money sense than most biaohang. Once you return to Bao An, we need to schedule a follow-up session to plan your financial strategy. Right now, I want to get a sense of your financial needs and expectations. Do you have any pending major expenses?"

"I'm in the middle of an expedition. It could get... intense. I was thinking of getting more supplies."

Mr. Feng's face grew stern.

"Do you *really* need them? I want you to think carefully about this question. Are you buying what you need? Or just buying new toys?"

Anger flared in Li Ming's heart.

"Throughout this expedition, we've fought bashe, hanba, shanxiao and zhenniao. We're hunting the biggest game in the Central Plains, and the job isn't anywhere near over. I've got no time to think about toys."

"Then you're only buying what you need. Good. I want you to listen carefully.

"As a biaohang, your greatest expense lies in three things: equipment, supplements, and medical treatment. The last is especially important if you choose to pursue an immortality treatment regimen.

"While bronze-grade gear and supplies aren't that expensive, now that you have so much money, if you rank up the costs will increase dramatically. Every year, Dayong spends millions of yuan on gear alone. The longer you stay in the business, the more expensive *everything* will be. Eighty-one million yuan will disappear faster than you know it. Not only that, you also need to beat the inflation rate, the tax collector, and unforeseen crises.

"How much do you need for supplies?"

"I don't know yet."

"Don't go overboard. Set yourself a budget. Not more than one million yuan, total. Spend it only on what you need, not what you want. What you want can wait for another three months.

"Do you plan on giving on charity?"

Li Ming blinked. That question had come out of the blue.

"*En...* Yes."

"Good. The government will levy a windfall tax of fifteen percent on the auction proceeds, above and beyond your individual taxes. Charitable donations will offset your total tax burden."

Taxes. He hadn't thought about them. Mr. Feng might be intense, but he had a point.

"After debts, expenses, taxes and charitable donations, what you have left is your capital," Mr. Feng said. "I want you to maximize this however you can. Reduce unnecessary expenses wherever possible. The more money you start with, the more you will create. The magic of compound interest should never be underestimated.

"How would you describe your investment personality and risk appetite?"

"I don't know. I haven't thought about investments before."

Mr. Feng shook his head.

"Now is a fine time to think about it. Since you are young, you should focus on wealth creation. This is *especially* important since you are a biaohang. It is an extremely high risk profession, with the threat of death and disfigurement around the corner. If you die, your wealth goes to your next of kin. But if you are crippled, if you can't work anymore, you need to find a way to sustain yourself and your family. It may not be pleasant to think about, but better to be prepared now than to be caught off-guard if the worst happens.

"Life insurance is an excellent instrument for growing wealth, if you know how to use it properly. Being a biaohang is a high-risk job, as risky as being an athlete, a policeman or a soldier. Your current insurance plan, while affordable, only covers the absolute minimum for a newcomer to the jianghu. As you level up and take on riskier assignments, your premiums will increase dramatically.

"I can help you find a life insurance plan that suits your needs and lifestyle. While you will have to pay a much higher premium, after ten, twenty, thirty years or more, you can cash out the policy when it matures. It is an easy and tax-free method of growing your wealth. In fact, super-rich biaohang buy customized high-priced insurance policies for this reason. And if something happens to you, you and your family will be taken care of.

"After life insurance comes other investment instruments. Gold and precious metals is the safe bet. It retains value over decades and centuries, but that also means gains are low and slow. You can invest in real estate, but that will be subject to real estate speculation and taxes. Other options involve securities, bonds, commodities, cryptocurrencies. The higher the volatility, the greater the risk—but also the greater the potential gains.

"Are you familiar with any of these options?"

"My father invests in farmland back home. He acts as a landlord and helps the farmers sell their goods elsewhere. He talks a lot about the business of investing and farming."

"Investing in farmland is a strong way to grow your income, if you choose the right properties and if you have the right business plan. It's not something I personally specialize in, but you could talk to your father and see how he made it work for him."

"I will."

Just like that, Li Ming had more to discuss with his father than just martial arts.

"What about the other options I've mentioned? Do you know anything else about them?" Mr. Feng asked.

"No. As I said, investments never crossed my mind."

"They should. It's going to take an awfully long time for me to walk you through everything, and I'm sure you have a lot of work to do. When you return to Bao An, we can talk about this in more detail. But for the time being, there are three things I'd like you to do.

"First, sort out all your debts and large expenses. *Necessary* expenses, not luxury items. Spend what you need to spend, and not one fen more.

"Second, open a new bank account for your windfall. Keep it separate from all your other accounts, then leave it alone. When we meet again, we can talk about how much should go into a savings account, how much should go to charity, how much we will invest, and so on.

"Lastly, think about investment options in your spare time. Eighty-one million yuan really isn't a lot when measured against your life, and the lives of those who come after you. If you want to become an immortal, eight-one million is *nothing*. Think about what kind of investor you are and your risk appetite, but prioritize growing wealth."

In the wuxia stories of Li Ming's childhood, heroes never had to concern themselves with money. Some took on dirty, dangerous and exciting jobs for a pittance, turning their noses up at the promise of wealth, pursuing instead higher and finer goals. Others had a seemingly inexhaustible supply of money, able to conjure it out of thin air whenever they needed it. Somehow Li Ming had found himself in a third category, in possession of a large amount of cash—but not infinite.

In the furnace of the real world, the romance of the jianghu always melted away.

On the other hand, he wasn't living in the jianghu of a fictitious golden age, an age of swords and emperors and gods. He swam within the rivers and lakes of this world, this age of Five States and Ten Corporations. If he did not align himself with the ways of this age, it would crush him.

He hadn't had to think about it much, but now he had to turn his thoughts to money. To wealth. To securing everything that wealth could bring him. Only then could he truly be free to pursue the Way.

But first, he had a job to do.

P aper was truth.

It was the foundation of the Xia civilization, and every nation descended from it. Paper recorded facts and figures, news and rumors, rumors and hearsay. Paper tracked the flows of men, money, goods. Paper placed everything in time and space, showing where everything had come from, where it was now, where it would go. Without paper there could be no civilization.

Blockchain built upon paper. Paper could be burned, altered, misplaced, or simply rendered illegible with the passage of years. A blockchain document management system retained the truth of paper and eliminated its flaws. Once recorded on the blockchain, a record could not be altered, copied, moved, deleted, not without leaving a trace. Every node within the blockchain network retained a copy of every version of every document, tracking changes over time, an unbreakable digital lineage stretching to the original ancestral documents. Should the network be disrupted, the blockchain and its records could be reconstituted from a single node. With tags, names, keywords and search engines, losing a record was impossible, finding one as simple as keying in the right search terms.

Blockchain wasn't just truth. Blockchain was eternal, as close to eternal as anything made by man could ever hope to achieve in this ever-changing cosmos.

Their consultations complete, Ghazan and Li Ming joined Cai Yan in examining the Jianghu Association's records. They studied everything. Everything that had to do with the Yudu military and the Ten Thousand Swords Society, every contract, email, note, missive, report, bounty, every interaction minor and major captured within the databases of the Jianghu Association's Yudu branch office.

With this information, they built up a picture of both groups. They plotted their movements over time, identified clients and patrons, trends and specialties. Captain Bao began issuing contracts three years ago, when he was merely a lowly lieutenant, and every contract he awarded was for hunting beasts. The Wanjianhui snatched up a healthy percentage of those in the early days, between one in three to one in two, but in the past two months that number dropped off to one in five.

But it was not for want of manpower or an excess of work. The Wanjianhui enjoyed steady growth over the years, marking a net growth of twelve biaohang in three years, for a total of fifty-two active biaohang, not including upper management. A year after Bao began issuing contracts, Chen Bingrong was appointed as the chief operations officer, and began leading teams in the field. Chen's signature appeared on almost every Wanjianhui contract, especially those Bao awarded.

Over the past six months, shortly after the events at the bunker, the Wanjianhui shifted its focus to direct contracts. Contracts offered by villages, towns, corporations, and private individuals directly to the Wanjianhui. It stayed off the open market, keeping its name out of the news. When the beast surge began, it dropped off the radar completely. It picked up only a handful of contracts, all of them from towns besieged by beasts, the latest being Shuanglong.

"There are too few contracts to keep a business as high-end as the Wanjianhui in the black," Cai Yan said. "With the gear and airships they've got, they'll need to bring in millions of yuan a month. The contracts aren't worth even a tenth of that."

"Maybe they have other sources of income," Li Ming suggested.

"Can they execute contracts without the Jianghu Association's knowledge?" Ghazan asked.

"Yes. The Jianghu Association acts like a broker and holds funds in escrow. But there is nothing stopping clients from contracting directly with the Wanjianhui."

"And the only records of such contracts would be with the client and the Wanjianhui," Li Ming said.

Cai Yan sighed.

"Yes."

The contracts revealed nothing more unusual than the Ten Thousand Swords Society doing too little work to stay profitable, and that could be easily explained away by direct contracts. The blockchain might be the truth, but it only recorded what truth was entered into the system. Everything outside it remained unknown.

The trio turned to movement. The movement of the militia and the Wanjianhui over time. Cai Yan summoned a map of the Central Plains on her screens and painstakingly marked the location of every contract over the past year. At the end of her labors, she saw random clusters of color-coded dots all over the region, concentrated in areas of high beast activity. Exactly what an ordinary biaoju would do.

Somewhere in the chaos of colors, there was a pattern. But Li Ming couldn't see it.

Wong-gor and Sarantuya returned at lunchtime. Over a room service meal, they reviewed Sarantuya's footage. Li Ming saw a perfectly ordinary pedestrian street, a hutong, filled with pedestrians and bikes and low-rise buildings that combined shops and homes into a single establishment. Midway down the hutong, a smaller, narrower, alley branched off the main road, its gate wide open. Extravagantly decorated doors revealed siheyuan, traditional courtyard houses. The signboard on the third house on the left carried three words, gold painted against black.

Wanjianhui.

Tall spikes tipped the head-high walls. A black camera dome watched the door. The intercom sported a security lens.

But there were no sign of guards, dogs, or any other physical security measures.

The rest of the video revealed the geography of the immediate area, and nothing more about the Ten Thousand Swords Society.

"Did you sense anyone inside the siheyuan?" Li Ming asked.

"No," Sarantuya said. "At least, I don't think so."

"It doesn't mean no one is home, only that she didn't sense anyone," Wong-gor added.

The team turned their attention again to the issue of paperwork, of attempting to divine meaning from paperwork. They studied the map and the contracts, they hunted fruitlessly for news on the Net, they threw about increasingly ludicrous suggestions.

"Why don't we just raid the Wanjianhui headquarters?" Ghazan suggested.

"Without evidence, without a warrant, without permission from the local authorities? We'll be arrested and thrown into jail for a long time. Or just shot on the spot," Wong-gor said.

"What about Captain Bao? We could interrogate him and find out what's really going on," Sarantuya said.

"If we can find him. If the military won't stop us," Cai Yan said.

"He's our prime suspect. Why *shouldn't* we go after him?"

"We have to, at some point. But I want to confront him with something more substantial than accusations and suspicions. We need leverage, evidence, something he can't deny or lie his way out of."

"And if we interrogate him, the opposition might escalate their plans," Wong-gor added.

As the team debated, Li Ming built a portrait of his enemy.

Following his participation at the Battle of Shuanglong, Chen Bingrong now ranked 8673 on the Jianghu leaderboards. An incredible achievement by any measure, marking him as among the top ten percent of all cultivators in the jianghu. A gold ranker and the chief operations officer of his biaoju, he had achieved heights most cultivators only ever dreamed of.

But that was all the publicly-available information the Society maintained on him. Awards, history, skills, everything that defined a martial cultivator was missing from his profile. Save for one word.

Immortal.

Of Captain Bao there was precisely nothing. He was not part of the Jianghu Association. He had no significant online presence to speak of. He was a ghost in a world of men. And that marked him as someone with something to hide.

Sarantuya's voice cut through Li Ming's musings.

"Why don't we look at where everybody *else* is going?"

The team went back to work, checking the news and consulting the Society's job boards. The beast surge had shifted to Shuanglong, and where the beasts went, biaoju followed. The pool of available contracts in Yudu slowed to a trickle, while those in Shuanglong boomed. Every major biaoju of the Central Plains had shifted their operations to Shuanglong, and many overseas ones too.

"I think we're the only gold-ranked biaoju still operational in Yudu," Cai Yan said. "All the others are taking jobs in the Shuanglong area."

"I bet the beast lords are stirring up beasts in Shuanglong," Li Ming said.

"No bets," Ghazan said.

"Assuming the beast lords are responsible for the beast surge—and we don't have evidence of that—then they aim to draw biaoju away from Yudu," Wong said.

"Which leaves the Wanjianhui," Sarantuya said.

"And us," Cai Yan finished.

"What could the Wanjianhui be plotting that requires every other biaoju to leave Yudu?" Wong asked.

"A beast invasion, like Shuanglong," Li Ming said.

"Doesn't make sense. Why destroy their own city?" Cai Yan asked.

"Maybe a coup?" Wong asked.

"A coup needs leaders. Figures known to the public. The Wanjianhui doesn't have any," Ghazan said.

"But by swooping down into Shuanglong, they increased their public standing," Li Ming said.

"You think they're planning on doing something similar?"

"It doesn't make sense," Cai Yan said again. "This is a high-risk and resource-intensive move. They wouldn't risk so much just to pull off a giant publicity stunt."

"They wouldn't need to target biaoju either, but they went after us," Li Ming said.

"Revenge?" Ghazan suggested.

"That could be part of it, but why suck in the rest of the Central Plains jianghu into this?"

"I think there's something going on in Yudu, either now or very soon," Cai Yan said. "To make use of that event, they must look like heroes, or else they're planning to use the situation to their advantage. They need the other biaoju out of the way to make it happen."

"We should call Ms. Zhang and ask her to help us dig up information on upcoming events in Yudu," Wong-gor said. "Especially low-profile events that aren't covered in the news."

A cold thought struck Li Ming.

"Whatever that event is, I think it's going to happen soon. The Wanjianhui and the beast lords have been steadily escalating. They tried to kill us twice already. Now that most of the Yudu biaoju have relocated to Shuanglong, it's the perfect time for them to execute," Li Ming said.

"Agreed. We'll ask Ms. Zhang to look for events occurring in the next five to ten days," Cai Yan replied.

"Less," Sarantuya said. "The beast surge will not last forever. I would say one to three days."

"I'll make the call," Cai Yan said.

"We don't have much time to prepare," Li Ming said. "I'm going on a supply run."

"Me too. I'm low on ammo," Wong-gor said.

"We are *all* going," Ghazan declared.

"I'm not," Cai Yan said.

"Working overtime?" Li Ming asked.

She shifted uncomfortably in her seat.

"I have an appointment at an immortality clinic."

She was the only immortal among the team. Her beauty and grace came from a strict regimen of training, supplements, and rejuvenation treatments. She was what any woman could become, if only she had the time and money for it.

A single rejuvenation treatment would cure most chronic illnesses. Annual treatments would slow down the aging process, augment the immune system, and promote graceful aging. A monthly regimen would reverse the hands of time, revitalize the body from the inside out, and restore the patient to the flower of youth. Weekly rejuvenations would freeze someone in time and grant biological immortality. For as long as she kept to the schedule.

No one in the Li Family had achieved immortality. Not even Li Ming's father, who had chosen to spend his wealth on his hometown instead of himself. But now, with eighty-one million yuan at his disposal, Li Ming could become immortal too.

But not today.

Immortality was nice to have, but not a necessity. Not now. He'd think about it after his next consult with Feng. Not before.

"I'll be back late," she continued. "Don't wait for me. We'll meet up back in the room."

"Just remember: we still have a job to do," Ghazan said.

Chapter Twenty-Three

World of Wealth

The Bridge of the Martial Immortal was quieter than Li Ming had remembered it. The tourists and the civilians were still out in force, strolling along the river and the promenade, taking in the sights and sounds, patronizing the many craft stores in the vicinity. But the martial cultivators, the men and women this street was dedicated to, were mostly gone. The weapon stores were peaceful, the supplement shops empty.

Inside the Three Worlds Emporium, Li Ming counted maybe two dozen people, of whom half were staff. The employees gazed eagerly at the Dayong team as they entered, practically salivating over the prospects of landing a sale. All their favorite customers had gone to Shuanglong, leaving only a trickle of shoppers and three floors' worth of inventory.

Strolling among the selections, Li Ming felt... light. Open. Free. He could pick and choose anything he wanted without having to look at the price tag. Hell, he could probably buy up everything in sight if he pleased. Cost was no longer a concern. The only thing that mattered was quality and fit for purpose.

Was this what financial freedom felt like? The ability to buy what he needed without a care in the world? To swipe a card, sign a check, blink at a bar code, and know immediately that he would get what he wanted?

If so, he could get used to this.

Still, Feng's advice rang in his head. One million yuan for gear and supplies. No more. Li Ming knew he could be flexible if he needed to, but that was just burning the future for the present. The rich could buy anything they wanted in the world, but the wealthy held on to their wealth, grew their wealth, and so continued to remain wealthy.

Li Ming strode up the escalator and strode between the shelves, making his way to the infinity gun selection. The Viper was still there, still in the same place he had left it, as though it had remained untouched, waiting for his return. When he showed his biaohang card, the counter staff was only too eager to allow him to handle it.

The huge handgun melted perfectly into his grip. The moment he wrapped his fingers around it, the textured handle gripped him right back, locking his hand into place. A dot-in-circle reticle glowed a reassuring red in the window of the reflex sight. He cycled through the settings, brightening and dimming it, switching between different kinds of reticles. A traditional crosshair, a dot within a circle within a crosshair, a small dot.

The employee launched into an enthusiastic spiel about the weapon's capabilities, rattled off its spec sheet, assured him that it was ideal for hunting dangerous beasts. Li Ming listened with half a ear, his attention focused on the weapon. On what he could do with it.

His mind returned to the paddy fields of An Le. To the shanxiao leaping through the air. The bolt from the Hellion disintegrated long before it came close to the beast. With the Viper, he could slay the shanxiao long before it hit the ground.

And with an overheat capacity of fifty shots, he could burn down a shielded cultivator at long range.

Li Ming asked for the Force Multiplier kit. The employee eagerly removed it from the display, dropped the Viper in place, and locked the pins in place. Mouth running like a river, the employee demonstrated and expounded on its capabilities. Li Ming filtered out the hyperbole, focusing on the practical and the tactical.

At last, the employee handed over the weapon. Li Ming faced an empty wall, weapon held in both hands, and relaxed.

And blurred.

And now the Viper was up in the ready, red dot burning into the wall, just like that.

It was *fast*. Faster than an infinity gun, easier to handle and manipulate. The fire selector and mode wheel was within easy reach of his master hand, leaving his other hand free to drive the gun to the target. He folded, unfolded, extended and retracted the telescoping stock, then adjusted the cheekpiece.

It was excellent. But not perfect.

He went on a treasure hunt. Sling, backup iron sights, light-laser combo, upgraded internal modules, a drop-leg holster that spanned the length of his thigh. Everything he was lawfully allowed to buy, everything that would add to the weapon's capabilities, he bought. The employee gleefully racked up the total, tallying up the cost and drawing up the upgraded spec sheet.

Range: 120 chi (+20)

Sustained rate of fire: 12 shots / second (+4)

Maximum rate of fire: 20 shots / second (+5)

Overheat capacity: 60 shots (+10)

Overheat cooldown time: 25 seconds (-10)

The bill came to 223617 yuan. There was a time Li Ming would have balked at the price. Even now, his heart quaked at the sight of the figures. But with a deep breath and a series of eyeblinks, he banished the emotions and paid the bill.

Was this what it was like to have money?

His shopping spree had only begun. On the top floor, he hunted among the reality shapers on offer, looking for shapers with the best stats.

Speed was everything to him. If he needed magic, he needed it *now*, and he might need a follow-up shot in an instant. Power came second. It did no good to overkill a single threat if the shaper took too long to address his buddies. Price was... not something he needed to care about anymore.

A staff member offered to help. Li Ming described his requirements. She sped off, and seconds later returned with a Five Mountains Type 18.

Qi saturation point: 1000 points

Qi recharge rate: 450 points / second

Discharge time: 0.03 seconds

Crystal optimization: Five Elements (+100 qi saturation, +50 recharge rate, -0.015 discharge time)

It wasn't the most powerful. It wasn't the fastest to recharge. But it fired the fastest, and it was designed for use with the five elements crystals. Best of all, he could trade in his old Type 12 for a discount. He placed it in his shopping cart without a second glance.

A shaper was useless without a crystal, of course. He selected a pair of 2000-point five element crystals, the most powerful crystals a copper-ranked cultivator could buy. And discovered, to his pleasure, he could throw in his old crystals for a discount too.

Between the trade-ins and his biaohang discount, the store charged a mere 21872 yuan. He paid for them without hesitation, and paused.

'Mere'. He wondered where that word came from. Was he diving too hard and too fast into this strange new world of wealth?

He wandered among the supplements and sundries section. He could buy anything he wanted, including the high-end pills and potions. If he really wanted to, he could book a consultation with an immortality clinic. Every bottle and every packet promised a shining future, a future of eternal youth, vitality and strength.

But this time, he bought nothing.

Every cultivator had different needs and physiques. If he downed a random collection of pills and potions, the effects wouldn't be as pronounced as a targeted regimen. It might even unbalance his qi circuits. He made a note to book a consultation with a specialist when he returned from the Central Plains.

There were few things the Emporium didn't, wouldn't, *couldn't* stock. Explosives were chief among them. Dayong hadn't replaced the mines they had expended on the bashe. Purchasing explosive munitions needed special paperwork and permits, and a lengthy processing time, even in the Central Plains. Fortunately, the team still had plenty of explosives and grenades on hand.

The Emporium offered many other goods. War belt, plate carrier, armor, soft goods, hard goods, camping supplies, everything a martial cultivator needed to hunt the beasts of the earth and sky. But all these he could do without.

The one thing he really needed was the Belt Bag. A man-portable interspatial storage machine. It was worth its weight in gold and then some. Dayong's bags were rented from an exclusive supply company in Dayong. When he returned, he could buy a brand new Belt Bag. Or another bag with a larger capacity.

Although, last he remembered, Belt Bag was priced as much as a studio apartment. Not that he couldn't afford it, just that it exceeded the million-yuan budget. And anyway, it wasn't urgent now. He made another note to follow up on it after the expedition.

Li Ming stepped out the main entrance to find the others waiting for him. Wong-gor wore an amused expression on his face.

"Our shopping prince returns in triumph!"

Li Ming couldn't help but laugh.

"I had more stuff to buy than you guys."

"We're still on the clock," Ghazan said.

"Would you rush a gear purchase?"

"Only if I knew what I needed."

"Ghazan is right," Sarantuya said. "We don't have time to waste. I want to go back and look through the data again."

"Me too," Wong-gor said. "I need to do some more research on the military and the Wanjianhui."

"I am going to see the Wanjianhui's headquarters with my own eyes," Ghazan said.

"They may know your face," Li Ming said.

"I'll be careful." Ghazan grinned like a shark. "Besides, I am a biaohang, just like them. They can't do anything to me on the street."

"They may step up their schedule if they see you," Wong-gor said.

"Then they are giving us a reason to strike at them."

"You guys go on ahead. I need to test my new gear," Li Ming said.

"Don't take too long," Wong-gor said. "We have to be ready to go at a moment's notice."

The quartet went their separate ways. Li Ming's map claimed the nearest shooting range was just three blocks away, behind the Bridge of Martial Immortals. His Raptor drew a solid red line over the road, showing him the way in augmented reality.

Li Ming walked the red route, strolling down the length of the street. The swordbreaker at his hip and the Belt Bag slung over his shoulder signaled his status to the world. Passers-by who recognized his gear and understood what it meant gave him a wide berth. Shopkeepers called out to him, yelling out special prices and promotions. Prices became numbers, empty of meaning; Li Ming saw only goods and what he could do with goods.

Once again, the certainty that he could buy everything in sight gripped him. That feeling emanated outwards from his heart, altering his body from the inside out. His back straightened, his head lifted, his limbs floated freely through space. His eyes flickered from left to right, looking down at street carts and signboards and vendors and people. He had no name for this feeling, but it felt... right.

At the end of the street, he made a left turn. Just like that, the shopping area ended. Money and color and goodwill fled the world. The flagstone path turned to a cracked asphalt road. Grimy high-rise apartments rose from concrete plots to carve out neat blocks and orderly grids. Street-level shops carried commonplace brands and no-name products, catering to the everyday needs of ordinary people. Every building in sight was painted the same tired shade of pale yellow, differentiated only by the huge block numbers painted on their sides.

Here the real Yudu. The Yudu that never made it to guidebooks, websites, and popular entertainment. The Yudu for everyone who wasn't an immortal, a cultivator, a white collar, for people whose luck had banished them to the edges of the Capital of Fortune.

The sidewalks were narrow, the roads wide. The few pedestrians stared nakedly at him, as if unable to believe that such an exalted personage would walk these streets. Shopkeepers stayed within their establishments, unwilling to poke their heads out. Gone was the warmth and respect he had enjoyed just a street away.

He was in the wrong part of town to be displaying his status so openly.

He picked up the pace. He was sure he could handle himself, but no sense sticking around longer than he had to. People stared at him, eying him like a deer that had wandered among a pack of wolves. He held himself erect, projecting his qi field in every direction, hands close to his hips, head on a swivel. He kept his gaze soft and wide, watching everyone, challenging no one, without shrinking away from hard stares.

Eyes burned into his back. Eyes rapidly approaching his position. Li Ming looked over his shoulder.

Halfway down the street, a young man stuttered in mid-swagger, his gaze locked on Li Ming's. Spinning around to face him, Li Ming registered a white shirt, black leather jacket, blue jeans, cheap black sneakers, cheaper smartglasses.

And a nose broken in many places.

"We meet again," Li Ming said.

"I knew it was you," Broken Nose said.

"We're a long way from the Bridge of Martial Immortals."

"You are a long way from home."

"I go where the work is. We're both from the jianghu, you should know how it works."

"Foreigners like you take all the work."

Li Ming spread out his hands.

"Luckily for you, my team and I aren't taking any contracts right now. You want work, now is your chance."

Broken Nose snorted and kept on walking.

"So long as outsiders like you are still around, you're snatching our rice bowls."

Anger twitched through Li Ming's heart.

"We took open contracts on the Jianghu Association's job boards, just like everybody else. You want a job, you can find plenty on the board. I have other things to do."

Broken Nose spat, taking another step forward, his eyes sweeping side to side.

"Foreigners like you, you take on all the high value contracts and leave us with the dregs."

"I started working 'dregs' too and worked my way up. You can do the same and build yourself an iron rice bowl."

Li Ming's words stretched out, his vowels elongated, slipping into his countryside accent.

"There's one more thing," Broken Nose said.

"Which is?"

"You cheated the last time."

Li Ming wagged his right index finger, sneaking his left hand to his pommel.

"I never accepted the match. You tried to fight me anyway."

"I demand a rematch."

"I refuse."

Broken Nose glanced at a spot behind Li Ming's left, then to the right. What was he looking at?

"You are a member of the jianghu. Have you no pride?" Broken Nose demanded.

"I don't fight when I don't need to."

Li Ming stepped to his right and swiveled counterclockwise, turning to look behind him. On the other side of the street, a man with a big mole hustled across the road. Two arm's lengths away, another man with a set of crooked lips strode towards Li Ming.

Li Ming's blood ran hot. He'd allowed Broken Nose to distract him, to pin him in place while his buddies moved in from behind. He should have crushed them back at the bridge. He had to end this. Now.

"So much for honor," Li Ming said.

"You cheated first," Broken Nose said. "You—"

Li Ming lunged.

Leaping off the ground, hands forming hooks, he closed in on Broken Nose. Broken Nose stepped back, sinking into his guard. Li Ming formed a spear hand and jabbed at his eyes. Broken Nose leaned back, voiding Li Ming's fingers, parrying with one hand, then rocketed his right fist towards Li Ming.

Li Ming vanished.

Flowing with the energy of the parry, Li Ming twirled through a clockwise spiral, raising his elbow to the vertical, shielding his head even as he advanced on Broken Nose. The fist shot past Li Ming's head, his elbow clipped Broken Nose's face. As Broken Nose staggered back, Li Ming swiftly stepped out, gaining Broken Nose's back.

And jumped back.

Broken Nose spun around. Big Mole brushed past him, rushing Li Ming. Crooked Lips picked up the pace, sprinting towards him.

Li Ming raised his hands, bent his knees and gathered his qi, taking up the three powers stance. He reached for the qi dormant in his shapers, flashing it to fire—

No. Not fire. They appeared unarmed. Some things were too much, even for the jianghu.

Instead, he erupted.

Twin palms blasted forth. Wood qi erupted from his shapers, an invisible shockwave of pure force howling from his hands, bowling Broken Nose and Big Mole over.

Crooked Lips stopped and gaped.

Li Ming smoothly drew his swordbreaker, lifting it from his scabbard, drawing it through a clean arc, bringing the handle to his right hip, taking it in both hands, tip pointed at the challenger.

Crooked Lips shook off the stupor. Yelling a word, he raised both hands.

Li Ming punched the swordbreaker out and away from him, holding the blade perfectly upright, sending metal qi cracking down the length of the weapon. Steely gray energies sheathed the blade, becoming a glittery wedge, a sharply-angled shield aimed at the hostile cultivator.

A huge bolt of golden light blasted from Crooked Lips' shapers. The bolt struck the apex of the wedge. The swordbreaker quivered in Li Ming's hands, splitting the spell in twain. Hot, bright energies roared past Li Ming's ears, drowning out the world in light and fury.

"What the devil?" Crooked Lips exclaimed.

Li Ming slashed.

The wedge leapt off the swordbreaker. Crooked Lips covered his face with his forearms, too little, too late. The heavy metal bar blasted into and through him, blowing him down.

Bone cracked loudly in the street. Crooked Lips rolled up into the fetal position, shrieking in pain, his shattered arms curled up beneath him.

Broken Nose and his buddy were back on their feet, surging towards him. Big Mole, the closer of the two, reached under his jacket and pulled out a—

Li Ming leapt and swung.

Steel crunched into bone. The handgun fell away. Big Mole cried out, gripping his broken hand. Li Ming turned around and swung for his head—

No. He was unarmed.

Li Ming changed the angle at the last moment. The heavy swordbreaker fell like thunder, splitting Big Mole's collarbone, destroying his balance, driving him down to the sidewalk.

Li Ming looked for the Broken Nose—

A heavy weight crashed into his side, taking him off his feet. A qi shockwave exploded through him, disrupting muscles and nerves, popping his fingers open. His swordbreaker tumbled from a suddenly-open palm. Powerful arms wrapped around his waist, taking him down, down, down to the hard asphalt.

Li Ming twisted at the last moment, taking the fall on his shoulder. Broken Nose pinned him down with his body weight, his qi hot and bright and powerful, fist rising up to pound him. With a thunderous roar, Li Ming torqued around, swinging a hammerfist, concentrating his qi in his hand.

The blow caught the man in the temple. Broken Nose recoiled away. Li Ming jerked his hips sharply, arching his back, bucking like a wild horse. Unbalanced, Broken Nose fell off. Li Ming scrabbled aside, arms and legs forming a bone shield, and picked himself back up.

In a flash, Broken Nose got up too, then leapt forward with a long-range jab. Li Ming rolled his shoulder away, the fist flashing past his eyes, then flowed back around and impaled his belly with his fist. Flesh hardened, qi erupted, and Li Ming's blow stopped cold.

Iron Shirt gongfu.

Broken Nose swiveled away, hands rising to the guard. Li Ming chased him, probing high, probing low. Stepping to the right, Li Ming's left forearm found his enemy's, and Li Ming spun into a low line hook. The rider dropped his elbow, covering his side. Li Ming seized his wrist, wrenched him off-balance, and blasted a splitting palm into his shoulder.

Concentrated qi reinforced his arm. But the complex force vector, the laws of physics, and Li Ming's own qi overpowered the Iron Shirt. With a sickening pop, Broken Nose's arm dislocated. Li Ming maintained the momentum, pulling him down, releasing him at the point of no return.

Broken Nose smashed facedown onto the road. Li Ming stomped his kidney, driving his bodyweight down into the vulnerable viscera, eliciting a piercing cry of agony.

Li Ming turned around, looking for his swordbreaker. It lay by a lamp post. He held the weapon up in both hands, still scanning. All three men were down, offering no further resistance, clutching their broken bones.

Fury coursed through him. How dare they attack him in broad daylight! This wasn't a match, it was a revenge attack! They could have *killed* him! He should have—

He exhaled.

And scanned.

A car stopped in the middle of a road. A middle-aged woman stood by it, cursing at him. Other cars rolled past, speeding through the red lights. Pedestrians stared at the sight, capturing the scene on their devices.

Li Ming spat an oath.

Sheathed the swordbreaker.

Awoke his Raptor.

And called the police.

Chapter Twenty-Four

Consequence

Every punch carried a consequence. In the Zhongxia Republic, the cops would launch an investigation, call in a prosecutor, notify the media and the Jianghu Association, and determine if they had to press charges against the participants.

Here, the cops rewarded Li Ming.

"Fifteen thousand yuan," Superintendent Wen said, all smiles and good cheer.

Words tried to form in his mouth. Only one emerged as coherent sound.

"Ah?"

"The men you brought in were wanted for harassment, assault and robbery. They preyed on cultivators entering and leaving the Bridge of Martial Immortals. The local shopkeepers offered a fifteen thousand yuan reward for their capture."

"Weren't they biaohang?"

"Not at all. They were freelancers. They floated at the edges of the jianghu, taking on odd jobs for martial cultivators who weren't too scrupulous about who they hired, occasionally targeting other cultivators they thought were easy prey. Today, they made a mistake."

"I never heard of shopkeepers offering a reward to arrest criminals before."

"You're not from around here?"

"I came from Zhongxia. Only the police issue bounties for capturing bandits, and only rarely these days."

"Ah. In Yudu, we like to encourage ground-up initiatives like this. It gives biaohang like yourself an extra incentive to keep the streets safe. Thank you for your hard work."

He'd beat up three men badly, sent them to hospital, and the people *paid* him for it? Unbelievable.

There'd been an investigation, of course, but it was a cursory one. Once the police had gathered statements and camera footage, they were satisfied that Li Ming was the victim. Being outnumbered and facing hostile cultivators, Li Ming was justified in using magic and his swordbreaker. Superintendent Wen and the prosecutor were quick to gloss over Li Ming's use of force, focusing instead on the aggressors' behavior. Li Ming was a biaohang, after all, one who worked for one of the most prestigious biaoju on the continent. He was the man who saved Shuanglong and slew countless beasts. The police couldn't possibly inconvenience him any further, not for mere criminals.

Li Ming thought he should be happy. He was merely relieved. The law might have smiled on him, but would his conscience? Was this a fight he could have avoided?

Maybe Ghazan was right. Maybe he should have crushed the trio the first time he'd met them. Maybe he should have accepted the challenge, established his dominance in the hierarchy of the jianghu, and ensured they could never take seek vengeance against him.

Or maybe Li Ming should have just stayed away from sketchy places.

The latter instinctively disgusted him. He was a biaohang. Who was he to flee from the dark and dangerous places of the world? And yet, he didn't know how well Broken Nose and his brothers would have fought. He didn't know how the crowd would have reacted. He didn't know if someone else would seek revenge or glory. There was so much he didn't know.

What was he supposed to have done?

The best he could, he supposed. To use his gongfu and his gifts the right way, to protect the innocent from the wicked, to avoid bringing more suffering to the world.

High ideals to live up to. He wondered if he could ever do it.

He returned to the suite shortly after sunset, where he found Wong-gor, Ghazan and Sarantuya in the living room, surrounded by piles of equipment and supplies. Armed with cleaning cloths and bottles of solvent, they were cleaning and inspecting their gear when Li Ming stepped in.

"Took you long enough," Wong-gor said. "We were about to send a search party for you."

"Got into a fight," Li Ming reported.

Ghazan perked up.

"What happened?" the Yue asked.

Li Ming recounted the incident, repeating what he'd told the police nearly word-for-word.

"That sounds intense," Wong-gor said. "You alright?"

"Yes."

"I told you to crush them back at the bridge," Ghazan said. "The world of the rivers and lakes respects only force."

Li Ming sighed.

I didn't think it was necessary then."

"Now you know why. Did they survive?" Ghazan asked.

"Yes."

"Pity."

"Pity? You're saying I should have killed them?"

Ghazan shrugged.

"You were outnumbered by martial cultivators. The law would understand."

"But I didn't have to."

Another shrug.

"You won. I suppose that's the only thing that counts."

"And he got paid for it too!" Wong-gor added.

"I would like to congratulate you, but you could have prevented it," Sarantuya said. "If you'd stayed away from the area, if you'd traveled in a group, or just destroyed them back at the bridge, this couldn't have happened."

Li Ming dipped his head in acknowledgment.

"I'll remember that for next time."

"*Tamen naxie danda baotian de hundan*," Wong-gor muttered. *Those audacious bastards.* "They'd dare assault a martial cultivator in broad daylight?"

"If they tried doing that to me, I'd simply blow them away," Ghazan said.

Sarantuya laughed.

"Literally."

Li Ming wanted to tell them about his state of mind. About how he was just one step away from destroying them where they had stood, and instead chosen to spare them. He wondered what they would have said. But he didn't trust Sarantuya enough to tell that story, he didn't know Wong-gor all that well either, and he feared Ghazan would simply lead him down the wrong path.

Instead he asked, "Have we heard from Ms. Zhang?"

"Not yet. Lady Boss said Ms. Zhang will call us the second she learns something," Wong-gor replied.

"Learned anything new from the paperwork?"

"Nothing," Sarantuya said.

"Without fresh material, we'll simply be going round in circles," Ghazan said.

"Any leads on where this fresh material may come from?" Li Ming asked.

"The Wanjianhui's office," Wong-gor said.

"Captain Bao's brain," Ghazan said.

"Both of which are out of bounds. At least unless we have no other choice."

"What do we do? Sit and wait for something to happen?" Sarantuya asked.

"There's one more thing we can do."

"Yes?"

"Maintain our gear. And prepare for war."

Chapter Twenty-Five

Of Course It's A Trap

Ms. Zhang dropped the bombshell the following morning.

"The Coordinating Council of the Central Plains Merchant Association have arrived in Yudu. They are going to hold an emergency meeting with the Jianghu Association tomorrow morning."

Seated around the dining room table, the team stared at Cai Yan's slate. At Ms. Zhang's face splashed across the tiny window.

"What's the meeting about?" Li Ming asked.

"The beast surge. The higher-ups are tight-lipped about the agenda, but I heard the Coordinating Council wants to organize a joint strategy with the senior members of the jianghu, militaries and governments of the Central Plains to deal with the beasts."

"Is the Wanjianhui on the guest list?" Cai Yan asked.

"Yes. So is White Tiger and the major biaoju of the Central Plains."

"No other foreigners?"

"No. It's a closed-door session. If you haven't heard of it, you're not invited."

"How did you find out about it?" Wong-gor asked.

She smirked.

"I have many friends. They like talking to me."

"Where is this meeting going to take place?" Cai Yan asked.

"The Merchant Association headquarters building."

"Could it be a coup?" Li Ming asked. "With so many important figures in one place—"

"They'll burn down the forest they live in," Wong-gor interrupted. "If the Wanjianhui does something like that, they will have no place to hide."

"If they cause widespread chaos in the area, they can take control of the Central Plains."

"With just fifty-odd bayonets? Not likely," Ghazan said.

"If they're plotting something, it is far more subtle than the use of naked force," Sarantuya said.

"Something that has got to do with beasts," Cai Yan said.

"Maybe they think they can steer the beast control strategy?" Ms. Zhang opined.

"Why would they spend so much time, resources and energy on creating a crisis and taking out biaoju just for something like this?" Wong-gor asked. "It doesn't make sense."

"There's something we're not seeing," Li Ming said. "Something that will explain what they're up to."

"Contracts? Maybe by creating up a crisis and offering the solution, they hope to make a make a killing," Cai Yan said.

Li Ming rubbed his chin.

"They incite the beasts of the Central Plains to attack the cities. Then they unveil their beast control technology, the same technology they use to agitate the beasts, but this time they use to direct the beasts elsewhere. Either for the slaughter, or simply move them away from the cities."

"I can see that happening," Ms. Zhang said. "Beasts have plagued the Central Plains for centuries. If they have such a technology at their disposal, they could demand sky-high prices to keep the cities safe."

"I don't think it's that simple," Ghazan said.

"How so?" Li Ming asked.

"You and I heard Commander Chen's speech as he left the hotel. Honor, strength and gongfu. The commercial and corporate corruption of the jianghu sickens him. Why would he chase money?"

"Maybe he's lying. He *is* the chief operations officer of an elite biaoju," Sarantuya said.

"Or maybe money is simply a means to an end," Li Ming said.

"Or maybe he's not after money, but prestige," Cai Yan said. "A biaoju that can shield the Central Plains from beasts would become the heroes of Xiazhou."

"Heroes of all mankind," Ms. Zhang said. "The farms of the Central Plains feed the entire world. The Central Plains is the single largest producer of rice, tubers, tea, and other fruits and vegetables on the planet. Anything that threatens the farms threatens the rice bowls of humanity."

"With prestige comes networks and influence," Cai Yan continued. "Very useful for a secret society."

"Assuming they are a secret society," Ms. Zhang said. "I hope you've found proof that they are criminals."

"We haven't," Cai Yan admitted.

Now Li Ming saw the genius of their plan. Beasts were everywhere. They were cheap, dangerous and expendable. The appearance of a single beast would send a town into a panic. Beasts could be slaughtered by the dozens, hundreds, *thousands*, and nobody would blink an eye at their loss. Beasts were the perfect shock troops, and the perfect pawns.

The beast control technology they used left no traces behind. It could be deployed from long range, and the operator would have plenty of time to erase his presence and flee. The only clues that something was wrong were beasts acting weirdly and cultivators sensing the qi. Nothing a law enforcement agency could act on. No evidence that lasted long enough for an investigation.

The beast lords were truly formidable.

"Without proof, there's nothing we can do. I can't even lodge a complaint against the Wanjianhui," Ms. Zhang said.

"We still have time," Li Ming said. "We have one day."

"If it's not a coup, if lives are not at risk, we can take our time building our case against them," Cai Yan said.

"We can't let the Wanjianhui become more powerful than they already are," Li Ming said.

"Agreed. But as Ms. Zhang said, without proof, we can't do anything."

Li Ming clenched his fists. Maybe Ghazan was right. Maybe it was time to raid the Wanjianhui office, to pry Captain Bao's mouth open, to force their hand somehow.

But Dayong was still bound by the laws of men and the laws of the jianghu. If they did that, they would be declaring war on the rivers and lakes *and* the Yudu military. That would not end well.

"There is one thing you can do," Ms. Zhang said.

"What is it?" Cai Yan said.

"The Jianghu Association issued an urgent request ten minutes ago. A beast hunt. Only gold-ranked biaoju are eligible."

"Are we the only gold rankers in the Yudu area?" Cai Yan asked.

Ms. Zhang went pale. She glanced at another screen, clicking a mouse and clacking her keyboard.

"Yes. Every gold-ranked biaoju except Dayong and the Wanjianhui have relocated to Shuanglong, and the Wanjianhui are not accepting any contracts."

"The Wanjianhui are involved," Li Ming said. "It's a trap."

"It's also an emergency," Ms. Zhang said.

"Tell us more," Cai Yan said.

"Early in the morning, many shanxiao overran the Zan Family Cooperative Farm. The Zan family and most of their workers have safely evacuated, but there are at least forty people not accounted for. The survivors claim that the shanxiao are gobbling up their crops, slaughtering their livestock and destroying their homes. They've issued a request for assistance through the Jianghu Association."

"Where is the farm?"

"Near the town of Jiuling, at the western end of the Central Plains. It's as far west as you can go before you cross into the Yue Homelands."

"Shanxiao aren't common in the homelands," Sarantuya said. "Usually they invade us from the Central Plains."

"The farm is extremely remote. It'll take half a day to drive there from Yudu," Ms. Zhang continued.

"If we go, we will give the Wanjianhui a window of opportunity to act here," Li Ming said.

"I'm just singing the opposite tune here, but what if this is really an emergency? What if the Wanjianhui *isn't* responsible?" Wong-gor said.

"What the Wanjianhui is planning to do will affect the Central Plains. It will affect the entire continent, the whole world," Li Ming argued.

"We still don't know what they're planning," Wong-gor said. "We *do* know what the monsters are doing."

"The Zan Family operates one of the largest farms in the area," Ms. Zhang said. "One thousand *mu* of farmland, ten thousand sows, all kinds of fruits and vegetables. It's the single largest employer in Jiuling. It's also a prime ecotourism location, attracting hundreds, if not thousands, of foreigners every year.

"Forty lives are at risk. Not only that, the livelihoods of everyone in the town is at stake. If the shanxiao destroy the farm, it would cause severe supply chain shocks across the region and affect hundreds, even thousands, of jobs. It will also affect our international standing. The repercussions would be felt all the way here in Yudu, and beyond.

"What the Wanjianhui may or may not be planning is hypothetical. What is happening at the farm is real."

Real enough that it would draw away any biaoju dedicated to the ideals of the rivers and lakes. A biaoju like Dayong.

They were caught on the horns of a dilemma. Stay in Yudu to guard against the Ten Thousand Swords Society, and allow forty people to perish and an entire town to suffer. Deploy to the farm, and allow the Wanjianhui to carry out their plot.

The Wanjianhui were truly beasts in men's form.

"Why can't the militia take care of this?" Li Ming asked.

"The Jiuling militia is on high alert and is defending the town. They do not have the numbers, training or firepower to defeat the shanxiao. The Yudu Military Forces are mobilizing to cordon the area. But the military prefers to send in professional beast hunters to deal with the shanxiao."

Li Ming shook his head. In the Zhongxia Republic, the military was keen to snatch work from the private sector. If deployed on a beast hunt, they would conduct a cordon and search operation to clear the area of beasts. They wouldn't wait for biaoju to mobilize, not unless the biaoju were already on the scene.

"How many shanxiao are there?" Ghazan asked.

"Witnesses report between thirty to fifty."

"Fifty? I've never heard of such a large pack of shanxiao before," Sarantuya said. "They are mainly solitary creatures."

"We've already faced zhenniao that fly at night and prey on men. Why not social shanxiao as well?" Wong-gor said.

"The Jiuling militia fear the shanxiao can overwhelm them at any time," Ms. Zhang said.

"There's only five of us in this room. If the militia is afraid of being overwhelmed, don't we have even more reason to be afraid?" Cai Yan said.

"You're scared?" Ghazan remarked.

"We didn't come here to throw our lives away."

"You came here to protect people, didn't you?"

Ghazan was facing the screen, but his words were aimed at Li Ming.

"You came here to hunt beasts, didn't you?" Li Ming replied.

Ghazan grinned.

"Of course."

"Are you mad? You're actually thinking of taking on *fifty* shanxiao?" Cai Yan exclaimed.

"Fifty shanxiao spread out over a thousand *mu*. If we set up on high ground, we can snipe them from afar and destroy them before they can even reach us."

Wong-gor stroked his chin.

"That makes sense. What's the terrain like?"

Cai Yan called up a map app on her screen and searched for the Zan Family Cooperative Farm. Zooming into the planet at high speed, the camera displayed a vast stretch of green. A huge river snaked through the world, branching off into thinner streams, feeding the town of Jiuling and its neighbors. The camera panned west, west, further west, following a branch of the river, and came to a stop above a floodplain.

Dozens, hundreds, of plots of produce blanketed the plains, ending at the edge of a dense forest, itself marking the foot of a grand mountain range. In the center of the farmland stood a small walled compound, dwarfed by the plots around it. Smaller outbuildings were scattered across the property, each serving different purposes.

"The ground looks nice and flat," Wong-gor said. "No cover and minimal concealment for the shanxiao."

"There's still fifty of them," Cai Yan said.

"It's not a suicide mission. Not if we work carefully," Li Ming said.

Everyone turned to him.

"How?" Cai Yan asked.

"We clear and hold the main compound. We set up at the windows and the roof and snipe every shanxiao in sight. Then we work our way westwards, moving from building to building. We'll leave Wong Biaohang and a spotter at the compound to cover us. When we find survivors, we call in the militia to pick them up and evacuate them. The forest will be the limit of our advance. Once we've eliminated the shanxiao, we back clear the area and return to the farmhouse."

As he spoke, Li Ming knew he was damning them to the mission.

"You sounded reluctant to leave earlier," Ghazan said.

Li Ming massaged his temples.

"We're the only ones who can respond to this. Can we live with ourselves if we pass it by?"

"We could let the militia take care of it," Cai Yan said.

"*Ng...* The Yudu military doesn't exactly specialize in monster hunting," Ms. Zhang said uneasily.

"What do you mean?"

"They *can* do it, they're just not experts at it. They don't have your level of experience and skills. If they go in, there might be many casualties. They might even burn down the farm while trying to save it."

"Your military is overreliant on biaoju," Li Ming said.

"It's how things have been done since the Summer Revolution," Ms. Zhang replied.

"This could be a trap," Cai Yan said.

"Of *course* it's a trap," Ghazan said.

"Only if the Wanjianhui were involved," Wong said, "and we still don't have proof."

"We don't know what the Wanjianhui is planning," Li Ming said. "But we do know what shanxiao can do to the farm and the town. If this were a trap, we can be prepared for it."

"If they know that we know that it's a trap, they can pre-empt us," Cai Yan said.

"Then we must be smarter than them. We must be ready for anything. We must pre-empt *them*."

She ran her hands through her hair.

"I... I don't know about this," she muttered.

"Who must do the hard things? He who can," Li Ming said.

"If we do this, we'll have to abandon Yudu."

"I'll keep an eye out," Ms. Zhang said. "If anything happens, I'll let you know. And if Captain Bao, the Wanjianhui, or whoever else does anything suspicious, I'll send the Jianghu Association after them. It may not stop them, but it will buy you enough time to come back here."

"It'll take too long. By the time we get back, it'll be all over."

There had to be a third option. Something that would allow them to do both. They just had to see it.

Time was of the essence. They needed speed. But the road was long and winding, and ground vehicles were limited to...

Ground. Road. What if they didn't travel by road? What if...

"Let's charter a private airship," Li Ming said.

"Airship? Can we charter an airship?" Cai Yan asked.

Everyone turned to Ms. Zhang.

"Can we?" Li Ming asked.

Chapter Twenty-Six

The Killing Work

T hey could.

Rush fee, booking fee, passenger fee, the charges all added up into the hundreds of thousands of yuan. Li Ming couldn't even imagine spending that much money in a single transaction. But they were rich now. Filthy rich. Wealth opened doors peasants could barely imagine.

Ms. Zhang smoothened the booking process. By the time Dayong reached the airport, the airship was waiting for them. Most commercial airships used gas bags and rotors to sail through the skies in slow but stately majesty. This one, sleek and aerodynamic, used state-of-the-air thrusters powered by wind crystals, defying gravity and physics to scream through the air at five hundred *li* per hour, as fast as a military airship. What should have been a grueling three-hour drive became a pleasant two-*ke* cruise.

Inside the passenger compartment, the biaohang fell into a deep silence. They tamed the heart, emptied the mind, focused the spirit, psyching themselves for battle the only way they could.

Wong-gor cradled his coilgun close to his chest, protecting it from sudden shocks. Ghazan, weapon aimed at the floor, clicked through the fire selector, rotated the fire mode wheel, deployed and stowed his bayonet. Sarantuya stared out the window, studying the ground below. Cai Yan ran her hands down her reality shaper, pouches, straps, gear, checking and double-checking that everything was secured in its place.

Li Ming sat and breathed.

He was ready. He had meticulously inspected and cleaned his Avenger. His new Viper rode in a drop-leg holster, calibrated and accessorized to his exacting requirements. The weight of his helmet and armor bore reassuring down on his body. His pack was strapped tightly to his body, his Belt Bag secured to its back. Qi hummed smoothly through his circuits. He was ready.

Still, an iron skein of tension ran through him. It vibrated like the string of a guzheng, plucked by an unseen hand. His nerves and sinews resonated with it, falling out of harmony with his body and spirit, denying him the totality of mind-body-spirit integrity needed for maximum performance. Thoughts bounced and rattled in the corner of his skull, endlessly reverberating and repeating, threatening to overwhelm him. Muscles compressed and locked into place, robbing qi from his reserves. His qi field frayed at the edges, a sword in a worn-out leather scabbard. There was only one antidote for this.

He sat and breathed.

In the breath, he drew attention to his inner self. Starting from his crown, he brought his attention into his body, identifying and releasing areas of tension, aligning his bones and posture, stabilizing his qi.

His neck and shoulders loosened. His spine drew up straight. His skull tilted higher, now perfectly level with the earth. His hands and feet and arms and thighs shifted and relaxed. His weight shifted, now falling straight down his coccyx, and the rest of him became light and free.

He breathed, and fell into timelessness.

Then a voice over the intercom dragged him back to reality.

"One minute out," the pilot called. "Lowering exit ramp."

The ramp dropped. Light flooded the dark compartment. Howling wind buffeted the biaohang. A long, loose strap, tied across the opening, flapped violently. Through the opening, Li Ming saw green farmland and white rivers rushing past.

Wong-gor unstrapped himself from his seat. One hand braced against a bulkhead, the other gripping his weapon, he made his way to the lowered ramp. A second later, Li Ming got up and joined him.

As the airship slowed, the men duck-walked to the ramp, fighting the wind. Li Ming drew a lanyard from a pouch, locked one end to a strap on his armor carrier with a carabineer, then secured the other end to a handrail with a second carabineer. Then, crouching deeply, he rested his infinity gun on the strap, master hand on the grip, support hand gripping the weapon, his angled forward grip, and the strap.

Standing next to Li Ming, Wong-gor anchored himself to another rail, his coilgun slung around his shoulder.

"With an infinity gun, sniping is dead simple. Place the reticle on target and press the trigger," Wong-gor said.

Li Ming had taken several long distance shots in his life. It was the not the same as being a sniper.

"It's my first time shooting from the air," Li Ming said.

"Don't worry. It's also my first time spotting a first-time airborne shooter."

Li Ming chuckled darkly.

The men had fiercely debated this issue during the drive to the airport. Wong-gor was the sniper, but Li Ming had the infinity gun. The airship, under thrust, vibrated in every possible direction. A sudden shift would throw off a shot. The stabilizing strap would mitigate it, but not by much.

Li Ming felt Wong-gor would be more confident taking the shot. Wong-gor insisted that the vibrations and the backwash from the thrusters could deflect his flechettes off target. Li Ming argued that the plasma bolts could set the farms on fire. Wong-gor fell back on military doctrine: the more experienced man spotted targets, the less experienced man fired.

"Don't worry about the shot," Wong-gor said. "Take your time. We're not shooting against a clock."

"It's not the clock I'm worried about," Li Ming said.

His sight picture jiggled and jittered in a loose circle. The bright red dot swam here and there, shifting left to right, up and down, its movements unpredictable and unfathomable. His hands locked into iron vices, but it didn't help much. The airship slowed dramatically, but the vibrations remained.

"Relax. You can do this," Wong said.

The airship slowed to a hovering halt, as close as any aircraft could halt in mid-air. Fields of green and brown filled Li Ming's field of view. White walls closed off a residential compound with a half-dozen buildings. The main building, a three-story mansion, anchored the compound. Single-story outbuildings, long and squat, flanked the mansion. A huge garage sat at one end of the gate, a shed at the other. Dark dots roamed the land, as tall as his thumbnail.

"Holding position and altitude. I'll do the best I can to give you a stable shooting platform," the pilot said.

The pilot was a civilian. He'd never even been in the military before. But he'd gamely accepted the biaohang's request. Wong had taken him aside and briefed him thoroughly on the pilot's role on an airborne shooting platform. But it was the first time the pilot had done this.

It was the first time for *everyone.*

"We'll clear out the compound first. I see six targets," Wong-gor said.

"Six targets, roger," Li Ming confirmed.

"By eye, go to the main gate."

The gates, once tall and sturdy, had been battered down, reduced to shattered chunks of wood and stone. Li Ming widened and softened his gaze, looking for signs for the beasts that had done this.

"Contact."

"By eye, move to the garden at the fourth hour, three mils."

The garden was a long, rectangular plot of green against pale concrete. A pair of brown dots frolicked among them.

"Contact."

"Go to glass."

Li Ming brought his eye to the optic and cranked up the zoom to 10X. The image resolved into crystal clarity, revealing a brown-furred beast with two muscular arms and a single hoofed foot. It wriggled about like a snake, hips and spine undulating from side to side, dragging its hoof behind it. Reaching out with both hands, it tore the blooms from a flowing bush and shoved them into a yawning mouth.

"Contact. I see a shanxiao feeding on a bush."

"That's the target. Engage."

The reticle found its chest. The airship trembled and the dot trembled with it, rising and falling, swaying from side to side. Li Ming clicked off the safety and touched his finger to the trigger. He breathed out, exhaling his thoughts with them, dissolving his ego into the universe. He held a single, focused intent, to shoot and hit the target, and allowed his body to act in harmony with all things.

His finger closed.

The gun snarled.

A white-hot bolt speared the shanxiao through the chest. Pink mist erupted from the massive wound. It slumped over, suddenly still, sprawling over the bush.

"Target down," Li Ming said.

"Next target. Third hour, one mil."

Li Ming swiveled to his right. The shanxiao stared quizzically at its fallen companion, unable to understand how it had grown a huge hole in its back. Li Ming planted the red dot on its shoulder, squeezed—

—the airship jerked—

Its head vanished in pink.

"Grape shot," Wong-gor said. "But let's not get fancy."

"Vibration," Li Ming said.

Wong-gor chuckled.

"By eye, go to the shed by the main gate."

Li Ming swung around.

"Contact."

"Go to glass."

The scope magnified a tiny circle of the world, revealing a shanxiao leaning out the doorway, exposing its neck and head. Li Ming eased his weapon slowly, smoothly, inexorably taking the red dot over its ear—

The creature shrieked.

Li Ming heard only the screaming of the thrusters. Through the lens, he saw its jaw drop, its head tilt back, the dot wobbling about. He shifted through a final, minute correction, saw red dot over brown fur, fired.

"Grape shot." Wong-gor leaned away and keyed his radio. "Pilot, bring us around and over the main gate. We need a better angle."

The thrusters flared. Li Ming jolted. He thumbed the safety on and relaxed. Down below, the world spun around. Li Ming's stomach roiled one way, then the other. Wong-gor bumped against his shoulder and recoiled away. The dropship came to a halt again, and now they were right above the gate, with a clean shot into the central courtyard.

"Three targets, courtyard, by the mansion," Wong-gor said.

Li Ming snapped his weapon to the closest brown dot. The shanxiao reared up, staring at the sky, foot planted on the ground, body coiled and tensed.

"I see a shanxiao," Li Ming said. "He's preparing to jump."

"Engage all three targets at will."

Li Ming fired.

The bolt caught the beast in its upper right breast, spinning it around. Li Ming swiveled right, shot the second beast in the sternum. Rotated right and down, found the third target, a red ruby glowing in its forehead—

A white bolt seared the sky.

Li Ming mashed the trigger. The bolt burst its right eye and knocked it down.

And the airship dropped from the sky.

"We're taking fire!" the pilot yelled.

White bolts seared across Li Ming's sight, fingers of destruction reaching for the airship.

The party had expected beasts. They hadn't expected Evolved beasts capable of powerful long-range magic.

"Drop us on the roof of the main building!" Wong-gor yelled.

Li Ming unclipped the stabilization strap. With a clean jerk, the retention lanyard came free.

Multicolored bolts streaked from the ground, zeroing in in the airship. The violent dive threatened to throw Li Ming out the door. He latched on to a handrail, planting his knees against the hard metal floor. Behind him, Sarantuya shouted in Yue. A heavy hand seized Li Ming's retention carabineer and unsnapped it.

Ghazan. Li Ming knew his touch anywhere.

The airship abruptly pulled up. The ramp scraped against the roof of the mansion. Ghazan barged past Li Ming and jumped out onto the sunbaked concrete. Cai Yan followed, arms outstretched, a shimmering shield materializing in mid-air. Next came Sarantuya, Wong-gor, and now Li Ming rose to his feet and leapt off the ramp.

"Last man! Last man! Get out of here now!" Li Ming yelled.

The airship soared into the air, ramp raising into place. The biaohang fanned out, infinity guns blazing. White bolts shattered against the shield. Li Ming took his place at the left-most end of the formation, closest to the roof access door.

Leaping on powerful hoofed feet, the shanxiao converged on the compounded, rushing forward in great bounds. Ten, twenty, thirty of them, trampling on fruits and vegetables, jumping into the air, landing on crops, taking off again. They screeched and shrieked and screamed, their voices carrying across the vast expanse of the farmlands. The Evolved among them fired with every leap, loosing a bolt the moment they cleared the high walls of the compound. The shots flew wild and high, but with every jump they came every closer to the biaohang.

Lying prone on stable ground, Li Ming hunted for the Evolved. The lesser shanxiao could wait. These had to die *now*. He tracked them by the flashes of their crystals and the flight of their bolts, white and bright, his visor darkening to shield his eyes.

The closest Evolved loosed a bolt. It lanced high above him, barely registering in his consciousness. Li Ming anticipated its landing, weapon already in motion, and the moment its foot touched the ground he blasted it in the chest.

Another shanxiao grew aggressive. It launched a fusillade of bolts the second it took off, resting only when it hit the ground. Burning in from far away, the bolts were small and weak, but they slapped loudly against stone and concrete. Li Ming breathed out, filtering out the blizzard of incoming and outgoing fire, and took it in the face when it landed.

Li Ming fired and fired and fired. He was in the zone, perfectly cool and calm, his blood singing through his veins, his nerves and muscles moving in perfect harmony with his mind. Every time he fired, a shanxiao went down. A few survived a single shot. None survived a second.

Then a thought exploded in his head.

You haven't cleared the farmhouse!

And the roof access door blew open.

Li Ming rolled over on his back and aimed between his legs. A shanxiao slithered out the door, massive claws digging into the hardened concrete, drooling lips parted to expose saber-like teeth, red crystals crawling down its limbs and across its face.

Li Ming fired.

And fired and fired and fired, working his way up its torso, its neck, its face.

"CONTACT LEFT!" he screamed.

And the sight picture cleared and Li Ming lowered his weapon and now he beheld the mess he had made of the shanxiao.

And more shanxiao screamed from within the house.

"Beasts coming up the stairs!" he shouted.

He picked himself up and sprinted to the door, staying clear of the fatal funnel. In the stairwell beyond, claws scraped against wood, fur brushed against stone, beasts panted heavily. His ear protection took every subtle sound and amplified it, filling his brain with noise. He switched his weapon to his left shoulder, leaned out and—

Empty.

The stairwell was empty. But heavy thumps and soft scratching echoed up the length of the stairs.

"Contact, lower floor!" Li Ming called.

A shield exploded in dazzling light and thunderous sound. The coilgun cracked once, twice, thrice.

"Off the roof!" Cai Yan yelled. "We're taking too much fire here!"

"We've got to clear the house!" Li Ming shouted back.

A heavy hand thumped his shoulder.

"With you!" Ghazan shouted.

Li Ming hopped over the shanxiao's remains and clambered down the stairs. He extended his qi sense, trying to feel the remaining beasts, but the shaft was too cramped, his heart too agitated, and all he felt were the walls closing in on him.

He emerged into a wide landing. He flowed right, weapon ready. Two open doors stood before him. The stench of blood and waste filled his nose. As boots trampled behind him, Li Ming moved to the left-hand door and spun through an arc, sweeping the corners of the room.

"Clear!" Li Ming yelled.

Wong-gor rushed inside, taking to the window.

"I'll engage the enemy from here! Keep clearing!" Wong-gor called.

He flung the window open, hefted his coilgun to the shoulder, and cracked off a shot.

Li Ming didn't stay. He stepped back out to the landing and flowed to the next room. Also empty.

"Clear!" Li Ming shouted.

"Clear!" Ghazan called.

Li Ming popped his head out. The other three biaohang emerged from more rooms to the left side of the landing.

"Cai Yan, over here! Set up by the window and support Wong-gor! Sarantuya, watch the rear window! Ghazan, on me!" Li Ming ordered.

The biaohang raced into position. Cai Yan brushed past Li Ming, calling out her presence. Sarantuya ducked back into the master bedroom. Ghazan fell in behind Li Ming. Together, the men rushed down the stairs to the ground floor.

The stairs fed into the living room. Qi, hot and expanding, surged from below. Li Ming leapt down the steps, landed heavily on the ground floor, spun around—

Crashed into a shanxiao.

Man and beast bounced off each other. Li Ming staggered, stunned for a moment. The shanxiao shrieked, raising its killer claws. Li Ming leapt back, spearing out his muzzle at its face. The beast recoiled—

Ghazan blew its head off.

More beasts screamed. The men rushed to the main entrance. The door had been ripped off its hinges and flung deep into the living room. Through the windows, Li Ming saw a shanxiao clear the wall and land in the courtyard. And another. And another.

The coilgun cracked. One went down. Ghazan blasted, taking down another.

"Keep clearing! I'll hold them off!" Ghazan shouted.

Li Ming worked clockwise through the ground floor. Living room, study, dining room, kitchen, laundry, study. He combined speed with caution, slowly slicing around angles, suddenly rushing into rooms. It was suicidal, it completely violated close quarters combat doctrine, but he was alone and he had to make the most of the situation.

All around him, guns snarled, monsters howled, qi erupted. His blood ran hot, his qi surged through his limbs, but he ignored the call to run to the guns and focused on his duty.

"Clear! The house is clear!" Li Ming called.

"Li Ming! Get over here! Beasts coming from the front and sides!" Ghazan yelled.

Li Ming planted himself at by window at the other end of the living room from Ghazan, just in time to see a shanxiao hop over the wall. He snapped up his weapon and fired—

Glass shattered. Blinds burned. Heat washed over Li Ming's face. The shanxiao twisted away, part of its arm dropping off. Li Ming pressed the trigger again and the beast went down in a broken heap.

"I thought there were only thirty to fifty shanxiao? There's at least a hundred of them!" Ghazan exclaimed.

"Intelligence is always wrong!" Li Ming yelled back.

Howling, shrieking, more shanxiao jumped over the walls and landed behind the outbuildings. Balls of blazing white light arced above the roofs of the longhouses, falling towards the mansion.

Li Ming ducked away. The balls burst against the sturdy walls. The walls shook, glass shattered, dust fell from the ceiling.

"No shot! They're using the buildings as cover!" Li Ming shouted.

"We've got to get back up on the roof!" Ghazan yelled.

"Let's go!"

Ghazan led. Li Ming followed. As they raced up the stairs, qi flared from Wong-gor's position. Thundercracks split the air. Explosions rocked the world. Monsters screamed. In pain, then in rage.

They burst back out on the roof. Without a word, they dashed to the corners, Ghazan going left, Li Ming going right. Standing at the edge of the roof, Li Ming had a clean line of fire at the beasts hiding behind the outbuildings.

There were ten of them, a moving, writhing mass of fur and hide and claws and teeth, and ruby red crystals fused into beast flesh. One of them pointed at him, howling at the top of its lungs. He blasted it in the face. The others wheeled around instantly, turning to the new threat.

Paws raised. Crystals flashed. Bolts of searing fire leapt from fingers and faces, from wherever the shanxiao had fused the primordial crystals into their bodies. Li Ming scrambled away, bolts smashing into the concrete around him, cursing his utter recklessness, his rank stupidity. What the devil was he thinking, rushing up to the enemy like that without cover, concealment, or even a shield?!

He needed a grenade. No grenade. He needed fire support. No artillery or gunships around. That left him with—

A dark blur launched up into the air and landed before him. Shanxiao.

He crashed into it, punching his muzzle into its throat. The beast screamed, its voice dissolving into a choking, gagging, fit. Li Ming pounced away and blasted it in the face.

And two more shanxiao landed just behind it.

He snapped to one. Fired. Pivoted to the other. Fired again. Back to the first. A second shot. Snapped right. Fired.

He went back and forth, blasting the moment the red dot found dark flesh, and suddenly his sight picture cleared and he lowered his weapon.

And punched his fist into the sky.

With a titanic scream, he launched a qi pulse into the heavens, fusing it with intent. High in the cosmos, the qi packet unfolded and exploded, manifesting his will. A lance of pure flame blasted down, searing the spot where the shanxiao had gathered, detonating on impact.

He punched his other fist. A second fire lance, smaller and weaker but still deadly, carved through the air and burst against the earth.

Abruptly the lances vanished, leaving pillars of smoke. He paused for a moment, gulping down more qi, allowing his shapers to recharge. Then he cast a shield, a small but thick plate of metal qi floating away from his body, and approached the edge of the roof.

The flame lances left twin craters in the ground. Severed limbs and blasted bodies lay scattered across the ground, the wall, the roof. Most of them twitched. Li Ming didn't have time to assess them all, he just fired and fired and fired, firing at everything that moved and looked like a torso with an attached head.

A chorus of howls tore him from his grim work. More shanxiao rushed towards the compound, more and more and more, fast-moving black dots bouncing closer and closer and closer.

"You sure there were only a hundred of them?" Li Ming called.

"Two hundred," Ghazan replied.

Glee crept into the Yue's voice. Li Ming shook his head, scanning for more targets at ground level and—

"The Yudu Military Forces just called me," Cai Yan radioed. "They're sending a pair of gunships to provide fire support. They're coming in from the east."

Li Ming heaved a sigh of relief. Finally. The military was finally getting its act together. Once the gunships arrived, they could turn this around and—

He paused.

"Did we ask for fire support?" Li Ming asked.

"Negative. The pilots claimed their superiors ordered them to assist us. No one told me anyone was coming to help us," Cai Yan replied.

"I have eyes on the gunships," Ghazan said. "Ninth hour, high, six hundred *chi* out."

The Yue had excellent eyes. Li Ming could scarcely make them out. Against the infinite blue skies the gunships were fast-moving black blurs, growing larger and faster.

Something wasn't right here, but—

The coilgun cracked. Lightning bolts flashed. Li Ming turned his attention back to the field. The shanxiao redoubled their attack, closing in.

Li Ming shot at movement, at color, at everything that drew his eye. He missed more than he hit, but with so many beasts here, volume of fire counted more than accuracy. He could let Wong-gor do the killing work, he had to keep the beasts at bay. He maintained a steady cadence, keeping the gun from overheating, shooting as soon as he had a sight picture, one shot every five seconds.

The screaming of the gunships' thrusters grew louder and higher-pitched. Glancing up, he saw that they were now dead ahead, oriented towards the mansion, half a *li* out and closer. He fired and—

And a wave of weird qi passed through him.

It penetrated his skin, his flesh, his bones, his soul. It carried a message of hate, of anger, of war, filling him with red rage. His body quaked, his soul ignited, his qi drew forth, ready for—

He exhaled.

The rage remained, but now it was only skin deep. He allowed it to flow around him, as if he were a rock in a river. Deep within, he went completely, totally still. In that stillness, he saw.

He knew.

"Wong-gor, kill the left gunship! Ghazan, engage the one on the right!"

Kill a gunship. With man-portable small arms. Madness. Modern gunships were so heavily armored, the only way to do that was to shoot the pilots through the thin cockpit glass. A long shot. A difficult shot. But it had to be done.

Ghazan didn't question him. He simply swung his weapon up to the aim. Li Ming reset the zoom on his scope and shouldered his own weapon. In the world of 1X vision the gunship was a black dot. The qi waves continued to pound him, shaking his heart, firing his nerves, swaying his scope. Li Ming ignored it all, centering the reticle on the target, and dialed up to 10X.

The gunship now loomed bright and clear in his scope, a sleek black bird of prey crafted by human hands. A large ball turret jutted from under its chin. The cannon swung around and blasted.

Sun-bright bolts slashed through the air, destroying everything they touched. Earth fused to glass, concrete shattered, grass burned, beasts disintegrated. Li Ming ignored it all, releasing all thoughts of impending doom from his mind, his attention narrowing down into the red dot. He placed it over the cockpit, clicked off the safety, rotated the fire wheel to double power, fired.

And fired, and fired, and fired.

He fired as fast as he could press the trigger, putting bolts through a melon-sized circle. Ghazan fired too, bolts ripping through the air. Bolts crashed against the gunship's armored fuselage, dissipating in flashes of light. Still he fired and fired, the turret blazed brighter, the explosions drew closer—

The gunship went down.

The gunship spiraled in mid-air, struggling to retain control, its chin turret silent. Li Ming poured on the fire, shooting every time red clashed against black. Something inside the aircraft exploded, and the gunship fell like a brick.

He clicked back down to 1X and hunted for the other gunship. It swooped down from the heavens, gun blazing. Rage crept into Li Ming's heart, rage at Wong, rage at the beast lords, rage at the world entire. He grabbed the rage, forced it out with his breath, and touched his finger to the trigger and—

And the gunship went down.

Down, down, down it went, locked in an inescapable death spiral. It smashed into the field, the sound of the impact carrying all the way to the mansion, a colossal shriek of metal and glass shattering and collapsing under titanic forces, and went still.

Suddenly the rush of rage vanished, leaving a mind as empty as the void, a heart as calm as still water.

"Li Ming, you want to tell me what I just did?" Wong-gor asked.

"The gunships were hostiles," he replied. "They were equipped with beast control tech. They were directing the shanxiao to attack us."

As he finished his words, the shanxiao screeched again, but this time in fear. They peeled away, forming loose packs, fleeing the farmhouse at top speed.

"The beasts are breaking!" Cai Yan exclaimed, joy creeping into her voice.

Li Ming exhaled. Tension melted from his body. That threat was over. He rotated the fire wheel to standard power and put his weapon back on safe.

And Ghazan fired.

And fired.

And fired again.

"Ghazan, what are you doing?" Li Ming asked.

"The more we kill, the more we're paid."

"They're running away!"

Ghazan fired.

"Good."

And fired again.

The shapers fell silent. The guns went quiet. Only Ghazan's continued to bite at the backs of the fleeing beasts. A cool breeze carried the scent of smoke and fresh butchery.

Ghazan had a point. But now, Li Ming had more wealth than he could possibly dream of. What was the bounty of a single shanxiao compared to eighty-one million yuan? It was one thing to kill a dangerous beast in combat. But this... this was slaughter for its own sake.

"Don't waste your heat," Li Ming said.

Ghazan fired.

"Every kill brings us a bounty. It's not a waste."

"There could be other threats."

Another shot.

"Do you see any?"

Li Ming scanned. The shanxiao had well and truly broken. They were bouncing off at top speed, making for the relative safety of the distant forests and mountains. Fires raced among the fields, consuming the crops at dizzying speed, turning gold and green to black and crimson.

"Cai Yan, alert the local emergency services. We have an uncontrolled blaze in the farms," Li Ming said.

"There's another fire around the back," Sarantuya said. "I'm trying to put it out."

"Roger. Who the devil is shooting?" Cai Yan asked.

"Me," Ghazan replied, and fired.

"Are there any more threats?"

"There are still plenty of targets."

"The Zan Family won't be happy if we burn down their farm."

"They'll understand."

"We still have civilians downrange."

"We can't get to them until the shanxiao clear out anyway." Another shot. "Call in the military. They can evacuate them by air."

The coilgun cracked.

"Don't be too eager to rack up kills. Watch your shots and stay away from the buildings," Wong-gor warned.

"Roger," Ghazan said.

Now two guns spoke, Wong's and Ghazan's. The bloodlust was infectious. Or maybe Wong-gor was simply trying to clear the field before Ghazan could burn it down.

Tiny buildings stood at the horizon, each the size of ants and gnats. Far beyond the range of an infinity gun. Li Ming didn't have to worry about Ghazan burning them down, yet. He continued his sweep at—

The gunships!

Li Ming went to glass, zooming in on the gunship he had downed. The wreck lay at the terminus of a deep trench, surrounded by flattened and burning sorghum, shrouded in smoke. The cockpit was a ruin of broken polymer. Shanxiao bounced up to it, still fleeing Ghazan.

The port side door popped open. A soldier staggered out. And jerked upright in shock.

He fired at a shanxiao. The beast blew apart, screaming of its death to the world.

A second shanxiao pounced on the trooper and tore him apart.

A third shanxiao slithered into the open crew compartment. Light flashed from within. Blood splashed across the windows.

Li Ming fired. A muscular leg blew off. He continued firing blindly, peppering the fuselage, shooting at where he thought the beast was.

"The shanxiao are attacking the gunships! Take them out!" Li Ming called.

"You're trying to *save* the enemy?" Ghazan wondered.

"We need answers. Dead men don't talk."

Ghazan paused.

"Good point."

Ghazan shifted fire, his cadence rapidly picking up. The coilgun cracked multiple times. Li Ming shot the shanxiao savaging the hapless soldier. Zooming out, he picked up no more threats. He swiveled to the other gunship, saw a pile of shanxiao bodies. An enormous beast had crammed itself into the fuselage, peppered with bloody holes. It had gone still, but the windows were splashed with red.

Li Ming regretted his earlier words. If he had acted quicker, realized the threat to the gunships, maybe he could have prevented this. Maybe more people would be alive. Maybe...

He didn't deal in maybes. He had to work with what he had now. And now, the shanxiao were a threat to life and limb, and to the mission.

Li Ming took up his gun and fired.

Chapter Twenty-Seven

Delicate Work

The scent of life and death hung think over the air. The deep rich aroma of fertile earth and the iron-rich tang of blood, the odor of waste and fertilizer, overlaid with toxic smoke loaded with plastics and metals. Downrange, there was no sign of sentient life, man or beast.

The women paired up to search the gunship Li Ming and Ghazan had downed. Li Ming and Ghazan headed to the other. Wong-gor hung back, covering them from the roof of the mansion.

The hunter in Li Ming wanted to handle his kill himself. The soldier recognized that the gunship Wong-gor had targeted was in better shape. The survivors in the second wreck would be better able to put up a fight.

If there were any.

Ghazan took point. Li Ming hung back, spraying down stray fires with water from his shapers. He wasn't battling the blaze so much as keeping it away from them and the crash site. It was the best he could do, at least until the scene was secure.

As they patrolled to the site, the men warily examined the shanxiao corpses. Many of them lay amid burned, blackened patches. The bulk of their bodies had smothered the flames the plasma bolts had started, or at least tamped them down to embers. Some of them still twitched, even after death.

Under more ordinary circumstances, they could wait for the shanxiao to bleed out. They had no time. They shot every shanxiao they saw in the head, sparing only those that no longer had intact heads. A small part of Li Ming quailed at the loss of valuable beast matter. His superego reminded him that his life was more important than money, that he already had plenty of money, that he was here not to make money or slay beasts but to save people.

A circle of fire surrounded the crash site, rushing outwards to consume the sorghum, creeping inwards to the shattered gunship. As Ghazan covered, Li Ming summoned water from the heavens. A ring of rain fell, dousing the flames but leaving everything else dry.

It was delicate work, mixing precision with power, capability with sustainment. Li Ming held focus, gulping down qi and channeling it to his crystals, augmenting the shapers' natural recharge rate. He used just enough qi to manifest rain without depleting the crystals, five hundred points' worth of qi and no more, allowing a steady flow of energy through the devices.

When it was over, he stood before a blasted furrow, the fire extinguished, the surviving grain dry, the wreckage untouched.

It didn't come close to the exquisite control and gentle power Cai Yan had displayed in Shuanglong, but it was Li Ming's finest magic working yet. Li Ming allowed himself a moment of pride in work well done.

Ghazan didn't comment.

Weapons raised, they circled the crash site, inspecting the downed aircraft. The fuselage was mainly intact, but the bubble canopy was completely starred over, a cluster of neat holes tracking across the pilot's and the gunner's seats. The men lay slumped forward in pools of blood, the pilot's helmeted head shattered, the gunner's chest riddled with wounds. Their qi was completely gone, and with it, their souls.

A huge shanxiao lay stuffed inside the passenger compartment, its mass blocking off the open door. Blood spilled from unseen wounds, forming a dark patch in the thirsty earth. Deep inside the compartment, a weak qi field slowly dissipated into the universe. Ghazan prodded the body with his bayonet. It remained still.

"*Wei!* We're here to help! Is anyone alive inside?" Li Ming called.

Someone groaned.

"We've got to move the body," Li Ming said.

"I'll cover you," Ghazan said, shouldering his weapon.

Li Ming rooted himself into the earth and grabbed the shanxiao's single leg. It was a huge, muscular organ, reminding him of a snail's foot, but covered in fur and slick with blood. With a loud grunt, he pulled.

The beast didn't move.

He pulled again.

It budged, slightly.

"It's stuck. Feels like it's caught on something," Li Ming said.

"We could carve it up," Ghazan suggested.

Li Ming blinked. Blinked again.

"Going to use magic."

Li Ming breathed the essence of fire into his limbs. His muscles ignited, his blood burned, ready for sudden, explosive force. Into the flame he added wood, reinforcing the fire, his hands and arms becoming tight cords of thews and sinews.

He gripped the monster's dead weight, propelled his weight into the soft earth, and pulled.

The body met resistance. Claws scratched against metal. Something cracked. And suddenly the obstruction was gone and the body slid on a puddle of thick blood and a cloud of flies burst forth from and Li Ming stumbled.

Li Ming caught himself. Seized the beast once more. And dragged it clear of the door.

The shanxiao was a mess. Its claws were caked in blood, its face a wasteland of plasma-burned holes. Red crystals gleamed brightly among the meat. Flies swarmed and buzzed about, settling on the meat, the blood, Li Ming's body. As Li Ming shooed them away, Ghazan switched shoulders and leaned into the compartment.

"We've got a live one," Ghazan declared.

Ghazan let his infinity gun swing free and drew his handgun. It was a hand cannon, a different model than Li Ming's but no less dangerous. Li Ming drew his Viper and...

And with the stock folded and telescoped, it was awkward to handle with one hand. Not impossible, just not ideal. He should have worn his Hellion somewhere on his body, maybe an ankle holster or something.

Ghazan ducked his head and clambered into the compartment. Li Ming followed and stepped into a world of blood.

Blood dripped from the ceiling. Blood splashed across the bulkheads. Blood covered the aisle between the two parallel rows of interior seats, lined flush against the walls. The savaged ruins of dead men lay strapped to the interior seats. Blacked lines played across the inside of the compartment. One of them lay slumped forward, his throat and jaw a torn-off mess, his hand still gripping a pistol.

Someone groaned.

Li Ming approached, weapon at the ready, keeping low and to the right, Ghazan right beside him. His boots sunk into the blood. Flies smacked against his visor and his face. The smell of soap and burned pork, blood and blasted metal, mingled to overpower his nose.

The survivor moaned again, shaking his head. Still strapped into his seat, he was spattered in blood, but Li Ming saw no wounds. An infinity gun was slung around his neck, pointed at the ground. His hands remained on his lap.

"Easy, easy. We're here to help," Li Ming said soothingly, holstering his weapon.

In a single, smooth motion, he lifted the infinity gun from the man's neck and slung it around his neck. The trooper offered no resistance.

"Can you hear me?" Li Ming asked.

The man whispered incoherently, his voice slurred, yet somehow familiar.

Li Ming drew his pocketknife and clicked the blade open.

"I'm going to cut you out. Stay still."

With swift, clean strokes, he cut through the safety webbing. The trooper fell forward. Li Ming caught him with his free hand and stowed the knife.

"We're done here. Let's go," Li Ming said.

Li Ming pulled the man off the seat and wrapped the soldier's arm around his neck. One hand gripping the casualty's own, the other supporting his waist, Li Ming retreated from the crew compartment.

Ghazan cleared a small circle from the grain, far away from the crash site. Li Ming set him down on the earth.

"He looks familiar," Ghazan remarked.

Li Ming unstrapped his helmet, set it aside and lifted his head to reveal—

"Captain Bao," Li Ming said.

Captain Bao groaned.

As Ghazan covered him, Li Ming unclipped the prisoner's plate carrier and set it aside. Then he pulled off his gloves and tore open his belt-mounted first aid kit. He hunted among the plastic-wrapped packages and produced a pair of disposable nitrile gloves.

"Beginning sweep," Li Ming said.

Li Ming slipped on the gloves and brought his fingers to Captain Bao's nose. Weak streams of air caressed his gloved skin. Li Ming touched Captain Bao's carotid artery. His pulse drummed in a steady beat.

Li Ming touched the back of the wounded man's head, then steady felt around the rest of his face. His gloves were clean, and he found no swelling or breaks.

Working his way down, Li Ming swept the rest of Captain Bao's body. Neck, arms, torso, groin, legs.

"Patient is conscious. Vital signs present. No bleeding or breaks. Looks like a concussion," Li Ming reported.

He rolled Captain Bao over on his side in the recovery position, an arm and leg bent to brace him against the soil, his neck tilted and mouth open, his other hand under his chin to support his head.

"Cai Yan, Ghazan. We've captured a prisoner. He appears to be concussed and requires medical attention."

"Understood," Cai Yan replied. "No survivors here. We'll make our way to you."

"Cover him. I'm going to check on the others," Li Ming said.

Ghazan readied his infinity gun. Li Ming discarded the nitrile gloves, put his tactical gloves back on, and approached the downed airship.

He knew the others were dead. There was no life force lingering in the wreckage. But he couldn't formally declare their deaths without inspecting them.

He cut the pilot and gunner free and dragged them aside. Their blood soaked his sleeves and pants. He brushed off what he could and plunged into the crew compartment. Breathing through his mouth, he cut one man free, then another, then another. He tried not to think about what he was touching, who he was handling. They were just dead weight, no different from the hundreds of carcasses he had processed in his life.

But the torn faces, the severed limbs, the gaping wounds, the gore sloshing about, and worst of all, the smell... His stomach rebelled, his limbs weakened. He breathed out the sensation, breathed in new strength, and willed himself to carry out.

As Li Ming brought out the fourth casualty, Ghazan returned. Together they extracted the remaining bodies and laid them all side by side.

There were eleven of them. Eleven men who, barely a half hour ago, were calling down beasts and firing on Dayong, in the final stages of an airborne assault. Li Ming guessed that Dayong had shot down the gunships right before the troopers were able to jump off. Now they were little more than punctured sacks of meat and bone and blood, empty of life.

Li Ming felt like he ought to say a prayer. Instead he and Ghazan got down to business, searching their pockets and pouches. They hunted for wallets, documents, devices, anything that could betray the troopers' identities and mission.

They were all sterile. They carried only their weapons, reality shapers, and tactical tools.

But they all wore the patches of the Yudu Military Forces.

The men returned to the women. As Sarantuya covered Captain Bao, Cai Yan stood over him, hands held out. Gentle, soothing light enveloped Captain Bao's head.

Healing a head injury was delicate work, more delicate than putting out a fire. Li Ming quietly drew a pair of zipties from his Belt Bag, then turned on his helmet-mounted cameras' video recording mode and approached Sarantuya.

"Found any survivors?" Li Ming asked.

"None. Whoever the crash didn't kill, the beasts finished," she replied.

Li Ming stood in silence, watching Cai Yan at work, until at last the light receded and Captain Bao moaned.

"I... Where...?"

Li Ming strode over.

"Captain Bao?" Li Ming asked.

"I..."

His eyes focused. His jaw dropped. His breath stopped.

"You!"

Ghazan touched the point of his bayonet to Captain Bao's throat.

Captain Bao went completely still.

"You tried to kill us," Li Ming said.

"We saw you were in trouble. We conducted a gun run and—"

"*Hushuo!* We sensed the qi waves from your gunships. From whatever it is you used to control the beasts."

Captain Bao shifted.

"This is a mistake—"

"Keep still," Ghazan said.

Li Ming seized Bao's shoulders and roughly sat him back up. He wrenched Captain Bao's hands behind his back and ziptied them together.

"You don't have to do this! I'm on your side!" Captain Bao protested.

"Your gunships fired on us," Cai Yan said.

"We were shooting at the beasts!"

Li Ming scoffed.

"You're a terrible liar. When making a gun run, you never shoot towards your allies. Only away from them, or parallel to their position. Even the Yudu Military Forces isn't that incompetent."

Bao opened his mouth. Cai Yan cut him off.

"Save your breath. We know you have a means of compelling beasts to attack humans. You've used it to stir up the beasts of the region, create a beast surge, and lure biaoju to Yudu. You used it again to launch a terrorist attack on Shuanglong, diverting the biaoju away from Yudu. You used it to organize no less than *three* beast attacks against us. You will tell us why."

Captain Bao closed his mouth.

Li Ming clenched his fists. He wished he knew how to make men talk. He was no interrogator, and the entirety of his training and experience was focused on breaking things and shooting living things. He had no expertise in situations that demanded the reverse. He had to play this by ear.

Li Ming knelt, glaring at him with the eyes of a tiger.

"The world of the jianghu is merciless towards those who make war on us. If you do not cooperate, you will be shipping yourself to the underworld."

"What are you going to do, torture me?" Captain Bao demanded.

"A tempting offer," Ghazan said.

"If you do, the courts will throw out any case you may make against me," Captain Bao said triumphantly.

"You seem like a brave man," Li Ming said. "You might just be a smart one too. Look around you. You are surrounded by a group of biaohang you miserably failed to kill, as well as many shanxiao corpses. You are in the middle of the wilds and there are no other witnesses. You're in a poor place indeed."

Captain Bao quivered. His qi field shivered. And rallied.

"You've got a big mouth. But you don't have the guts to touch me," Captain Bao replied.

Ghazan touched the tip of his bayonet to the soft skin just under Captain Bao's eye. The prisoner flinched, sucking in a deep breath.

"You're a cat pretending to be a lion," Ghazan said.

"That's all you can do?" Captain Bao sputtered. "I'm not scared of you!"

"You protest too much for a courageous man," Ghazan retorted. "You're as cowardly as a mouse."

"We don't have to go down this route," Li Ming said soothingly. "Tell us what we want to know. Tell us why you organized these attacks."

Captain Bao stuck out his chin and bared his throat.

"Go ahead, do your worst!"

Captain Bao was goading them to kill him, and so preserve the secrets of the beast lords. A truly brave man, Li Ming admitted to himself. How did you break someone who welcomed death?

"We don't have to do anything," Li Ming said.

"What do you mean?"

"Your gunships are mostly intact. Whatever device or method you used to control the beasts can be salvaged from the wreckage. The craters the cannons left behind will prove that they were firing towards us when we shot you down. We have all the evidence we need to press charges of attempted murder, terrorism, and unlawful use of magic.

"We could hand you to the justice of the jianghu. With charges like these, you'll spend the rest of your existence in maximum security, locked up alongside other criminal cultivators who still feel a measure of loyalty towards the world of the rivers and lakes. You can imagine what they will do to someone like you.

"If you cooperate now, however, we can plead for leniency. As a gold-ranked biaoju, our words will carry weight with the prosecutor. You may not be afraid of death, but how much suffering do you think you can endure?"

"More than you ever will."

"It will be less than what you'll experience in maximum security. But why suffer when you don't have to? We already have a good idea of what's going on. We simply need you to confirm a few things for us."

"I can confirm that your acting skills are terrible. Where'd you learn that line from? Some third-rate crime drama?"

A bestselling thriller novel, actually. The writer had assured him that the line would reduce the psychological threshold to confession, making him feel as if he weren't giving up something that wasn't already know. Reality, of course, was much messier than the pages of a book.

"We know you are in league with the Ten Thousand Swords Society. What is your goal?" Li Ming asked.

Captain Bao twitched. His eyes widened.

"You know nothing, do you? You're just firing from the hip!"

He was. But Captain Bao's reaction had betrayed him.

"Biaoju go where beasts go," Li Ming said. "They want the riches and the glory that come from hunting the most dangerous beasts in the land, and selling their meat and bones. Create a beast surge, and every biaoju in Xiazhou will come running.

"You and the Wanjianhui counted on it. And it worked like a charm. You drew beasts from all over the region, pulling the biaoju along with them. Where hunters and biaohang spent their strength and risked their lives destroying the beasts, the Wanjianhui consolidated its position and preserved its forces. It allowed the Wanjianhui to swoop down on Shuanglong at the last minute and portray themselves as heroes.

"With the beast surge at Shuanglong, you planned on pulling biaohang and beast hunters away from Yudu, leaving it defenseless. But we foiled your plans. Instead of returning to Shuanglong after destroying the zhenniao nest, Dayong headed to Yudu.

"There was only two other gold-ranked biaoju left in Yudu. The Wanjianhui and us. You created a crisis that only a gold-ranked biaoju could solve, then the Wanjianhui refused to respond to it. This attack was meant to draw us away from Yudu and force us to stay away long enough for the Wanjianhui to do what they're doing.

"We've seen through your plan. We all know what you've done. Now you're going to tell us what you've planned in Yudu, and why."

Captain Bao clamped his lips shut.

"Too scared to talk? Where did your bravery go?" Ghazan asked.

Captain Bao remained silent and looked away.

Li Ming seized his head with both hands and forced it forward, bringing his eyes level with Bao's.

"What is the Wanjianhui planning in Yudu? What do they want? What do *you* want? Who else is involved in this scheme?"

Captain Bao lashed his head forward. Li Ming released him, bringing his hands back, just as his jaws snapped at the air.

"These are simple questions. The more you resist, the more you will pay for it later. Talk to us. Now," Li Ming said.

Captain Bao glared and said nothing.

"He's stalling for time," Sarantuya said.

And the only reason he would do that is…

A cold wave washed over Li Ming.

"It's going down now, isn't it?" Li Ming demanded. "The Wanjianhui is executing the final phase of its plan in Yudu, yes?"

Satisfaction gleamed in Captain Bao's eyes.

"What is going on? What are they planning? What do they want?" Li Ming asked.

"You'll find out," Captain Bao said.

"You're working for them, aren't you?"

He blinked. He tensed his lips. He said nothing.

"Or maybe you're working *with* them."

His qi field hardened. His eyes became twin shields holding against a laser-hot glare, and failing.

"I'm not saying anything to you," Captain Bao said.

"You've partnered with the Wanjianhui. That makes you co-conspirators. Terrorists."

Cai Yan stepped away, whispering urgently into her palm. Captain Bao's eyes flickered to her, and his lips curled upwards in satisfaction.

"Look at me," Li Ming said. "I want you to understand this. We are returning to Yudu and we will hand you over to the police and the Jianghu Association. Terrorism is punishable by death. Confess now and we'll put in a good word for you."

Captain Bao said nothing.

"You're a hard man. But the Wanjianhui isn't worth it. They're going to drag you down into the underworld. You don't have to follow them. Answer our questions and we can help you."

"Why should I help you uphold a world that rewards only wealth and power?"

"Help us understand where you're coming from. Why are you working with the Wanjianhui? What do you get out of it? Where did you get the beast controlling technology from? Is it new technology?"

"Nothing we use is new. Guns, armor, magic, the gunships, reality shapers, everything you see around you was salvaged from the bones of the Yue Dynasty and the Celestial Empire."

"It's a Yue relic?" Ghazan asked.

Captain Bao smirked and said nothing.

Ghazan pressed the point of his bayonet into his throat.

"Talk! Where did the technology come from?"

"I won't say anything to *yuegui*."

Ghazan flushed. His qi erupted. His hands clenched his weapon.

"What did you say?"

Li Ming grabbed Ghazan's shoulder.

"He's trying to rile you up. Don't fall for it."

Ghazan exhaled sharply.

Captain Bao laughed.

Cai Yan ran back to the men.

"Beasts have invaded Yudu," she announced.

Chapter Twenty-Eight

Loaded for Dragon

"What's going on?" Li Ming demanded.

Cai Yan held up a hand.

"Hang on a second. I'll bring you into a conference call."

She pulled her scroll from her pouch and tapped a few buttons. A pop-up window appeared on Li Ming's heads up display, notifying him of the new connection.

"Ms. Zhang, the rest of my team is on the line. Please brief us on the situation," Cai Yan said.

Ms. Zhang's voice, breathy and panicky, filled Li Ming's earpieces.

"Yudu is under attack! Jiaolong have surged up from the Yu river and are wreaking havoc across the city! They just attacked the hotel!"

Jiaolong. Aquatic dragons. An endangered species, but also extremely dangerous. Li Ming had never seen one before, but he'd read many horror stories while in the military.

"Are you safe?" Wong-gor asked.

"Yes. I'm taking shelter inside the metro station. The news says the jiaolong have been spotted in at least five locations. The city is locked down and emergency services are mobilizing."

"How many jiaolong are there?" Cai Yan asked.

"I don't know. I personally saw two. The news says between ten to twenty."

A single wrathful jiaolong could flatten a village. Ten was a calamity. Twenty could destroy a nation.

"Where's the Wanjianhui?"

"We don't know. My colleagues in the Jianghu Association are trying to reach them."

"Is there anything major going on in the city? Anything that might be a political target?" Wong-gor asked.

"I'm finding out now."

"Do you have any contacts in the military or police?" Cai Yan asked.

"Yes. What do you need?"

"We are returning to Yudu by air. We need expedited clearance to enter the city and assist with beast subjugation operations."

"We also have a prisoner," Li Ming added.

"A prisoner? Who?"

"Captain Bao of the Yudu Military Forces."

"Captain Bao?! Impossible! What happened?"

"While clearing the Zan Family Farm, he and his men attacked us from the air with a pair of gunships. We shot them down. Captain Bao was the sole survivor."

"*Tian ah…* I knew you suspected him, but…"

"There is a terrorist plot unfolding Yudu," Cai Yan interjected. "Captain Bao might have answers. We need to drop him off with the security forces for questioning."

"*Rigorous* questioning," Ghazan added.

"Understood. I'll make a few calls."

"Excellent. We'll get moving. I'll call you back."

"We need to clear a landing zone for our airship," Li Ming said.

"How large a zone do you need?" Ghazan asked.

"Thirty by thirty *chi*. But not here. We need flat land, free of loose material and obstructions—"

Ghazan turned about and held out his hands and shouted a word.

A pillar of white light speared from the heavens, striking a patch of sorghum. The column of energy flattened everything it touched, producing a perfect square, and vanished just as abruptly. Blinking against the sudden glare, Li Ming realized that everything within the square had simply ceased to exist. No crushed stalks, no grain, just blackened earth.

"The Zan Family isn't going to happy with us," Li Ming said.

Ghazan shrugged. "They can always plant more crops."

Li Ming and Ghazan hauled Captain Bao to his feet and frog-marched him to the landing zone. Sarantuya scanned the forest, covering them. Wong-gor jogged out the compound, coilgun cradled in his hands. Cai Yan spoke into her scroll.

"We've killed most of the shanxiao. The rest have been dispersed." She paused to listen. "We can't secure the area. There's only five of us. But there are no more beasts and terrorists in sight if that's what you're asking." Another pause. "No, no survivors found. We don't have time to look for survivors. We're needed back in Yudu. We need you to conduct search and rescue operations and... No, it's not about cleaning up *our* mess. Jiaolong are attacking Yudu. There are no more beasts here. We have to go."

Li Ming patted down his pockets, scrolled through his Belt Bag, and frowned.

"What's wrong?" Ghazan asked.

"I need something to mark the landing zone with. Streamers, auxiliary lights, something like that."

"I have a colored smoke grenade."

Li Ming blinked.

"Why do you have a smoke grenade?"

"Why don't you have one?"

Li Ming shook his head. "Never mind. Once the airship approaches, pop smoke and drop it at the edge of the landing zone."

Cai Yan harangued into the scroll some more, then hung up and headed over.

"Airship is on its way. Five minutes. The local forces will take over the scene. They're not happy, but they'll do it."

"Will our kills disappear?" Sarantuya asked.

"Of course they will," Ghazan replied.

Captain Bao laughed sardonically.

"Shut up," everyone said at once.

"We need to recover the bodies," Sarantuya said.

"No time," Cai Yan said. "We have to go."

"We could leave someone behind to coordinate recovery operations," Ghazan suggested.

"Jiaolong are all over the city. We can't afford to go in with a missing man."

"We need to retrieve the dead soldiers at least," Li Ming said. "They need to be identified and investigated. We can't afford for them to disappear."

"While we do that, we can photograph the shanxiao corpses. If we document the kills, we can at least be paid *something*," Sarantuya said.

"You three go ahead. I'll watch the prisoner," Cai Yan said.

Li Ming, Ghazan and Sarantuya dispersed. The men drew their meat coolers from their Belt Bags and unceremoniously tossed the dead men inside. They deserved more dignity than that, Li Ming knew, but no one had brought body bags.

Sarantuya jumped high into the air, and stayed there. Her skin glowing white, she rotated in a slow circle, her helmet cameras taking in the scene, focusing on the dead shanxiao. And the gunships.

They returned to Cai Yan just as Wong-gor marched up to them. In the distance, the airship's thrusters screamed.

"We got everything?" Wong-gor asked.

"Yes," Cai Yan said. "Did you—"

"I documented the dead beasts as I left. That's why I took so long. The militia isn't going to steal *our* kills."

Captain Bao laughed again.

"Don't count on it. They'll chop up the beasts and sell them on the gray market," Captain Bao said.

"That's illegal," Li Ming said.

"So? You biaohang get paid for completing the mission, the militia enjoy a bonus for risking their lives. Win-win all around. It's how the Central Plains works. No one will bother pressing charges."

Li Ming gritted his teeth. After what he'd seen here, he had no reason to doubt Captain Bao.

"Since you're feeling talkative, how about you tell us what's going on in Yudu," Wong-gor said.

"Never."

The airship drew closer, a glittering bee swooping from the heavens.

"This is your last chance to confess. If you don't talk to us, you'll be talking to the security forces *and* the Jianghu Association. They'll be a lot harsher than us," Li Ming said.

Captain Bao squashed his lips together and said nothing.

The screaming of the thrusters grew louder and closer. The airship was visible now, making its final approach. Li Ming turned to Ghazan.

"Pop smoke. We are leaving."

The flight was the longest twenty minutes of Li Ming's short life.

The cabin was quiet. Everyone had retreated into their inner worlds, reorienting themselves for this new mission. Ghazan and Sarantuya watched the prisoner. Wong-gor checked and double-checked his pouches, his pack, his weapons, but handled his coilgun with immense care. Cai Yan made a non-stop series of calls, bouncing between the authorities and the Jianghu Association and Ms. Zhang. Li Ming placed his palms on his knees, straightened his back, held his head upright, and breathed. But for the screaming of the thrusters, and Cai Yan working the phone lines, there was hardly a sound.

Other than Cai Yan, only once did the biaohang speak.

"Are we loaded for dragon?" Li Ming asked.

"Jiaolong have thick scales. The cultivators among them can harden their natural armor, strengthen their claws, spew energy beams. A full-power coilgun shot *should* be enough tear through the scales," Wong-gor said.

"Should?" Ghazan asked.

"I've never hunted jiaolong before. The only flechettes I have are for soft targets. Worst comes to the worst, I could try shooting one in the eye."

"It won't necessarily be a fatal shot," Sarantuya observed.

"Better than nothing."

"My infinity gun is infinitely more powerful than your coilgun," Ghazan said. "If your gun doesn't work, then stay behind us."

Beast hunters didn't choose kinetic guns because they were powerful. They used them to minimize collateral damage. It was enough to kill a beast; blowing it up with a plasma bolt would merely reduce the richness of the bounty. However, many beasts with the magic to resist kinetic fire still roamed the world.

A small smile crept across Wong-gor's face.

"We'll be counting on you."

"If infinity guns don't work, we'll use magic," Li Ming said.

"You use Sima Clan Avengers, don't you? Your guns are more powerful than your magic," Sarantuya said.

"What about *your* magic?" Li Ming said.

"Me? I'm not much of a magical combatant. Mainly I use it for support roles."

"Not you. Ghazan."

Ghazan lifted an eyebrow. "What about me?"

"I saw the magic you used on the zhenniao. I saw what was left of them. That's way more damage than what a single infinity gun bolt would do."

Ghazan's eyes narrowed. Li Ming held his gaze.

It was an indirect accusation. For all but top-tier cultivators, the magic power they had at their disposal was but a candle against the firestorm that an infinity gun offered. An infinity gun offered focused power, reality shapers provided tactical flexibility. A silver-ranker like Ghazan shouldn't have access to so much power.

Li Ming hadn't meant to phrase it that way. But the words had tumbled out of their own accord. Once spoken, they could never be retracted.

"If our guns fail, my magic will not," Ghazan said at last.

"You sure are confident in your magic," Li Ming said.

"Of course. Yue magic is the most powerful magic in the world."

"I've seen only a few cultivators more powerful than you. They were all martial immortals or gold rankers."

A shark-like smile spread across Ghazan's face.

"I follow a strict dietary and training regimen, customized to my unique physiology."

"And supplements?" Li Ming asked.

"Of course. Without supplements, you can never reach the apex of power."

Li Ming almost asked him about qi eating. Almost. But the others hadn't heard about it yet. Dropping that bombshell here and now would shake their hearts before the mission even began. And Captain Bao was listening to every word.

"Your lifestyle sounds complicated. I could never do what you do," Wong-gor said.

"You're not bad yourself. You're the only one among us who knows how to use a coilgun," Sarantuya said.

"Thanks."

Wong-gor settled into a relaxed sprawl. Most ordinary people would be awed, terrified, or insecure in the presence of such martial immortals. Yet he was so... self-assured. Where did his confidence come from?

His expertise in sniping with a coilgun, Li Ming thought. It was a skill Dayong valued but few possessed. With this skill, even someone reduced to half a man would win respect from martial immortals.

Li Ming decided this confidence was something to learn from, to emulate, and one day, to embody. But what skill should he master? What would he make the bedrock of his identity, one that all needed but few knew?

The answer came to him in a flash.

The Li Family Magic Weapon Style.

But it was a long way to mastery, and he had merely taken the first few steps on a journey of a thousand *li*.

His thoughts turned back to the battle at hand. He triple-checked his gear and the configurations of his weapons and electronics. He pulled up the Yudu news services on his scroll and cross-referenced jiaolong sightings against the street map. He called up the Jianghu Association's database on jiaolong and absorbed what few facts hunters of ages past had learned in blood. And when his gear was ready and the facts known, he sat and breathed and did nothing more.

"We are five minutes out," the pilot announced.

"Is the airport safe?" Cai Yan asked.

"The military and police have locked down the area. No jiaolong reported in the area, but they're not taking any chances. All flights have been canceled and directed, except ours. How did you arrange that, anyway?"

Cai Yan smiled.

"We have friends in high places."

The airship landed on empty tarmac. Heavy-duty bunkers sheltered the remaining civilian craft within the airport. Soldiers hustled about, setting up defensive positions along the perimeter. A group of uniformed cops met them as they disembarked.

Four of them grabbed Captain Bao and unceremoniously marched him away. Li Ming emailed a copy of the interrogation video to the senior officer. Another four cops escorted the biaohang through the airport, whisking them past security, locked doors, and checkpoints, and deposited them at the parking lot.

All around them, the city cowered in fear. Civil defense sirens wailed on every street at ear-splitting volumes. Cars sat abandoned on the streets. The sidewalks were completely empty. Digital signboards flashed emergency warning messages. In the distance, an explosion thundered.

"We're going to hunt jiaolong?" Wong-gor asked.

"There's twenty of them, five of us," Cai Yan said.

"Good odds," Ghazan said.

"I've never hunted jiaolong before, but from what I hear, it sounds dangerous."

"Which is why we're not going to hunt jiaolong," Li Ming said.

"Then what are we here to do?" Cai Yan asked.

"We're going to hunt the Ten Thousand Swords Society."

Chapter Twenty-Nine

Raid

Biaoju did not make war on other biaoju. It was a rule of the jianghu that didn't need writing down. Any biaoju that did this would be banished from the world of the rivers and lakes and hunted like beasts. Turn against your fellow cultivators and there will be no place that will shelter you.

And yet...

"We know the Wanjianhui is involved in this. We have to stop them," Li Ming said.

"We don't have proof they're involved," Wong-gor said.

"Captain Bao admitted it."

"He didn't deny it. Besides, we have no other evidence pointing to the Wanjianhui."

"That's why they used beasts. So that there'll be no evidence. The only way we'll find proof is if we raid the Wanjianhui headquarters."

"Without a warrant? No. If we don't find proof, the Jianghu Society will shut us down. If we *do*, the courts will not allow the evidence to be admitted."

"The city is burning and you're thinking about legalities?" Cai Yan demanded.

"I'm thinking about our long-term safety. Raiding the Wanjianhui office won't do us any good if we're shut down too."

"This isn't police work. This is war," Ghazan said.

"Yes, exactly. They made war on us. We must make war back," Li Ming said.

Wong-gor sucked in a breath. His mask of confidence had fallen off, revealing anxiety and indecision.

"I... I don't know about this..."

"Don't know about what?" Cai Yan asked.

"If we do this, we're going to cross a big black line. No matter what we do, there will be consequences."

"I cannot live in a world where the Wanjianhui is allowed to carry out its plots unopposed," Li Ming said.

"Me neither," Cai Yan said.

"If you're so worried about the law, then we should leave no evidence behind," Sarantuya said.

Everyone turned to her.

"You're saying we should act like bandits?" Wong-gor said.

"Masks, infinity guns, magic. We strike hard and fast, erase our traces, use different vehicles…"

"So we should act like bandits."

"We should protect ourselves from all consequences," Sarantuya said.

"I can't believe I'm hearing this from a biaohang."

"Believe or disbelieve all you wish, but the time for argument is over. Beasts rampage through the city, and the lords of beasts are moving in the shadows."

"Do you want to sit this out?" Cai Yan asked.

Wong-gor clenched his fists. Gritted his teeth. And sighed.

"Let's go before I regain my senses."

Racing through the city, they tore down deserted streets and empty alleys at top speed, blasting past traffic lights and speed cameras. The wailing of the sirens followed their every turn. Distant eruptions hounded them. They stopped only twice, both times at police checkpoints, and the moment the cops saw their biaohang cards they waved them through.

They parked their vehicle three blocks away from the Wanjianhui office. They donned ski masks and tactical gloves, ripped off everything that identified them as biaohang, left behind their identification documents. Stepping outside, Li Ming glanced around to see shuttered doors, closed windows, abandoned cars.

There were no human witnesses.

Li Ming called up a minimap, placing it at the lower left corner of his heads up display. A crimson arrow pointed the way to the Wanjianhui in augmented reality, coursing down the road, swerving around a streetlight, and piercing through a locked gate.

Automated gates secured the narrow hutong feeding deeper into the district. The direct descendants of the gates of dynasties past, they protected the homes and businesses beyond from beasts and bandits. Security cameras watched the entrances, computers controlled the massive doors. They wouldn't stop jiaolong. But they could prevent mere humans from passing through.

So they took to the roofs.

Li Ming ran to the nearest building. A two-story coffee shop, it was built to resemble the houses of ages past, with a huge overhang that doubled as the second-floor balcony. With every step, he charged his legs with fire qi.

And jumped.

He rocketed off the ground, hands outstretched. He rose higher and higher, past the overhang, past the balcony and its empty tables and chairs, flying through a steep parabola, and landed on the roof.

The steeply-arched tiled roof.

His feet slipped. Instantly he dropped his weight, hands scrabbling for purchase. His kneepads struck hard tile, the impact mostly absorbed by hard polymer and flexible foam. He caught himself just before he fell off, then picked himself back up, this time planting his feet on surer ground.

Ghazan and Sarantuya had simply leapt up on the rooftop in a single bound and stayed upright. Cai Yan grabbed Wong-gor and flew on a column of wind. None of them had suffered a landing as ugly as his.

At least they didn't comment.

The augmented reality software went haywire. The crimson arrow circled around him, tracing the layout of the street, acting as if he were still at ground level and had simply stepped into the coffee shop. Li Ming switched it off, oriented himself to the Wanjianhui office, and ran.

Sprinting across rooftops, leaping across alleys and roads, they cut through the district. Li Ming kept to flat roofs when he could, treaded carefully when he couldn't. The others pulled ahead of him, surer in their footing and their magic.

Several blocks away, other men took to the roofs, taking up arms or running to new positions. Drones and airships screamed overhead. Large sinuous forms glittered in the gaps between buildings and streets, following the path of the city's many rivers. Distant thundering threw up great clouds of smoke. Infinity guns snarled, and the beasts answered with great ululating howls.

Li Ming kept low and continued running.

A block away, past the final set of gates, the biaohang returned to street level. Ghazan and Sarantuya dramatically jumped off, landing with feet spread wide apart, arms outstretched to arrest their momentum. Cai Yan grabbed Wong-gor again and descended on wings of wind.

Li Ming stepped off the roof, manifested earth qi, and fell as gently as a flower petal.

He found himself in a narrow hutong, flanked by one- and two-story buildings. The windows were closed, the doors shut. Dozens of qi fields burned bright deep within them, clustered close together. Bikes leaned against walls and lampposts, unguarded and unlocked.

Far away, a jiaolong roared.

Silently the biaohang formed up. Li Ming and Ghazan up front, Cai Yan in the middle, Wong-gor and Sarantuya at the rear. Li Ming led the way, keeping to the right side of the alley, sweeping the world ahead.

The hutong looked familiar. The recon video had encapsulated the entire block. But Sarantuya had walked this place from the other direction, and it took Li Ming a few moments to reorient himself.

"Head for the third bend on the left," Sarantuya whispered.

Li Ming counted the turns as he stalked down the hutong. Every time he passed an opening to his right, he swiveled around to sweep it, trusting that Ghazan would cover his left.

At the third entrance, a gate barred their way. It wasn't a particularly tall gate, barely taller than a single story. Li Ming didn't bother going around it. He just leapt straight into the air and hauled himself up on top of the structure. He sat atop the arch of the structure and trained his weapon on the alley before him.

"Clear," he reported.

As he covered them, the biaohang scaled the gate one by one. Wong-gor didn't need magical assistance. He simply jumped like Li Ming did, pulled himself up and over, and lowered himself carefully on the other side.

Sarantuya was the last to clear the gate. After she reached ground level, Li Ming slung his infinity gun and dropped to the road, using just a touch of earth qi to cushion his knees.

The team headed off again. Now Li Ming was the rearguard, watching their backs. The alley here was even narrower than before, a passageway of old brick so cramped a man could extend his arms and touch the walls with his palms.

An electric crackling filled the air. The scent of ozone drifted into his lungs. The sound grew louder, sharper, like sparks jumping the gap between a pair of live wires. Halfway down the hutong, Li Ming saw the source of the sound.

A gigantic white-blue dome covered a courtyard house in a protective bubble. Composed of thunder energy, it would electrocute—or vaporize—anything that touched it. Through the force field, Li Ming saw only the steep peaks of arched roofs. Squat boxes ran at regular intervals down the wall, anchoring the dome. Above the main gate, a black signboard with gold characters screamed 'Ten Thousand Swords Society'.

"We're here," Cai Yan said. "Breach the gate."

Ghazan aimed his palm at the huge double doors.

"Breaching!"

White light exploded from his hand, engulfing the doors. A tremendous boom reverberated in the street. Dust billowed from the point of impact. The doors were gone, shattered, *vaporized*.

And blue-white energies walled off the doorway.

"Thunder screen! No go!" Ghazan reported.

"On me!" Li Ming yelled.

He stepped away from the wall and rotated the fire mode wheel. One click, two clicks. Raising the weapon, he glanced to his sides. Sarantuya stayed safely to his side him. Wong drew his hand cannon. Behind the wall, someone yelled.

"Breaching!" Li Ming warned.

He pressed the trigger.

A cone of blinding light leapt from the muzzle, consuming all in its path. Everything caught in the nova-hot blast ceased to exist. Superheated gray smoke poured from the point of impact. The stone and brick around the edges turned to slag. The air itself exploded, rocking Li Ming with a titanic shockwave. His infinity gun expelled steam and shrieked its overheat alarm.

The dust cleared to reveal a melted mirror, half of a sink, a tap with the head snapped off, water spurting from broken pipes, a shattered toilet bowl.

A toilet bowl.

Li Ming laughed.

He couldn't help it. Something about the absurdity of the moment seized his heart and sent him into laughing fits. Even so, he released the overheated gun and drew his Viper. As he snapped the stock into place, Sarantuya brushed past him and raced to the hole. She held out her hands and shouted at the top of her lungs. Spheres of incandescent light flung from her hands and detonated against the edges of the breach. More brick and stone collapsed, making a hole large enough for two men to burst through.

Wong-gor rushed in, Viper shouldered. Li Ming trailed him. Water splashed across his visor and carrier and down his back, shockingly cold in the heated air.

The blasts had blown the toilet door off its hinges. Sunlight streamed through a cloud of smoke. Boots pounded from the hutong. As Li Ming stacked on the door, he heard a distinct *CLINK*.

Li Ming burst out the door and spun to his right. Two men stood before him, kitted in helmet and body armor, the closer with an infinity gun, the other grasping a long cylinder in one hand and a cotter pin in the other.

Li Ming fired.

Plasma bolts shattered against invisible shields. Blinding light forced his visor to darken. Li Ming advanced on the duo at an angle, hosing them down, charging at the grenadier. The gunner screamed, his gun flashing. A plasma bolt sizzled past his helmet. A second. Then Li Ming lunged.

His muzzle speared the grenadier at the base of his throat. Gasping, the man folded into the blow and went stumbling away. His hand sprang open and the grenade went flying.

The other shooter rammed his shoulder against Li Ming. Li Ming lost his balance. Turning in mid-air, he landed on his back against hard concrete. The shooter swiveled around, the muzzle of his infinity gun a great yawning hole promising oblivion.

Time slowed.

The shooter moved in a slow, dreamlike crawl, his weapon languidly rising to his shoulder. Li Ming's body languidly responded, bringing his own gun to bear, but he was far behind the curve, too slow to beat the aim. His mind raced ahead, urging his body own, but he was too slow, too late.

The grenade exploded.

White light and thunder drowned out the world. A concussive blast washed over Li Ming's prone form. The shooter winced, hesitating for a fatal fraction of a second.

An infinity gun howled.

A stream of bolts hammered the shooter's shield from behind. Li Ming got his own gun up, firing as fast as he could press the trigger. The shield sparkled, weakened, failed.

And Li Ming fired.

And the team fired.

And the shooter's upper body dissolved into a red cloud.

Li Ming stared stupidly at the pink mist. Then a familiar shape loomed over him.

Cai Yan.

"Come on!" she yelled, holding out one hand, smoking gun in the other.

Li Ming grabbed it. Cai Yan pulled him back up. As he rose, Li Ming scanned.

They were in a long, rectangular courtyard. Small rooms stood on either side of the gate, facing deeper into the compound. A gravel path wound through a patch of grass, leading to a flight of steps that fed into a gate. A small black patch marked the spot where the stun grenade had detonated. Ghazan stomped the grenadier in the throat. On either side of the courtyard, tall doors led to smaller yards.

This place was a siheyuan. Past the gate, Li Ming sensed a huge flare of energy. The cosmic tap powering the dome, no doubt located in the main hall.

"Split up and pass through the side doors," Li Ming said. "We'll pass through the side halls and hit the main hall from both sides!"

Li Ming ran to the left. Cai Yan and Wong-gor followed. Sarantuya paired off with Ghazan and headed right. The door before Li Ming was tall and sturdy, no less stout than the main gate. To his utter lack of surprise, it was locked, and when he kicked it, it refused to budge against his boot.

Cai Yan sank her hands to her belly, drawing in qi from the world. With a shout, she blasted her palms forward, sending out an invisible shockwave of pure force. The cosmic battering ram smashed the doors open. Instantly a thunder screen veiled the opening.

Without missing a beat, she raised her infinity gun, clicked it to breach mode, and aimed at the closest patch of wall.

"Breaching!"

Nova-hot plasma roared forth. The wall crumpled and collapsed in the face of the blast. Dust and debris blew into the world beyond. Viper high, Li Ming burst into the opening, spinning around to find—

Nothing.

Just a patch of dead ground. And no doors leading to the side hall.

Li Ming checked his infinity gun. It had cooled off completely, or at least close enough for government work. He angled off from the adjoining wall, checked the blast zone, and aimed.

"Breaching!"

Light. Fire. Thunder. The detonation blew in bricks and mortar, blew out glass and shrapnel. Choking smoke and steam spewed from fresh fires. Through his ski mask he scented burning plastic and fabric. Instantly his mind carried him back to another time and place, to another siheyuan he had to fight his way through.

Wong-gor rushed past him. Li Ming shook away the memory, raised his Viper, and moved to cover Wong-gor, entering—

Another toilet.

And more water splashed down on him.

Just his luck.

The men barged out the washroom and entered a waiting room. The plasma blast had wreaked its havoc here. The glass coffee table was a ruined mess, the carpet burned under Li Ming's boots, the furniture had been tossed about and set alight. As the men penetrated deeper into the room, Cai Yan worked her magic, extinguishing the blazes with precise hits of water magic.

Infinity guns screamed. Bolts blasted through the windows, digging divots into the walls. Li Ming ducked.

"Contact! Enemies in the main hall!" Cai Yan called.

Li Ming swore. He should have gotten his shields up while Cai Yan was breaching. Too late for that now. Staying low, Li Ming scrambled to the closest window and peeked out.

On the other side of the inner courtyard, the main hall loomed, boasting two wings and a taller, sharper roof. Gunmen crouched by the windows, tearing up the side halls with fusillades of fire. The thick stone held against the full-power shots, but they wouldn't last long.

Qi spiked from the other side hall. A hand popped up at a window. A scorching ray of prismatic light blasted forth. A ripple of explosions—shattering stone, bursting steam, fluttering clothes—carried across the courtyard. And suddenly the biaohang were no longer taking fire.

"Shields up! We have to keep moving!" Li Ming yelled.

Keeping low, Li Ming generated a shield out of the air, a torso-sized plate of thick metal qi reinforced with earth. Straps flowed out the underside, wrapping around his right forearm. Li Ming switched his Viper to his left hand and pressed on, orienting the shield to the window. Wong trailed Li Ming, keeping behind the shield, blasting a steady cadence of fire through the blasted windows. Cai Yan accelerated, catching up to Li Ming.

The door at the far end opened into yet another courtyard, this one shaped like an upside-down 'L'. Through windows on the right-hand wall, Li Ming saw the main hall and the main doors. Left of the door, smoke wafted from wrecked windows, marking the spots where the Yue had unleashed their devastating magic. On the other side, the windows were still mainly intact. Qi gushed out into the world.

And gunmen fired.

Plasma bolts rained on the biaohang. They cracked the stone wall, burned through the wood and glass windows, struck Li Ming's shield. Everyone ducked, shrapnel raining down on them. Wong stuck his Viper up and over the hole, blasting blindly at the shooters.

"Keep moving!" Li Ming yelled.

They cleared the bend, weapon raised. And saw only a blank wall.

"Do you sense anyone in the side hall?!" Li Ming yelled.

"No!" Cai Yan replied.

Ghazan's voice cut through Li Ming's earpieces.

"Li Ming, Ghazan. We're in position and ready to breach the main hall."

"Roger. Breach on my mark. Break. Cai Yan, on me. Wong-gor, cover us."

Wong-gor raised his Viper. Cai Yan and Li Ming raced to the windows of the side hall. Through the smoke and fires, Li Ming saw only an empty office, filled with cubicles. No surprises would come this way.

Li Ming pointed at the blank wall of the main hall and pumped his fist into the air. Cai Yan shouldered her infinity gun and moved up. Li Ming discharged wood qi into the office, all sound and fury and nothing more, the booms echoing like a stun grenade.

In the main hall, the qi fields shifted. He couldn't *quite* pin them—he was too tense, the enemy too fast—but he sensed the defenders shifting positions, preparing for an assault through the empty side hall.

Li Ming placed himself beside Cai Yan and glanced at her. She nodded.

"Breach on my mark," Li Ming said. "Three. Two. One. Mark!"

Two simultaneous explosions rocked the house. The wall disintegrated in a flash of destroying light. Li Ming chased the dying star, rushing through a thick veil of chalky powder to step into the room beyond.

A gunman crouched by a window next to the door, stunned by the double blasts, splashed in red. Emerging from a cloud of gray tinged with pink, Ghazan entered from a fresh hole on the other side of the building, infinity gun raised.

Li Ming could leave the threat to Ghazan. The moment he cleared the hole, he turned left.

Three men knelt behind heavy desks, still reeling from the explosion, all of them turned towards the side hall, all of them armed.

Li Ming's training took over. His heart went still, his brain fell silent, he saw nothing but targets to be engaged and destroyed. His hands rose, fast as lightning, bringing the Viper to bear on the closest threat. The second he saw a head framed in the reflex sight, he squeezed the trigger.

He didn't pause to look for a reaction. He snapped to the next threat, fired, flashed to the third, fired again. He swung back to the first, saw he was still up, fired.

He hammered the gunmen in a hail of rapid fire, engaging one threat at a time, as if he were shooting at three points on a triangle, degrading their shields. More shots rang out behind him. Bright lights flashed in front of him. He didn't think, he didn't notice, his attention was hyperfocused on the act of shooting, of killing.

The outflanked men scrambled, racing for cover. Li Ming fired at movement, at moving man-shaped silhouettes, pressing the trigger as soon as he had a target, moving on to the next the moment he sensed a flash. Qi washed over him, silk sheathing steel, and he knew Cai Yan was right beside him, taking cover behind his shield. She extended her palm past his ear and yelled.

Blue-white lightning leapt from her hand, blasting into the nearest target. The bolt jumped to the next man and exploded. The detonation birthed a second bolt, tearing into the last man.

Li Ming fired another triplet of shots, and the other biaohang fired also, and suddenly they were all down. Li Ming lowered his smoking gun and scanned, saw only thick red mist and blood-spattered furniture.

The biaohang flowed through the massive room, checking every corner, peering into every nook and cranny. Li Ming registered desks, monitors, computer equipment, words and images flashed across screens. He suspended apprehension, looking only for threats and signs of threats.

"Clear!" Li Ming yelled.

"Clear!" Ghazan called.

Li Ming, Cai Yan and Wong-gor breached the door to the side hall. Once more Li Ming stepped into smoke and fire. He gave the office a quick once-over, long enough to confirm there were no living things here. Cai Yan poured out the essence of earth into the fires, extinguishing the flames in a blast of dry smoke. Back in the main hall, Li Ming found Ghazan and Sarantuya standing watch.

"Area clear!" Li Ming reported.

"All clear!" Ghazan confirmed.

Spreading out, the men checked the enemy casualties while the women covered them. Li Ming found an arm flopped against a chair, a head lying on the floor staring wide-eyed at the ceiling, a man sawed clean in half. He found no intact bodies, and there were too many limbs and too few torsos for there to have been only five men.

This was a hose job, no question about it. He remembered a time when the sight and the smell would have sickened him. Now it was business as usual.

He didn't know how he'd gotten to this point.

But before he could brood on it, Ghazan called out.

"I've got a live one!"

It was the gunman by the window, the sole survivor of the Wanjianhui crew. He lay sprawled out on the floor, unconscious but breathing.

"What happened to him?" Li Ming asked.

"I kicked him in the head," Ghazan replied. "Gently."

"'Gently'," Li Ming repeated.

"He's alive. And I don't think I broke anything."

As Li Ming covered, Cai Yan patted him down, cuffed him, then cast a healing spell.

"Can you bring him back around?" Li Ming asked.

"He's suffered significant head trauma. Stabilizing him is no problem. Reviving him… it will take more time than we have."

"Do what you can."

And now, at last, the biaohang stood down.

Li Ming folded the stock of his Viper and returned it to his holster. He dissolved his shield and patted himself down for wounds. He found nothing, but when he touched his helmet he felt a deep gouge of melted polymer.

He shivered. That was *too* close. He hadn't even sensed the hit.

"Everyone all right?" Cai Yan called.

"I'm okay!" Li Ming said.

"We're good!" Sarantuya replied.

"Spread out and search the area. Let's see what we've got," Li Ming said.

Chapter Thirty

Smoking Gun

As his blood cooled and his heart settled, Li Ming's brain pieced together everything he had seen of the main hall into a single contiguous reel. He walked the room once more, picking up the minor details he had missed during the initial sweep.

Clusters of industrial steel desks formed rows and bows, demarcating the hall into discrete workstations. Every table sported processors, scrolls, stationery. Military-grade radio sets and telephones occupied a corner of the hall. An overabundance of keyboards, touchpads and mice inhabited the tables.

Huge screens mounted on stands dominated the walls. Collectively the main screens showed a map of downtown Yudu. Dozens of red dots congregated at a half-dozen clusters. At the edge of the display, two teams of five blue dots each closed in on a single cluster. A third team stood their ground in a large building in the center of the map. More blue dots flew solo, orbiting the red groups.

Smaller screens at the side of the hall tracked other information. Live news broadcasts from the city's major media channels. Updates on the beast surge from online newspapers. Media feeds from the Yudu police, military and city government. More maps, these showing the airport, the highways, the port.

This was a tactical operations center. He'd been in too many in his short military career to ever forget what one looked like. The radios were a dead giveaway. But there were no monitors, holographic windows, or any other displays on the desks.

They didn't need external displays, Li Ming realized. The dead all wore headsets, no doubt serving as display and input devices. He pulled one off the nearest corpse and looked through the lenses. The lock screen showed the time and date, and demanded a password and vital signs.

"Are the dead men's headsets locked?" Li Ming asked.

Everyone checked the headsets.

"Locked," Ghazan confirmed.

Li Ming took a mental step back, taking in the room in its entirety, ignoring the corpses and the gore. The Wanjianhui was coordinating a major operation. Two teams of shooters were engaging hostiles, most likely the jiaolong, a third team was staying put. The solo dots must be drones or aircraft. They were drawing open source intelligence and aerial imagery to drive their decisions.

But this was not a smoking gun. There was nothing here that pointed to the Wanjianhui's plot.

Dread chilled his heart. Was the Wanjianhui truly on the level? Were they truly a legitimate biaoju that served and protected the people?

Had Dayong just slaughtered a group of fellow biaohang?

He breathed them out. Fear clouded the mind, and there was never a good time to panic. There had to be something else he could work with, something that revealed the Wanjianhui for who they were. He just had to see...

The monitors.

"Which computers are the monitors hooked up to?" Li Ming asked.

The team spread out, questing for the answer. They followed the long cables to three separate processors.

"These computers aren't locked," Li Ming declared. "We should go through them."

By the main screens, Ghazan withdrew a cable from his Belt Bag, wired the processor to his scroll, then extended the screen of the flexible device to its full length. Li Ming peeked over the Yue's shoulder, staring at the device.

Ghazan deftly navigated a series of prompts, all in the Yue language. The small display reproduced the maps on the main screens in miniature. This time, Li Ming made out a bar running along the bottom length of the screen filled with icons. Including a vertical ellipsis.

"Open the menu," Li Ming said, pointing at the icon.

Ghazan touched the button. A host of options appeared.

Including 'Beast Controller Status'.

Without prompting, Ghazan selected it. The screen refreshed, now showing a long list.

Controller-1

Status: Active

Program: Rage (directed)

Targets: 3

Controller-2

Status: Autonomous

Program: Fear (general)

Targets: 2

Controller-3

Status: Standby

Program: Pacify

Targets: 0

On and on the list went. There were ten of them in all. Ghazan clicked on the first option, revealing yet another list, this time with eighteen entries. Li Ming glanced at the top.

Target type: Jiaolong, adult male

Status: Rage

Influence: Active

The remaining entries followed the same fashion, differing only in the type of target. There were adult males and females, juveniles, and a pair of elder jiaolong.

"This is it," Li Ming said excitedly. "The Wanjianhui are controlling the beasts!"

"Is there a way to shut down the drones?" Sarantuya asked.

Ghazan swiped through menu after menu after menu. He found weather reports, force trackers, maps, everything but an option to shut down the controllers.

"I think this computer only collates and displays information from the other workstations," Ghazan said.

"Maybe one of the other computers controls the controllers?" Sarantuya suggested.

"We need to hack into the computers to find out, and I'm no hacker," Li Ming said.

"Me neither," Sarantuya said.

"We've got hunters and biaohang in Dayong, but no hackers," Cai Yan said, strolling over. "Never thought we needed one on a job like this."

"What do we do now?" Sarantuya said.

"Photograph the evidence. We need to document this for the authorities," Li Ming said.

"I'll do one better. I'll image the computer on my external storage drive," Ghazan said.

"Go for it."

Ghazan produced a solid state drive from his Belt Bag and plugged into the processor. His interspatial storage device was like a cave of wonders. Every time the team needed something, Ghazan just had to reach pull it out. Li Ming wondered what else he had inside the deceptively small device.

I really, really have to buy one of these, Li Ming resolved.

As Ghazan went to work, Li Ming turned his attention back to the maps on the main screen. He photographed the screens with his helmet-mounted camera, then compared the photographs to his street maps.

And blinked.

"What the devil is the Wanjianhui doing at the Merchant Association headquarters?"

Cai Yan pulled Li Ming into a conference call with Ms. Zhang. The second she picked up, Cai Yan repeated Li Ming's question.

"The Coordinating Council is holding a secret meeting today," Ms. Zhang answered.

"Wait a second. What's going on? Why didn't you tell us?" Li Ming demanded.

"I just found out about it myself. The Coordinating Council is holding a preliminary meeting today, in preparation for the meetings later this week."

"What's this preliminary meeting for?"

"The members of the Coordinating Council come from all over the Central Plains. They represent the major cities, the Ten Corporations, the guilds and unions. Before they officially act as one body, they usually come together to negotiate, strike backroom deals and align their positions."

"Was the Wanjianhui hired as security?"

"One moment. I'm going to check my scroll."

The moment dragged into a minute.

"There are no records of the Council hiring the Wanjianhui through the Jianghu Association. Likewise, the police paperwork on the meeting states that the Council will rely on in-house security," Ms. Zhang said.

"When the attack went down, the Council must have hired the Wanjianhui directly," Cai Yan said.

"Or the Wanjianhui acted on their own and swooped down like big heroes," Li Ming added.

"How do you know the Wanjianhui is at the Merchant Association headquarters?" Ms. Zhang asked.

"We raided their office."

Silence.

"You... *what?*"

"We raided their office."

"You raided... Why? That's... How did you even—"

"No time to explain. Listen up. The Wanjianhui set up a tactical operations center. We found tech that lets them control beasts. They use their controllers to agitate their emotions and draw them to a location. They are coordinating the beast surge, *and* their own response to it."

Ms. Zhang uttered something harsh and bitter in the local dialect.

"They created a fake crisis?" she whispered.

"Looks like it. They must have gotten word that the Coordinating Council will be meeting today. By attacking the city with beasts, they cause the Council to panic. Then they come in and save the day and win their adoration. Shuanglong was just a dress rehearsal. This is the main event."

"But this doesn't make sense! The Wanjianhui is already one of the premier biaoju in the Central Plains. What more do they want?"

"The tech," Cai Yan said. "They must be using this invasion as an opportunity to show off their beast controlling tech. It will open many doors to them."

"More than that, they'll prove that the private sector is superior to the military in handling beasts," Li Ming said. "It'll win them influence in the highest levels of power in the Central Plains. With *guanxi* like this, they could use the Central Plains as a base to spread their tentacles across the Continent."

"All this sounds like speculation to me," Ms. Zhang said.

"We have their computers. We have a prisoner. The police can pick them up. Call them and dispatch them to the Wanjianhui headquarters," Li Ming said.

"Understood."

When Ms. Zhang hung up, Cai Yan frowned at the screen.

"The Wanjianhui has fifty shooters, yes?"

"Thereabouts," Li Ming said.

"There were about ten men here. We're tracking thirty on the screen. But that leaves ten shooters unaccounted for. For an operation as major as this, wouldn't they want everybody in the fight?"

Li Ming's blood chilled.

"Those ten men could be a quick response force. They could be coming back here."

Cai Yan cursed.

"Everyone! Enemy reinforcements may be inbound! Grab everything you can and shove them in your Belt Bags! We have one minute!"

"And the prisoner?" Wong asked. "We're taking him with us?"

"We'll drop him off at the nearest police station."

"Wait!" Li Ming said. "We need to make sure the Wanjianhui or their allies don't rescue him too."

"We're undermanned. We cannot afford to leave one man behind to guard him."

"Ms. Zhang," Wong called out. "We pick her up too and take them to the police station."

"That works," Li Ming said.

Cai Yan and Li Ming paired up and worked the front of the hall. His Belt Bag swallowed up everything he threw into it: computers, keyboards, headsets, weapons. As he worked, a thought struck Li Ming.

"Why is the Merchant Association team stationary? Shouldn't they be evacuating the Coordinating Council?"

Cai Yan froze, the confiscated infinity gun in her hands stuck halfway in a black hole. And looked up at the map.

"You're right. There's no reason for them to stay put. There are no jiaolong in a five-block radius around them. Unless..."

"They're protecting the building," Li Ming finished.

"And the only reason to protect the building is if the principals are still on site. Maybe there's a bunker and they're holding out for reinforcements?"

"Or maybe the Wanjianhui launched a coup."

Chapter Thirty-One

You Cannot Stop Us

Ms. Zhang was a fixer, not a fighter. So she fought the way a fixer would.

By the time Dayong reached her position, the entrance to an underground metro station, they found a squad of biaohang standing guard. They carried a hodge-podge of kit, mostly low-tier guns and gear and no-brand shapers and armor, but they were united in purpose. In the center of the formation stood Ms. Zhang, her pistol clutched in her hands.

Ms. Zhang climbed into Dayong's rented vehicle, squashing her in next to Li Ming. Her protectors followed in their own cars. As they sped off, Cai Yan updated Ms. Zhang.

"You launched an unauthorized raid on a gold-ranked biaoju?" Ms. Zhang exclaimed. "Are you courting death?"

"Captain Bao confessed to collaborating with the Wanjianhui," Li Ming said.

"You didn't have a warrant. We have rules here!"

"*Now* she says the Central Plains has rules," Ghazan remarked.

"The laws of the Jianghu Association allow biaohang to act freely during 'exigent circumstances'. This counts," Cai Yan said.

"Pray your lawyer can hold up this defense in court. I can't."

"We just need you and your protectors to guard the prisoner and the evidence," Cai Yan said.

"We can do that."

"Where did your biaohang come from, anyway?" Li Ming asked.

Ms. Zhang squirmed in her seat. Her skin, shockingly cool and soft, brushed against Li Ming.

"I issued an urgent contract. These biaohang kindly responded."

"We'll pay for it," Cai Yan said.

"Don't worry. I'm authorized to use the Association's emergency funds for this."

"These biaohang look like they're bronze-rankers at best," Ghazan said.

"They're good enough for the job."

Ms. Zhang chattered into her headset, switching seamlessly between Xiayu and Yuhua. She kept up the patter all the way to the police station.

The police station stood alone on the street, a high-walled bastion of law and order. High gates sealed off access to the compound. Shutters guarded the building's doors and windows. As the biaohang spilled out their vehicles, unconscious prisoner in tow, a distant jiaolong screeched.

Windows shook. Trees shuddered. Ms. Zhang recoiled. But the biaohang, one and all, stood firm.

Ms. Zhang placed a call. The gate slid open on silent tracks. Shutters lifted, unblocking the main door. Inside the lobby, a squad of heavily-armed cops nervously regarded the biaohang. And their prisoner.

"What's going on here?" the senior officer demanded.

Ms. Zhang took him aside, showed him her identification card and whispered to him in the local dialect. As the officers stared, dumbfounded, the Dayong biaohang retrieved the gear they had confiscated.

"Every single one of these items have been documented," Li Ming said. "If any of them disappear, we will hold you responsible."

The cops continued staring dumbly. The local biaohang nodded grimly.

As the Dayong shooters turned to go, the senior cop called out to them.

"Just a minute! I have questions for you!"

The biaohang continued walking. Li Ming tossed his head over his shoulder.

"We don't have time! We've got a city to save!"

"Hold on! Where did this... this *stuff* come from? And what did you arrest this man for?"

"Ms. Zhang will explain," Cai Yan said. "We have to go."

The senior cop strode across the lobby.

"You're not going—"

Ghazan executed a parade ground about-face. Every bootstep rang in the cramped lobby. Infinity gun held at port arms, his bayonet glinted in the light. Marching up to the cop, Ghazan's eyes burned with an inner light, boring into the cop.

"Your city is burning. Only we can save it. Do *not* get in our way."

Quaking in his shoes, the policeman went pale.

"We have questions. We can't just let you leave."

Ghazan glared at him for a long moment. Then turned his searing gaze on the other cops. His qi field blazed. A sudden heat filled the lobby. Suddenly Li Ming felt like he was standing behind a furnace—and had no wish to know how the others felt.

"You cannot stop us."

It wasn't a threat. Just a simple statement of fact, delivered in a low, growling monotone.

Sweat spilled out over the cop's cheeks and neck. Wet patches appeared in his armpits. Ghazan stared at him for a second longer, then spun around and followed the team out.

None of the cops tried to stop them.

Chapter Thirty-Two

Thunder

The city howled in a hundred voices. The wailing of civil defense sirens, rising and falling in sync. The screaming of police, ambulance and fire engine sirens bouncing and echoing off empty streets. Primal shrieks of enormous beasts. Explosions randomly punctuating the discordant chorus. Guns crackling in the distance.

Barreling down desolated streets, the team raced for the city's heart. Ghazan drove the way he fought, pedal to the metal, tightly gripping the steering wheel, taking every turn at top speed. Wong shouted out directions and warnings in equal measure. Sarantuya kept her weapon close to hand, staring out the window. In the backseat, Cai Yan and Li Ming conferred with Ms. Zhang and plotted their next step.

"I can't reach anyone inside the Merchant Association headquarters," Ms. Zhang said. "No one's answering the phones."

"Is there a bunker inside the building?" Li Ming asked.

"I heard there's a safe room. I haven't seen it."

"What other physical security measures are there?"

"Cameras. Gates. Keycards. Nothing that would hold you back."

"And the guards?" Cai Yan asked.

"Nobody knows what happened to them either."

"Are there any other strange events around the city? News stations going dark, military activity, manifestos being published, things like that?" Li Ming asked.

"Nothing like that. Just little groups of biaohang, police and soldiers running around, doing what they can."

"At least it's not a coup," Cai Yan said.

"Yet," Li Ming added.

"What's the plan?" Sarantuya asked.

"We need to do three things. One, find out what's happening at the headquarters. Two, disrupt the Wanjianhui's plot. Three, neutralize the Wanjianhui," Li Ming said.

"How do we do that? Walk up to the front door, ring the bell, and ask them to let us in?"

"Why not?" Cai Yan asked. "We *are* fellow biaoju. We can say we're here to help."

"They could stop us from entering," Wong-gor said.

"Tell them I sent you," Ms. Zhang said. "Say the Jianghu Association has dispatched you on a mission to locate and secure the Coordinating Council. You cannot leave until and unless you have proof they are safe. That should get you through the front door."

"What we're doing will rock the rivers and lakes," Cai Yan said. "You sure you want your name associated with this?"

"We're all in this together."

"Thanks," Cai Yan said.

"Once we go in, the Wanjianhui might open fire," Wong-gor said. "They may start shooting *before* we enter."

"Then it is proof of hostile intent. We smash through them and carry on," Ghazan said.

"What about the guards? They can't all be in league with the Wanjianhui. I don't want to fight people who just happened to be in the wrong time and place."

"I'm putting together the paperwork for an official single-source contract," Ms. Zhang said. "Between that and your biaohang cards, you should be able to convince the guards that you're the good guys."

"How do we convince them that the Wanjianhui are the bad guys?" Li Ming asked.

"When they start shooting at us," Sarantuya suggested.

"I don't want to give them a chance to shoot at us. And wouldn't the guards join in too?"

"We may have to shoot the guards," Cai Yan said soberly.

Wong-gor cursed.

"You have magic. Can you take them down non-lethally or something?" he asked.

"I'll try. No guarantees," Cai Yan said.

The plan was simple. It had to be simple. Anything more complicated than that and it would fall apart at the worst possible time.

Even so, it had too many holes. Too many ways it could go wrong. Li Ming could think of a dozen ways the Wanjianhui could foil them before they even got to the front door. But there was no time left for talking. Now was time for action. They just had to improvise and adapt if—*when*—things went wrong.

Like now.

"What the devil is that?" Wong shouted.

A huge bulk blocked off the street. Green iridescent scales shone wetly in the sun. Finned spines flowed down the length of the enormous mass. Thick crimson blood oozed from a dozen gaping wounds, coating the road in red. The thing was so massive it dwarfed the car, blocking out the view from the windshield.

"Jiaolong," Sarantuya whispered. "I've heard they could grow to huge size, but..."

"Hang on!" Ghazan called.

Ghazan spun the wheel and pumped the pedals. The vehicle screamed through a J-turn, throwing everyone to the left. Li Ming's seatbelt locked in place. His shoulder crashed into Cai Yan's. The women screamed. Li Ming gritted his teeth.

The car slowed dramatically, tires smoking and shrieking. Just as suddenly it shot off again, tearing down a side road.

"We'll approach the Merchant Association headquarters from the west. Half a minute out," Ghazan called.

Clacks and pops and rustles filled the car. A final round of checks and calibrations, tugs and pats. Li Ming discovered he had left his Avenger on breach mode. Hurriedly he reset it to standard power and inspected the rest of his kit.

Ghazan blew through another hard turn. Now the team saw the head of the fallen jiaolong, facing away from the team. A pair of great horns sprouted from its temples, branched like antlers, curving upwards to form a bony crown. A third horn jutted out its dome-like forehead. A pair of thick whip-like whiskers extended from its muzzle to flop against the road. A great hole tunneled through its skull, leaking red and gray fluid.

The car struck a whisker. It lifted the vehicle skywards for a heart-stopping moment. Wong-gor crashed his helmet against the ceiling. The moment the car hit the road, it bounced off the other whisker. Cai Yan slammed her shoulder into Li Ming's.

"Who taught you how to drive?!" Sarantuya shouted.

"We're in one piece, aren't we?" Ghazan replied.

A third turn. A fourth. And now the team tore down a wide six-lane boulevard. Empty cars occupied the outer two lanes, leaving a straight shot down to the jiaolong. And the Merchant Association Headquarters.

An imposing pagoda of glittering steel and glass, it speared into the heavens, looming over the world around. Dramatic upswept roofs divided every floor, each shaped like an octagon folded upwards to form sharp points aimed at the world. A golden finial, a dome tipped with a delicate needle, crowned the skyscraper.

And the structure crackled with blue-white light.

A force field. Pure thunder, as with the Wanjianhui's office, but this one extended ten, twenty, thirty, *fifty* stories into the sky. As they approached, the raw qi from the shield washed over the car. Displays brightened and flickered. Unseen currents crawled across Li Ming's skin, seeking to penetrate his being. His whole body trembled, resonating with the barrage of high-frequency energy waves.

It was a marvel of magic, a work of technological genius, an awesome marriage of multiple disciplines to create a nigh-impenetrable defensive barrier. It consumed an unimaginable amount of power, easily enough to run a town, maybe even a small city. Nothing short of a concentrated assault by a reinforced battalion of armored infantry with artillery and air support could hope to penetrate a defensive screen like this.

There were only five Dayong shooters, armed with whatever they had on hand.

Ghazan mashed the brakes. Rubber burned. Tires locked. The car screeched as it slowed, coming to a halt right in front of the building. Li Ming unbuckled his seatbelt and burst out the car, kneeling beside the passenger door, orienting himself to the entrance.

No guards. No incoming fire. No sign of hostile activity. Nothing but the impenetrable wall of thunder.

Warily the team approached the building. This close to the force field, the raw qi was a tangible force, electrifying Li Ming's blood. His palms tingled, his feet crackled, his lungs drew lightning with every breath. He'd never felt such a fearsome amount of qi before. He didn't think staying here for long was healthy.

The moment his boots hit the sidewalk, the main doors opened. Two men in gray overalls stepped out, kitted for war. Full face helmets with mandibles and visor that protected the entire head, armor carriers fitted with hard plates, gorgets and groin protectors, auxiliary plates covering their legs and biceps, the entire ensemble supported by a powered exoskeleton. Their forearms mounted bulky reality shapers, up-armored for additional protection, their hands held sleek black infinity guns, and handguns rested in drop-leg holsters.

"Halt! Identify yourselves!" the taller one said.

"Dayong Biaoju! We've been contracted by the Jianghu Association to secure the Coordinating Council!" Cai Yan called.

The men glanced at each other. Stepping out, weapons pointed at the ground, they swept the group with their helmet-mounted lenses. They were assessing the group's qi. A reflexive gesture in the jianghu, but with the thunder field between them, any readings they received would be highly distorted.

"Show me your identification!"

Cai Yan slowly fished her biaohang card from her pouch, hands away from her weapons, and held it up.

"You can verify this with Zhang Mei Lin of the Jianghu Association," Cai Yan called.

"We have the situation under control," Mr. Tall said. "You can stand down."

"We can't leave until we make contact with the Council and receive orders directly from them."

The shooters looked at each other and exchanged a few lines in dialect. Mr. Small walked back inside.

"My colleague will verify with our superior," Mr. Tall said.

"You don't mind if we set up security positions around here, do you?" Wong-gor said.

"Be my guest."

The biaohang fanned out. But only Wong-gor turned around to check their backs. The others remained oriented on the main door.

Li Ming crept a few steps closer, scanning the guard. He had no nametag, no patches, nothing that identified him as police, security, or something else.

"Do you work here?" Li Ming asked.

"Excuse me?" the guard answered.

"Are you security?"

The guard hesitated.

"Yes."

"Ah. A fellow biaohang."

"I didn't say that."

"We were told the Wanjianhui is on site. That's you, isn't it?"

"I…"

"You're obviously not wearing a police uniform. The local cops don't use the same kit you're carrying. That means you're Wanjianhui, yes?"

The man stiffened.

"Yes."

"Ah. Pleasure meeting a fellow professional here."

Mr. Small stepped back outside. He whispered into Mr. Tall's ear. Both men tensed.

"We have been told not to allow any outsiders into the building. We can, however, pass a message from the Coordinating Council. They say they are all alive and unharmed. The Wanjianhui stopped the jiaolong before they could breach the building. We will be staying here until the emergency is over," Mr. Tall said.

"That's not acceptable. Under the terms of the contract, we must receive word from the Council in person. Not from a messenger," Cai Yan said.

"Sorry. We have our orders. You cannot enter."

"If it's about the money, you can go hunt jiaolong. You have the gear for that," Mr. Small suggested.

"We're not leaving until we see the Coordinating Council."

"Be prepared to wait a long time."

Mr. Tall leaned over and murmured to Mr. Small. Both men turned around.

"*Wei!* Come back here!" Cai Yan called.

The double doors slid shut behind them.

"Now what?" Sarantuya said.

Li Ming walked right up to the force field. A high-pitched hum filled his ears, bypassing his ear protection. His organs vibrated unpleasantly in his body. His visor darkened against the brilliant light. Now he saw the source of the field.

A small black box hid under every upturned eave, aimed at the world. Qi drilled outwards from the boxes like geysers, transforming into a pillar encapsulating the skyscraper. Deep underground, a wellspring of qi surged, betraying the presence of a powerful cosmic tap. The entire building stood behind the forcefield. There would be no blasting through a wall this time.

The beauty of the five element magic system was its ability to immediately counter any kind of magic the user faced. Thunder was classified as wood. Metal would cut through it. But there was so much thunder here, it might overwhelm what metal he could bring to bear, the same way chopping down many trees would blunt and damage an axe.

Or would it?

There was a chapter in the Li Family Magic Weapon Style manual that covered a situation like this. When confronting an insulting element, use the generating cycle to reinforce the conquering element. An earth-augmented cut with the swordbreaker, immediately changing to metal qi, would boost its destructive power against wood.

Or would it?

He didn't know. He hadn't practiced that far yet. He was only beginning to grasp the fundamentals, never mind advanced techniques like this. If he failed, the thunder shield would destroy the swordbreaker on impact. And him.

"I don't see how we can defeat the shield," Li Ming admitted.

Ghazan stepped up.

"I do," Ghazan replied.

"How?"

"The magic of the Night."

"You can burn through the shield?"

"I can step through it. While carrying someone."

"*How?!* It's made of pure thunder!"

Ghazan grinned.

"Even lightning from heaven must surrender to the Night."

"You've tried this... magic before?"

"Yes. But I can only carry one person at a time. Once we make entry, expect stiff resistance."

"We'll break into the lobby and clear it out. Once it's secure, I'll provide overwatch while you bring in the others."

"Sounds solid. Let's do this."

"Wait a second," Sarantuya said. "Are you going to use Night Step?"

"Yes," Ghazan said.

"I can use it too. I'll fight alongside you."

"Let's do this."

Li Ming fixed his bayonet. Ghazan fired his own spring-loaded bayonet. Sarantuya half-closed her eyes, drawing her qi into herself. Cai Yan and Wong-gor spun on their heels, covering the street.

"You ready?" Ghazan said.

There was no such thing as being ready for something like this.

"Do it," Li Ming said.

Standing beside and behind Li Ming, Ghazan seized his left shoulder with fingers like iron hooks. Li Ming instinctively yielded to the force, sending it down his torso, his leg, his foot, and into the earth. A strange energy, a cold, howling darkness whipped up around Li Ming.

"Stepping," Ghazan called.

The world disappeared.

Li Ming now stood in a universe of shadows and insubstantial form. All around him was nothing but blackness and intangible silhouettes. He stood on a blanket of thin smoke, as tenuous as a cloud, so impossibly thin it felt like it would give way under his weight and send him plunging into nothingness. Before him, the pagoda soared into an empty night, glowing a faint white. Waves of qi cycled through its shell, like a manmade fountain varying its flow at precise intervals, spraying outwards from the transmitters and falling back into the boxes, becoming a shimmering curtain.

Darkness engulfed the street, the world, everything. The buildings lining the boulevard were ghostly wirework skeletons, thin lines hinting at size and form and no more. Curved and blocky blobs suggested the existence of road vehicles, their cosmic taps cubes of incandescent light. Cai Yan and Wong-gor were blurs of prismatic colors, him a shrunken head and thin torso floating in mid-air, her a full-formed woman embraced in a thick, glorious aura.

Ghazan was darkness.

A darkness deeper than night, a total absence of light, emanating black, bone-chilling qi. Li Ming didn't see so much as *felt* him, sensed him by the shape of his gnawing, freezing qi field, a void in the shape of a man, accoutered in helmet and armor and infinity gun. His gear was suspended in space, as if completely untethered from reality, but when Ghazan moved, they moved also.

"Where the devil are we?" Li Ming spoke.

As he opened his mouth, shrieking cold invaded Li Ming's lungs, stealing his breath, fracturing his mind. It took all his willpower just to finish his sentence.

"Night," Sarantuya replied.

Like Ghazan, she, too, was an avatar of pure Night, no more than a silhouette of a woman, outfitted in armor and weapons.

Ghazan's grip tightened.

"We are outside the bounds of normal space-time. We can go anywhere, so long as I can hold on to the magic. Once I let go, you'll fall back into reality," Ghazan said.

Li Ming sucked down a breath. An evil wind froze and burned his insides.

"Is it dangerous to breathe here?"

"No. But you need to get used to it."

Another breath. And it hurt less. Slightly.

"I've never seen magic like this before."

"You have."

"Where?"

"Your people call it interspatial storage."

"*What?!*"

"Come on. Time's wasting."

Ghazan hauled him along by the shoulder, firmly but gently. Li Ming didn't walk so much as *float*, his feet effortlessly propelling him forward. Friction felt weak here, gravity a mere suggestion. The thunder shield, once fierce and crackling, now seemed nothing more than a thin veil of sluggish electricity.

"How are we going to bypass the shield? Just walk through it?" Li Ming asked.

"Yes," Sarantuya said.

And did just that.

Li Ming blinked.

Blinked again.

He saw it. He wasn't sure if he believed it. The Yue woman had simply walked right through the shield as if it weren't there.

"Come on," Ghazan said. "Our turn."

They stepped through.

Qi washed over Li Ming's skin. It was pleasantly warm, like a hot shower on a cold winter's night. His body instinctively sucked some qi down. Electricity jolted through him, concentrating in his liver, then dispersing to his organs and extremities.

And just like that, they were through.

The double doors proved even less of an obstacle than the thunder field. Passing through it was like walking through mist. Now they stood inside the entrance hall. Divided into two halves, the public area was a vast open space of sofas and sculptures and pillars and potted plants, while the secure zone funneled down to two separate lift lobbies. A long desk and a longer line of automated barriers demarcated both sectors.

Two blurs of buzzing gray light, one tall and one short, sat at the reception desk. Two more stood in the left-hand lobby. Another man crouched in the other lobby, half-way through a squat.

All had helmets, body armor, shapers and infinity guns.

"We have a bit of time. We should plan our assault before we return," Ghazan said.

Looking closer, Li Ming realized the men were frozen in time. The squatting man was locked in an awkward position, neither fully upright nor completely lowered, a posture that would strain the thighs and calves before long. The men in the other lift lobby were leaning towards each other, as if in conversation. The duo at the desk—Mr. Big and Mr. Small—gazed intently at the entrance, guns cradled close to their bodies.

"Do you think we can disable the thunder field?" Sarantuya asked.

"How?" Li Ming asked.

She pointed.

Deep underground, past two large voids filled with spectral vehicles, a large structure blazed with light. Bright and blinding, Li Ming could barely look at it. It must be the cosmic tap he had sensed outside. A dozen people were clustered in an adjacent room, hunched over ghostly consoles and tables.

Across a hall, a gang of eight men occupied a large room. Three of them sat and stared at screens. The others, carrying long objects in their hands, lounged about, sitting or standing close together, relaxed yet monitoring the displays.

A third group of humans glowed bright, almost as bright as the cosmic tap. A hundred of them, packed tightly together, spread across the largest room of all. Looking at them, Li Ming vaguely remembered an illustration from his high school chemistry textbook, showing water molecules randomly bouncing off each other in crazy vectors.

The first group were the technicians managing the cosmic tap. The last group had to be civilians, locked away in a bunker. That meant the second group was the security team.

The security office would control the thunder field. The cosmic tap powered the shield. Knocking out either, or both, would knock out the shield.

Or would it?

"No," Li Ming said. "We'll have to bypass the security protocols. If we can't, we'll have to fight our way up, and I can't see a route back up to the surface. The enemy could defeat us in detail while Ghazan brings in the others."

"We destroy the enemies here, then destroy them below," Ghazan said.

"Wait a second."

Li Ming looked up.

High above, a fuzzy cloud glowed a faint white, individual colors spilling out at the edges. A qi field, the kind formed by bringing a group of people together.

"Are those people?" Li Ming wondered, pointing at the field.

"Have to be," Ghazan said.

"What are they doing there?"

"Boys, hurry up. I'm running low on qi," Sarantuya interjected.

Li Ming pointed at the solo guard.

"We take him from behind. I'll neutralize him. You two cover me. Then we do the others," Li Ming said.

"Roger," Ghazan said. "Hang on."

Ghazan *flew*.

He didn't run. He zipped across the entrance hall, his feet levitating off the floor, dragging Li Ming with him. The men phased through a sofa, a pillar, a barrier as if they were nothing. All Li Ming felt was a full-body sensation of softness, as if he had flown head-long into a field of feathers, parting before him.

Ghazan halted right behind the squatting guard. Sarantuya took her place next to Ghazan.

"Ready?" Ghazan asked.

"Go!" Li Ming said.

Ghazan released.

Color and sound and sensation flooded back into the world. Dazzling lights reflected off warm marble floor and gilded walls. A crack reverberated in the hall. Hot qi flowed back into him, driving out the coldness that had infiltrated his being. Li Ming blinked, dazed and disoriented, half-blinded by the sudden light.

The guard froze.

And twisted around.

And Li Ming pounced.

In a single, swift motion, he kicked out the back of his knee, wrenched his head back with his left hand, wrapped his right arm around his throat—

Neck protector!

The gorget blocked off the guard's throat, keeping Li Ming from accessing his neck. The guard recovered, reaching up to claw at his forearm. Li Ming snaked his hand in between the mandible and gorget and gripped the man's chin. Twisting around, he wedged his knee against the back of the shooter's leg and threw him down, smashing his head against the marble floor with a thunderous boom.

"What the devil was that?!" a man yelled.

Li Ming turned back around, bringing his gun up, and in his peripheral vision he caught sight of a black dome mounted on the ceiling.

Camera.

"Ah Guo! Are you okay?"

Wheels rolled. A chair squeaked. Boots echoed in the entrance hall. Shadows danced across the illumed floor. Qi, hot and bright, surged through the world.

Should have taken out the other two guards first!

Ghazan eeled himself to the closest wall, in the blind spot around the corner. Li Ming rushed to Ghazan's side. Sarantuya angled off, qi crackling off her.

Mr. Tall stepped around the corner, weapon at his shoulder, muzzle sweeping towards—

Ghazan struck.

Stepping in, he snapped his infinity gun in a clockwise circle, smashing Mr. Tall's infinity gun away. Quick as a snake, he swooped low, sinking the bayonet into his belly, into the gap between the armored vest and groin guard. The shooter doubled over with a loud whoosh.

Ghazan fired.

Heat and light and sound blasted in the confined space. But Mr. Tall remained standing, his flesh mostly intact. Ghazan swiftly retracted his bayonet, pivoted around, and rammed his shoulder into Mr. Tall.

Mr. Tall went flying.

He crashed into Mr. Small, knocking him down, and sprawled out over him. Ghazan raised his weapon and hosed them down with a spray of continuous fire. Shields sparkled, struggling vainly against the barrage.

Li Ming yanked a stun grenade from a pouch, pin the pin, tossed it high round the corner.

"*Zhen dan!*" Li Ming warned.

The grenade erupted in blinding light and deafening thunder. Li Ming sensed none of it. Ghazan crouched and pivoted around the corner. Li Ming leaned out, his muzzle above and past Ghazan's helmet.

The blast had caught the two surviving guards in the open. Their high-tech helmets had saved their senses, mostly, but the detonation had thrown them off-guard. In that fatal split-second, Li Ming snapped up his infinity gun and fired.

Left and right, right and left, he went back and forth, firing them up, pumping out bolts as fast as he could pull the trigger. Ghazan added his gun to the weight of fire, drowning both men in a searing string of explosions.

The right-hand man's shield failed. Bolts smashed into his body armor, rocking him back. Li Ming continued firing at both men, stitching them up. The target raised his gun, then a lucky bolt struck the weapon. The cosmic taps blew, destroying the gun and his hands. Then a bolt burned through his visor and reduced his head to steam and shrapnel.

The other man fell back, retreating for the other lobby. As he rounded the corner, a stream of bolts slammed into him, destroying his shield, dissolving his arms and neck and face.

Li Ming turned to Mr. Big and Mr. Small. Both shooters lay sprawled on the floor in a pool of blood. Mr. Small squirmed out from his partner, reaching for his—

"GUN!" Li Ming warned.

And fired.

He deluged them in fire, aiming for center mass. A stray shot struck the floor next to Mr. Small's hand. Belatedly he realized he ought to have set his gun to double power. He compensated by working the trigger, keeping up the fire and—

A blast of star-hot fire washed over the men.

In its aftermath, there was only ashes.

And fingers.

Li Ming stared at the scene for a second, until at last his brain realized what he was looking at. Then he swept the lobby.

"Clear!" Li Ming called.

Sarantuya's voice carried from the other lobby.

"Clear!"

Li Ming glanced behind him.

And the man he had thrown down was moving.

His fingers twitched. His chest heaved. And his neck lay twisted at an unnatural angle.

Why wasn't he dead? Li Ming should have finished him off!

But... maybe some good could come from this.

"Ghazan, on me! Sarantuya, check on the enemy casualties!" Li Ming yelled.

He leapt over to the downed man. The patient's hands twitched, trying to curl up. His breathing came in quick, desperate bursts, faster with every passing moment. His qi swirled around him in chaotic whirls, vainly trying to organize.

Li Ming grabbed the man's infinity gun. The patient spasmed, as if trying to resist, but the best he could do was to lift his hands slightly off the floor. Li Ming delicately lifted the man's head, just enough to clear the sling, then unslung the patient's weapon and threw it aside.

"Ghazan!" Li Ming called.

"Here," Ghazan said, kneeling by Li Ming.

"Stabilize his head. I'm going to disarm him."

Ghazan braced the helmeted head in both hands. Li Ming pulled the patient's handgun from his holster and tossed it into another corner. Then he unstrapped his reality shapers one at a time and flung them away. The patient offered only grunts and scant resistance. Li Ming crouched by the patient's head, looking him in the eyes.

"How badly are you hurt?" Li Ming asked.

"Go... die," the man replied.

"It looks like a broken neck. Stay still and breathe deep."

The patient glared.

"Where are you from? The Wanjianhui?"

He said nothing.

"Where is the Coordinating Council? Are they in the bunker?"

"I've got... nothing to say... to you."

"Do you still need me?" Ghazan asked.

"Not right now," Li Ming said.

"I'll get the others."

"Go."

Ghazan released the casualty and stepped back. His skin burned black. His eyes glowed white. And he *vanished*.

At the other side of the hall, a loud crack split the air.

Li Ming blinked, marveling at Ghazan's sudden disappearance for a moment. Then looked back down.

"Tell me where the Coordinating Council is, and I'll help you."

"You'll... kill me... anyway."

"No. You're going to live. But if you don't tell me where the Council is by the time my friends get back, we have to leave you here."

A flash. A crack. Then:

"Coming in!" Wong-gor announced behind him.

"That's one," Li Ming said. "One more. Where is the Council? Where's the rest of the Wanjianhui?"

"Heading out!" Ghazan yelled.

The downed man whispered something, lost in Ghazan's voice.

"What did you say?" Li Ming asked, leaning closer.

"Go to... your mother."

A green light flashed. Li Ming looked up.

The lobby hosted a bank of four elevators, two on either side. A door at the far end led to the emergency stairs. The indicator light above the closest elevator flashed green.

The car was headed up.

"Incoming!" Li Ming yelled. "Take cover!"

Li Ming leapt away and scrambled behind a corner. Wong-gor rushed to him. Li Ming leaned out, crouching low. Wong-gor went high, bracing his coilgun against the wall.

Qi flared from the elevator shaft. People, lots of people. Li Ming exhaled sharply, relaxing into his breath, and held out his palms. Wong-gor clicked a lever.

"When they come out, I'll douse them in fire," Li Ming said. "You finish them off."

"Understood," Wong-gor said.

Another flash. Another crack.

"Coming in!" Cai Yan announced.

The elevator doors opened.

A man in a suit stumbled out.

An unarmed man.

More people spilled out the doors. A woman in a bright floral dress, a trio of janitors, a child—

"They're civilians!" Li Ming called. "Don't shoot!"

Gunfire roared from the *other* lobby.

"CONTACT!" Cai Yan yelled.

The civilians shrieked. Panicking, they scattered in every direction.

"DOWN! DOWN! HEADS DOWN!" Li Ming yelled.

They threw themselves to the floor, curling up in balls. The man in the suit grabbed the woman and yanked her down, covering her with his body. The child screamed, running back into the elevator. The infinity guns continued to scream.

A string of blasts thundered in the hall. White light washed over the hall.

"Li Ming! Over here!" Ghazan called.

"Can you cover them?" Li Ming asked.

"Yes. Go!" Wong-gor said.

Li Ming broke away, bringing up his gun. The women crouched by the corner of the other lobby. Ghazan stood out in the open, wreathed in golden flame.

"Stairwell!" Ghazan shouted, pointing at a door.

Next to the door, a line of smoking holes drilled through the wall.

"With you!" Li Ming replied.

Ghazan charged the door. Li Ming followed. The Yue was *fast*, faster than any man had a right to be. Light and heat poured off the Yue, as if he were a living furnace. Li Ming channeled fire into his muscles, struggling to keep up.

Ghazan bulled through the door. It blasted off its hinges and flew into the shaft beyond. Still running, Li Ming gaped, then followed him into the stairwell.

Blood.

A lake of blood covered the landing. Pink steam swirled and vanished in the harsh electric lights. Five bodies lay flung about the floor, the guardrail, the steps, the walls. All of them had been drilled clean through, leaving enormous gaping wounds. Bloody divots, five of them, marked the far walls.

Li Ming gaped. The magic had penetrated the thick concrete wall, lanced through hard armor rated to resist a plasma bolt as if it were butter, and blasted deep into the innermost structure of the stairwell.

Ghazan had done this?

As Li Ming processed the sight, a downed man next to Ghazan stirred. Still clutching his infinity gun, he drew a ragged breath. A sucking sound emanated from his chest.

Ghazan kicked him.

The visor shattered. Bone crunched. Gore splashed. Ghazan lowered his boot, and the man went still.

"Clear," Ghazan said.

Li Ming rushed to the guardrail and looked down.

"Downstairs clear!"

Ghazan aimed his weapon upwards.

"Upstairs clear!"

"All clear!" Li Ming called.

Ghazan exhaled loudly. The qi flames extinguished. His skin darkened to a dusky hue. The light and heat faded away. Now he stood once again as a man, a mortal, a celestial embodiment of war who had willingly, if reluctantly, abdicated his divine birthright.

"What happened?" Li Ming asked.

"Enemy reinforcements rushed up the stairs. We took care of them," Ghazan replied.

"They sent civilians up the elevator in the other lobby."

Ghazan's eyes narrowed.

"A distraction."

Li Ming's blood ran cold.

"Human shields."

If Li Ming hadn't seen the unarmed man's hands… if he'd unleashed the flames without checking his target… if he'd struck the child…

He didn't want to think about it. Only that he *hadn't* done any of these.

As Ghazan and Wong-gor guarded the lobbies, the women tended to the civilians. Cai Yan coaxed the child out of the elevator, then brought out everybody else. The civilians remained prone on the floor, hands protecting their heads. Sarantuya kept a close eye on the shooter with the broken neck. Li Ming collected the discarded weapons from the fallen, shoving them into his Belt Bag.

"Is anyone injured?" Cai Yan asked. "We're here to help."

Silence.

"Who's in charge here?"

The man in the suit looked up.

"I think that's me," he said. "What's going on?"

Cai Yan knelt, looking him in the eye.

"What's your name?"

"Xu Weixiang, General Manager of the Administration Department."

"We're from Dayong. We're here to help."

"Help?" General Manager Xu glanced to his side. "Isn't he from the Wanjianhui?"

"We think the Wanjianhui launched a coup."

"A coup? How?"

"They used magic to stir up jiaolong and sent them at the city."

"That's impossible! The Wanjianhui has always protected the Central Plains!"

"General Manager Xu, focus. We have questions."

"Wait a minute. You just accused—"

"The Wanjianhui sent you up here to draw fire," Li Ming interrupted.

General Manager Xu's jaw dropped.

"We want to help, but we need to know what happened here," Cai Yan said. "What happened when the jiaolong invaded Yudu?"

"I... I was working at my desk when the sirens sounded. Security hit the lockdown alarm. They ordered us down to the bunker in Basement Four."

"Was the Coordinating Council with you?" Li Ming asked.

"Yes."

"When did the Wanjianhui arrive?" Cai Yan asked.

"About fifteen minutes after we reached the basement. The security chief called the Wanjianhui for backup. When the Wanjianhui came, they activated the forcefield. How did you break through anyway?"

"Magic," Li Ming said.

"Magic? But—"

"Focus!" Cai Yan interjected. "How many Wanjianhui members were there?"

"I don't know. Only a handful came down to the bunker. Five, six, I think. They said they will hold the building against the beasts and told us to stay. And then... Their leader, Commander Chen, he entered the bunker and asked the Coordinating Council to follow him."

"What did he want?"

"I don't know. I saw him whispering to the Council, but I didn't hear what they said. They just followed him out."

"Followed him where?"

"They didn't say where they were going. I asked Commander Chen, but he just told us not to worry and that they'd be back soon."

"Why did the Wanjianhui bring you up here?"

"They didn't explain either. They just grabbed a bunch of random people and said we were needed up at the entrance hall. The Council wanted to speak to us. The Wanjianhui herded us into the lift, pressed the button, and sent us off. Next thing we knew, we got sucked into a firefight."

"What's at the top floor?" Li Ming asked.

"Private art gallery. Sometimes used as a function room. It opens out into the roof."

"The Council is there," Li Ming said. "Them and Commander Chen."

"How do you know?" Cai Yan asked.

Intuition, Li Ming's heart whispered.

"I saw them," Li Ming's mouth replied. "While traversing the Night, when I looked up, I saw a group of people clustered on the top floor. Has to be them."

"But what are they doing *there?*" Cai Yan asked.

"Nothing good," Wong-gor chimed in.

"We're burning time," Sarantuya said. "We have to go."

"Return to the bunker, barricade yourselves inside, and tell the security team to call the police. The *real* police, not any other biaoju," Cai Yan said.

Li Ming didn't like leaving potential hostiles at his back. Standard operating procedure would be to search and restrain the hostages, then evacuate them. But they were all trapped in here, the biaohang had to maintain their momentum, and most importantly, they had no time left to waste.

They had to go.

"Where are you going?" General Manager Xu asked. "What are you going to do?"

"Save your city," Li Ming said.

Chapter Thirty-Three

Essence of Fire

Fifty stories was a long way to fly.

Security could jam the elevators. Climbing fifty stories on foot would take more time and energy than they could spare. That left them with magic.

With their magic arts, they ascended the stairwell. Cai Yan grabbed Wong-gor, claimed the stairs in the western lobby, and lifted off on a column of howling wind. The Yue Night Stepped their way up the eastern stairwell, flashing in and out of existence every few stories.

Li Ming blasted up the shaft on spears of fire, burning the air around him to become a human rocket.

Every ten flights, Li Ming paused to recharge. Ten deep breaths, enough power to send him soaring another ten flights. It was the limit of his capability.

It was slow.

Ghazan was the first to arrive. He was like a demon, the way he blinked up the stories, taking only a second to rest in between steps. Cai Yan and Wong-gor were next, her flight continuous and uninterrupted. Next was Sarantuya, scant seconds after Cai Yan. Li Ming took up the rear.

Ghazan was a beast. Cai Yan was an immortal, and she had hauled Wong along for the ride. But Sarantuya? Her qi levels hovered at around fifteen hundred points, not much more than Li Ming. How did she beat him? Was Night Step more energy-efficient? Did she have more practice? Or was there something else there?

At the landing between the forty-ninth and fiftieth floors, Li Ming hauled himself up and over the guardrail to find Ghazan covering the steps leading up to the top floor, Sarantuya supporting him.

"About time," Ghazan said.

Li Ming grunted.

"All call signs, Li Ming. I'm in place. Hold position. The enemy might have set up an ambush for us."

"Any ideas?" Cai Yan asked.

Li Ming turned to Ghazan.

"We'll recon with Night Step."

Ghazan grabbed Li Ming's shoulder. Sarantuya moved up to take his place.

"Ready?" Ghazan asked.

"Do it."

As the words faded, the world bled out. Colors, sounds and shapes dissolved to black. Once again, he was back in the void outside space and time, a ghost observing the mortal realm from the great beyond.

Ghazan was a titan of cold and darkness, a living emptiness in the world, swallowing all around him. Behind him, Sarantuya was a figure of lesser shadow, but only slightly less. Past the thick, transparent wall in between them, Li Ming identified Wong-gor and Cai Yan, him by his half-formed aura, her by her immense qi field. Now oriented, Li Ming looked up, seeing past shadows of matter to hunt for signs of life.

The door fed into a small foyer. Ten men fanned out in a narrow semi-circle, crouching behind heavy shields, their weapons aimed at the elevators and stairs.

"Wanjianhui," Li Ming said, defying the shocking cold to enunciate every word.

Ghazan grunted.

Past them, the foyer opened into a wide hall. Specters of chairs and tables were scattered across the empty space. Outlines of paintings hung on the walls. A huge chandelier presided over the hall.

It was completely empty.

Outside the hall, two dozen men congregated at the northern end of the roof. They gathered around a singular figure, waving his arms like a conductor. His qi was a bonfire burning among candles, outshining the assembly, brighter even than the ten men lying in ambush.

"A martial immortal," Ghazan mused.

"Chen Bingrong," Li Ming said.

"How do you know?"

"How could he not be here?"

"We'll have to break through his men before we get to him."

"We could head downstairs and strike them from below with magic. We take them out at once and—"

"No. A single Sky lance capable of doing this *and* defeating personal shields *and* armor in one blow will consume a vast amount of qi. I expended most of my reserves during the fight and the flight up the stairs."

Was there consternation in his voice? Resentment? Or just Li Ming's imagination?

"Could you step out into the real world quietly? Without emitting sound and light?"

"It'll cost more qi, but yes."

"How's this: the two of us will step out into the main hall, while the others move up on to the fiftieth floor landing. I'll shock the enemy with a stun grenade, then you and I will burn them out from behind. If any try to run, the others will intercept them."

"Set up a crossfire with the others. We'll have more guns in the fight."

"No go. We're right in their line of fire. We have to do this, just you and me. We call them in only if the enemy turns away from the doors."

Ghazan gritted his teeth. Then grinned.

"More kills for us."

Ghazan whisked Li Ming up and through the wall. Li Ming blinked, but dared not resist him. The men emerged in a corner of the main hall. As colors rushed back into his vision, Li Ming dropped to a knee, blinking hard, breathing smoothly and softly.

He was just as disoriented as the first he flashed back into the world. He had no idea how the Yue did it without aftereffects.

As he recovered, Ghazan air-typed a message, his hands dancing in front of his face, working an augmented reality keyboard only he could see. A text window appeared in Li Ming's heads up display, describing the plan.

"Roger," Sarantuya replied.

Cai Yan sent a thumbs-up.

Li Ming's senses returned. His skin and nose reported cool, stale air. His eyes registered furniture, paintings, the chandelier. Shafts of sunlight beamed through tall windows into the gloomy hall and reflected off fine-grained parquet. Great doors on the three sides of the hall he could see led out to the roof.

Crouching, Li Ming crept to the foyer entrance. No door here, just a wide opening. In the chamber beyond, display cases and pedestals glittered in warm amber light. Delicate pottery, statuettes of fo and pusa, carvings and ancient relics rested behind the thick protective glass. A few members of the Wanjianhui squad arranged themselves around the displays, crouching low behind their shields to minimize their profile. The others formed an interlocking shield wall, each man covering his buddy. They were so intently focused on the doors before them, they didn't look at the biaohang was behind them.

Li Ming gestured his thumb at Ghazan, then pointed to the corner opposite him. Ghazan nodded and Night Stepped out. He reappeared an instant later on the other side of the opening, and slowly lowered himself to a high kneel.

Text messages flashed across Li Ming's visor.

In position, Sarantuya sent.

Ready, Cai Yan said.

With hard blinks and eye movements, Li Ming typed out his reply on his own augmented reality keyboard.

Execute on the bang.

With great care, Li Ming reached for his other stun grenade, mounted high on his chest. The noiseless buckle silently surrendered to his fingers. He lifted the grenade free, held it tight in his right hand, threaded his finger through the huge ring, and pulled.

CHING

"Anyone heard that?" a Wanjianhui shooter whispered.

Li Ming threw.

The cylindrical grenade sailed through the air. Ghazan raised his gun. Li Ming sucked down qi.

A shooter turned around.

The grenade exploded.

A shockwave of light and sound thundered through the confined space, washing over Li Ming. His visor darkened, his headset shut off, saving his sight and hearing. Glass shattered. A man yelled in fright. Ghazan loosed a steady stream of shots, shooting so fast it was like he was firing on continuous fire. Li Ming raised his hands, touching the essence of fire—

The artwork!

—Switched to metal and produced a shield. The thin plate hovering before him, he raised his infinity gun, placed the red dot on the nearest helmeted head, fired.

Flash. Bang. He swiveled right, his world shrinking down his optics. The red dot found a broad back and his finger pressed. He turned, saw a man turning to look over his shoulder, blasted him in the middle of the visor—

"THEY'RE BEHIND US!" someone yelled—

—kept turning, saw his buddy swivel around, shield high, gun rising—

—Li Ming fired—

The bolt smashed into the shield.

The shooter returned fire an instant later. Star-hot bolts smashed into the wall a hand's breadth from Li Ming's face. The shield captured a burst of bolts and disintegrated. Stone shrapnel raked his helmet. Li Ming flinched away, back into cover.

"Magic! Use magic to burn them out!" Ghazan shouted.

"The art! We can't damage it!"

Ghazan gaped.

"Are you kidding me?!"

The Wanjianhui shooters adapted quickly. Laying down a hail of suppressive fire, they scrambled for cover, calling out orders, dragging their wounded to safety. The bolts came thick and fast, a white-blue blizzard searing past Li Ming's face, promising death and debilitation with the slightest contact. As the bolts chewed up his corner, Ghazan retreated. Pressing himself against the floor, Ghazan extended his hand around the corner, drawing qi into his shaper.

Above the hellstorm of fire, Li Ming heard a distinct *clink*.

The shooting slackened. The bolts tracked high. Li Ming went low and poked half his head around the corner.

A shooter stepped out around a display case and flung a—

"GRENADE!"

The grenadier retreated. Magic blasted from Ghazan's hand. A great black wall appeared, sealing off the opening. The grenade struck the wall and—

Disappeared.

"Blocking team, breach, bang and clear!" Li Ming whispered.

"Roger," Cai Yan replied.

An uneasy silence fell in the main hall. The shooters whispered. Ghazan lowered the black wall. A shooter poked his head up.

Li Ming blasted him in the face.

At that moment, the stairwell doors burst open. A second sun went supernova in the hall, whiting out the world. Infinity guns chattered. A coilgun screamed. Men shrieked.

And a pair of men with heavy shields pivoted around the corner and into the opening.

Throwing himself against the wall, Li Ming fired a shot. The plasma blasted harmlessly against the shield, its heat searing Li Ming's skin. Momentum carried the shield man through the opening. The wall arrested Li Ming's own. The enemy turned, orienting himself towards Li Ming, but the shield was heavy and awkward, and he was pressed up against his buddy, slowing him down for a fraction of a second.

Li Ming thrust.

His weapon drilled through a tight counterclockwise turn. His bayonet sank into his exposed armpit and lanced his heart. His muzzle struck with the force of Li Ming's entire mass in motion. The spiraling blow exploded through the shooter's body, overcoming his resistance and structure, blasting him against his partner.

Both men dropped.

Li Ming and Ghazan shot them in the head until there was nothing left but blackened craters and pink steam.

"Clear!" Cai Yan called.

"Clear! Sarantuya shouted.

"Clear!" Li Ming yelled.

"Coming in!" Cai Yan said.

"Come in!"

Li Ming and Ghazan pivoted outwards, covering the windows and doors, flowing along the walls. The others trooped in, weapons raised. Stray bolts had incinerated tables and chairs, starting small fires. Smoke began to fill the hall. Cai Yan doused them with precise blasts of water.

"Outside! We need to secure the Council!" Li Ming called.

As he rushed to the exit, he generated a fresh shield. Metal once more, this time reinforced with earth. The Wanjianhui must have set their guns on double power, just like him. A standard shield wouldn't be enough.

There was no time to stack on the door. Through the windows, Li Ming saw the crowd turning around, looking at the source of the commotion. He prayed they weren't armed. He hoped they wouldn't use magic of their own. Just in case—

"*Zhen dan shang!*"

Cai Yan moved up, holding out a shield of her own with her left arm, her right arm gripping a stun grenade. Li Ming flung the door open. Cai Yan tossed the grenade through.

The crowd screamed. The grenade detonated. Li Ming stormed out to the roof. The glaring sun and shimmering thunder field shone off the white floor, half-blinding him. Squinting, he swept the crowd, weapon ready.

"DOWN! DOWN! EVERYBODY DOWN!"

The civilians quickly complied, falling to their knees and faces. Cai Yan caught up with him, shouting the same orders. At the edge of the roof, one man remained on his feet.

Dressed in gray overalls, he stood tall and erect, gazing out into the waters of the Yudu River. He spread his arms out, his reality shapers glowing with bright blue light. He had a helmet and body armor, but no drop leg holster or slung long gun.

His qi field burned like a pyre.

It was like staring full-on at the sun. Li Ming squinted involuntarily, half-closing his mind's eye. Tongues of ethereal flame licked at Li Ming's qi. The civilians parted, creating an open lane between the two martial cultivators.

Li Ming hard blinks and eye gestures, Li Ming activated his qi assessment app. His cameras scanned the cultivator's aura and returned a figure.

16738 points.

"Shut down your shapers now!" Li Ming yelled.

The cultivator pirouetted.

He moved with supreme economy of motion, of effortless grace married to concentrated will, supreme relaxation untied with distilled purpose. As he spun, his arms extended outwards. Qi discharged from his shapers, thick clouds of cold blue energy, dissipating harmlessly into the air. He held out his open palms, but a smile crept across his face.

"We've been waiting for you," Commander Chen Bingrong said.

Chapter Thirty-Four

Justice

"Chen Bingrong! You are under arrest for conspiracy and terrorism! Remove your reality shapers and surrender now!" Li Ming yelled.

Chen Bingrong smirked.

"Arrest? You're not police and I've committed no crimes. Do you even have a warrant?"

"We've been empowered by the Jianghu Association to locate and secure the Coordinating Council of the Central Plans Merchant Association."

"You slaughtered your way through *my* men, who were hired to *protect* the Coordinating Council. *You* are the terrorists!" Chen Bingrong said.

"We were safe until you arrived!" one of the civilians cried.

The Council murmured among themselves. Li Ming suppressed the urge to shout them down. These were the rulers of the city, of the region, and a single misstep would damn all of Dayong.

"The Ten Thousand Swords Society placed *all* of the Central Plains at risk," Cai Yan said. "They agitated the beasts of the region to incite a beast surge. They used beasts to assault and murder biaohang and hunters. They created this crisis and aimed to profit from it!"

"A bold claim. But you have no proof," Chen Bingrong said.

"We raided the office of the Ten Thousand Swords Society," Li Ming said. "We found a tactical operations center coordinating a citywide operation—"

"We were trying to save Yudu!" Chen Bingrong retorted.

"By controlling beasts?" Li Ming asked.

Chen Bingrong smiled.

"In partnership with our overseas branches, we have developed a prototype technology that empowers us to control beasts. Why, I was giving a live demonstration of this capability before *you* arrived."

"That's right," the civilian shill said. "Jiaolong were swarming the district earlier. Commander Chen sent them back into the river!"

"Does saving the city include sending the jiaolong into a destructive rage?" Li Ming asked.

Cai Yan pulled out her scroll and called up a set of images.

"Here!" she shouted, holding up the device. "We took these photos inside the operations center. They were using unmanned aircraft to enrage the jiaolong!"

Chen Bingrong sniffed.

"Anyone can create imagery and claim it is proof. Even now, my men are bringing the remaining jiaolong under control—"

"You deny that you enraged the beasts?" Li Ming interjected.

"The beast controllers have that capability, but I did not use it. I sought to pacify the beasts."

"*You* didn't use it, but your men did. Isn't that right?"

"How do I know *you* didn't raid the office and reprogram the controllers?"

"How could we? Most of the computers were secured. We didn't have the time or ability to hack into them, never mind use tech we've never seen before."

"You could have coerced my men into doing it. Where were you when the crisis began, anyway?"

"We were working a contract to clear shanxiao from the Zan Family Farm. Shanxiao *you* summoned."

"More baseless allegations!"

A gray-haired man in a gray suit rose to his feet with grave dignity. Deep lines highlighted a high forehead and sharp cheekbones. His thick moustache flowed into a full beard, framing a pair of thin, unsmiling lips. Through his smartglasses, his eyes were hard as steel.

"You speak with foreign accents. Are you from Zhongxia?"

"Yes," Cai Yan said.

"I do not know the law where you came from, but here, biaoju do not make war on other biaoju without warrants and evidence. From our perspective, *you* are the terrorists."

"You admitted you raided our office," Chen Bingrong said. "Without a warrant, that's a crime."

"Exigent circumstances. We were acting based on a confession from a prisoner we captured at Zan Family Farm," Li Ming said.

"And who is this prisoner?" the gray man asked.

"A soldier from the Yudu Military Forces."

"A grave accusation. Tell me what happened at the farm."

"The attack on the Zan Family Farm was an ambush. The beasts lured us in. When we were pinned, two gunships swooped down on us. We destroyed the combined enemy forces and recovered a survivor from the wreckage of a gunship."

"And what did he say, exactly?" Chen asked.

"He confessed to the conspiracy. Using beast control technology, the Wanjianhui would create a crisis, then seize the opportunity to ingratiate themselves to the highest levels of the military and government. Like what you are doing now."

"I want to hear his words. If he even exists."

"The police have taken him into custody," Li Ming said.

A jiaolong roared. A heavy grinding sound filled the air. The Council covered their heads. But the gray man, and Chen Bingrong, and the biaohang, remained on their feet. The others looked around for the source of the threat. Li Ming locked his eyes on the Wanjianhui operative.

"Let me guess: this prisoner is Captain Bao or one of his men," Chen Bingrong said.

"How did *you* know that?" Cai Yan asked.

"During the prototyping phase of our beast controlling technology, we partnered with Captain Bao and his men. We aimed to test the technology together and determine the best ways to use it.

"As testing continues, however, he revealed his true colors. We learned that he reached his position through a combination of blackmail and bribery. He offered to work with us to overthrow the government of Yudu, using beasts to threaten the city.

"We had no desire to participate in such a scheme, of course. We reported him to the relevant authorities, and together we formed a plan to trap him. We pretended to agree to his plan, so that we could identify everyone in the conspiracy and uproot it completely.

"He must have learned of our betrayal. He must have kicked off his coup attempt early. When he failed, he decided to turn you against us."

Li Ming gritted his teeth. Chen Bingrong was selling out his partner to save himself. He was a monster in man's clothing.

"That's ridiculous," Wong-gor said. "If Captain Bao wanted to launch a coup, why would he bother with us?"

"He mentioned to me that Dayong was giving him trouble. He wished to get rid of you. I advised against it. Evidently, he didn't listen. He deployed his forces without my knowledge and paid the price."

"The police stations are intact, the media is broadcasting freely, his men aren't here. Captain Bao didn't even make a statement. If this were a coup, it's a terrible one," Li Ming said.

"He was delusional. He ranted about how he would expose the corruption of the city government, show the weaknesses of the authorities, and inspire to people to revolt. He was like every half-bit revolutionary out there, all sound and fury and nothing more. But we needed to know if anyone else were backing him, so we pretended to play along," Chen Bingrong said calmly.

"We could simply interrogate Captain Bao now and see what he says," the gray man said.

"We don't have to do that," Li Ming said. "I only need to ask Chen Bingrong one question."

"Really. Ask away," Chen Bingrong said.

"How did you know Captain Bao attacked us?"

Chen Bingrong twitched.

"Why wouldn't he? He was the leader—"

"I said 'gunships'. I didn't say anything about troops in the gunships. And Captain Bao and his men were *infantry*. Not gunship pilots and crew."

Chen Bingrong said nothing.

His qi field crumbled, taking his essence with it. He seemed to hollow out, his face becoming a fragile mask guarding an empty husk.

"Furthermore, we never actually identified ourselves," Cai Yan said. "How did you know who we were?"

Chen rallied. His qi burned brighter, hotter, washing over Li Ming.

The distant jiaolong howled again. Its voice reverberated in the streets, filling the emptied city. It was closer now. And much angrier.

"We met. At the roof of the hotel in Shuanglong. Remember?" Chen Bingrong said.

"Only once. I remember your speech about how the current world sickens you, and how the Wanjianhui stands for honor, strength and gongfu."

"Yes, honor. We wouldn't stoop to treachery!"

"Tell that to my brothers, the ones your brothers killed," Cai Yan said bitterly.

"We've only met Captain Bao three times," Li Ming said. "The first two times, we accepted a contract from him, and he used beast control technology to send beasts to kill us. The third time, he showed up personally to wipe us out."

"We've done nothing but hunt beasts ever since we arrived," Cai Yan said. "The paper trail we left with the Jianghu Association proves it.

"There's no way we would pose a threat to any other biaoju. Not unless they happened to be beast lords, men manipulating the same beasts we were hunting for their ends. And only if we were in the Yudu region."

"Biaoju go where the beasts go. We kept our return to Yudu low-profile. The only way Captain Bao would know we were back here is if he kept tabs on us."

"And having two simultaneous beast surges, one in Yudu, another half a day away by car, both so deadly they need a gold-rank biaoju to handle, is too much of a coincidence, even for the Central Plains."

The gray man turned to Chen Bingrong.

"Do you have anything to say, Commander Chen?"

Chen Bingrong clicked his tongue.

Smiled.

And shrugged.

"This was a tragic misunderstanding. Captain Bao had lied to them, and Dayong had fallen for his schemes. Bao manipulated Dayong into raiding my office and killing my men."

"You are the liar!" Li Ming cried. "The evidence is stacked against you!"

"What evidence? Photos?"

"Don't forget, the police have Captain Bao in custody. And one of your men. Their testimonies will expose your lies," Cai Yan said.

His smile, fake and brittle, remained unchanging.

"There is one thing you haven't considered."

"Which is?" Li Ming said.

"*I* am a lord of beasts."

His shapers glowed red.

Red qi, hot and rising, thick and thunderous, blasted across the world. It tore into Li Ming, into his being, burning his blood, pounding his mind, quickening his heart. A scarlet curtain fell over his eyes. A murderous rage erupted within, filling every cell of his being, commanding his body to rip and tear, to kill and crush, to destroy everything in sight.

He breathed out.

In the breath he released the qi.

Now it was a torrential red river, passing through him, yet not touching him. He was empty, a void, a yielding nothingness that could not be felt or touched. Behind that nothingness was a deep, firm, stillness, immovable as a mountain, the seat of his soul, immaculate and unbreakable.

The qi departed as quickly as it arrived.

Li Ming breathed in.

And a jiaolong screamed.

A second.

A *third*.

The calls came from the south, from the flanks, somewhere in the city below. Li Ming's blood went cold.

It was all a big distraction. While they'd argued with Chen Bingrong, he'd been driving beasts to their positions. And the only reason he'd do that is—

He snapped his fingers.

The thunder shield cut out.

Clean, cool air assaulted Li Ming. The sun glared down, finally unobstructed. His skin calmed, suddenly free from the backwash of the murderous, crackling qi. The gray man's gaze switched to Chen Bingrong, to Li Ming, back to Chen Bingrong.

The beasts screamed again.

Three, four, five, a half-dozen, *more* of them, all of them converging on the Merchant Association headquarters, on the biaohang and the Coordinating Council. Metal shrieked, glass shattered, alarms blared, heralding the passage of aquatic dragons drowned in a berserker rage.

"Let me go, and I'll send the jiaolong back to the river," Chen Bingrong said.

"No," Li Ming said.

"Are you mad? Every jiaolong in the city is coming here. They will destroy everything in their path. You can't hope to kill them all."

"Here's my counteroffer: call off the beasts, lay down your shapers, surrender, and you will be treated in accordance with the law."

"I can't do that."

"Then we have a stalemate."

As Chen Bingrong spoke, he slowly stepped back, retreating to the guardrail.

"Stop! Don't move!" Li Ming said.

Chen Bingrong took another step back.

"I mean what I said. Let me go, and I'll call them off."

"You're as trustworthy as a snake."

A third step.

"It's not that hard. Just step aside, and you'll never see me again."

The gray man crept away, out of the men's line of fire. The rest of the council followed his example, opening a space between them.

"The jiaolong are coming closer!" Wong-gor yelled.

"Prepare to engage!" Cai Yan shouted.

"Ghazan," Li Ming said.

"Yeah?"

"Kill a jiaolong for me, will you?"

"With pleasure."

"Thanks," Li Ming said.

And detonated his shield.

He concentrated the force forward, transmuting it to a fist of fire and wood, striking Chen Bingrong square in the chest. An invisible shield flared into existence, long enough to shatter the spell in mutual annihilation. Chen Bingrong flinched, stumbling backwards.

Li Ming lunged.

With a single, powerful step, Li Ming ate the distance between them. Chen Bingrong stomped his rear foot, rebalancing himself. Li Ming thrust high. Chen Bingrong brought both hands up, smashing the handguard aside with his reality shaper.

Li Ming yielded to the blow, augmenting it with a powerful step and twist of his hips, slamming the butt of his weapon against the cultivator's helmet. Stunned, Chen Bingrong staggered again, hands scrambling for the guardrail. His shapers flared green, the crystals within summoning the essence of wind.

You don't get to fly away, not now, not ever.

Releasing his weapon, Li Ming charged in. His palms became blades, chopping at the threat's neck. Chen Bingrong blasted his hands up, coming up from under to deflect the double blow. Li Ming circled his hands down to his hips and stepped in with a crushing fist.

His knuckles caught Chen Bingrong square in the belly, just above his groin guard. Chen Bingrong staggered back, his balance broken, back bending over the rail—

Li Ming rushed in. Caught his collar with his right hand and pulled back upright. Seized the back of his elbow with the left hand. Spiraling clockwise, Li Ming wrapped his hand around the threat's back, sank his knees, and blasted his hip into his belly. Still turning, Li Ming popped his knees and hips back up, lifting Chen Bingrong off the ground, and slammed him down against the hard concrete roof.

Li Ming scrabbled for the threat's flank, bending over, going for his arm—

Chen Bingrong twisted around and slapped Li Ming in the temple.

There wasn't much power in the shot. Li Ming's helmet absorbed the brunt of it. But the blow carried a payload of qi, and on impact the ethereal warhead detonated, sending shockwaves through Li Ming's skull.

His ear rang. His vision blurred. Stars swam across his eyes. His hands shot open and he stumbled away.

Shaking his head, Li Ming touched his hand to the impact zone, sending healing energy into his brain. As his vision cleared, he looked up and scanned.

Chen Bingrong was back on his feet, sprinting for the open doors. All around him, the biaohang were busy engaging the incoming jiaolong. Amidst the screaming guns and the howling magic, the fight had gone unnoticed.

"HE IS RUNNING AWAY!" Li Ming yelled.

Cai Yan smartly spun around and extended her hands. Qi poured forth from her shapers, forming twin lances of light spearing the heavens.

The spears rained back down, tens, hundreds of them, surrounding the gallery. They ignited as one, becoming a wall of white-hot flame, sealing off the doors and windows. Chen flinched away, hands raised to protect his face.

"Give up! There's nowhere to run!" Li Ming shouted.

Chen Bingrong snarled.

Spinning around, he pulled something from his pocket.

And ran.

At Cai Yan.

White energies spilled from his shapers, crackling through his body. He launched himself off the ground and flew at top speed, rushing Cai Yan. Her shapers drained, she scrambled for her gun, but he was too fast, she was too slow—

Li Ming exploded.

Fire erupted from the soles of his boots, blasting him towards Chen Bingrong. His mind emptied, his heart stilled, his eyes widened, seeing the world as forces and vectors and qi. He adjusted his own flight, placing himself on an intercept course. Chambering his infinity gun by his hip, he coiled his muscles, a spring ready to explode.

Chen Bingrong startled.

He stomped the ground, blasting his qi down into the earth, killing his forward momentum. Spinning around, he turned to face Li Ming, spreading his arms out—

Li Ming thrust.

The bayonet sunk into his armor carrier. The tip parted toughened fiber, sinking deep into him—

And struck the trauma plate.

The colossal blow propelled Chen Bingrong backwards. Something cracked. The bayonet *wobbled*. Li Ming rechambered his weapon and closed in on Chen Bingrong.

Chen Bingrong was off-balance, his posture awkward, left hand covering the spot where he'd been struck. But as Li Ming approached, a river of qi poured into his dantian. Suddenly he sprang forward, thrusting his right hand forward.

Red and white light flared. Li Ming instinctively hollowed out his belly, shooting his weapon down to his groin. The handguard met a beam of burning light tinged with crimson.

And *sizzled*.

Li Ming jumped back. Chen rushed in, a sword of fiery qi in his hands, slicing away with huge, powerful strokes. Li Ming hopped back, back, trying to gain room. Chen gathered his qi and pounced, his sword crashing down in a double-handed slash. Li Ming leapt back and held up his weapon to block—

The blade cleaved the infinity gun in two.

Not again!

Chen Bingrong thrust. Dropping the useless weapon, Li Ming bounded off-line to his left, gaining his flank. Li Ming swiftly pivoted towards Chen Bingrong and stepped in with a double palm strike.

His dantian and spine undulated, sending power running up his scapula, down his arms, and into his palms. His left hand found the threat's helmet, his right smashed into his bicep. The combined force blasted Chen Bingrong off the ground, sending him sprawling. The weapon carved neatly through the concrete, leaving a smoking black scar.

A sunsword. A magic weapon, the raw power of Fire contained within the crucible of Heaven. A weapon that could cut through almost anything.

But Li Ming had a magic weapon of his own.

He seized the handle of his swordbreaker with his left hand, lifting it free of his scabbard. Twisting to the right, he brought the weapon to his hip, shifted his grip and took the weapon in both hands. He thrust the swordbreaker forward, assuming his guard.

Chen Bingrong picked himself back up, his reality shapers now recharged.

"It's over! Drop your weapons now!" Li Ming ordered.

Chen Bingrong barked a laugh.

And lifted off.

"He's flying away! Take him down!" Li Ming yelled.

Sarantuya shouted a word and punched the air.

A gigantic fist roared forth from her hand, black as night, a fist the size of a man. It streaked through the air, fingers extending to form a palm.

Chen Bingrong jinked, trying to avoid it. The hand blurred, and suddenly it was on him, all five fingers crushing down into an inescapable grip. He yelped, his breath suddenly gone. The hand spun about in midair and flung him down to the roof.

He fell like a shooting star. Yelling a curse, he spread his arms, turning to face the ground. Moments before impact, shockwaves of white light exploded from his palms. A cruel wind gusted through the world, blowing through Li Ming, rocking him back.

Li Ming winced against the sudden shock. Looking back up, he saw Chen Bingrong back on his feet, sunsword in hand, sucking qi down into his shapers.

Li Ming ran.

With every step, he filled his swordbreaker with energy. Cool water qi gushed from the five element crystal in the pommel, transmuting the weapon. The heavy blade lightened in his hands, the tip dancing in a lively circle.

The blade of a sunsword was composed of two elements, Heaven and Fire. Heaven represented the element of metal. Fire melted metal, creating a destructive combination. A sunsword was an incredibly dangerous weapon, one that demanded total respect and intense training to use. But metal also produced water. If a water-infused swordbreaker struck a sunsword…

What would happen? He swore he'd read the combination effects table in the Li Family magic weapon manual, but when he tried to recall it all he saw was a blank space in his head, and now it was too late to think. It was time for battle.

Chen thrust. Li Ming slipped to his left, the blade hissing past his ear. Li Ming stabbed out, but Chen Bingrong had used the thrust to cover a sudden retreat. Chen Bingrong stabbed high, probed low, seeking an opening, establishing range. Li Ming stayed wary, keeping his distance. Chen Bingrong was deliberately shortening his reach, trying to lull Li Ming into complacency.

But Li Ming couldn't stay out forever. He couldn't wait for Chen Bingrong's shapers to recharge and allow him another shot to escape.

So Li Ming punched.

A brown fist of wood energy leapt out from his left-hand shaper. Chen Bingrong shot out his sunsword in both hands, intercepting the fist, burning it up in a flash of light. Li Ming leapt in behind the flash, swordbreaker held low. Chen Bingrong lunged, throwing his left arm high and back, stretching his chest, extending his arm to its full length, the point of the sunsword lashing in like a snake.

Li Ming flicked his swordbreaker through a tight circle.

The blades struck.

White steam erupted from the point of impact. Vibrations ran down Li Ming's hands. Chen Bingrong's sword arm blasted across his chest. Li Ming muscled through the explosion, aiming his swordbreaker high, and thrust.

The armor-piercing point pierced Chen Bingrong's throat protector and kept on going, sinking through flesh. Li Ming twisted the blade, tearing the hole wide open, and leapt out of range.

Chen Bingrong staggered. Blood gushed through the wound. A horrific liquid gurgle escaped his lips. He slapped his left hand over the hole.

Green light flashed.

Chen Bingrong breathed.

Coughed.

Spat out a gob of blood.

Straightened.

And smiled through a mouthful of bloody teeth.

"You'll need more than that to stop me," he said.

He switched his weapon to his left hand, aimed his palm at the ground, gathered his qi—

Li Ming slashed.

Water flashed to metal. In an instant, the swordbreaker glowed gray, becoming the core of an energy sword. As the swordbreaker slashed down, the metal qi tore free, forming a sharp crescent. The energy blade howled through the air, seeking flesh.

Chen Bingrong cut.

The sunsword sundered the metal crescent, dividing it in half. He flowed with the momentum of the stroke, slipping away from the swordbreaker, then hopped in and whirled around with a backhand cut, going for Li Ming's throat.

Li Ming side-stepped, torquing through a cut of his own. Earth qi surged through the swordbreaker, solid and heavy, turning the blade into a leaden weight. The swordbreaker was slow to rise but fast to fall, cutting through a tight arc, and crashed against Chen's sword hand.

Bone shattered. The hand opened. The sunsword fell at Chen's boot.

Li Ming lowered his swordbreaker and burst in with a left-handed palm strike. His palm spiraled as it rose, spiraled as it fell, a textbook metal fist from wuxingquan, and crashed into Chen Bingrong's helmet.

And sent a blast of wood qi through him.

Wood was light, fast, straight as an arrow. What an arrow struck collapsed into the point, be it fabric or flesh. The wood qi blasted through his spine like an arrow, tearing up and collapsing his nervous system, his energy circuits, everything in its path. Chen Bingrong screamed and spasmed uncontrollably, as though he were being electrocuted—and, indeed, the effects were not so different.

Chen Bingrong fell.

Li Ming caught his shoulder and flung him backwards, away from his sunsword.

Chen Bingrong struck the concrete and continued twitching. He tried to say something, but all that emerged was an incoherent scream. Li Ming aimed the point of his swordbreaker at his throat and carefully rolled the sunsword away.

"I need backup!" Li Ming yelled.

"Here!" Wong-gor yelled.

The hunter hustled over and aimed his massive coilgun at Chen Bingrong. Li Ming sheathed his swordbreaker, drew a pocketknife and flicked it open.

"What are... you doing?" Chen Bingrong muttered.

Li Ming knelt and cut through the straps of Chen Bingrong's reality shapers. He picked up the pieces and threw them aside. Then he stowed the knife, drew a set of zipties, and secured his hands behind his back.

"You are under arrest for conspiracy, terrorism and attempted murder," Li Ming said.

Chen Bingrong laughed.

"What's so funny?" Li Ming asked.

"You've just doomed the whole city."

"Call off the jiaolong. Now."

"I'll need my shapers for that."

"Tell me how to use your beast control tech."

"It's not tech. It's magic. I can't use it without my shapers."

"If we give them back to you, you'll just try to run away again," Wong-gor said.

"My offer still stands. Let me go and I'll send the beasts away."

"Show me how to use your magic," Li Ming said.

Chen Bingrong just laughed.

Then the beasts shrieked.

The call echoed through the city streets. One by one, jiaolong after jiaolong took up the howl, forming a primal chorus.

And the ground rumbled.

"They're fleeing!" Cai Yan shouted.

Chen Bingrong went pale.

"What?"

"The jiaolong are fleeing for the river! Do *not* engage! Target only those that still put up a fight!"

"You're lying! That's not supposed to happen!"

"Let's see for ourselves," Li Ming said.

He grabbed Chen Bingrong by the collar, hauled him up, and frog-marched him to Cai Yan. To the edge of the roof.

Far below, a great green dragon slithered through the city streets. It hauled itself along on four-clawed feet, spine surging and coiling and unwinding. Its scales glittered in the sun, a prismatic parade flowing like water. It maneuvered its head with great care, keeping its antlers and horns from tangling with cars and wires. It was stupendously long, as long as a train, as long as a street. Even from fifty stories up, Li Ming could see it with his naked eye.

And it was leaving.

Two streets north, the jiaolong hauled itself to the bank of the Yu River. It regarded to the guardrail for a moment, then arched itself over it and continued crawling. An instant later, the rail collapsed under its stupendous weight. It ignored it and kept going.

As it dipped its head into the river, it sped up, its spine rolling like waves, until at last its tail sank between the waters and disappeared.

Li Ming was suddenly glad he didn't have to kill such a magnificent creature. And such a magnificently dangerous one too.

All along the riverbank, other jiaolong took to the waters. The biaohang, the Council, and Chen stared at the scene, in awe, in terror, in reverential silence.

"This... is not supposed to happen," Chen Bingrong said softly.

"The effects of the magic doesn't last long. If it's not maintained, the beasts will flee once the magic cuts out. Great beasts like dragons, intelligent enough to cultivate qi, can resist the effects by releasing the hold the magic has over them. Humans, especially cultivators, can do the same. All I had to do was keep you from re-casting the beast control magic until the magic wore off," Li Ming said.

Chen Bingrong shook his head.

"You... I never thought someone as weak as you would be so formidable."

The gray man walked up to Li Ming.

"I suppose events proved your theory right after all," he said. "Thank you."

"You're welcome. What's going to happen next?"

"There will be an investigation. The guilty will be brought to justice. We will do everything in our power to prevent this from happening again. And, of course, you will be richly rewarded for your services to the people."

"We were only doing our job," Cai Yan said.

"I'm sure you were. Now there is one more thing I must ask of you."

"What is it?"

"During the commotion, I called the police. They are already downstairs and are swiftly headed up. I expect your full cooperation with the lawful authorities, for as long as it takes to sort this mess out. Clear?"

"Yes."

"Wonderful. After all this is over, we will speak again."

"About what, if I may ask?"

His eyes glittered.

"Business."

Chapter Thirty-Five

Hegemon of the Central Plains

Li Ming had always wondered how rich people lived. Today, he finally had some answers.

The mansion stood alone at the edge of a sparkling lake, walled off from its lesser neighbors by a combination of high fences and a garden so luxuriously overgrown it was better described as an exotic forest of brilliant blooms and sturdy trees. Past the main gate, a bubbling waterfall marked the center of the property, the anchor around which all other buildings oriented themselves. The mansion itself was a three-story edifice of brick and tile, every floor sporting a huge upswept roof, supported by sturdy oak pillars sunk into concrete. Two open-air pavilions served as its wings, jutting out into the water. The garage was the size of a small dwelling, enough for a family of six, or four cars.

Inside, the mansion boasted every modern comfort. The floors were gleaming cream marble streaked through with blue-gray veins, accented by thick red carpets woven with intricate designs. Crystal chandeliers illuminated the major rooms, highlighting the warm colors and bringing out a pleasant shine. Paintings hung on every wall. Cream leather furniture with dark wooden frames awaited in every room. Twin staircases in the foyer majestically swooped up to the second story, to a landing that could serve as a second living room.

There were so many rooms. Grand room, dining room, study room, reading room, three bedrooms, three bathrooms, recreation room, rooms Li Ming had no name and whose purpose he could not begin to divine. The interior design drew upon Western sensibilities, but every room, every bed, every table and chair, was subtly and immaculately arranged in accordance with fengshui principles.

It was the grandest home Li Ming had ever seen. And the most opulent prison.

Armed drones patrolled the grounds, air and waters at all hours of the day. A squad of ten guards, martial cultivators with top-tier infinity guns and reality shapers, stood watch at the doors, the gates, and every possible exit. A team of servants prepared the meals and cleaned the house at regular intervals but refused to speak about anything not related to their duties.

No one was allowed to leave or send messages to the outside world without prior approval. The holovision was strictly limited to a small selection of news and entertainment channels. Every phone was disabled, every electronic device confiscated. The guards handled security, the servants took care of chores, leaving the team with nothing to do and nowhere to go.

The authorities called the team 'guests of the state'. A polite term for house arrest.

When the police finally reached the rooftop gallery, Dayong offered no resistance. They surrendered the prisoners to the tactical team, then themselves and their equipment. For the first three days the cops held them at Central Police Station, far away from the regular prisoners, isolated from each other.

The days followed the same routine. Wake up, breakfast of thin rice porridge and fried dough sticks, then a grueling interrogation lasting through the morning. After a quick break for lunch—more porridge, a few vegetables, maybe an egg—the interrogation continued. Dinner was the last event of the day, more porridge, more vegetables, a slice or two of pork, then wash-up and enforced bedtime.

Hour after hour, day after day, the police bombarded Li Ming with hundreds, thousands, of questions. They were all variations of the same themes: what the team did when they reached the Central Plains, their encounters with Bao and Chen, the beasts, the terrorist plot, the actions they took. Li Ming answered them all the best he could, leaving nothing out, repeating the answers so many times he could recite them by heart.

Li Ming repeatedly requested for a lawyer. Every time, the police just laughed in his face and cited the Yudu antiterrorism law, which allowed for indefinite detention without immediate access to a lawyer.

But on the fourth day, everything changed.

A tactical team in riot gear gathered the team from their cells and marched them to a blacked-out van. They carried out their work with cold professionalism, yet lacked the sternness Li Ming was accustomed to. And they didn't apply handcuffs. When Li Ming asked them where they were taking them, the leader's answer was terse and ambiguous.

"A better place than prison."

By every objective measure, the mansion was surely a better place than a dark and dingy cell. Dayong had free run of the place, so long as they stayed inside the walls and away from the lake. And yet, with so many restrictions, and *still* no access to a lawyer, the mansion was merely a gilded cage.

Li Ming made the most of it.

He awoke at his usual time, three *ke* before dawn. After a quick wash, he headed outdoors, to the banks of the great and nameless lake. By the clear, still waters, he cultivated.

Zhan zhuang. Five Fists. Twelve Animals. Every form and every drill he had learned over his two decades of life. He worked deep and slow, every movement clean and precise, utterly relaxed and perfectly synchronized, his body moving as a single integrated unit. Qi coursed powerfully through him, hot and electric and welcoming, making up for the time he had lost in prison.

Sometimes Cai Yan joined him. Sometimes he trained alone. Always he heard Ghazan training somewhere close by, his booming stomps and sharp exhales betraying his presence. He never saw Sarantuya train, but he'd caught her sneaking into the garden in the morning and leaving it in time for breakfast.

Every meal was magnificent. The chef could prepare any kind of food from anywhere in the world on demand. From simple steamed buns to elaborate multi-course feasts, with a single day's notice the chef and his team could work culinary wonders Li Ming had never seen before.

Even so, he couldn't begin to appreciate the sumptuous fare. He might be a multimillionaire martial cultivator now, but before that he was a humble conscript sustained on military food, and at heart he was still a dirt bun from a farming village. He still had the tastes of a simple farmer's son.

He recognized good food when he tasted it, but that was the limit of his gustatory capabilities. Cai Yan seemed pleased with the meals and discussed the food with Wong-gor, using exotic terms he had never heard before. Li Ming contented himself with simple, stark meals of rice, vegetables and meat, occasionally choosing steamed buns and noodles for variety.

Ghazan and Sarantuya chose even plainer fare. Their meals came in two main colors, red and white, reflecting the cuisine of their homeland. At every meal they brought out dishes Li Ming had never seen before. Barbecued mutton, spiced beef and lamb dumplings, stews, noodle soups, fermented milk, yoghurt.

Despite their markedly different tastes, they still had one thing in common. After every breakfast and every dinner, they broke out their supplements. Bottles of beast essence, herbal pills, potions made from strange fungi and exotic creatures, supplied by the household staff. Even Wong-gor drank beast essence. Li Ming limited himself to beast essence—and reminded himself to consult a pharmacist to assemble an optimum supplement mix for the future.

If there was one.

As with their time in prison, the interrogations continued. After breakfast, a team of plainclothes interrogators visited the house, speaking to them privately in separate rooms. While more polite and formal, they were no less firm than the uniformed cops who had handled the initial round of questioning. They called themselves investigators from the Yudu Public Security Bureau, which meant they were secret police.

They retread the same ground the police did, with greater depth and subtlety, digging up every last bit of information Li Ming could recall. They invited him to comment on Chen Bingrong, on Captain Bao, on the team. Li Ming spoke only well of his colleagues, and of his enemies he gave only a frank assessment of what little he had seen.

The interrogators allowed Dayong to lunch in peace, then once again divided and questioned them until the early evening. The second they left, the team was free to live as they pleased until the morning, so long as they remained on the mansion grounds.

Naturally, they trained.

Weights and machines in the gym. Runs by the lake. Bodyweight regimens in the pavilions. And sparring. Lots of sparring.

The team congregated one last time for dinner. Then they retired for the evening. To the grand room to watch the holovision, to the recreation room and its old-fashioned diversions of card and board games and pool, to the library and its enormous shelves lined with classics, to the richly-appointed bedrooms with silk sheets and plush settees.

Seven days passed like this. Days of comfort, but also days of stagnation. While the world moved on, they were all stranded here, trapped in a realm of luxury and leisure. Li Ming didn't know how long this would continue.

But they were allowed to cultivate. To train. That had to count for something.

After the tenth day, the interrogators stopped showing up. With their newfound free time, the team continued doing more of what they'd done for the past week. More training, more martial arts, more cultivation.

Left in a world of their own, their biaohang desperately sought new ways to remain engaged. Wong-gor secluded himself in the library for hours on end. Cai Yan negotiated an employment contract with Sarantuya, then stuck close to her. Li Ming and Ghazan, of course, cultivated. And sparred.

Though they only had empty hands and fallen branches salvaged from the garden, their sparring matches were no less intense. Both men quickly built up an impressive collection of bruises. Forearms, chest, cheeks, every major muscle group. In the daylight they fought, in the evening they rubbed down their injuries with medicated oil and discussed techniques and tactics, the following morning they got up to do it all over again.

Ghazan needed an outlet for his energy. Li Ming wanted to study the methods of an undefeated prize fighter. It was a win-win situation.

Li Ming just wished it didn't have to hurt so much.

On the twenty-second day of their confinement, the gray man visited them.

Now he came dressed in silver. Three-piece hand-fitted suit that shimmered in the light. Cufflinks on both sleeves, bracelet on his left hand, extravagantly complex watch on his right. A pair of rings on either hand. Everything he wore was in shades of silver, complementing his sleek gray hair and chiseled face. Only his shoes were black, and even so, when he entered the house he removed them to reveal silver socks.

He came with a retinue of bodyguards. Twenty of them, martial cultivators one and all. The bodyguards speedily but thoroughly swept the mansion, then left as briskly as they had arrived, leaving him alone in the grand hall with the team.

He sat alone, back straight, legs spread and planted firmly on the ground, hands relaxed on the arm rest. With that gesture, he elevated a club chair into a throne, and himself the sovereign of all under heaven.

"I trust your stay has been pleasant," he said.

"Not bad," Ghazan said.

The visitor laughed.

"'Not bad'! I can see why you'd say that."

"We have no complaints," Cai Yan said.

"Wonderful. You must be wondering why I came to visit you."

"It's not every day the Chairman of the Central Plains Merchant Association Coordinating Council pays you a visit," Li Ming said.

For the past two weeks, Chairman Lu Feng dominated the news cycle. He promised justice for the dead, vowed to visit the vengeance of the heavens upon the terrorists who had attacked the city, and praised the security forces and the jianghu for swiftly restoring law and order. Li Ming saw his face every day, twice a day, on the holovision.

Every time, he felt like kicking himself for treating Lu Feng like an ordinary civilian.

The ghost of a smile graced Lu Feng's face.

"You've been sequestered here for two weeks. You must be starving for news."

"Absolutely," Cai Yan said. "We are most especially eager to learn about our current legal status."

Lu Feng's eyes twinkled.

"You saved Yudu. You exposed a conspiracy. You defeated a gang of devil cultivators with the power to turn beasts into living weapons. *And* you preserved the priceless artwork stored at the gallery at the Merchant Association headquarters. Under these circumstances, it will be exceedingly difficult to find a prosecutor willing to press charges against you or a judge willing to hand down a sentence. Rest assured that you are not liable for any charges under the Yudu Criminal Code."

An invisible weight sloughed off Li Ming's shoulders. He savored the moment with a deep breath.

"If we're not going to face charges, why were we confined here?" Ghazan asked.

"You are all guests of the state. We had to protect you from retaliation, until we were certain we have rounded up every member of the conspiracy."

"We were also questioned from dawn to dusk," Wong-gor said.

"The security agencies needed to find the truth. I trust they comported themselves in a professional fashion?"

"No complaints," Li Ming said.

"Wonderful. You'll be pleased to know that they have concluded their investigations and are satisfied that you acted in accordance with the laws of the Jianghu Association, foiling a devastating plot that had claimed the lives of hundreds."

There would never be a confirmed body count. The death toll of the jiaolong incursion stood at two hundred and sixty-seven. A hundred and twelve more lost their lives at Shuanglong. Beasts slew at least two hundred more civilians and hunters in the field and ate some of them. Their remains had yet to be recovered. Li Ming doubted they ever would.

"What about the conspiracy?" Li Ming asked.

"We will make the official announcement later, but since you asked, I am pleased to say that it's been smashed. The computers and devices you've recovered from the Wanjianhui office contain plans, memos and emails describing a plot to undermine the lawful authorities of the Central Plains by manipulating beasts.

"Chen Bingrong confessed to the conspiracy following *rigorous* questioning. His statements confirmed your own. The other prisoners you took corroborated them as well. The security forces have swept up many of the remaining Wanjianhui members in Yudu and the surrounding region. They will be prosecuted for conspiracy, terrorism, murder, and illegal use of magic.

"After learning that Chen Bingrong broke down, Bao Wang also confessed. He revealed to us his co-conspirators in the Yudu Military Forces and the security agencies. They have also been arrested. In addition to the above charges, they will also be charged with mutiny and treason.

"We expect the trial to be swift and decisive. Those who plead guilty will be sentenced to life imprisonment. Those who do not will face the death penalty. Either way, they will never see daylight again."

"A fitting end," Wong-gor said.

"Regretfully, some members of the conspiracy escaped before the security forces mobilized. We are still hunting them, but we believe they are no longer in the Central Plains."

"Who are they?" Cai Yan asked.

"A handful of *former* soldiers from Captain Bao's unit who provided material support for the conspiracy. Some low-ranking Wanjianhui operatives who attempted to make a show of hunting the jiaolong, then escaped when the jiaolong fled. Most importantly, the top three executives of the Wanjianhui. The President, Vice-President and the Director of Human Resources.

"We have circulated arrest warrants around the world and the Jianghu Association. Should you happen to encounter them in the future, take them into custody and hand them to us. We will be extremely grateful."

"On the bright side, the Wanjianhui can no longer do business in the open," Wong said.

"I'm surprised you even allowed the Wanjianhui to operate in Yudu," Cai Yan said.-gor

She tried to hide it, but heat smoldered in her voice.

"The Central Plains is a land of merchants and farmers. We do business with everyone, so long as they do not bring harm to us.

Her voice broke.

"The Wanjianhui killed my father and my brothers."

"My condolences for your loss. Nonetheless, until recently the Wanjianhui stringently obeyed our laws within our lands. There was nothing we could do about them."

"They were bandits, murderers and terrorists, and you couldn't do anything about them?"

"Our own laws forbid it. I, myself, am but a businessman, and so is everyone who sits on the Coordinating Council. We have no power to decide who is innocent or guilty, who to punish and who to release. That is up to the local governments. It is the way of the Central Plains."

Li Ming gestured at the expansive room around them.

"Businessmen put us here?"

"We do have some measure of influence over the local authorities. But our jurisdiction is strictly limited to business. We cannot command, only suggest. We are pleased that the Yudu Public Safety Bureau elected to follow our suggestions."

Li Ming didn't believe Lu Feng one bit. On paper the power of the merchants might be limited, but he who controlled the money controlled the world. Even emperors and immortals had to bow to the one who produced wealth.

Li Ming suspected the Coordinating Council allowed the Wanjianhui to continue operations in Yudu because they calculated that it would bring continued profits to the Central Plains. Once the Wanjianhui revealed their true natures and turned against the

Council, and the cost-reward ratio tipped the other way, the Council moved to crush them.

In this land that worshiped only wealth and power, it was the only logical course of action.

"What was the Wanjianhui's goal? Why did they concoct some a scheme to begin with?" Sarantuya asked.

"Influence."

"I knew it," Li Ming said.

Lu Feng smiled.

"Young man, it goes much deeper than you think it does."

"How deep?"

"To understand this, we must first discuss the timeline of events.

"You were correct when you surmised that the Wanjianhui sought political influence. Using beast control technology, they drew the beasts of the Central Plains to Yudu—and lured the biaoju of the world.

"They summoned beasts from every corner of Xiazhou and sent the most dangerous among them to attack hunters and biaoju. This created the perception of a crisis, one that the Coordinating Council fell for.

"The Coordinating Council quietly reached out to gold-ranked biaoju across the Central Plains, seeking proposals to solve the crisis. The Wanjianhui claimed they had the ability to control beasts. We sent a small team of observers to verify their claims, and they sent back a glowing report.

"The Council organized a meeting between the Wanjianhui and the security forces of the Central Plains to see how we can use this beast control magic to end the crisis. Privately, we arranged for *another* meeting, one to discuss crisis *and* the implications of this magic, only among members of the Council.

"Through a contact in the security department of the Merchant Association head-quarters, the Wanjianhui learned of the meeting. They suspected that they'd been found out, so they chose to escalate. They sent zhenniao to attack Shuanglong.

"Their goal was to draw away every major biaoju from Yudu. They succeeded. After your encounter with the Wanjianhui, Chen Bingrong decided you were too dangerous to leave alive, so Captain Bao arranged for the mission to wipe out the zhenniao nest.

"You were supposed to die there. Instead, you returned to Yudu and launched an investigation. Worse, Mr. Li fought with a group of thugs, and the news reached the ears of the Wanjianhui."

Li Ming looked away. If he'd refused the original encounter, or if he'd destroyed them, would things have turned out differently? He didn't know.

"The Wanjianhui adapted their plan. They incited the beasts at the Zan Family Farm, knowing you would swoop in to save the day, buying themselves time to summon the jiaolong that lived along the lengths and depths of the Yu River. To guarantee your deaths, they sent in Captain Bao and his gunships. They didn't count on you surviving—or returning by air.

"When the jiaolong attacked, the headquarters building went into lockdown. The security chief—one of Mr. Chen friends—hired the Wanjianhui for 'assistance'. We welcomed their help at first. This was the first time so many jiaolong had rampaged through Yudu at once. When Mr. Chen offered to show us a live demonstration of his beast control magic... I admit, it seemed too good to be true, but with beasts destroying the city, we were desperate for a speedy resolution.

"We followed Mr. Chen up to the roof, where he put on a show of sending a jiaolong back into the river. After that, my colleagues were quite prepared to offer the Wanjianhui an exclusive sole-source contract to drive back the beasts across the Central Plains. Then you came in.

"The Wanjianhui was banking on that contract. It would have made them the most powerful biaoju in the Central Plains, more powerful even than the military. By calming the beasts and sending them back into the wilds before the eyes of the jianghu, they could elevate their status and be seen as the saviors of the Central Plains. Of all of Xiazhou.

"With this one stroke, they could have rehabilitated their image. It would win them allies and supporters in the Central Plains. Recruits, sponsorships, contracts and equipment would quickly roll in. They could then rapidly expand their influence and connections, creating a base of operations to pursue their goals.

"If anyone resisted... they had the power to summon dragons. Who could stand against such strength?"

"I didn't know you'd gain so much wealth and political influence simply by controlling beasts," Ghazan said.

"Then it might surprise you to learn that beasts are a critical component of the economy of the Central Plains."

"How so?" Li Ming asked.

"The Central Plains is a land of abundance. Animals breed quickly here, and where there are prey animals, there will be predators. Beasts are the apex predators of the food chain. While highly dangerous, they are also highly valuable.

"When beasts appear, hunters follow. Where hunters go, they spend money on food, lodging, supplies, equipment. They inject cash into the economy and sustain local businesses. By hunting beasts, they gain wealth and satisfaction, and remove danger to the people. A win-win situation all around. For this reason, the Central Plains has long sought to attract hunters from all over the world to hunt the most dangerous beasts of the land.

"Many industries rely on the existence of beasts. Zoos, extreme safaris, animal husbandry, pharmaceuticals, outdoors and survival specialists, weapons and reality shapers. They slaughter beasts, they appreciate beasts, they defend people from beasts, but in some shape or form they are dependent on the existence of beasts. Economists estimate that beast-linked industries account for no less than twenty-eight percent of the gross domestic product of the Central Plains.

"What do you think will happen if the beasts go away?"

"The money stops," Li Ming said.

"Precisely. Hunters will stop coming. Safaris will have to find something else to do. Businesses that cater to martial cultivators and hunters will see a sudden loss in business. Pharmaceutical companies will experience a shortage of supply of valuable beast parts."

"If the Wanjianhui can use magic to drive the beasts out of the Central Plains, they can disrupt the economy," Cai Yan said.

"Yes. By giving them the single-source contract, we would be buying the rope they would use to hang us with. With such power at their disposal, they could make even more demands in the future. Should someone refuse, they will send in dragons."

"With power like this, the Wanjianhui could destroy any biaoju who opposes them," Wong-gor said. "Out in the wilds, there are shanxiao and zhenniao and dragons. Anything could happen out there, and no one know."

"As you have yourself experienced," Lu Feng said.

"By becoming the lord of beasts, the Wanjianhui will become the hegemon of the Central Plains," Li Ming said.

"He who controls the Central Plains controls all under heaven."

The bloody annals of history had proven the truth of this statement over millennia. The Central Plains was the breadbasket of Xiazhou. Every ruler who sought to unify the land must first conquer the Central Plains, or all his efforts would quickly go to naught.

"The Central Plains under the rule of a secret society," Wong-gor said. "A scary thought."

"Instead, it is ruled by a society of merchants," Ghazan said.

Lu Feng laughed.

"True. But it is precisely because we are merchants that we were entrusted with the care of the Central Plains."

"Why is that?" Li Ming asked.

"During the Summer Revolution, the Alliance was incredibly fragile. Through raw charisma and sharp diplomacy, Generalissimo Jiang forged a coalition with mutually hostile factions. Getting the leaders of every faction to sit at the same table was a feat worthy of a Fo.

"When they discussed how to divide the territory of the Celestial Empire between them, the hottest debates revolved around the Central Plains. Everyone knew that he who ruled the Central Plains ruled all of Xiazhou. Yet no single faction was powerful enough to dominate the alliance, not even the Republican Army. Everyone lusted over the Central Plains and scrambled to keep everybody else from claiming it.

"Generalissimo Jiang came to us with a proposition. In exchange for supporting the Revolution, the Merchant Association would be granted the right to govern the Central Plains, and transform it into a haven for businesses and merchants.

"We accepted the proposal. Soon, all the other factions did."

"I do not understand. Merchants ruling a nation? Why would anyone accept it?" Ghazan asked.

"We are businessmen. We understood that there were huge profits to be made from this arrangement. Everyone from emperors to peasants need to eat. By selling food to everyone, we would make lots of money and forge strong relations with every faction. Every faction, in turn, would be guaranteed a steady supply of food, *and* be assured that none of their rivals would control the flow of the five grains. Everybody wins."

"This agreement became the seed that grew into the Five States and Ten Corporations," Li Ming said.

"You do know your history, Mr. Li."

"You speak as if you personally knew Generalissimo Jiang," Cai Yan observed.

"I was there."

The room fell quiet.

"I was part of the team that negotiated with Generalissimo Jiang, and later with the leaders of the other factions. Mind you, I was just an aide at the time, but I learned much from the experience."

"From an aide, you became a Chairman. Well done," Wong-gor said.

Lu Feng nodded in silent acknowledgment, a sovereign receiving his due praise.

"The Summer Revolution was over a hundred years ago," Li Ming said. "How old *are* you?"

Lu Feng laughed.

"Very young. Only a hundred and twenty-two years old."

"You look like you're only half that age," Ghazan said.

Lu Feng's eyes twinkled.

"Thank you. I work with some of the finest doctors in the region."

Lu Feng was an immortal. But where most immortals chose to return to the flower of youth, he had instead retained the gravitas of age. Lu Feng enjoyed the excellent health that came with immortality treatments, and the automatic respect accorded to elders. The best of both worlds.

He was not a man to be trifled with.

"You're not a cultivator," Ghazan said.

In his words lay a faint accusation. Lu Feng laughed it off.

"I am an old man, and I much prefer counting coins to swinging swords. I'll leave the hard work to you youngsters."

Everyone laughed.

Li Ming marveled at Lu Feng's tact. In two sentences, he had deftly defused the situation and diverted attention from Ghazan's true meaning: that Lu Feng had seized power and immortality without putting in the work. Without gongfu.

"What will happen next?" Cai Yan asked.

"Next we talk about the one topic that unites merchants and biaohang: money."

"I'm all ears," Wong-gor said.

Lu Feng chuckled politely.

"Between the contract to clear the Zan Family Farm and the recovered bodies of the shanxiao and jiaolong you slew, the Jianghu Association will pay a bounty of ten million yuan. The Coordinating Council is prepared to match it from our personal funds, for a total payout of twenty million yuan."

Split five ways, that would be four million yuan per biaohang. Three million, after Dayong took its cut. Not bad for a day of hard work. Li Ming would have been overjoyed to receive even a tenth of the amount for twice the labor and thrice the risk, but now that he was eighty-one million yuan richer, three million was…

Not bad.

"Thank you very much," Cai Yan said.

"You deserve far more than that for saving the Central Plains. Please forgive us for such a small and humble token."

"We are grateful for everything you have done for us."

"You're most welcome. And with this, I have a favor to ask of you."

"What is it?"

"Leave the Central Plains and do not come back."

The room chilled. An unseen demon stole the breath from Li Ming's lungs. Ghazan bristled, ready to erupt into flames.

"May I ask why?" Cai Yan asked.

"You have made many enemies in Yudu and elsewhere. The Ten Thousand Swords Society has ten thousand allies in every corner of Xiazhou. Raiding a fellow biaoju's office… such an audacious act has never been seen in Yudu since the Summer Revolution. Worse, you acted without a warrant or even a formal authorization from the police. If you hadn't recovered actionable intelligence, if you hadn't stopped the plot, you'd find yourself in an awkward set of a circumstances.

"As it stands, there is a concerted attempt to smear your name. An army of lawyers has flooded my office with demands to investigate Dayong. Elements within the police force and the judiciary are also calling for your arrest and imprisonment. The Jianghu Association is arguing that you acted in accordance with the exigent circumstances doctrine, but even their influence only reaches so far. The only reason you are not rotting in a maximum security prison is because the Coordinating Council saw you save the city with their own eyes. Without their influence, you'd be having a different kind of conversation with a different person."

"Shouldn't you investigate these allies instead?" Wong-gor asked.

"The Wanjianhui has forged many connections with every echelon of society. Purging their influence will take a long and grueling campaign. Simply assembling a team of incorruptible investigators requires heroic effort. We must obey our own laws in our investigation, lest we undermine our way of life. It will take time. A long time."

Lu Feng spoke mildly, but in every word, Li Ming heard a ringing condemnation. Every action had consequences. Break the law, choose expedience over prudence, deviate from the Way of doing things, and there would be a price to pay.

The payout was a bribe, Li Ming realized. A payoff to sweeten this demand. If Dayong took the offer, it would be a win-win situation for everyone.

"After you remove these allies from power, we can return, yes?" Sarantuya said.

"The situation is more complicated than that, I'm afraid."

"Please explain," Li Ming said.

"The lifeblood of the Central Plains is its farms and beasts. The actions of the Wanjianhui have devastated both.

"Beasts are apex predators. When too many are gathered in one spot, they ravage the land and decimate the populations of flora and fauna lower on the food chain. The beasts agitated by the Wanjianhui have destroyed farms and ranches, gobbled up livestock, disrupted roads and shipment routes.

"Altogether, the beasts caused over three *billion* yuan of damage to crops, farmland and ranches in the past two months. But that's not all. The beast surge caused massive supply shocks through the food and agriculture sector. We've released our emergency reserves into the market to mitigate the impact, but now there are reports of price hikes and food shortages in the outlying towns. This will have knock-on effects on other sectors, including pharmaceuticals derived from herbs and beast parts, sundries, transportation, and more.

"In their quest for power, the Wanjianhui created the worst economic crisis of the decade. Maybe even two decades."

"With the beasts gone, the problem can be managed," Li Ming said.

"As I said, it is more complicated than that. Remember what I said about farms and beasts. The beast surge drew in biaoju from across the land. We declared open season on beasts. *All* kinds of beasts. No bag limit. With the Wanjianhui engineering clashes between hunters and beasts, the Yudu region saw many record bounty claims.

"This policy was *too* successful.

"Beasts are the apex predators of the food chain. What happens when you depopulate the apex predators?"

"The lesser species enjoy a population boom," Sarantuya said.

"Precisely. Without the apex predators keeping the lower animals in check, they will breed quickly. Many of them are herbivores, and they will encroach on farms. We've already seen this during the beast surge.

"The surge was not caused by a sudden spike in the population of beasts. It was caused by the Wanjianhui gathering large numbers of beasts from vast ranges and concentrating them in key locations to create the impression of a population explosion. In regions the beasts vacated, herbivores multiplied and caused severe damage to farms and forests.

"This was why we were so eager to accept the Wanjianhui's offer. With the beast control magic, we had hoped to redistribute the beasts and restore the delicate ecological balance of the Central Plains. It would have been the best possible outcome. It's too late now. There are too few beast clusters left for meaningful redistribution.

"By destroying so many beasts in such a short time, we have created another ecological crisis of our own, one that will play out over the coming months, one that cannot be resolved through gunfire and magic."

"You could simply encourage hunting of nuisance animals," Sarantuya said.

"That's the part of our policy measures, yes. We will offer hunting permits for nuisance and invasive species. But we must, of course, prioritize our own people over foreigners. Likewise, we cannot pay a bounty for turning in the carcass of a nuisance animal. Such an animal, after all, isn't likely to directly threaten life and limb.

"You could try applying for a hunting permit, but even if you get one, I fear you will find such a hunt far less rewarding than hunting beasts elsewhere.

"Further, we will impose an immediate moratorium on hunting most beasts in the Central Plains. We need to give the beast population time to recover. Only beasts directly threatening human settlements may be lawfully harvested and turned in for a bounty. Foreign biaoju must also apply for a special permit to accept beast control contracts. Beasts in the wild must be left alone.

"Under these circumstances, work for beast hunters in the Central Plains will dry up very soon."

A moratorium on hunting most beasts. Permits and other restrictions to destroy the most dangerous among them. Li Ming had never heard of such things before. There were no limits or regulatory restrictions in the Zhongxia Republic where beasts were concerned.

But the Central Plains had their own circumstances, and they governed themselves the way they saw fit. As they always had.

"It seems we now have little reason to stay in the Central Plains," Cai Yan said.

"Indeed. We have reserved a first-class flight to Bao An for you later this evening. Our parting gift to you. May you return home safely, with good health and unforgettable memories."

It was a most pleasant way of pronouncing a sentence of exile. But exile it most definitely was.

"Thank you," Cai Yan said. "Our experience in the Central Plains has been most memorable."

What more could Cai Yan say? Martial cultivators they may be, but before the true hegemon of the Central Plains, there was nothing they could say or do to sway him.

"We wish you the best in your future endeavors," Lu Feng said.

"Just one more question, if I may," Li Ming said.

"Go ahead."

"What will happen to the beast control magic?"

Lu Feng's eyes sparkled.

"We will study it. Who knows, we may find a way to use it to mitigate this new crisis."

Everybody had won. But the merchants had won most of all. They could hold on to their power, chart a new course for their nation, and take possession of one of the most dangerous magical technologies in the world. And all they had to do was to pay off a biaoju and banish them.

This was the Central Plains. And the Central Plains lived by their own rules.

Chapter Thirty-Six

Yin and Yang

The Hegemon of the Central Plains had spoken. His underlings scrambled to carry out his will.

The second Lu Feng took his leave, his bodyguards filed into the grand room, this time bearing the team's personal belongings. Their backpacks, their clothes, their weapons, everything the police had confiscated from them. The biaohang took their time going through the items, checking them one by one, down to the smallest detail, before finally acknowledging receipt.

After a grand dinner, courtesy of the housekeeping staff, a team of grim-faced men whisked them away to the airport, where a private plane waited.

And Zhang Mei Lin.

She stood at the waiting area by the main entrance, her eyes fixed on the automated doors. In her pink beret and boots, off-white blouse and black dress, she stood like a willow bending in a strong breeze. As the biaohang approached, her lips smiled but her eyes remained dull.

"Glad to see you again. Are you all right?" she asked.

"We lived," Cai Yan said. "The authorities took us into protective custody. They released us only an hour ago. What about you?"

"Same. The police brought me to a safe house in the middle of nowhere, then interrogated me for days. Then they told me you were leaving the Central Plains and asked me if I wanted to see you one last time. So here we are."

"Thank you. We've been exiled. I don't think we'll ever come back," Cai Yan said.

"Exiled? For saving the Central Plains?"

"And breaking the law and showing up the local authorities in the process," Li Ming said.

"*Qian she bu an diantou long*," Wong-gor added.

It took Li Ming a moment to realize he had reversed the original idiom. *A strong snake cannot subdue the local dragon.*

"It wouldn't be politically acceptable to prosecute the people who saved the region, but the Coordinating Council couldn't turn a blind eye to it either. They paid us off, and now they are sending us away," Cai Yan said.

Ms. Zhang sighed.

"It's a shame... But, you know... I lost my job too."

"What? Why? You weren't directly involved with us," Li Ming said.

"When you went to rescue the Coordinating Council, I generated the paperwork to cover your tracks. An emergency assignment from the Jianghu Association, made out in my name. But I hadn't sought approval from the higher-ups."

"Why not?"

"They would throw a fit. The Wanjianhui are the heroes of the people. If I told them I was going to take out a contract against them, the Wanjianhui would have greeted you with all guns blazing. Branch Manager Qiu tried to defend me but the Regional Director himself got involved. He argued that I violated regulations and contributed to the crisis, and got me fired."

"*Gaisi...*" Li Ming muttered. "Are you going to appeal?"

"I'm going to try. But..."

"You don't like your odds," Ghazan said.

"The Regional Director is the most powerful member of the Jianghu Association in the Central Plains. I am only a fixer."

"You could come with us," Cai Yan said. "You could find a new job in Zhongxia."

She shook her head, the smile still plastered on her face, posed and hollow.

"The Central Plains is my home."

"What will you do next?"

"I have a lawyer friend who is willing to help me pro bono. I still have connections inside the Association. After what you did for them, and how I helped you along the way, the Coordinating Council owes me too. I'll find a way to survive. Don't worry."

That's a relief. But if you ever find yourself in Bao An, reach out to us," Cai Yan said.

"Thank you. I will." Ms. Zhang extended her hand. "May you be healthy and prosperous."

Cai Yan shook.

"May you also be safe."

Morning, again. This time in Bao An. The city he had settled in, but never called home.

Dayong had arrived in the city well after dark. The moment they returned to the Dayong compound, they reverted to their post-mission routine. Lay out weapons and equipment, strip and clean and inspect everything, stow it all away carefully, and only then turn to personal hygiene. And sleep.

Vague nightmares haunted Li Ming through the early hours of the morning. He tossed and turned, sleeping in short fits, waking suddenly only to lose consciousness minutes later. He made out impressions of dragons and shanxiao, of zhenniao and unnamed monsters, of the myriad beasts that roamed the Central Plains. Yet they were off somehow, not quite pure beasts, slowly mutating into forms unmistakably humanoid. But not *quite* human.

A half hour from dawn, he finally rolled out of bed, neither rested nor fatigued, existing in a twilight state in between both. He was back in the biaohang house, the residence the Cai Yan family maintained for its biaohang. When he stepped out of his room, he heard a string of thunderclaps. Ghazan, once again training in the secret courtyard attached to the house. Did the man ever feel tired? Or was training more important than sleep?

Armed with his swordbreaker, Li Ming stepped out of the biaohang house. The main courtyard was empty, as it always was this time of day. Wong was still fast asleep, the household staff were tending to their chores elsewhere, and there were presently no other resident biaohang.

Autumn had come. The clean, crisp air chilled Li Ming's lungs with every breath. Piles of dead leaves gathered at the foot of the trees planted within the courtyard. The cries of birds and insects rolled out from every direction in the predawn darkness, interposed with the endless stomps echoing from the secret courtyard.

Li Ming stood in the middle of the courtyard, arms at his side, weapon sheathed, eyes wide open. He stayed there for a moment, taking in the world, feeling the rhythms and flow of qi, letting the energy flow in and out with his breath, reconnecting once again to the grand dance of the cosmos.

And he flowed.

Palms parallel to the ground, he drew his arms through a small circle and rooted himself into the earth. He dropped his left hand to his hip, pushed off his left foot, extended his right fist at the level of his heart, and stepped his right foot forward, angling it out fifteen degrees. Stepping again, he brought his hands and feet together, cocking his left elbow. He stayed there for a moment, adjusting the interplay of muscles to optimize his weight balance. Then, in a single coordinated motion, he blasted his left palm through an arc, retracted his right hand to his belt vessel, and planted his left foot forward.

And stood.

And breathed.

In stillness, motion. In motion, stillness. It was the fundamental practice of zhan zhuang, the foundation of wuxingquan, the anchor of every practitioner of the art. Whenever the world upended itself, when black became white and white became black, when all the cosmos blurred into shades of gray, he could always root himself here, in the Three Powers Stance, and find his way back into truth and light.

Outwardly he was still. Inside, he made a hundred minute adjustments to his posture. He curled his fingers, he relaxed his shoulders, he turned his feet just so, seeking that perfect balance of looseness and tension. All at once he felt a sudden weightlessness, his entire being falling straight through the soles of his feet and into the earth.

There he stood.

And breathed.

Qi flowed into him, electrifying his fingers and hands, his soles and legs. He breathed deep, allowing it to gather in his dantian and circulate through him. He kept his awareness at the Huiyin point, at his perineum, the point where yin and yang converged. Vital energy flooded him in successive waves of liquid lightning, chasing away the chemical cocktails of sleep and fatigue.

Timing himself with his breath, he stayed there for five minutes. Five minutes of standing, breathing, circulating qi, and no more.

One last breath, and he moved again. He closed his hand into a fist, turning it palm-up. Half-stepping forward, he crossed his right hand over his left forearm, forming a wedge of bone and muscle. He adjusted his weight a fraction. Then, as a single an explosive movement, he launched his right palm out and drew in his left hand and stepped his right foot forward.

He stood.

He breathed.

He circulated qi.

Another five minutes passed.

His hands closed into fists. His upper body sank, his right arm bending with it. As his left foot half-stepped forward, his left fist rocketed out, his right hand pulled back to his liver. Qi crackled through fist and forearm. He twisted his fist, angling it upwards ever so slightly, and a second wave of qi, softer and more diffuse, swirled through his body. He paused, breathed, rooted his weight. Stepped off and fired his right fist.

Beng Quan. The wood fist. The simplest of the five fists, the fist he used to cultivate qi.

He marched through a line, punching as he went. At the end of the courtyard, he spun around, shot out his fist and foot, and stepped forward into a deep crouch, his front foot angled sharply outwards to torque his legs into the character for the number eight. He rose with a punch, bringing his rear foot forward, and continued punching.

Over and over he repeated the process, punching and stepping and turning, never stopping. Two hundred strikes later, he was back where he had begun, in the middle of the courtyard. One last pair of punches, then he drew his arms to his dantian, twisting his body and sinking his knees, drawing in qi.

And stood.

And breathed.

Hands loose, eyes closed, he breathed, letting the qi roar and rush through him. Energy spiraled up his legs like coils, feeding into his dantian. Energy surged up his hands and arms, leaving them hot and heavy. Energy filled him from head to toe, revitalizing and rejuvenating him.

After ten breaths, he stepped out into the Three Powers Stance.

The remaining four fists followed. Metal, fire, water, earth. The conquering cycle, the cycle for practicing combat. He practiced each fist two hundred times, pulling in the qi of the world, blasting it out into the cosmos, reabsorbing it into his body.

When he was done, he stood in the center of the courtyard once again, the first rays of the sun pouring down from the heavens. The trees were like torches, their crimson leaves blazing in the light. A cool breeze blew, yet his inner furnace burned bright and hot. Sweat poured off him, pasting his clothes to his skin.

Hidden from sight, Ghazan continued stomping.

Li Ming resumed training in silence.

Wuxingquan was billed as a combative art, a system of rapidly destroying all enemies before you, but it was first and foremost a system for cultivating qi, and without internal power the practitioner would never reach the heights of gongfu. With total awareness of the qi flows within and without, Li Ming practiced the sets. Baby Chase Butterfly, Five Element Linking Set, Twelve Animals, Assorted Set, every solo set in the art he had knowledge of.

When he was done, he stood in the courtyard like a human pyre, burning with an inner flame. His body brimmed with vitality. His blood sang. His eyes and ears and skin drank in the world around him. His lungs pumped like a bellows, sucking in fresh air and qi, blasting out waste, sending his fire burning ever hotter, ever higher, ever brighter.

Now he was ready.

His qi score now hovered around 14400 points. A respective score for someone of his age. But it wasn't enough. Three times in his life he had battled cultivators far more powerful than him. The first two times they had underestimated him. Chen Bingrong was more focused on trying to escape than fighting seriously. Li Ming had been lucky. But he couldn't count on luck forever.

He had to get stronger, quickly. Someday he would run into a powerful enemy, one who could destroy him as easily as crushing an ant. At his current level, picking a fight with such a foe was suicide.

The smart move would be to break contact, run away, flee before the enemy even knew he was there. But if he couldn't? If a client or an innocent or one of his fellow biaohang were in danger? He couldn't run. He'd have to fight.

To stay in the jianghu, he had to cultivate. A martial cultivator was nothing if he didn't cultivate. In this dog eat dog world, the weak were meat for the strong. The only option was to be strong.

With a flourish, he drew his swordbreaker. He sank the motion deep within him, ingraining the quality of movement, seeking perfection and efficiency. Weapon in hand, he cut.

The five elements expressed different ways of moving. Rising and crashing, powerful thrusts, torquing and twisting. Li Ming manifested them all, swinging his weapon as though it were a one-handed staff, thrusting as if it were a sword. A hybrid weapon like this demanded hybrid movements and tactics.

Now warmed up, he glanced around. Still no one in sight. He pumped metal qi into the blade, feeling it harden and contract, its quadruple ridges sharpening into the beginnings of edges. He stepped and swung once more, letting the qi guide his movements.

As he flowed through the steps of every set, he cycled his qi through the different elements. With every change he sensed the blade change, altering its properties, favoring certain movements and fighting against others. He went deeper, reinforcing the elements, studying the interplay of energies.

The Li Family Magic Weapon Manual prescribed a set of drills, built upon the five elements and twelve animals, specifically for practicing magic with weapons. His ancestors had painstakingly compiled correspondence tables, cycles, charts, but there was no substitute for seeing the effects firsthand.

His swordbreaker flashed through dazzling colors. Gray, blue, green, red, brown, the colors of the elements. It became lively, then heavy; swift, then powerful; explosive, then sinking. Qi swirled all around Li Ming, becoming a pillar of whirling energy, and he was the eye of the storm.

A final thrust. A reset to the neutral position. A quick sweep.

And, at the edge of a courtyard, Cai Yan watched.

"Good training?" she asked.

"Yeah. And you?"

She yawned, covering her mouth.

"I just woke up. Don't you boys ever sleep?"

"An hour here, an hour there. It is sufficient for heroes such as ourselves."

She blanched.

"Heroes? *Ni tai guofen le!*"

You're too much!

She giggled. He laughed with her. The qi around him slowly began to disperse.

"Were you practicing magic weapon arts?"

"Yes."

"I didn't know you knew how to do that. Where did you learn it from?"

His mind warned him to say nothing. Martial cultivators always kept their deepest secrets to themselves, lest their enemies learn how to defeat them, and their friends become enemies. His heart said she was his boss. More than that, she was... well, she was the woman he had fought alongside for the better part of a year. If he refused to say anything, how would that affect their relationship?

Heart and mind warred for a moment, neither side refusing to give in. At last they found a compromise and called a truce.

"Ancestral martial style," Li Ming said.

"From your great-grandfather?"

The men of the Li Ming line were soldiers, police and biaohang. Ever since the first Li Ming settled in Fuyang during the days of the Celestial Empire, they had shed blood on a hundred battlefields and a thousand streets. Li Yan Shun had fought in the Summer Revolution, and for his sacrifices he had been gifted the swordbreaker from the hand of Generalissimo Jiang himself.

"And his son," Li Ming said. "They created a family style, one meant specifically for the use of magic weapons."

"I'd like to see that."

"Become a Li and you just might."

A smile crept across her face.

"Was that a proposal?"

"You sound eager to receive one."

She turned away, pouting.

"Are you so desperate?"

"You heard it as a proposal. Aren't you the desperate one?"

"*Tao yan!*"

Li Ming bowed.

"Thank you."

She humphed.

"*Zhen shi de!*"

Still, the smile remained in her eyes.

The old Cai Yan was back. Her grief had lifted, if only temporarily. He'd like to keep it that way.

"It *is* a family style. I can't show it to outsiders. Unless they become part of the family," he said.

"Or unless you fight them."

"That too."

She held her hands behind her back, cocking her head up at him.

"Do you plan on doing any more fighting in the future?" she asked.

"Fighting is dangerous."

"Yet here you, training for fighting."

"We can't always choose not to fight. If violence is forced upon us, we must be ready to answer."

"Being a biaohang means exposing yourself to violence every day."

"Comes with being part of the jianghu."

"Are you going to stay?"

There it was, the other option lurking in the back of his mind.

He could quit the world of the rivers and lakes forever. Leave the sword behind, take up an honest trade, perhaps be a gentleman farmer like his father. Or some other profession that would take him far from the field of battle. With eighty-four million yuan in the bank, he could live a life of ease and leisure.

But if he did that, who would he become? Someone he wouldn't recognize, that was for sure.

"I'm still signed to Dayong," Li Ming said.

"You said that the last time."

"I meant it both times."

"What are you planning to do once you complete your contract?"

The real question, of course, was: Will you stay with Dayong?

"I don't know."

She frowned.

"That doesn't sound like you at all."

"Eighty-four million yuan changes a lot of things. Your life, your worldview, your priorities. I hadn't counted on ever seeing even a tenth of that amount. Now... I don't know what to do next anymore."

"Are you going to wash your hands in the golden basin?"

Retirement at the age of twenty-one. Practically unheard of. But eighty-four million yuan makes a lot of things possible.

Even so...

"I didn't join the jianghu just for money."

"Why did you join, then?"

"To become a youxia."

Her smile illuminated the courtyard.

"That sounds exactly like you."

"Gongfu is the one thing I'm good at. I should make the most of it."

"And with so much money... you can be free. Free to float from place to place, take only the jobs you want, focus on cultivating and becoming an immortal. It's the dream of a martial cultivator."

Her face darkened. Her eyes cast down at her feet.

"You could come with me," Li Ming said.

"I... I have responsibilities. The company, the biaohang, the family... it's not easy for me to just drop everything and travel the world."

"You managed to travel to Yudu with me... *us*."

"That was work."

"Being a youxia is work too."

"Just not part of Dayong."

"Does it have to be that way?"

Her eyes sparkled.

"You sound very eager in traveling with me," she said.

"We make a great team, don't we?" he replied.

"That we do."

Li Ming sensed now he and she stood on a knife's edge. A single word would send them tumbling into an abyss from which they'd never recover. Or into a brave new world no one had seen before. The air itself felt fragile, a mass of ice crystals ready to shatter at the slightest touch.

"A lot can change in the next few months," Li Ming said.

"There's also a lot of work to do too."

"Yes. I... appreciate everything you've done for me. The opportunity to work here, the jobs..."

His breath caught in his chest. His heart thudded. His words battled in his throat. He breathed out, steeled himself, spoke again.

"The time we spent together."

She glowed.

"Me too. I'm glad to have met you."

There were still five months left on his contract. He wasn't going anywhere until then. After that... He'd figure it for now. Here and now, it was just him and her in the whole world.

And, for now, it was enough.

He extended his hand.

"Would you like to push hands with me?"

She laughed. Sighed. Shook her head.

And touched her wrist to his.

"Sure."

Chapter Thirty-Seven

Crouching Tigress, Hidden Dragon

The world of the rivers and lakes respected only wealth and power. It was the first lesson Ghazan had learned when he had started his martial journey, transmitted from his grandfather, who had walked through the dark world and survived to tell the tale, a lesson Ghazan had taken to heart. The naive would deny this. The idealists would attempt to change things. But how a man felt about reality changed nothing about it. A man dealt with the world as it was, not as what he wanted it to be.

When he wasn't working, he was training. When he wasn't training, he was working. Every day he worked to grow his wealth and power, usually both. It was how he had risen through the ranks in the military. How he had become an undefeated fighter in the Taiping prizefighting circuit. How he had, with his own hands, secured wealth beyond his wildest dreams—and a legendary relic from the Yue Dynasty.

It wasn't enough.

Eighty-four million yuan was a stupendous figure, but there were many gold rankers with billions at their command, who possessed so much wealth they could buy armies and nations at whim. At around 16800 qi points, Ghazan was formidable, but still a candle compared to the top thousand martial cultivators to walk the land. He had gone far, but the peak of martial mastery was still a long way off.

He knew the others thought of him as obsessed with gongfu. So be it. You did not become the best in the world at what you did if you were not obsessed with it. If you did not live, breathe, eat and sleep gongfu, the dream of martial supremacy was further than the highest heavens. Even with the legacy of his ancestors, The Way of Conquering Heaven and Earth, he could not afford to be complacent. Superior gongfu it might be, it was still gongfu.

And the very meaning of gongfu was hard work.

So it was with mild surprise that he found himself in a high-class restaurant in the Cultivator Quarter, tucked away in a private booth, behind soundproof curtains. Even more surprisingly, he had company.

Sarantuya.

In the morning, he had emerged from the secret courtyard, drenched in sweat, and saw her waiting at the dining room table in the biaohang house. In her sports bra and leggings, her long hair wild and free, she'd covered everything and concealed nothing. She wasn't his type—insofar as he *had* a type—but he appreciated what he saw.

And he also noticed that she was drenched through with sweat.

She'd been training. Not in the secret courtyard. Not with Li Ming in the inner courtyard—he could see him pushing hands with Cai Yan through the window. That meant she'd practiced in her room, alone.

"*Ugluunii mend,*" she said. *Good morning.*

"*Ugluunii,*" Ghazan muttered.

She had a bottle of beast essence in her hand, the seal broken and the cap twisted off. She tossed her hair, brought the bottle to her lips and threw her head back, highlighting her curves as she drank.

"Been training hard?" she asked in Yumen Khel.

The Xia called the language Yueyu. In his mind, he'd never thought of it as anything other than its native name. The name 'Yue' was taken from the Yue Dynasty, but in their own tongue his people called themselves the Yumen.

"Yes. I see you've been training too," he replied, also in the same tongue.

Her eyes twinkled.

"Training never ends."

"Never."

"I've never heard of a training method that requires such… forceful stomps before."

"It is the martial art of our people. The Fist of Ten Directions."

"Ah. Shifangquan. If I recall, Xia vassal soldiers developed the art."

"It was later adopted by the armies of the Great Yue, and so became part of our legacy."

"Shifangquan is a spear and fist art, yes? I heard of it, but I never had a chance to train in it."

"What did you train?"

"Bits and pieces from all over. I don't have a formal style. I practice the best of what I've picked up and call it my own."

"An interesting approach, but it can only take you so far. Without grounding in the fundamentals of a style, you won't make much progress."

"I haven't settled down in one place long enough to properly train with a teacher."

"You signed a contract with Dayong, have you not?"

"Standard six-month contract. I'll be staying here for at least that long."

"Plenty of time to find a teacher and learn from him."

Her eyes twinkled.

"Like the man before me?" she asked.

Ghazan chuckled.

"I am not a recognized instructor," he said.

"Yet you have used your skills in war. That counts."

"You want to train with me?"

"If you don't mind."

"What about Li Ming? I train with him sometimes."

She glanced at the window and shrugged.

"Well, sure, but I think it would be easier if I trained with a fellow countryman. Someone with the same language and culture," she said.

"I begin my training a half hour before dawn. Starting tomorrow, you can join me in the courtyard behind the kitchen."

"Sounds good. Thank you."

"You're welcome."

"There is another favor I'd like to ask of you."

"Which is?"

"I'd read much about the Cultivator Quarter. Would you show me around?"

"Sure."

With that one word, he'd allowed her to drag him around the section of the city reserved for martial cultivators. In Dayong, days off were few and far between, but the Cais had ordered the expedition members to stand down until the end of the week to sort out their affairs and their gear.

When lunchtime came, they visited Tenger, five-star restaurant specializing in Yumen cuisine. They'd requested for a private booth, and when they flashed their biaohang cards, the staff scrambled to comply. Now here they were, seated in the far corner of the establishment, seated across each other.

Ghazan felt distinctly underdressed for the occasion. He'd dressed to disappear into the background. Gray shirt, blue jeans, trusty leather boots, a ball cap pulled low over his head. The outfit of a day laborer, an engineer, a technician, someone who worked with his hands in the great outdoors. His long sleeves hid his military-grade shapers, his handgun rested in a belly band. His pale hair and dusky skin already marked him as an outsider. Better for people to see what they want to see instead of who he was.

It made tactical sense on the street, but here in the Tenger Restaurant, where the men wore three-piece suits and glossy shoes and flashy shapers for a mere salad, he was a peasant among nobility.

Sarantuya was dazzling. She wore a navy blue deel with a bright gold floral pattern running from shoulder to hem. A wide scarlet sash encircled her narrow waist. Dark handles protruded from the underside of the sash, blending against her dress. Like the women around her, she had chosen shapers engraved with elegant designs, shapers that blended high fashion and functionality, while hiding the primordial crystals behind sleek brass shields.

There wasn't a more mismatched couple in the restaurant. He was the shadow to her sun. He'd caught more than a few men looking her way, some of them more than once. Those who deigned to look at him gave him a cursory look, seeing only his hair and skin and clothes and no more.

Here and now, he wondered if she'd planned this. To string him along so she could place him in a private booth in one of the fanciest Yumen eateries in the city.

No, he didn't wonder. He *knew*. Things had played out too perfectly for this to be spontaneous. The only question was what she wanted.

The menu offered a creative mix of traditional Yumen and fusion fare, written in Xia and Yumen script. He thought it a nice touch, but there were too many dishes and strange food combinations he had never heard of.

Ghazan had had more than enough rice in his time in the Central Plains, so he ordered a bowl of tsuivan, noodles stewed with meat and vegetables. Sarantuya had gurital shul instead, a hearty soup of thick fried noodles and lamb. Tenger offered a wide selection of alcohol, but today they both ordered airag.

Traditional Yumen fare. Heavy on meat, dairy and carbohydrates, light on vegetables. The food of nomads and conquerors. It was one of the few things he missed after leaving the Yumen Homelands to find his destiny in the Zhongxia Republic.

"Thanks for accompanying me," she said.

"We're Yumen in a foreign land. We have to look out for each other."

"You've been looking out for me since I signed up. I'm... grateful."

"No problem."

"What's it like, working for Dayong?"

"You're asking me now, after you signed up?"

"Better late than never, right?"

Ghazan couldn't help but chuckle.

"Dayong is one of the premier biaoju in the province. Maybe even the country. Even after the beating we took at the hands the Wanjianhui, our services are still in high demand. Work with us and you'll experience a huge range of jobs. Training, security audit, personal detail, beast hunting. No two jobs are the same. The work is hard and fast-paced, but it also pays well."

"That explains the high-end gear and five-star restaurants."

"The Cai Family are skilled in investing their earnings in the company."

"It shows. I've worked with many hunting groups in the Homelands, and I've found that the best bosses are those that invest in their gear and people."

"The Cai Family is... competent."

"Competent? You don't say."

"Mostly I worked under their father. Cai Meng Yang. After he passed on, Cai Yan took a backseat. The Yudu expedition was her first major job. All things considered, I'd say she did well. She has room for improvement, of course, but I have no major complaints."

"Me neither. I think I'll enjoy working with you."

"I hope so too."

Was there a touch of longing in *his* voice? He hadn't meant to sound like that, but... once spoken, a word could not be unsaid. And already her eyes lit up.

"Are there any other Yumen in Dayong?"

"No. It's just you and me. In fact, there are very few Yumen who work as biaohang in Bao An."

"Really? Come to think of it, I haven't seen many Yumen on the streets at all."

"Most Yumen biaohang tend to work in Taiping, or in other cities with a large Yumen population. Bao An may be a provincial capital, but compared to the major cities, it's practically a backwater."

"I think Dayong will pair us more often in future jobs."

"Of course. We're both Yumen, and the Cai Family will want me to show you the ropes."

"Not Li Ming? Or one of the senior staff?"

"Li Ming is the second-newest hire after yourself. Too junior for a mentorship role. The others... They do not share our heritage, our language, our culture. The job is stressful enough. We do not need cultural barriers making things worse."

"I noticed the others call you Ga San."

"They still don't know how to pronounce my name." He sighed. "Well, everyone except Li Ming."

"He's an earnest young man, isn't he? After yourself, I don't think I've met anyone quite as intense."

Ghazan's mind returned to the bazi master they had met at Yudu. Ghazan didn't want to put much stock in divination, but maybe the old man had gotten one or two things right.

"You're lucky. Your name is easier to pronounce in the Xia tongue."

"Sa Ran Tu Ya," she sang, and giggled.

"Exactly. Noticed Li Ming was the only one among them who tried to pronounce it the way you did?"

"He tries his best, doesn't he?"

"All the time. However..."

"However?"

"He is Xia. We are Yumen. We see the world differently."

"We live in the same world, though."

"Yes. But so long as we hold different worldviews, there will always be a gap between us. It is simply how the world is, and nothing can change that."

"At least we have the same heritage."

"Indeed."

"Does that include the Way of Conquering Heaven and Earth?"

Ghazan's heart thudded in his chest. His blood froze. The world around him blanked out, leaving only Sarantuya seated before him, smiling in her blue dress.

"That is a name out of myth and legend. A lost art, if it ever existed," Ghazan said.

"For a lost art, you used it quite well during the zhenniao attack."

"It was merely a high-level application of Sky and Night magic."

"And the Way of Conquering Heaven and Earth is the highest level of Sky and Night."

"What did you see me use?"

"The first three methods of the Way. Killing, pillaging, storing. Transmutation of captured qi. Scavenging raw qi."

"As I recall, you were far behind me, taking cover among the trees."

"Yes. I sensed the qi signatures of the magic you used. The methods of the Way are unmistakable if you know what they look like."

"And how do you know them?"

"I, too, study the Way of Conquering Heaven and Earth."

Ghazan glared at her. She met his gaze, matching his intensity, revealing the steel that lay behind her silk.

"You said it was a lost art," Ghazan said.

"Yes. My family retained fragments of it, passed down from my great-great grandfather, who had served in the Kheshig. After the fall of the Yue Dynasty, he retired to the life of a nomad, and hid from the hunters who sought to purge the remaining government officials and high-ranking soldiers.

"He'd transcribed the Way of Conquering Heavens and Earth, but his training was incomplete, and much information was lost over the centuries. When his legacy passed into my hands, I sought to complete my studies. To find a surviving manual of the Way. You have one, don't you?"

"If I did, it would be a priceless cultural artifact."

"A dangerous one, too. It would turn anyone who mastered the Way into a living weapon of mass destruction."

"What do you want from me?" Ghazan asked.

"I want to learn the Way of Conquering Heaven and Earth. All of it."

"Why?"

"This world respects only wealth and power. The Way is a method of obtaining both. With what little I have learned, I transformed myself from a common person into a cultivator in the space of a year. With the full method... our potential is limitless."

She had seamlessly switched from 'I' to 'our'. A ploy to hook him in. Ghazan noticed it. But her views didn't seem too different from his.

"Why do you chase wealth and power?"

"Once the Great Yue ruled a continent and stood astride the globe. Now it's been reduced to a rump state, a pitiful existence dependent on the largesse of the Ten Corporations. We were khans and conquerors. It is well past time to remind the world of this."

"You're a Yumen revanchist?"

"I can trace my ancestry to the golden age of the Yumen people. Do you not wish to bring back that golden age? Why do *you* train?"

Why indeed. He paused for a moment to collect his thoughts.

"This world is distorted. The reins of power go not to the strongest or the wisest, but to those who control wealth and the means of production. The jianghu honors not the most skilled or the most powerful, but those with the right connections and marketing skills. Those with true gongfu, those worthy of rule and power, are shunned or destroyed.

"We live in a soft age of soft men. It sickens me. I want to see the world made right again. But to do this I need power. The power to conquer Heaven and Earth."

She smiled.

"Ambitious. I like ambitious men."

She laid it on thick. But, he had to admit, it felt good.

"Our goals sound similar," she said.

"We are only two."

"It only takes two to start a revolution. And surely there must be others who think the same as us."

The Ten Thousand Swords Society. Chen Bingrong had said something similar to this, hadn't he? Ghazan simply hadn't voiced what he'd wanted to say back then.

Yesterday the Wanjianhui were enemies. They did owe him a blood debt for betraying Dayong at the expedition site. But the men responsible for that were all dead, most of them by his hand. The Yudu cell was also destroyed.

If he could dominate his enemies, gain their allegiance, turn them towards a new purpose... Wasn't this how the great khans of history had created an empire that shook the world?

"You're thinking of something," she said.

Ghazan shook his head.

"Nothing important. But there is one thing I need to ask."

"Yes."

"You said you wish to learn from me. But what can you offer me in return?"

Licking her lips, she leaned in towards him, baring her delicate neck, the swell of her breasts pressed against folded arms, her eyes dilating in the half-dark.

"Everything."

His heart jolted. His blood stirred. Something else stirred too. It had been a long time since a woman had looked at him like that.

But he was more than his hormones. And he held all the cards here.

"How do I even know you're worthy of being taught?" he asked.

She leaned back and smiled.

"You saw what I did at the Wanjianhui office."

In his mind's eye, he saw it clear as day. As the guards rained fire on Li Ming and Cai Yan, she'd stuck her hand above the parapet of the short roof. Qi bubbled up from a hidden dimension, her own wellspring of stored and stolen life, surging through her. Fiery spears of Sky blasted from her fingers and palms, obliterating everything they'd struck.

It was what he would have done. And her magic was only slightly less powerful than his own.

"You also saw how I kept Chen Bingrong from escaping," she added.

The Night fist was incredible. It demanded great concentration and precision to manifest a hand like that, never mind track and capture a fleeing target. Ghazan's specialty lay in offense and defense, not in support skills like this.

"If I learn the Way of Conquering Heaven and Earth, and pair it with the Fist of the Ten Directions, I can be of great use to you." Her cheeks colored. "In addition to anything else you may ask of me."

Her perfume filled his nostrils. Sweet, thick, but not cloying, like honey and fresh cream. It was intoxicating. Fire surged in his heart, sweeping through his body.

He breathed it out.

The Xia had a saying. *Wohu canglong.* Crouching tiger and hidden dragon. It referred to a master who had concealed his talent, and so remained unnoticed by society. A term of praise, but also a warning to never underestimate anyone around you. Especially in the jianghu.

Sarantuya was a crouching tigress. And surely he was a hidden dragon.

"I expect to work closely with you in the future. I also expect much from you," Ghazan said.

"I am ready," she said.

"If we are to conquer heaven and earth together, I expect you to take direction from me. I will take any suggestions you have, but I will have the final say."

"Of course. It is only proper."

"I have the complete manual of the Way of Conquering Heaven and Earth. But I have no master to learn from. Everything I know of it, I learned through trial and error, and obsessive study. Our goal is to reconstruct the Way, to master it, and then master the jianghu."

"We will do it together."

"Of course."

At this time, the waitress chose to enter. She set down two glasses of airag on the table and departed.

Ghazan lifted his glass. Smiling, Sarantuya did the same.

"*Uukhai!*" Ghazan said.

"*Uukhai!*" she repeated.

They clinked glasses, and drank.

<<<<>>>>

Chapter Thirty-Eight

Preview of Spear of the Night!

Thanks for reading Lord of Beasts! Turn the page to see a preview of Book 3: Spear of the Night!

Chapter Thirty-Nine

Avatar of Shadow and Night

A bodyguard's job was to protect his client. He didn't have to like him.

Every day for the past two weeks, Li Ming had to remind himself of that. He was not here to pass judgment on a man's life. He was here to defend it. When the job was over, he would never speak of the things he had seen.

But it was so tempting to make an exception just this once.

Han Tao was undoubtedly a great man. He had survived the cutthroat corporate world and risen above his peers to become Vice President of Global Sales Operations at Jinshi Mining Group. He would never climb any higher. The Liang Family reserved the top seats for themselves and their relatives. Nonetheless, responsible for trillions of yuan of revenue, he was a man of remarkable genius, and even more remarkable wealth and power. With it came the greatest prize of all: immortality.

He was most assuredly not a good man.

Charged with spearheading Jinshi's expansion into the Yue Homelands, Han Tao traveled to the capital city of Kharodon to conduct high-level negotiations with a staggering array of stakeholders. With him was a retinue of beautiful young women and soft men who looked like women. Beneath their delicate exteriors, they were sharp, aggressive, focused, perfectly willing to parlay their appearances into strategic advantages.

But not enough for Han Tao.

He demanded one hundred and ten percent from them every day, every hour, every minute. When they fulfilled his requests, he showered them with effusive praise. When they failed to completely carry out his orders or live up to his standards, he lashed out with a torrent of abuse unbecoming of his refined station.

Save for one person.

The most gorgeous woman among them all, a goddess of beauty made flesh, the woman he claimed was his Special Executive Assistant. Dressed always in tight silks and skirts, she decorated his arm during critical meetings, smoothened tensions between everyone, kept the mood light whenever she was around. Every night, after the close of business, he would return to his luxury suite with her, banishing the others to their rooms.

He was married, with children, but not to her.

Li Ming had stood guard outside their room for many a lonely night. The sounds that emanated through the door left nothing to the imagination.

When dealing with his counterparts, Han Tao was a maestro. He flattered, he cajoled, he delivered dazzling presentations with style and panache. But when it came to negotiating terms, he dropped the mask and revealed himself as the great white shark he truly was.

Li Ming had listened in as he discussed strategies with his staff, stood watch as he played hardball with his counterparts, readied himself to intervene when the stakeholders responded to his provocations and prevarications. There was only enough truth in his words to sell Jinshi to the stakeholders; Li Ming had overheard him boasting about his lies to his staff in the after-hours closed-door meetings.

Once, when a negotiation session with a government agency reached a stalemate, Han Tao sat down with his counterpart and presented him with a thick file folder. The second he opened the folder, all the blood drained from the hapless official's face. The official shut the folder and meekly accepted Jinshi's terms.

Li Ming hadn't seen what was inside the folder. He wondered if he should have. Or that if he could live with such knowledge.

Within the rivers and lakes, the weak were meat to the strong. But in the world of the Ten Corporations, the waters ran darker and deeper, and in their fathomless depths lurked beasts greater and more fearsome than any that trod the realm of mortals.

Just as well that the job was almost over. One last night, a blow-out banquet with stakeholders to celebrate the success of their joint venture, then a day to wind down and enjoy the sights of Kharodon, and the client would fly home to Taiping. After that, the Dayong team would return to Bao An. And *then*, Li Ming would catch the first bus to Fuyang. Just in time to spend the New Year with this family.

In truth, Li Ming didn't have to take this job at all. He didn't even need to work at all. With almost ninety million yuan in the bank—the payout from a series of high-profile jobs, including the discovery of a Yue ruin and rescuing the Central Plains from the clutches of the Ten Thousand Swords Society—he didn't have to work at all. Most of his money was safely parked in a diverse portfolio of investment vehicles. No matter which way the market swung, he would always profit. The funds he kept in his checking accounts would allow him to live like a king for a century.

But this was the highest profile job Dayong had run since the mission to the Central Plains. Twelve protectors on the team to escort six principals. Half of the team were newcomers to Dayong, and half of *those* were running a job overseas for the first time. The Cai twins had personally requested Li Ming's help. As a veteran, he could help anchor the rookies, show them the ropes, pass on his knowledge and experience.

Some veteran he was. He hadn't even been on the job for a full year yet. He just had the fortune—or perhaps *mis*fortune—to have been swept up in events greater than himself, than Dayong, and to have somehow pulled through intact.

But to the rookies, that was enough.

Dayong needed him. The Cai Family needed him. Which meant the clients needed him too. Who was he to turn them down? The truest currency was a man's honor, and a man who walked away from those in need of his skills was no man at all.

On the other hand, after a year of near non-stop operations, he would be glad to take a break.

He breathed deep. Released that thought. Emptied his mind. And returned his focus to the mission.

Argent House was one of the finest and hottest restaurants in all Kharodon. Aimed at an international audience, it offered exquisite fusion cuisine that blended the best tastes and freshest ingredients from around the world. Its signboard was written in the Yue and Xia scripts, the staff were all multilingual, even the menus came in several languages. A fitting place to conclude an agreement between a minister of one nation and a prince of another.

In a private banquet room on the upper floor, Han Tao and his retinue entertained his guests. It was a small gathering, only thirty-six participants, all of them high-powered government and corporate officials and their spouses. The stakeholders had forbidden the presence of protectors in the room. No doubt there would be even more frank exchanges of confidential information, more negotiations smoothened over with delectable food and wine, more venomed daggers hidden behind empty smiles.

That left most of the protectors manning the bar outside the banquet room. The bartender stood nervously at his post, under the eye of no less than six close protection agents, four of them from the State Protection Service. Six more were scattered around the bar, dominating the corners and power points, including four from Dayong.

Li Ming stood by the guardrail, looking down on the main dining room. Crystal chandeliers cast warm golden light on gleaming oak floors and white-clothed furniture. Frescoes on the walls depicted the vast steppes of the Yue Homelands, heroic horsemen standing tall against blue skies, snow-capped mountains rising above lush pasture. Wait-staff in formal red uniforms circulated the dining hall, some carrying large serving plates, others cleaning up after the patrons. Civilians ate and drank and chattered, almost entirely oblivious to the event on the upper floor. Past the dining area, a pair of staircases swept up and outwards, two halves of a crescent moon, feeding into the second floor.

The dozen men and women on duty on the second floor was only the most visible layer of security. The innermost perimeter. Government agents stood guard in the kitchen and the back door. More plainclothes agents watched the main entrance, masquerading as restaurant staff. A fleet of cars surrounded the block, ready to extract the protectees at a second's notice. Altogether, there were forty-eight protectors on site.

Li Ming had never been part of such a large combined detail before. On the other hand, he had never protected such a powerful group of individuals before.

C-suite officers from the largest mining conglomerates in the Yue Homelands. Labor union chiefs. The Commissioner General of the National Police Agency. The Ambassador of the Zhongxia Republic and his commercial attaché. Members of the State Great Assembly. And the most august of all, the Minister of Mining and Heavy Industry.

None of them were cultivators. But if they willed, they could send ripples through the jianghu and touch the lives of everyone who dwelt within.

One-quarter of the Yue economy rested on mining. Precious metals, minerals, coal, and most of all, primordial crystals. The Yue were the first to harness the raw potential of primordial crystals and marry it to Xia cultivation methods to create the first reality shapers. The first formalized methods of magic. Armed with this technology, they conquered the continent and established a dynasty that endured for a thousand years.

The Yue Dynasty was no more. Now, in the era of the Five States and Ten Corporations, there was only the Yue Homelands, a shadow of its former glory, confined to the westernmost reaches of the continent. Among the Five States, the Zhongxia Republic stood ascendant. Of the Ten Corporations, Jinshi commanded the mining sector, and was based in Zhongxia.

By expanding into the Yue Homelands, Jinshi would bring with it the wealth and influence of the Zhongxia Republic. Money would flow into the coffers of the Yue Homelands, and the treasures of the earth would pour out into the factories and ateliers of the Zhongxia Republic. From these manufactories would come the wonders of modern civilization: vehicles, machines, shapers, guns, everything that used primordial crystals to shape and manifest energy. These goods would flow out into the world of men, the world of the rivers and lakes, and irrevocably change the balance of wealth and power.

Li Ming intuited it all, though he didn't have the schooling to predict the precise effects. He didn't think anyone could, not even the immortal state economists and their machine intelligences in both nations. All he knew, all that he needed to know, was that whatever happened in this small room would influence the entire world.

And it was his job to make sure nothing would stop it.

A voice cut into his earbuds and through his thoughts.

"Third course coming up."

Ghazan. Standing next to the bartender, the Yue was the leader of the inner perimeter team, and the principal liaison with the State Protection Service. In his navy blue deel, dark silk sash and high boots, he was virtually indistinguishable from the other Yue guests downstairs. But there was no mistaking him for a civilian.

A powerful aura radiated from his body, an ethereal bonfire on the verge of visibility to the untrained eye. He held himself tall and erect, his weight perfectly balanced, moving with ease and grace. His thick coat concealed the tempered muscles beneath, but could not hide his broad shoulders, thick neck, and sturdy limbs. Most of all, he had the Look.

Behind his smartglasses, he watched the world with the eyes of a tiger. The lenses were tinted, but his gaze carried a palpable weight, an unseen force that engulfed everything within its domain, sizing it up, feeling it out, ready to seize and pounce and kill. Many times this night alone Li Ming had felt his eyes on his back.

Only recently had Li Ming sensed this gaze. Maybe Li Ming had grown more sensitive. Maybe Ghazan had become more powerful. Maybe both.

On the ground floor, an army of waitstaff assembled at the stairs. The State Protective Service agents took their posts, arming themselves with millimeter wave scanner wands and turning on their smartglasses. Two Dayong rookies stood to by the door to the banquet room, flanked by their government counterparts. Li Ming glanced around him, monitoring the room. When Ghazan entered the center of his field of view, Li Ming blinked hard, three times.

The sensors of his Raptor smartglasses captured an image of Ghazan's aura, analyzed the energies they had detected, and returned the results.

Qi score: 17389 points

Ghazan was only a silver-ranked biaohang, but with a qi score like that, he was on the verge of going gold. And Li Ming suspected he was hiding his true strength.

Even a gold ranker could not simply charge into a horde of beasts and slay them all with nothing but magic and bare hands.

Li Ming continued his sweep. Off to his left, by the wall, a woman stationed herself at the dumbwaiter. The only woman among the inner perimeter, but with her long black hair tied up in a neat bun, she could pass as a man. She wore her dark brown deel the way Yue men did, with wide sleeves and a loose fit, concealing her silhouette. Like Ghazan, she also wore a wide sash around her waist, this one made of black-dyed silk.

Li Ming had seen the figure under the deel before. Like Ghazan she was tall and clean-limbed, all sharp bones and sleek muscle. Her narrow lips and hard jaw lent her a severe look, emphasized by her high forehead and angular cheekbones. No matter how she tried to disguise herself, she was a warrior princess of the steppes.

She was one of Dayong's newest recruits. Her journey into the rivers and lakes had taken her down strange paths. She began her career as a beast hunter, working for some of the most prestigious hunting guilds and companies in the Yue Homelands over the course of eight years. Li Ming and his team had met her in Shuanglong when beasts and terrorists raided the city. She had acquitted herself well and had proved herself in the jobs that followed. After leaving the Central Plains, she had signed on with Dayong.

Despite her work experience, Li Ming was technically her senior. Only two years ago, she'd been recognized as a cultivator. Not that he could tell.

He trained his smartglasses on her and activated his qi assessment app.

Qi score: 12381 points

A score like that made no sense at all. A person's qi score fluctuated naturally over the course of a day, week, even month. But with an intense cultivation regimen, daily and perfect practice, a person could increase his qi score by two or three points a day. With supplements, that could be increased to perhaps five points daily.

The last time he'd seen her score, she was in the low 11000s. Even with supplements, she shouldn't be able to break into the 12000 point regime, not in such a short time. How had she increased her qi score by over a thousand points in just half a year?

It wasn't unheard of. Cultivators sometimes experienced sudden and permanent qi surges while cultivating. But the older you got, the more powerful you became, the closer you reached your natural biological limits, the less likely and powerful these breakthroughs became. At the highest level of cultivation, cultivators needed a stringent supplement plan just to squeeze out an extra point or two.

He made a note to ask her about it. He wondered if she would answer, or at least answer truthfully. Ever since the Central Plains job she'd been practically attached to Ghazan's hip. They were fellow Yue after all, and he had to admit, they made for a handsome couple. But they denied all rumors of anything even resembling romance. They were just colleagues, but because of their shared heritage, Dayong paired them up for large-scale jobs.

Whatever it was they had between them, it seemed to work well for them. Li Ming didn't care to pry too much into their personal lives, so long as it didn't affect the mission.

The waitstaff climbed the stairs. At the top, the station protection agents wanded them down, scanning for concealed weapons. Those that passed were shepherded to the dumbwaiter. Sarantuya personally observed them removing trays holding huge bowls of piping hot soup from the small elevator. More protectors escorted the servers to the doors of the banquet room.

As the procession continued, Li Ming maintained his vigil, watching the hall below. Four paces to his left, Wong Wan Lung joined him.

Hailing from the South, Wong-gor was easily the most experienced Dayong protector within the inner perimeter. With twelve years of experience behind him, he was ranked silver within the hierarchy of the rivers and lakes. Li Ming didn't expect him to rise any higher. After all, he was no cultivator.

He couldn't be one.

Savaged by a beast as a child, his arms and legs had been replaced by bionic prosthetics. With much of his organic body gone, he could never hope to develop a qi field on par with even the weakest cultivator. He threw himself instead into the art of long-range marksmanship. With his coilgun, he had won for himself a place among martial cultivators and immortals.

Wong-gor was Li Ming's senior. An older man, stress lines carved through his face, sinking his eyes even deeper into his face. Within a close-cropped patch of dark hair, a single strand flashed white. On the other hand, Li Ming had been in Dayong longer than Wong-gor, making him technically his superior. Wong-gor was deferential enough, but Li Ming still wasn't quite sure how to manage this relationship.

As obvious foreigners, there was no point trying to blend in with the locals. Their fair skin, dark hair and facial features would give them away. Instead, they presented themselves as something other than who they were.

Three-piece suits, gray for Wong-gor, black for Li Ming, paired with matching ties and steel-toed dress shoes. High-end smartglasses, plus a gold watch for Wong-gor, and silver cufflinks for Li Ming. Pocket squares, blue for Wong-gor and gray for Li Ming. Neatly-groomed with a confident bearing, they could be businessmen, aides, gofers, assistants to the rulers of the world.

But the suits had come from a small company specializing in high-end wear for low-visibility operations. A civilian would see elegance and luxury, a biaohang would discover little touches that made his life much easier.

Gusseted sleeves to facilitate rapid aim. Weighted jacket pockets and a snap button to ensure a smooth draw stroke. Cut-resistant sleeves on the outside, abrasion-resistant fabric on the inside. RFID-shielded pockets for storage of sensitive items. Reinforced belt loops to hold a gun belt. Trousers cut to accommodate an inside the waistband holster, sleeves loose enough for reality shapers. Clip-on tie that would detach the second someone yanked on it.

It was the finest suit Li Ming had ever worn. In it he felt like ten million yuan. Or like a secret agent.

The last server held his platter high, joining his comrades. As one, the doormen opened the doors. State protection agents swept in ahead of them. The servers marched in, efficiently fanning out to serve their tables. More protectors flowed in behind them, observing their every movement.

The waitstaff worked fast. Inside two minutes, they had set down their dishes, refilled cups of tea and water, cleaned up spilled food, cleared away the remains of the previous course. In silent unison, they filed out the banquet room and down the stairs.

"Third course served. Waitstaff headed downstairs," Li Ming reported.

"*Shan sia, seng sia ziu ge,*" Wong-gor said.

As always, Li Ming needed an extra moment to translate his Nanguang accent into standard Xiayu: *three down, nine left.*

Wong-gor was the very picture of stillness. Still as a rock, as a mountain, he scanned the world below, so still he didn't even look like he was breathing. Li Ming knew what it was like to stand like that, but it demanded conscious effort on his part, to enter and maintain that state. Wong-gor made it look effortless. Li Ming wondered how he did it.

Practice. Always practice. With enough practice, any skill and any art could be mastered. It was the definition of gongfu.

Something pricked the edge of Li Ming's consciousness. An intangible *something* that filtered through the chaos of the world to graze the outermost layer of his qi field. It was a ripple, spreading languidly but inexorably across the surface of a lake, heralding something falling into the depths.

Falling fast.

Li Ming crossed his arms and wrapped them around his body. The fingers of his left hand brushed against the grip of the Hellion 360 subcompact pistol riding on his right hip. His left armpit squeezed against his Viper personal defense weapon, a humongous hand cannon mounted in a brace, snug in its shoulder holster. His reality shapers weighed heavy on his forearms.

Wong-gor shifted his hands to his belly.

"Do you feel it?" Li Ming said.

"I feel *something,*" Wong-gor said.

Their eyes narrowed. Their faces hardened. Their jaws set.

The wise cultivator never discounted feelings like this. When running against top-tier predators, by the time the conscious mind perceived visible evidence of a threat, it would be too late.

Li Ming touched his tongue to the roof of his mouth, rounded his shoulders, hollowed his chest, breathed into his belly. His qi circuits aligned and connected, sending energy smoothly through his body. He stepped his left foot back, blading his body off. Right hand covering his left, he placed his hands on the break point of his jacket, just below the snap button.

Behind him, a government agent spoke a word in Yueyu.

The State Protection Service agents snapped to attention. A team swiveled out to cover the stairs and dumbwaiter. A second detachment made for the doors. The government agent continued speaking in Yueyu.

"Alert," Ghazan translated. "A martial cultivator jumped down from the roof across the street. He's armed with a—"

A thundercrack split the air.

In that moment, the world froze. Warm air caught in Li Ming's lungs. His heart hung suspended in his chest. His eyes sucked in everything before them—colors, shapes, details—the edges of his vision graying out and narrowing down.

He exhaled.

And the world exploded into chaos.

A woman screamed. The waitstaff turned to the door. A guest shrieked, then another, another, panic spreading like wildfire. The government agent spoke urgently into his mic, repeating a name.

"Stand to! Stand to!" Ghazan ordered.

Li Ming parted his jacket. His right hand shot to his armpit, seized the grip of his Viper, tore it free. Holding it at waist height, finger off the trigger, he unfolded the stock to its full length. The reflex sight glowed a bright, reassuring red. Digging the stock into the pocket of his shoulder, Li Ming wrapped his left hand around the forward pistol grip and raised the weapon to the—

The main door burst inwards.

A spectral horseman rushed into the hall. It was a being of pure energy, of muddy black qi, taking the form of a short furry figure riding a pony with no tail. The stout creature had the arms and legs of an ape, but its fingers and feet ended in wicked claws. Its eyes were coals burning with evil red light. Howling, it raised its right hand, holding high above its head a crude axe.

It was a devil summoned from an infernal plane. A yaomo.

All this, Li Ming absorbed in the milliseconds it took to bring his weapon to the aim. He had no idea what it was, only that it had to die. The bright red dot found a spot in between its eyes. He thumbed off the safety, touched the trigger, pressed.

Infinity guns screamed all around him. A fusillade of sun-bright bolts hammered the creature's torso and head, burning away the foul qi. The monstrous horseman screamed in pain and terror, and continued screaming even as half his body vanished in fire. The pony neighed, rearing its legs, and charged.

Behind it, another horseman rushed into the restaurant. And another, and another, and another, fanning out across the room.

"Almasty!" a Yue agent yelled.

"Burn them all down!" Ghazan ordered.

Li Ming continued firing, this time aiming for the tailless horse. Bolts ripped into its chest, into its heart, blowing it apart.

Glancing up, Li Ming scanned his field of fire. Three almasty, closing fast. He picked the one closest to the stairs. Axe held high, the almasty weaved between tables of screaming guests, yammering and screeching. He tracked it but held fire. He didn't dare risk a shot, not while it was mingled among innocents.

The demon had no such compunction.

Red eyes flared. Twin lances of searing crimson light slashed through the bar. Wet explosions erupted behind him. Cursing, Li Ming dropped to the floor. A Yue screamed, and suddenly his voice cut off.

More scarlet rays tore through the world. Li Ming unbuttoned his wrist cuffs and rolled up his sleeves, exposing his reality shapers.

"Cover me!" Li Ming yelled.

"Covering!" Wong-gor replied.

Raising his left hand, Li Ming touched the essence of earth. Earth qi, yellow and heavy, oozed out from the crystal stored within the shaper. It took form as a body bunker, wide enough for two men. With his other shaper, Li Ming injected water qi into the shield.

Water insulted earth. Too much water would wash the earth away and undo his shield. But the energy lances were filled with fire qi, and water conquered fire. Li Ming concentrated the entirety of his being into maintaining the balance of elements, fusing earth and water to create a wall of mud.

Wong-gor hustled over, still firing, and crouched behind the shield. A storm of bolts tore across the length of the dining hall. Scarlet beams answered, obliterating everything they touched. Shouting above the fusillade, the protective agents advanced on the threats, moving and firing, bounding from cover to cover. The civilians ducked, hiding under tables, chairs, each other, huddling up into small balls. An almas exploded, a second, a third, and yet more and more and *more* of them poured through the open doors, a horde of demonic horsemen fearlessly rushing into the wall of fire. Ghazan and Sarantuya rushed to the rails, their handguns barking, calling to each other in Yue.

Through the chaos, Li Ming sensed... *it*.

A ferocious wildfire of raw, hungry qi, burning with the fury of the stars, just outside the restaurant, slowly advancing on the entrance. Its qi field was enormous, the size of a house, a hill, the equal of giants and dragons. But in the heart of the field, Li Ming perceived... a man.

Li Ming snapped his consciousness away from the approaching monstrosity. There were other, more immediate threats in front of him. An almas charged the left-hand stairs, rays blasting from its crimson eyes, sweeping towards Li Ming. Li Ming ripped off a five-shot string, taking the rider from chest to groin. Wong-gor stitched it from chest to head. The almas vanished in a burning black cloud, but the horse continued onwards.

The wraith horse leapt up the final few steps, crashing into a pair of agents. A third man planted his pistol in its side and pumped the trigger, blowing it away in a choking black mist.

Four demonic horsemen galloped up the left-hand stairs. Li Ming wished he had a long gun, or at least continuous fire, but all he had was his civilian-grade Viper and his still-recharging shapers. Aiming down the left-hand stairs, he punched out a string of shots, one two three four, taking each almas in the center of mass, front to rear. As he worked his way back, Wong-gor fired.

Wong-gor's Viper had a mil-grade fire control unit. He hosed down the group with a stream of bolts, tearing into them, *through* them. The carpet burned. Steps exploded. The demons dissolved under the weight of fire.

Steam blasted from the muzzle of the Viper. The weapon emitted a high pitched scream. Overheat.

"Red!" Wong-gor yelled.

Lowering his Viper, Wong-gor scrabbled for his backup pistol. Li Ming swung to the other staircase, to the other monsters—

Ghazan.

Ghazan stood at the top of the stairs, pistol extended, aiming at the charging demons. Blackness rippled across his body, tainting him in darkness, transforming him into an avatar of shadow and Night. Red beams lanced into him, but the darkness swallowed up the energy. His pistol thundered, over and over, raining hellfire upon the horde.

One almas went down. Two. Three. Four. And the pistol overheated and there were still four more left.

Ghazan extended his palm.

"*UUKHAI!*" he roared.

Spears of light, bright and blinding, erupted from his palm, lancing into the demons. They sank into riders and horses alike and erupted milliseconds later, destroying from the inside out. At the same time, the blazing light of Sky blew backwards into him, tearing off the energies of the Night, painting him in a blinding white.

And suddenly there were no more threats.

Li Ming glanced about. The red eye beams had burnt black scars into the walls and carved tunnels through the floor. Pink mist drifted in the air. Severed limbs and half-vaporized torsos lay scattered everywhere. Sarantuya picked herself up from the floor, clutching her head. Wong-gor continued sweeping the world below, hunting for new targets. Ghazan stood his ground, right hand pointing his handgun at the floor, left palm extended.

There were no more government agents left.

And a man strode through the door.

He was dressed all in black, blacker than the night. Black body armor, a cuirass augmented with pauldrons, bracers, faulds, greaves. Black sash around his waist. Sturdy black pants and heavy-duty boots. Thin black gloves. Black veil wrapped around his face, tucked in under a helmet painted all in black. In his right hand he held a black spear, a spear as tall as he was, the butt planted firmly against the ground. Below the leaf-shaped spearhead, a tassel of red horse-hair shrouded a pair of violet crystal globes, each the size of his fist.

A magic spear, in the hands of a man with the aura of a monster.

His qi field was an all-consuming fire, rising from his core to drown everyone in the building. Ghostly heat washed over Li Ming's body, igniting the edges of his qi field. Red, bright and hot, washed over his sight. Naked aggression roiled off the intruder, married to bloodlust and raw power.

Li Ming blinked three times, activating his qi assessment app.

Error: outside sensor detection limits

"What the devil?" Li Ming whispered.

Deep within the kitchen, under the bar, a government agent shouted a phrase, too muffled for his machine translator to hear.

The spearman snapped down his spear, gripping it in both hands, aiming it like a long gun. A lance of blinding white light erupted from the crystals, faster than a plasma bolt, hotter than the stars. A muffled explosion reverberated in the restaurant, the popping of a huge water-filled balloon mixed with the shattering of stone.

"OPEN FIRE!" Li Ming screamed.

Plasma bolts rained down on the spearman. Li Ming brought his weapon up to the aim, saw the red dot over the threat's face, pressed the trigger and—

Gone.

The devil cultivator was *fast*, so fast he was a black blur, streaking down the length of the hall. The Dayong shooters opened up, their bolts blasting in the floor around and behind and in front of but never against him. The spearman glowed with an inner flame, white light against deep night, accelerating with every step. He leapt off the floor, suddenly weightless, rocketing right at Li Ming.

Li Ming flinched.

The spearman thrust.

The magic spear struck the shield. White light pulsed from the crystals, reinforcing the spearhead, biting and blasting into the shield. The mud wall exploded.

The force of the blast flung Li Ming aside. His hands opened and his Viper flew free. Automatically he curled his back. He thumped heavily against the hard wood floor. Instantly he slapped his palms, killing and reversing his momentum. His legs hung in mid-air for a moment, unsure whether to rise or to fall, then dropped and slammed against the ground.

As he lay stunned, the devil cultivator vaulted over the rails. Ghazan and Sarantuya cracked off a string of shots. His all-black clothing absorbed the plasma bolts completely, leaving no trace behind.

Wong-gor, still on his feet, still unsteady, lurched towards the devil cultivator, past the spearhead, reaching for the crystals—

The spearman reeled the spear into himself. His left hand slid up the shaft and his right followed, his fists now dividing the length of the weapon into equal thirds. He reversed his left-hand grip and spun into Wong-gor.

The steel-capped butt smashed into his exposed side. His ribs collapsed with sharp cracks. Wong-gor doubled over, clutching his side, staggering away. The spearman launched a sliding thrust, left hand shooting up to meet the right, driving the butt into Wong-gor's sternum. The strike blew Wong-gor backward. Wong-gor crashed into a table, bowled over and went still.

Li Ming shook his head, propping himself up into a seated position. Sarantuya hammered the devil cultivator again, this time with bolts of pure white light. Ghazan hung back, drawing qi into himself, charging up for a superpowered spell. The devil cultivator smoothly swung his spear back around, again bringing it to his shoulder, and fired.

The energy bolt tore through wooden guardrails and balusters and struck an invisible shield. The shield detonated, the force throwing Sarantuya down.

And now it was just Ghazan and the devil cultivator.

Ghazan sank into his guard. Bladed towards the enemy, weight on his rear leg, forward leg extended, he held his right fist over his liver, and extended the other. Qi flared from his body.

Light flashed. Thunder cracked. And a long spear of blazing Sky appeared in Ghazan's hands.

Li Ming's eyes widened. He'd never seen magic like this before. Was this a secret Yue art?

The devil cultivator spun to Ghazan. Went still for a moment. Then he shifted his hands and sank into his guard. The same guard Ghazan used.

The men bladed off, each the mirror image of the other, Sky white and Night black. Glaring at each other, their qi roared forth, each attempting to overwhelm the other. In the tiny space, their qi crackled like electricity, the backwash blanketing Li Ming's own.

A voice, harsh and hissing, filled the room. The voice of the devil cultivator, speaking in the tongue of the Yue people.

"We walk the same path. Why do you fight me?"

Ghazan shrugged.

"Because you fight me."

And lunged.

His spear drove forward, flying for the devil cultivator's head. With a laugh, the enemy batted it aside and counter-thrust. Ghazan nimbly danced away, swinging his rear arm up, stabbing for his enemy's foot. The devil cultivator stepped back, dodging the blow, then stomped down. Ghazan withdrew the spear just before the boot touched it, then circled back around to bat the spear aside. The devil cultivator lowered his weapon, evading Ghazan's own, then aimed the point at Ghazan's face and unleashed a qi bolt.

Darkness exploded against Ghazan's face. Screaming, Ghazan staggered aside. The enemy pivoted, readying for a thrust.

And Li Ming jumped in.

Right hand dipping for his pocket, he charged the devil cultivator. The man was shielded, but surely a shield wouldn't stop a slow blade. He dug out his folding knife and popped it open, left hand extended to reach for the threat.

The enemy spun around with preternatural speed. Li Ming twisted aside to his left.

And the devil cultivator lunged.

The spearhead whooshed past him, missing him by a hair's breadth. But as it retracted, it seized his qi and sucked it down into itself, into the paired violet crystals.

Strength bled from Li Ming's body. A sudden cold gripped his heart. Startled, Li Ming jumped back, left hand reaching for the enemy. His nerves fired in a jangled, confused sequence, clawing only empty air. The devil cultivator swiveled towards Li Ming, spear aimed at his head—

Ghazan thrust.

The spear of light rammed into the enemy's side. The devil cultivator staggered back, back towards the opening he had blasted in the guardrail.

Li Ming rushed in. Past the spearhead. Past the crystals. Past the hands. The threat spun towards him. Li Ming stepped off to his side and thrust for his throat.

It was like stabbing steel.

Force ran down the length of his knife, of his arm, all the way into his core and down his feet. Pain shot through his wrist and elbow. The enemy stepped back and torqued around to face him. Li Ming sank down, intercepting the shaft of the spear with his right forearm, knocking him off-balance. Li Ming exploded back up, pushing off his rear foot, hips twisting, spine uncoiling, left palm blasting into his temple.

It was like striking stone.

But now, now the enemy stumbled. One step. Two steps. Then an uncontrollable backwards flight, his arms flailing for balance. He struck the edge of the blasted rails and fell.

The sound of the impact reverberated in the restaurant.

Li Ming stowed his knife. Drew his handgun. Rushed to the gap. Ghazan joined him.

The devil cultivator stood tall, seemingly unscathed. Long cracks in the wooden floor radiated away from his boots. Tilting his head up, he glared at the men.

And behind the veil, Li Ming swore he *grinned*.

Sirens screamed in the night. Police sirens. Ambulance sirens. More sirens than Li Ming could count.

The devil cultivator slammed the butt of the spear against the floor and pointed at Ghazan. At Li Ming.

And spoke.

And blurred.

"STOP!" Li Ming yelled.

Too late.

He was a black streak, rushing into the kitchen and out of sight. Men swore in shock and anger. Ghazan swore too, something bitter and blasphemous.

"Are you okay?" Li Ming asked.

Ghazan nodded. "You're bleeding."

Li Ming touched his face. His hand came away wet.

"Just a scratch. We need to check on the others."

Wong-gor moaned. Li Ming turned to him, saw Sarantuya kneeling over his prone form. Li Ming hustled over.

"Wong-gor! Are you alright?" Li Ming asked.

Wong-gor groaned.

"Ribs... broken. Can't... breathe."

Sarantuya held her reality shapers over him. Warm white light washed over him.

"I'm going to use first aid magic. It'll take the worst of the pain away," she said.

"How about you?" Li Ming asked.

"Nothing to worry about."

Her voice was pained, her teeth gritted. But qi flowed smoothly from her hands, and her eyes were clear and focused.

"I'll check in on the others."

"I'm... not... going... anywhere," Wong-gor whispered, lips spreading into a smile.

Getting back up, Li Ming hunted for Ghazan. He stood at the door of the banquet room. The energies of Sky had dissipated, restoring him to a human form. He conferred briefly with a Dayong agent, then stepped away.

"The principals are all safe," Ghazan reported. "The authorities are on the way."

"What about the vehicles?" Li Ming demanded.

"The attacker flooded the street with an army of almasty riders. While we were fighting him, the drivers were battling the demons. They put down the last of them a minute ago, but the convoy is wrecked."

"*Gai si...*"

The attacker was powerful. More than that, he was *good*. He'd anticipated the evacuation attempt. He'd sent in the demons as cannon fodder, to soak up the gunfire and the magic, and to soften up the defenses. His only mistake was failing to account for Ghazan's raw power.

"What are our casualties?" Li Ming asked.

"Five Dayong biaohang wounded. But stable."

"And the government protectors?"

"Unknown. The detail leader and his deputy are gone. The others are trying to sort out the mess."

Li Ming swore again.

"What's the plan?" Li Ming asked.

"We're going to bunker down. The drivers and the vehicle team will form the outer perimeter. We'll hold out until the police come."

"Roger."

At the rails, Li Ming and Ghazan beheld the chaos below. Civilians hurried towards the exit, forming a crush of flesh and bone. People shouted and jostled and pushed, all of them trying to get away. In their wake, they left behind plates of half-finished food, overturned furniture, holes and cracks blasted into the floors and walls. Blackened spots on the carpet smoldered and smoked.

"What a mess," Ghazan said.

"Could have been worse. You stopped the attacker from breaking through into the banquet room."

Ghazan tilted his head.

"He was strong," Ghazan said.

"Stronger than you?"

He looked away. Sighed. Nodded.

"Yes."

"I tried to read his qi. I got an error message instead. Out of sensor detection limit."

"Me too."

Li Ming shuddered.

"What kind of monster was that?"

"Someone I don't want to fight again. If you hadn't landed that last blow... things would have gone very differently."

"I didn't do much. I couldn't. His skin was as hard as steel."

"You pushed him down. And you delayed him long enough for the police to arrive. It was enough."

Ghazan shrugged. "Thanks."

"What did he say at the end?" Li Ming asked.

Ghazan stiffened. Clenched his fists. Frowned.

"We'll cross spears again."

Acknowledgements

I would like to thank the following people for their invaluable contribution to this manuscript:

Everyone who backed Saga of the Swordbreaker on IndieGoGo. With their faith and support, what was supposed to have been a boutique series with far-out concepts easily became my most successful series yet.

The Story Forge and PulpRev, for helping to shape my fiction philosophy and direction.

Author Denton Salle, who shared his knowledge of the Kenny Gong lineage of xingyiquan, informing the combat and cultivation sequences in the series. Any errors and liberties I've taken with the internal martial arts are mine alone. A prolific writer, you can check out his bibliography on Amazon.

And of course, you, dear reader, for purchasing and reading this book. If you've enjoyed this book, please leave a review on Amazon. This helps other readers like yourself find this book and helps me continue writing more books that you'll love.

Also By Kit Sun Cheah

Fiction

Saga of the Broken Sword

Singularity Sunrise

Dungeon Samurai

Nonfiction

Pulp on Pulp: Tips and Tricks for Writing Pulp Fiction

About the Author

Kit Sun Cheah is Singapore's first Hugo and Dragon Award nominated writer. A blogger and martial artist, he is the Herald of the Pulp Revolution, combining the aesthetics and mindset of the pulp era with modern-day tastes and tradecraft. He has authored multiple series, most recently *Singularity Sunrise* and *Dungeon Samurai*.

Website: kitsuncheah.com
Twitter: @thebencheah
Facebook: benjamin.cheah.7
MeWe: bit.ly/2D1L2UK

www.ingramcontent.com/pod-product-compliance
Lightning Source LLC
Chambersburg PA
CBHW071726150726
47998CB00005B/1527